ALIX JAMES

BETTER LUCK NEXT TIME

FIRST IMPRESSIONS BOOK THREE

A PRIDE & PREJUDICE VARIATION

Cover Design by GetCovers.com
Cover Image Licensed by Period Images
Background image licensed by Shutterstock

Blog and Website: https://alixjames.com/
Newsletter: https://subscribepage.io/alix-james
Book Bub: https://www.bookbub.com/authors/alix-james
Facebook: https://www.facebook.com/ShortSweetNovellas
Twitter: https://twitter.com/N_Clarkston
Amazon: https://www.amazon.com/stores/Alix-James/author/B07Z1BWFF3
Austen Variations: http://austenvariations.com/

CONTENTS

The Author surely has many people to thank, but she also has a short attention span and a scattered brain, so this book is dedicated to her lap dog, instead, because she forces the Author to sit down and write.

CHAPTER ONE

London, May 11, 1812

L ADY ELIZABETH MONTCLAIR DID not set out to witness a murder.

In truth, she had set out to catch a glimpse of Mr. Henry Audley—the most devastatingly handsome young Member of Parliament in all of Westminster. That the evening would end in bloodshed and catastrophe was rather vexing, indeed.

At present, however, she was thinking only of how fetching her hair looked today—the one feature Henry Audley had ever noticed about her. She had every intention of making the most of it if she managed to see him today.

She was standing in the Ladies' Gallery of the House of Lords, idly fanning herself and suppressing a giggle, while her dearest friend, Lady Charlotte Wrexham, attempted to convince her that politics were of actual interest.

"Of course they are, Lizzy," Charlotte insisted, eyes bright with enthusiasm. "There is nothing so thrilling as a lively debate between gentlemen of good breeding and education!"

Elizabeth arched a brow, more amused than convinced. "Charlotte, I do not deny the importance of tariffs and tithes, but I have yet to hear a gentleman debate them with any real eloquence—let alone charm."

Charlotte gasped. "Politics are not meant to be charming!"

"Then they ought to be conducted more competently," Elizabeth said with a sigh, snapping her fan shut with a flick of her wrist.

Charlotte gave her a long-suffering look. "You are incorrigible."

"I prefer discerning."

Charlotte laughed. "Then why, pray, did you agree to accompany me here? This is hardly the opera or a musicale."

Elizabeth smiled, lowering her voice to a conspiratorial whisper. "Because, dearest Charlotte, Mr. Henry Audley is expected to speak in the House of Commons this very evening."

Charlotte blinked. "Henry Audley? That... earnest fellow from Hertfordshire who speaks of nothing but reform?"

Elizabeth exhaled, exasperated. "He is brilliant, Charlotte. Passionate. Intelligent enough to make the Lords appear slow-witted, and—if one studies him closely—rather handsome in a thoughtful, brooding sort of way." She paused, tilting her head. "At least, when viewed from the proper angle."

Charlotte snorted. "You are absurd. He really is rather plain, Lizzy."

"Not at all. He is precisely the sort of man I should marry—someday, when I am ready to endure the tedious reality of matrimony."

Charlotte gave her a knowing look. "Your father would never approve."

Elizabeth grimaced at the thought. Her father would rather set himself on fire than allow his only daughter to marry a mere Mister, no matter how intelligent or idealistic he might be. The Montclair name belonged in the House of Lords, not the House of Commons.

But her father was not here, was he?

That meant she could steal a moment for herself.

She straightened her posture and flashed a dazzling smile. "Fortunately, my father is closeted with some meeting or other this evening, and my mother has no idea where Westminster even is on the London map. We are chaperoned only by your mother, and she is presently engaged in conversation with that rather deaf Lord Witherspoon, which means she shall remain entirely occupied for the next half-hour at least. Therefore, I shall take a little walk, find some place where I might catch a glimpse of Mr. Audley in the House of Commons, and return before I am missed."

Charlotte frowned. "Lizzy, I do not think—"

Elizabeth cut her off with a cheerful wink. "Do not think, dearest. Simply pray that I do not lose my way in this infernal labyrinth of corridors. Or worse—that I am forced to listen to a dull speech about tax reform."

Before her friend could protest, she turned on her heel and slipped away, her heart thrumming with excitement.

S HE HAD NO DIFFICULTY avoiding detection. The halls were dimly lit, the grand marble floors muffled by thick carpets, and no one took note of a young woman slipping away from the crowd.

As she descended a narrow staircase, she glanced over her shoulder to ensure no one followed. She had never ventured this far before—and it was exhilarating. The House of Lords was filled with dignitaries, noblemen, and political minds of great consequence, but she found herself far more intrigued by the secrets of its corridors, the whispers in the alcoves, and the glimpse of something just beyond her reach.

As she approached the arched entrance to the House of Commons, her breath caught in her throat.

There—through the open doors, beyond the gilded railing—was Mr. Henry Audley. Her pulse quickened.

He was standing in conversation with another gentleman, his posture easy yet authoritative, his dark hair tousled with just the right amount of studied carelessness.

Elizabeth tilted her head, considering. Was he truly as handsome as she had imagined? Or had she exaggerated his charms in her mind? He did have a rather serious expression—perhaps too serious. And his spectacles did nothing to enhance the sharpness of his jawline, for it was rather... soft. But he was so easy and confident, and spoke so well—

She was so occupied with these vital contemplations that she did not immediately notice the strange tension in the air.

It was a shift, subtle at first—like the calm before a storm. She became vaguely aware that the conversation in the lobby had grown quieter, as if the air itself had turned thick and expectant. A few gentlemen glanced toward the entrance, their gazes uneasy.

Elizabeth barely had time to frown before—

A crack—an explosion of some kind.

The world split apart. The noise thundered through the chamber, reverberating off marble and stone.

Elizabeth jerked backward, the sound piercing through her bones. For a moment, she could not comprehend it. Had that been a shot? A misfire? A door slamming? She snatched her gaze around the room. Everyone was looking about them, but there appeared to be no singular point of crisis.

Then—a second report.

Closer. Muffled... an echo? No, for something tore through the air past her ear.

The world exploded into movement. A man staggered. Gasps. Screams. Running footsteps. The crash of a chair overturning.

Elizabeth clutched at the cold stone of the column behind her, her breath strangled in her throat. Someone had been shot.

She saw it—saw the man crumple, his hands clutching at his chest—but her mind had not yet made sense of it.

And then she saw him.

A man—one of the officials—staggered, his hands clutching his chest, his expression frozen in disbelief. Blood bloomed across his waistcoat, staining the fine fabric like ink spilled upon parchment. He swayed, confusion writ into every line of his face before his knees gave way.

Someone screamed. A woman? A man? The sound blurred into the thick haze of voices.

Men surged forward. Others backed away in horror. A pistol had been fired. Two pistols? No—one. Only one. She was sure of it... she thought.

Elizabeth could not move. She could only watch as the man—a man she recognized now as the Prime Minister himself—collapsed upon the marble floor.

Spencer Perceval was dead.

Somewhere, a man was shouting. "Bellingham! It was Bellingham!"

Elizabeth gasped and strained—a crush of men all descending upon a man with a pistol in his hand. Someone had seized him—the man named Bellingham.

He was fighting, struggling— "I am not mad! It was justice!" he cried as men wrestled him to the floor.

The walls tilted. The floor was slick with something dark. The scent of gunpowder stung the air.

Elizabeth's breath came short, sharp. Her ribs ached. Her eyes darted wildly through the chaos, searching for something solid to anchor to when—

There.

A figure, just beyond the crush of bodies. Not running. Not fighting. Not panicking.

Tucking a small pistol inside his coat, a glint of gold on his finger the only thing catching the light.

Moving backward. Calm. Unhurried.

Her mind stuttered, and she could not tear her eyes away. *Who?*

That was when his gaze flicked up. Met hers.

Her lungs seized.

He was looking at her. Not at the dying man. Not at the guards descending upon the one they called Bellingham.

At *her*.

Something dark flickered in his expression. Recognition. Calculation. A decision made.

A step backward. Another. Then he was gone, swallowed into the confusion, into the throng of bodies rushing toward the wrong man.

Elizabeth's fingers dug into the stone. The prime minister was dead. Shot, his life's blood even now spilling all over the pavers.

And she—Lady Elizabeth Montclair—had just witnessed the assassination of the most powerful man in England... but from a vantage that no one else had.

And worse... someone knew she had seen it.

Hertfordshire, May 11 1812

F ITZWILLIAM DARCY HAD SPENT the last six months balancing duty and discretion, maneuvering through the quiet battles fought in drawing rooms rather than on fields. The work demanded precision, patience, and a stomach for deception—a thing he abhorred above all others.

He had earned this respite.

Netherfield Park was, by any estimation, a ridiculous house. It was too modern, too ostentatious, and entirely too pleased with itself—as if it had been built not for comfort, but for the express purpose of announcing to the world that a very rich man lived there.

But it was also a mere three miles from Meryton, only twelve from London, yet a world away from the filth of Westminster intrigue. A place where he was known, but not watched. A place where he could, for a time, be simply Mr. Darcy of Nowhere.

Which was why, when Bingley's most recent, obscenely cheerful letter had arrived, brimming with tales of garden parties, trout fishing, and the unparalleled delight of "the freshest air in England," Darcy had written back with a single sentence:

"I am coming."

And so, here he was—riding up the long, tree-lined drive of Netherfield for the second time in his life, the house already familiar, the bright green fields and golden May sunlight welcoming him like a warm embrace.

For the first time in six months, he let the poisonous air out of his lungs.

Yes. This would do.

"**D**ARCY!"

The moment his horse reached the front steps, the door flung open and Bingley all but bounded down the drive, grinning like a man without a single care in the world. Darcy barely had time to dismount before his hand was seized and shaken with great enthusiasm.

"I knew you would return! You did not say how long you are staying, of course, but you never do, so I took the liberty of assuming indefinitely."

"Then you have set yourself up for disappointment."

"Nonsense. You have nowhere better to be. London is horrid this time of year, and you must be utterly exhausted from whatever it is you do when you disappear for months at a time."

Darcy handed the reins of his horse to the waiting groom. "You make it sound far more intriguing than it is."

"Yes, well, that is because you refuse to tell me anything, so I am forced to assume espionage or highway robbery—and between the two, espionage seems slightly more in keeping with your usual sensibilities."

Darcy snorted. "I will let you wonder a little longer."

"Wonderful. I shall entertain myself with theories. You are, of course, just in time—we are invited to dine at Longbourn tomorrow."

Darcy sighed deeply. "Bingley."

"Oh, do not look at me like that. You like Mr. Bennet, and you tolerate the rest of them well enough."

"You mean I tolerate them better than you tolerate your own sisters."

Bingley looked pained. "That is not untrue."

Darcy smirked. "Speaking of—where is Miss Bingley?"

"Oh, in the drawing room, trying to convince Louisa that country air is poisoning her complexion."

"How dreadful for her."

"Quite. Shall we go inside?"

The drawing room at Netherfield was precisely as Darcy had left it six months ago—tasteful, well-furnished, and entirely too orange.

Louisa Hurst was lounging indolently upon a settee, while her husband was already half-asleep in an armchair, snoring gently.

Caroline Bingley sat stiff-backed at the writing desk, penning what was no doubt an acidic commentary on country society to an equally disinterested acquaintance in town. The moment Darcy entered, her eyes flicked up, her expression briefly startled—before settling into cool politeness.

"Ah," she said. "You are here."

"As you see," Darcy replied.

She set down her pen. "For long?"

"Not if I can help it," he said, and she visibly relaxed.

Bingley coughed into his fist, his amusement poorly disguised. Caroline's disdain for him had become something of a morbid joke between the two of them. Upon their first introduction three years earlier, she had glanced at his tall figure, his stately posture, and taken him for what he ought to be—a man in possession of a large fortune and a comfortable estate with no other cares but the search for a bride.

But when she learned he was no more than a public servant, whose duties were so obscure that they lacked even a definition, and whatever claims he had once possessed to wealth and title were nothing more than a vague memory, why... she cared as little for him as he did for her. Which suited him well enough.

Darcy settled into a chair opposite Bingley, stretched out his legs, and let the warmth of the fire sink into his bones. It had been a long time since he had allowed himself the luxury of ease.

Perhaps he would even enjoy it.

May 12, 1812

F ITZWILLIAM DARCY SPENT THE next day deliberately avoiding the world.

The sun had been bright, the fields damp with the lingering breath of morning rain, and Charles Bingley had been in his usual good spirits as they walked the countryside, shot at pheasants, and exchanged only the most necessary words. It was, in every respect, the perfect way to disappear for a time.

They had returned to Netherfield late in the afternoon, just long enough to change before setting out for dinner at Longbourn—an invitation apparently extended weeks ago, before Darcy had even arrived. They could hardly alter their plans now.

And so, he found himself here once more, in the modest, lively dining room of the Bennet household, surrounded by familiar absurdities. Darcy had thought the Bennet females ridiculous last autumn, and nothing in the intervening months had softened his opinion.

Mrs. Bennet was as noisy and indiscreet as ever, clearly eager to see her daughters married to as much wealth as they could manage. And if wealth could not be caught, a redcoat would do. He, therefore, was safe from her on both counts, and she made no secret of that fact.

Misses Lydia and Catherine Bennet leaned toward one another, heads bent close, their hands fluttering to disguise—rather unsuccessfully—their whispering. Darcy had observed this habit last autumn as well; neither of them possessed any real talent for discretion. It was never difficult to determine what—or more often, *who*—had captured their interest. At present, their giggles and darting glances toward Bingley suggested they were still speculating on his marriage prospects, though Lydia, as the younger, seemed far more intent upon the entertainment of it.

Miss Mary Bennet sat slightly apart from her sisters, her posture rigidly upright, her fingers curled around the stem of her wineglass as though she had given great thought to the precise way a lady ought to hold it. She was discussing virtue and restraint, though not in the way one might expect from a sermonizing moralist. There was no firebrand energy in her speech—no dramatic declarations of ruin. Instead, she approached the topic as one might a philosophical problem, her tone grave but studious, as if she were considering the matter from a purely academic standpoint.

Darcy had met women who preached morality with the fervor of the righteous, but Miss Mary Bennet seemed to be working through her convictions in the midst of expressing them, arranging her arguments with care, though with little consideration as to whether anyone was listening.

Indeed, no one appeared to be.

The eldest, Miss Jane Bennet, was somewhat less of an oddity and somewhat more of a curiosity. She sat composed and quiet, offering the occasional polite remark but never volunteering conversation of her own accord. She was much as Darcy remembered—pleasant, mild, and largely indistinct.

She smiled often, though never with any particular animation. Her expressions were carefully modulated, never too pleased, never too affected, as if trained to rest in agreeable neutrality. It was difficult to tell whether she was truly engaged in the conversation around her or merely enduring it with practiced patience.

Darcy was not entirely certain which.

Had she always been so silent? He had noticed, last autumn, that she was not given to strong opinions or lively debates. Even now, she seemed content to sit back and let others speak, her presence felt only in the occasional murmured agreement or the soft laughter she offered at appropriate moments. Was it shyness or reserve? He did not know, and frankly, he did not care. It was of no consequence to him, except in how it pertained to Bingley.

And therein lay the question.

Months ago, he had thought he saw some interest in her for his friend—not in anything overt, certainly, but in the faint, unreadable shifts in her expression when Bingley was near. A slightly longer glance. A slight warmth in her tone. Perhaps nothing at all.

But if there *had* been anything, it was long buried now.

Miss Bennet looked at Bingley much as she looked at everyone else—polite, vaguely interested, but hardly as if she were pining away for him. If she had ever been inclined to him, it had been a fleeting thing, easily dismissed.

Bingley, for his part, was as oblivious as ever.

At present, he was engaged in an animated discussion with Misses Lydia and Catherine, while Miss Bennet sat serene and undisturbed, making no effort to draw his attention.

Darcy took another sip of wine. Either Bingley had never held her interest, or he had lost it. Either way, it was not his concern.

Mrs. Bennet, at least, had lost none of her enthusiasm.

"Mr. Bingley," she said, waving her hand in a vaguely grand manner, "you must be so very glad to have your good friend Mr. Darcy returned to Hertfordshire! Although, I daresay, you must hardly require more company, what with all the invitations you must receive."

Bingley smiled politely, but there was no mistaking the way Mrs. Bennet's gaze flickered—not toward him, but past him, to her daughters.

Darcy knew that look. He had seen it last autumn, when she had still imagined his friend might be inclined toward her eldest daughter.

Bingley, entirely unaware of the direction of her thoughts, merely said, "It is always a pleasure to see Darcy again, ma'am."

Mrs. Bennet tutted. "Well, I suppose that is fortunate for him, indeed."

Darcy caught the barest hint of a glance in his direction, but she did not address him directly. Of course she would not. He had nothing to offer her daughters—no grand fortune, no landed estate. And no red uniform.

That suited him perfectly.

He reached for his wine.

"I am certain," Mr. Bennet said idly, "that Mr. Darcy must be relieved to have a brief escape from London. I can only imagine how exhausting it must be—what with all the terribly important matters he attends to."

Darcy gave him a flat look, but Mr. Bennet only smirked, taking a leisurely sip of his own wine.

Oh, yes. At least one person at this table knew how to amuse himself.

They had just finished the second course when the commotion began. Footsteps in the hall. The murmur of voices. A moment later, Hill, the housekeeper, stepped into the dining room, looking slightly harried.

"Begging your pardon, sir," she said to Mr. Bennet, "but there is a rider at the door with an urgent express. He says it is of some importance."

Mrs. Bennet set her fork down with a gasp. "Oh, heavens! I knew it! It must be from your cousin, the parson—that patroness of his has surely died! I just knew this would happen," Mrs. Bennet continued, fluttering her hands. "And no doubt he means to take possession of Longbourn at once—oh, Mr. Bennet, he will throw us all into the hedgerows!"

"I suspect my cousin and heir has yet to learn how to claim an inheritance from the living, my dear," Mr. Bennet said dryly, pushing back from the table. "Excuse me, gentlemen."

It took only a few minutes before Mr. Bennet returned, looking altogether too serious for news of his relative. In his hand, he held a sealed letter.

Darcy straightened.

Mr. Bennet paused by his chair, then extended it. "It is for you, Mr. Darcy."

Darcy took it, frowning. "For me?"

"The messenger went to Netherfield first," Mr. Bennet said. "Upon being told you were here, he came directly." He lifted a brow. "He is waiting outside for a reply."

Silence settled over the table.

Darcy set down his napkin, rose, and inclined his head. "If you will excuse me."

He stepped into the hall, breaking the seal as he walked.

The message was brief, unsigned, and direct:

You are expected tomorrow at White's at two o'clock.

Nothing more.

But that was enough. Darcy's pulse quickened.

White's was not merely a gentlemen's club—it was where the most powerful men in England met in private. The very place where ministers, military officers, and men of influence conducted business the public would never hear of.

Whoever had sent this message had authority.

Something had happened. He had missed something.

Darcy folded the letter, tucked it into his coat, and strode toward the waiting messenger.

Chapter Two

London, May 12, 1812

Lady Elizabeth Montclair had never known what it was like to be needed.

She was *wanted*, certainly—coveted, admired, endlessly discussed in drawing rooms and gentlemen's clubs—but never needed.

And now, when it truly mattered, when she alone knew the truth of what had happened yesterday, she could not get a single soul to listen.

Not even her father.

The Ashwick townhouse was a grand, elegant building just off St. James's Square, with tall windows that looked out onto the streets of London and a staff that operated with quiet efficiency, whether its master was present or not.

Which was fortunate, as he rarely was.

The Marquess of Ashwick spent most of his time at White's, Tattersall's, or Parliament—depending on the time of day and whether the subject at hand was politics, horses, or the ongoing woes of the country.

Her mother, meanwhile, was nowhere near London.

She had long since removed herself to Devonshire, her family's ancestral estate, content to play lady of the manor while pretending she had not been exiled there years ago when she and her husband mutually declared that more children were not to be, and consequently, they could not abide the sight of one another.

As for Elizabeth, she had the townhouse, the maids, the carriages, the silk gowns, the endless social engagements—everything but purpose.

Until now.

Until she had seen a man murdered in the halls of Parliament and realized—with chilling certainty—that she had seen what no one else had.

And her father, a man of considerable influence, rank, and power, would not even look up from his desk.

THE STUDY SMELLED OF tobacco and old books, the heavy scent of some sort of meat and brandy clinging to the air. Papers were stacked in neat piles upon the desk, and a single lamp burned low, casting a golden glow over her father's disinterested expression.

Elizabeth stood before him, hands clenched at her sides. "You are not listening to me."

"I am listening, petal," the Marquess of Ashwick said, not looking up from the document in his hand.

"No, you are *hearing* me," Elizabeth corrected. "You are not *listening*."

Her father sighed deeply, set the paper down, and finally fixed her with a gaze that was both indulgent and distracted.

"Well, then, my dear," he said. "Do tell me again what you saw. I promise to apply my full attention."

She hesitated, suddenly uncertain. The moment felt too big, too important—and yet, here she was, standing in the same study where she had once begged permission to keep a stray kitten, feeling much the same sense of futility.

"I was at the House of Commons yesterday."

Her father's brows lifted a fraction. "Were you?"

"Yes."

He did not ask why. She was both relieved and vaguely mortified.

"I saw what happened," she continued, gripping her hands together. "I saw the shot that killed him. And it was not the man they arrested."

Her father's expression did not change.

"It was *not* Bellingham!" she pressed, heart pounding. "His pistol misfired. I saw it. There was another shooter."

"Mm."

That was all.

Not "Good God, Elizabeth, are you certain?" or "This is of vital importance! We must speak to someone at once!"—just a quiet, utterly indifferent murmur.

Elizabeth exhaled sharply. "Father!"

"Petal?"

"You do not believe me."

"I believe that you *believe* what you saw."

Her temper flared. "That is not the same thing."

Her father leaned back in his chair, regarding her with the same half-amused, half-dismissive expression he had worn for years.

"And you think," he said, tapping his fingers against the armrest, "that the Prime Minister of England was murdered in cold blood by an unknown second shooter, and that no one but my daughter—who had no business being there in the first place—managed to see it?"

"Yes."

He sighed, rubbing a hand over his jaw. "Elizabeth."

She knew that tone. The one he used when he was about to placate her with empty reassurances before sending her off to do something more ladylike.

"I am certain," he said, "that whatever you saw felt very serious indeed. But Parliament is full of ministers and officials. If there had been another gunman, it would have been noticed."

"No, it would not," she insisted. "Because I was not supposed to be there, so I was hiding. I had a vantage point no one else had. I saw something—"

"And I am sure the ministers will handle it."

She inhaled sharply, pressing her lips together. "You do not understand—"

"I understand," her father interrupted, pushing back from his desk with a heavy sigh. "I understand that Spencer Perceval's assassination is a tragedy, and that it has caused a great many headaches among those of us who actually have a role in government. I understand that I have spent the last day in endless meetings while the entire House of Lords determines how best to proceed. And I understand, my dear, that you are not involved in any of it."

Elizabeth stiffened.

"I am trying to tell you—"

"You are telling me a fine story."

Her hands clenched into fists. "I am telling you the truth."

Her father exhaled, then stood, pressing a kiss to the top of her head. "You are my brightest, most brilliant girl," he murmured. "But you let your imagination run away with you."

She stared at him, cold disbelief creeping into her veins.

That was it. That was all.

A pat on the head. A "Run along, dear."

The one man in all of England who had the power to do something—who could bring her to the right people, get her words in the right ears—had dismissed her entirely.

Elizabeth turned on her heel and walked out.

If he would not listen, she would find someone who would.

ELIZABETH HAD BARELY REACHED the door when a knock echoed through the house.

It was answered immediately, and a murmur of voices drifted from the entrance hall. A moment later, a footman appeared in the study doorway, bowing low.

"My lord, the Duke of Wrexham and Her Grace the Duchess have arrived. The duke asks to speak with you on an urgent matter."

Her father exhaled slowly, rubbing his temple. "Of course he does."

Elizabeth froze. The Duke of Wrexham? Here?

Charlotte's father.

Her mind raced as the realization struck—Charlotte had spoken often of her father's role in government affairs. He was a man of immense power and influence, one of the oldest and most respected dukes in the realm. If he was here, speaking with her father, then—

This was about the assassination.

Before she could even consider what to do, footsteps sounded in the hall, and then—Her Grace the Duchess of Wrexham swept into the room on the arm of her husband, the duke..

The duchess was a striking woman, tall and impeccably dressed, her dark hair arranged in a fashion that suggested effortless grace—but was, Elizabeth knew, the work of at least two maids and an entire morning's preparation.

She was not a warm woman, nor a sentimental one, but she was intelligent, well-connected, and powerful enough to walk into any room without announcing herself. She was also one of the few ladies of rank Elizabeth could tolerate for more than half an hour.

"Ah," the duchess said, her gaze flicking between Elizabeth and her father. "I see we have interrupted something."

Her father sighed heavily. "You have interrupted my daughter's latest conviction that the world is not operating to her exacting standards."

The duchess's lips twitched. "How dreadful."

"I was just leaving," Elizabeth said, her voice carefully light. "Shall I have tea sent to the drawing room for you, Your Grace?"

The duchess waved a gloved hand. "Lovely, dear girl. I should also like some company. Walk with me."

Elizabeth hesitated only a moment before nodding.

Her father was already dismissing her concerns. Perhaps the duchess—perhaps a *woman*, someone with sense and influence—would listen.

She gestured toward the hallway. "Shall we take tea in the blue sitting room?"

The duchess smiled, looping her arm through Elizabeth's with a practiced ease. "Lead the way."

Elizabeth kept a perfect posture as she poured tea, carefully measuring out the sugar with the calm precision of someone whose nerves were entirely intact. Mostly intact.

They had spoken first of nothing at all—who had been seen at court, which gowns had been admired, the usual inconsequential gossip. But beneath the pleasantries, the true conversation lingered like a storm on the horizon—unavoidable, gathering strength, waiting for the moment it would break.

At last, the duchess sighed, setting down her cup. "This business with Perceval is truly dreadful. The entire court is in an uproar—one cannot take three steps without hearing of it. And now my husband is closeted with your father, no doubt ensuring that the world keeps turning."

Elizabeth set down her spoon. She hesitated, then leaned forward, lowering her voice. "There is more to it than everyone thinks."

The duchess lifted a brow. "Oh?"

Elizabeth swallowed. "There was another shooter."

The duchess blinked. Then she laughed lightly, shaking her head. "My dear, such rumors—"

"It is not a rumor. I saw it with my own eyes."

The duchess stilled. "To say such a thing," she mused, studying Elizabeth's face, "one would have to have been in the House of Commons, but I recall perfectly that you were with Charlotte in the Ladies' Gallery yesterday."

Elizabeth inhaled slowly. "I slipped away."

The duchess's fingers tightened slightly around her teacup. "You were there?"

Elizabeth nodded. "I was in an alcove. Behind a support column. I knew I should not have been there, so I kept hidden. Charlotte knew—I left her in the Ladies' Gallery. She was the only one who knew where I had gone."

A flicker of something crossed the duchess's face—a reaction quickly masked.

"And I was not alone. The real shooter was hidden there as well. I saw him fire. And he—" She swallowed. "He saw *me.*"

The duchess said nothing at first, merely studying Elizabeth with the sharp, searching gaze of a woman who had learned to sift truth from fiction. Elizabeth braced herself for disbelief.

And at first, she got it.

Her Grace sighed, shaking her head. "Elizabeth, my dear, I am sure—"

"I *know* what I saw."

The duchess opened her mouth, likely to utter some soothing dismissal, but then—she again studied Elizabeth's face. The fear in her eyes. The lingering pallor in her cheeks.

The duchess set down her tea. "You truly believe this."

Elizabeth let out a shaky breath. "I do not need to *believe* it. I *know* it. They arrested the wrong man."

The duchess exhaled slowly, folding her hands in her lap. "Well. Something must be done."

Elizabeth blinked. "What?"

"Do you think I would sit here and allow you to be hunted?" The duchess scoffed. "Really, Elizabeth."

Elizabeth let out a breathless laugh—a nervous, unsteady thing. "I suppose," she said, attempting lightness, "that I might be in some trouble over having gone to the House of Commons alone, if it were spread abroad. But otherwise, it is unlikely the man could even know who I am. I am probably quite safe." Yes, if she repeated that enough times, she would persuade herself of it.

It did not work.

The duchess studied her for a long moment before shaking her head.

"No, my dear," she said softly. "You are not."

Elizabeth swallowed.

The duchess straightened, smoothing her skirts. "My husband the duke has the Prince Regent's ear. I shall see that you are heard. And protected, if necessary."

Elizabeth swallowed. "How?"

"That, dear girl," the duchess said, rising gracefully to her feet, "is a matter for the Prince of Wales to decide."

She turned toward the door.

Elizabeth stood quickly. "Your Grace—"

The duchess turned, and for the first time, her expression softened.

"Do not worry, Elizabeth. The Prince has a rather long arm."

White's, London—May 13, 1812

F ITZWILLIAM DARCY HAD ALWAYS known his place in the world.

He had been raised to understand the nuances of power—who wielded it, who sought it, and who would destroy themselves in its pursuit. He had been taught the art of caution, the value of discretion, and the wisdom of never reaching too high.

Yet here he was. Being shown back into the most private of rooms of White's, about to speak with one of those men of power.

He had arrived in London scarcely an hour ago, having risen at dawn to bid farewell to Netherfield after only one day. The express had been cryptic, but Darcy was not a man to ignore such messages—especially when they directed him to White's.

And he was not a man to walk into such a meeting blind. He had collected a broadsheet at the coaching inn, skimming the headlines over a quick meal.

The Prime Minister had been shot.

That, at least, he understood.

But the summons had offered nothing further. No details, no explanation—only a time, a place, and an unspoken command to appear. It had come with no official insignia, no government seal—yet upon his arrival, he had been taken up the back stairs, shown into a private room, and told to wait.

And Darcy had waited. He had no illusions about why he had been called.

He was useful.

He was discreet.

And—perhaps most importantly—he owed no man anything.

That last part made him valuable. Because it meant he could not be bought.

When the door finally opened, it was not some minister or private secretary who waited on him, but the Prince Regent himself.

Darcy, much to his own satisfaction, did not visibly react, though it was rather a long pause before he entered the room fully.

The prince was a large man, lavishly dressed in a blue coat embroidered with gold, a jeweled snuffbox in one hand, a half-drained glass of brandy in the other. He carried himself with the casual arrogance of a man who had never been denied anything of importance.

"Ah, there you are, Darcy." The prince waved vaguely in his direction as he crossed the room. "I wondered if you would make me wait. But no, here you are, like a good little soldier. Most commendable."

Darcy inclined his head politely, but said nothing.

The prince sighed and lowered himself into a chair with great theatrical effort, as though the very act of sitting were a burden upon his person.

"You are aware, of course," he drawled, reaching for the decanter with a watery sniff, "that our dear Mr. Perceval is now quite dead."

Darcy nodded once. "I saw the broadsheets."

"Ah, good! Good, good." The prince poured himself another glass, swirling it absently. "Then you are also aware that the trial proceeds even as we speak. A fine, efficient bit of justice, is it not? Shoot a prime minister on Monday, be sentenced to death by Friday. We shall see it done." He chuckled, shaking his head. "'Twill set a most delightful precedent."

Darcy remained silent.

The prince sighed again, studying him over the rim of his glass. "Tell me, my dear fellow—what do you make of it?"

Darcy hesitated, choosing his words carefully. "It seems... remarkably swift. Efficient. Tidy, Your Highness."

"Oh, quite. Which is why I am concerned."

Darcy's gaze flickered up.

"I have heard whispers," the prince said, leaning forward slightly, "that this little affair is not as simple as it seems."

Darcy blinked.

"Oh, do not look at me like that." The prince took a lazy sip of brandy. "I care not for your delicate sense of discretion. I have been told there is more afoot. And while I am perfectly content to allow our dear ministers to pat themselves on the back for swift and decisive action, I would be remiss—would I not?—if I allowed my own safety to be so thoughtlessly assumed."

He set the glass down with a sharp clink. "Because, you see, my dear fellow, when prime ministers start dropping dead, it does tend to make one wonder—who might be next?"

Darcy said nothing. He had spent too many years in the shadows of government affairs to entertain rumors. The assassination had been brutal, certainly—but it was not unusual for men to seek vengeance for perceived injustices. Bellingham had a motive. An old grievance. He would be swiftly tried and condemned.

The matter was settled.

"Your Highness," Darcy said at last, his tone deliberate and just skirting on the edge of patronizing, "it is highly unlikely that there is any truth to these whispers."

The prince scoffed, rolling his eyes. "Oh, well, that is a relief! Darcy has decided, so we may all rest easy." He gestured wildly toward the door. "Shall I call for a scribe? Shall we have it written into law?"

Darcy did not flinch.

The prince sighed with his usual theatrical flair. "Come, come, man. I care not for your reputation in the Home Office. I care not for your distinguished sense of principle. I care only that a man has been shot dead and someone has whispered in my ear that perhaps—perhaps!—there is more to it." He fixed Darcy with a shrewd look. "And that, my dear fellow, is where you come in."

Darcy exhaled slowly, weighing his options. He had no desire to involve himself in a fruitless hunt for phantoms. But neither did he think the prince was going to allow him a choice.

So—he might as well gain something for the trouble.

He leaned back slightly, his tone carefully deliberate. "Perhaps Your Highness might also reconsider my petition."

The prince stilled. Then, with exaggerated casualness, he reached for his brandy. "My dear fellow," he said airily, "I have no earthly idea what you are talking about."

Darcy's mouth twitched. "Your Highness is mistaken. You know precisely what I am talking about."

The prince sighed heavily, tilting his head back against the chair. "Must we discuss such dreary matters? The lands were transferred by royal grant, quite aboveboard, quite proper. Would you have me undo the will of a reigning monarch?"

Darcy raised a brow.

The prince rolled his eyes again, then sat forward, dropping the act. "You are insufferable."

Darcy inclined his head. "And yet, Your Highness summoned me."

The Prince groaned. "Very well! I shall take your tedious little matter under consideration."

"A most gracious concession," Darcy said dryly.

The prince waved him away. "Yes, yes, I am a beacon of mercy. Off with you. Do whatever it is you do."

Darcy rose, inclining his head. "Then I, too, shall take your matter under consideration."

"You are most tiresome, Darcy."

Darcy smiled thinly. "Your Highness may consider it a mutual affliction."

CHAPTER THREE

London, May 14, 1812

E LIZABETH WAS NOT EXPECTING a summons from the Duchess of Wrexham.

When the footman arrived with the note, she had been in the morning room, feigning interest in a book of poetry while half-listening to the voices drifting in from the study. Her father was at home today, which meant the house had a faintly altered air—not quite busy, but attentive, as if the very walls knew they ought to behave in the presence of their master.

The letter was delivered on a silver tray, and the seal alone was enough to make her heart jump slightly. She broke it open, scanning the words written in the Duchess's flowing hand:

> *Be ready in an hour. We are going to Buckingham House.*

Elizabeth was still reading when she felt her father's presence at her shoulder.

"A message from Wrexham?" The pleased note in his voice was unmistakable.

She turned, holding the letter aloft. "From the Duchess."

Her father took it from her fingers, reading quickly. His brows lifted, and a slow smile spread across his face. "To The Queen's House," he murmured. "Now, what have you done to attract such interest, petal?"

Elizabeth folded her hands, choosing her words carefully. "The Duchess and I have had some discussions about... recent events."

Her father gave a dismissive wave. "Ah. The assassination nonsense. The whole of London is in a frenzy over it."

"This is not nonsense, Father."

He barely seemed to hear her. Instead, he turned the letter over, as if examining the weight of the paper might tell him more.

"The Queen's House," he repeated. "Not a formal audience, I suppose—too short a notice for that. A private meeting." His lips curled slightly. "Interesting."

Elizabeth was not sure she liked the way he said it.

"You must dress well," he continued, handing the letter back. "The Queen is fond of modest refinement—no frills or French embellishments."

Elizabeth arched a brow. "Father, I am aware of how to dress."

"Yes, yes," he said vaguely, already lost in thought. Then, with a pointed look: "You realize this may bode well for you."

Elizabeth tilted her head. "How so?"

He chuckled indulgently, as if she were hopelessly naïve. "When a young lady is invited to the Queen's residence in the company of a duchess, it is not usually to discuss politics."

Elizabeth held her breath.

"She may be considering bestowing favor upon you. Perhaps something substantial. Preeminence among your peers... perhaps she has taken it upon herself to see you well matched. She *has* seemed rather taken with you this Season. A pity Montford is still in mourning; he would have made a solid enough husband, dull though he is. But there is Ferndale—charming fellow, very much in the Prince Regent's good graces. And there has been talk of Prince Nikolaos of Württemberg looking for an English bride, and I heard some murmurs that he found *you* rather fetching. Imagine that—my daughter, a princess! I do believe even your mother would have to approve of that."

Ah.

So *that* was what interested him.

Elizabeth sighed, folding the letter carefully. "Or, perhaps, she simply wishes to speak with me."

Her father chuckled. "Of course, petal. Of course."

E LIZABETH HAD STOOD BEFORE dukes and earls, princes and ministers. She had promenaded under the chandeliers of Almack's, dined in the company of lords, and parried words with the sharpest minds in London society.

None of it had prepared her for this.

The corridors of Buckingham House were cool and quiet, lined with high windows that let in the pale afternoon light. The air carried the faintest trace of fresh-cut roses and lavender, the hush of well-trained servants moving in silence.

At her side, the Duchess of Wrexham walked with absolute poise, her posture perfect, her steps unhurried but purposeful.

Elizabeth, by contrast, felt far too aware of her own movements, as if she had forgotten entirely how to walk like a rational person.

She had never met the Queen of England.

She had been presented at court, yes, but from a distance, a fleeting curtsy among a sea of glittering debutantes. Her Majesty had looked in Elizabeth's direction once or twice at balls, and there was even one occasion when Elizabeth happened to be leaving the retiring room the very moment Queen Charlotte passed by in the hall. But this—this was an *audience*.

And an audience granted on short notice.

That alone was enough to tell her that Queen Charlotte knew exactly why she was here, and was willing to listen to her statement.

So why, then, was she so terribly nervous?

They reached a set of double doors, manned by a footman in livery so crisp it seemed untouched by mortal hands. The man bowed. "Her Majesty will receive you now."

The duchess did not hesitate. Elizabeth followed, willing her legs not to tremble.

The room was sumptuously appointed but not ostentatious, its grandeur softened by the scent of fresh-cut roses and the faint crackle of a fire burning low in the hearth. At the far end of the room, seated in a high-backed chair, was the Queen.

Queen Charlotte had never been a beauty, nor had she ever aspired to be one. There was something severe about her, from her tightly curled white hair to the rigid line of her shoulders. She was dressed in dark silk, her gown adorned with an impressive lace fichu, a walking cane resting against the chair beside her.

She did not rise when they entered, nor did she even look particularly interested.

The duchess swept into a deep curtsy, her movements fluid and effortless. Elizabeth followed suit, lowering herself as far as she could, keeping her gaze fixed on the floor long enough to be appropriate.

A moment passed. A very *long* moment.

Heavens, were they ever to be permitted to stand again? Elizabeth stared at the floor under her feet, praying she would not topple over.

"You may rise," the Queen said at last.

Her voice was precisely as Elizabeth had expected—cool, measured, and edged with a faint German accent.

Elizabeth stood carefully, clasping her hands before her.

The Queen's dark eyes flicked over her with the same mild disinterest one might afford an adequate painting or a half-decent performance at the theatre.

"So," she said, at last, to no one in particular. "This is the girl."

Elizabeth's stomach tightened, and she tried to keep from staring at anyone in particular.

The duchess tilted her head in quiet acknowledgment. "Yes, Your Majesty."

A pause.

The Queen turned her attention to Elizabeth directly. "I understand you have something to say."

The words were not a request.

Elizabeth inhaled, carefully schooling her expression into one of quiet confidence—though her fingers felt cold where they rested against her skirts.

"Yes, Your Majesty," she said, keeping her voice clear but deferential.

She recounted what she had seen. She spoke carefully, precisely, omitting nothing—the first misfire, the second gunman with the quieter shot, the way he had slipped into the crowd.

The Queen did not react.

Not once.

Not when Elizabeth described the true shot that had killed the Prime Minister. Not when she spoke of the man who had seen her.

And certainly not when she described how no one else had noticed any of it.

By the time Elizabeth finished, her mouth felt parched, her pulse thrumming against her ribs. She had spoken the truth—all of it.

And the Queen was entirely unmoved.

For a long moment, silence filled the chamber.

Then— "I see."

That was all.

Two words.

Elizabeth's breath hitched.

Had she made a mistake? Had she imagined the significance of this meeting? Had she—?

The Queen exhaled, reaching for her cane. "I am told there will be a trial."

"Yes, Your Majesty," the duchess agreed.

"A swift one."

"As His Highness deems fitting, Your Majesty."

Another pause.

The Queen pressed her lips together. "So they wish to make an example of him."

Elizabeth frowned slightly. "Your Majesty, I do not believe—"

The Queen lifted a hand.

Elizabeth fell silent immediately.

"You believe much, Lady Elizabeth."

Elizabeth stiffened and dropped her gaze to the floor.

She could feel doubt creeping in now, a terrible, humiliating thought forming in her mind—*Am I wrong? Did I imagine it?*

The Queen tilted her head slightly, considering her. Then, at last, she sighed. "I shall refer the matter to my son."

Elizabeth's stomach dropped. "The Prince Regent?"

The Queen's expression was unchanging. "That *is* my son."

Elizabeth felt herself sway slightly. This was far more serious than she had thought.

If the Queen had already decided to involve the Prince, then she had known—before Elizabeth had even set foot in Buckingham House—that there was truth to what she had seen.

Elizabeth exhaled slowly, straightening.

The Queen lifted a brow. "You are trembling," she said, not unkindly.

Elizabeth forced her hands to steady. "I am not afraid."

The Queen's lips twitched faintly—not quite a smile, but something close. "Then you are a fool," she said mildly.

Elizabeth swallowed. "I hope not, Your Majesty."

The Queen adjusted the lace at her wrist. "That will be all."

The duchess curtsied. Elizabeth followed. They were dismissed.

It was not until they were back in the carriage, rolling away from Buckingham House, that Elizabeth allowed herself to breathe.

The duchess was silent, staring out the window, her expression thoughtful.

Elizabeth's mind was a riot of panic and indecision. Had she curtsied deeply enough? Had she spoken out of turn? Oh, goodness, her shoes—there was a tiny fleck of dirt on the heel! Had the Queen noticed?

Finally, after they rolled past the gates, she sighed deeply and sagged against the squabs. "She knew."

The duchess turned slightly, one brow lifting. "I am sorry?"

"She already knew everything I told her."

The duchess studied her for a moment. Then she simply nodded.

Elizabeth's stomach twisted. "What happens now?"

The duchess sighed. "Now?" She reached for the curtain, pulling it slightly aside to glance at the crowded London streets. "Now, the Crown will manage the affair."

FITZWILLIAM DARCY HAD SPENT the morning trying to be a normal man.

It was proving tiresome.

His chambers at Albany were neat, orderly, and entirely impersonal—just as they had always been. A bachelor's residence, suited to a man who required convenience rather than sentiment.

The sitting room was tastefully appointed, its furnishings modest but of excellent quality. The fire was always well-tended, the shelves lined with books, and the desk—a sturdy, well-worn piece of mahogany—was arranged with military precision.

Darcy had spent his first hour at that desk, sorting a stack of odd notes and sightings collected from his sources about London. Not one of them, as far as he could tell, had a thing to do with Perceval's murder. He would have to search somewhat farther afield to make a beginning.

But before he did that, he paused. It was high time he penned a letter to his sister, Georgiana. She was in London at present, and perhaps when he had liberty, he would pay her a call.

Had he the means, he would have set her up in a house of her own, with a companion of her choosing and the freedom to pursue her education and interests as she pleased.

Instead, she was living with their aunt and uncle—the Earl and Countess of Matlock—on the charity of their family.

Darcy had been told that his cousin, Lady Julia, treated Georgiana with kindness, and of course Richard and the Viscount doted on her. But that did not ease his discomfort. Georgiana deserved better than being the poor relation.

His pen pressed a little harder against the page.

My dearest Georgie,

I trust you are well and that your lessons remain engaging. You will, no doubt, be pleased to hear that I have left Hertfordshire and returned to town—though I regret to inform you that I have nothing of interest to report on the matter of my petition. No progress has been made, but neither has it been dismissed. We must continue as we are, for now, and hope that the tide turns in our favor.

I should like to hear from you soon. Let me know how you fare, and if there is anything you require. I shall always do what I can, and I intend to present myself at Matlock House when possible.

Yours,
Fitzwilliam Darcy

He sighed, sealing the letter before setting it out for his frequently absent manservant to find, whenever it suited him.

That was done.

Now—to make himself useful.

D

ARCY WALKED TO THE Home Office, rather than taking a carriage. It was not a long distance, and besides, he had always found that a man walking with purpose was less noticeable than one arriving in a fine conveyance.

The government offices were as he had left them—the same dark-paneled rooms, the same low murmur of conversation, the same suspicious glances exchanged in passing.

He was not a full agent—he was too much of a gentleman for that, but too penniless to be anything else—so he occupied a strange place in the hierarchy.

Not quite trusted.

Not quite expendable.

He had learned, over time, how to make himself useful without making himself vulnerable.

Today, he was merely observing. The broadsheets had already laid out the public narrative—a lone assassin, a close range shot, a swift trial, a grieving nation. But he wondered if anyone inside the Home Office was quietly doubting that narrative.

He took his usual route through the halls, pausing at an open door where a clerk was furiously copying out reports.

"Troubled times," Darcy murmured, as if making casual conversation.

The clerk barely glanced up. "A terrible business, indeed."

"The trial seems swift."

The man let out a soft snort. "Swift? That's one way to put it. They'll have him hanged before the week is out."

"Efficient justice."

"Political justice."

Darcy lifted a brow. "Oh?"

The clerk sighed. "The Home Secretary wants this buried. No debate, no fuss—just a quick execution and a return to order."

A pause.

Darcy let the silence linger, then asked, as casually as he could— "I have never yet seen a case so simple. Uncomplicated and clean, and perfect for the broadsheets."

The clerk stiffened.

Darcy leaned in slightly. "Have you heard any rumors?"

The man hesitated. Then, in a lower voice— "There was a whisper—nothing confirmed, mind you—of someone else in the lobby. But if there was a second man, he disappeared clean. The ministers don't want to hear it."

Darcy's fingers tightened into a fist behind his back.

Someone else.

He was not the only one who had heard the rumor.

He did not linger. The Home Office was not a place for idle loitering, and a man who asked too many questions soon found himself with more problems than answers.

By the time he stepped back into the grey afternoon light, he had already pieced together what he knew for certain.

The prince had called him in because of a rumor. That rumor had made its way inside the Home Office. And at least one man—possibly more—had doubts about the official story, but the Crown wanted the public knowledge to remain limited.

Darcy sighed. The Prince Regent had been right about one thing. There was more to this.

He was going to have to find out what.

D ARCY HATED LONDON AT this hour.

The streets were crowded, noisy, suffocating, filled with the mingling scents of sweating horses, unwashed bodies, and the filth of the gutters. The evening traffic of carriages and pedestrians moved in chaotic waves, forcing him to weave his way through the press of bodies.

He should have taken a carriage. He did not like to be jostled and delayed, and yet, he had chosen to walk. He needed the movement, the sharp bite of cool air, the sensation of his boots striking against the cobbles.

He needed time to think.

He had spent the afternoon in various clubs and pubs and back alleys, sifting through half-truths and whispers, and had walked away with little more than confirmation that the rumors existed. And that—supposedly, anyway—no one in power wanted them acknowledged.

And now, with night descending over the city, he was on his way to his cousin, Colonel Fitzwilliam. Richard would be at his flat by now, and Richard would tell him the truth.

If there was anything more to this affair—if there was something beneath the surface that only those in military and intelligence circles knew—his cousin would have heard of it.

He turned onto Jermyn Street, the familiar route toward St. James's Square. Fitzwilliam kept rooms in a respectable townhouse, neither extravagant nor meager. The kind of place a well-bred soldier might live, comfortable but practical.

The sound of hooves hammering the street reached him first. Then—the movement. Dark shapes shifting ahead, closing in.

Darcy stopped just in time.

Out of nowhere, a dozen men surrounded him—horsemen in the street. Foot guards flanking him on either side.

The King's Guard.

A sharp rush of irritation spiked through him. He did not move, his jaw tightening as the soldiers boxed him in, their polished boots and gleaming scabbards forming an impenetrable wall.

Good heavens, this was unnecessary.

He was no fugitive, no man on the run. If the Prince had wanted to see him, a simple message would have sufficed. Still, he kept his expression cool, detached.

"What," he said, voice edged with irritation, "is the meaning of this?"

The commanding officer—tall, broad-shouldered, wearing the expression of a man who had no interest in explaining himself—reined in his horse and looked down at him.

"Mr. Darcy," he said. "You are commanded to appear before His Royal Highness at once."

He exhaled slowly. So. It was to be now.

"Am I to assume," he said dryly, glancing at the armed men surrounding him, "that His Highness will not permit me to complete my business first?"

"You assume correctly."

The rumble of wheels on stone approached from behind. Darcy turned just as an unmarked black carriage rolled into view, its windows heavily curtained, its meaning unmistakable.

He sighed. "Very well."

He turned on his heel, ascended the carriage steps without hesitation, and pulled the door closed behind him. The moment the latch clicked, the carriage lurched forward into the London night.

CHAPTER FOUR

"**Y**OU HAVE BEEN QUIET today, my lady."

Alice's voice was soft but pointed as she tugged the laces at the back of Elizabeth's best dinner gown.

Elizabeth forced a small, absent smile, though she knew her maid was too astute to be fooled by it. "I imagine I am permitted to be thoughtful on occasion," she said lightly.

Alice huffed, adjusting the gown's shoulders, so they sat just right at her collarbone. "Thoughtful, yes. But you've the air of a lady waiting for something unpleasant."

Elizabeth's throat worked, shifting the pearls faintly in the mirror. *Had* she been waiting?

She had spent the afternoon reeling from her audience with the Queen, trying to content herself with the knowledge that the matter had been placed in the Prince Regent's hands. She had been assured that her duty was done. There was nothing more to worry about.

And yet—here she was, standing still as Alice shook out the layers of her skirts, the fine silk of her gown cool against her skin, the weight of pearls settling at her throat. She was expected to descend the stairs in half an hour, to dine with her father as if this were any other evening, as if the events of the day had not unsettled the very ground beneath her.

But her hands refused to stop trembling.

It was not fear—not exactly. It was anticipation, curling in her stomach like the first threads of a storm. A hundred possible explanations had turned over in her mind since she had stepped out of Buckingham House that afternoon, each one attempting to rationalize what had happened.

The Queen had been unmoved, cool and indifferent, as if Elizabeth had brought her nothing more than some idle bit of court gossip. And yet, before the hour was out, she had already acted upon it.

Elizabeth knew what that meant.

It meant there had been truth in her words—truth the Queen had already known, truth she had been waiting for someone to confirm. And now it was in the Prince Regent's hands.

Elizabeth had done all she could. She had been assured there was nothing more to worry about. So why did it feel as though something was coming?

A sharp knock at the door startled Alice into a flinch.

Elizabeth's stomach dropped. She exhaled slowly, carefully. There was only one person who would be knocking at this hour.

The door opened, revealing her father, the Marquess of Ashwick, standing on the threshold with an expression of considerable amusement. "Well, well," he drawled. "It appears my daughter has acquired the peculiar talent of being summoned to royal audiences twice in one day."

Elizabeth's spine went rigid. "What do you mean?"

The marquess stepped inside, holding a folded letter between his fingers. "A royal messenger just delivered this for you."

Elizabeth stared at it.

Her father beamed as he extended it toward her. "The Queen desires to be 'entertained' by Lady Elizabeth this evening, to banish her melancholy. I sincerely hope you have been practicing your Bach and your Clementi."

Alice gasped. "Her Majesty requests your presence?"

Elizabeth's mind raced as she reached for the letter, unfolding the thick, cream-colored paper. The message was brief—formal, polite, and utterly confounding.

There was no mention of their earlier meeting. No hint of its true purpose.

Just a simple, gracious command:

> *"Her Majesty, the Queen, commands the presence of Lady Elizabeth Montclair at Buckingham House this evening, that she might lend some agreeable company to dispel the melancholy which currently dims the light of the royal household."*

"You must have made quite the impression, petal."

Elizabeth's fingers tightened around the letter, and she blinked unseeingly at the paper. There was nothing about this that made sense. "Father," she asked, her voice a distant echo even in her own ears, "is the Queen known to summon the 'agreeable company' of someone with whom she is barely acquainted, and at such an hour?"

Her father paced idly, hands behind his back. "The Queen has always been a mercurial creature—the whims of royalty, of course. One mustn't read too much into it."

Elizabeth looked up sharply. "You are not curious about why she would send for *me*? This is hardly common."

"Hardly," he agreed. "But I imagine it has something to do with the unfortunate business with Perceval. The Queen must be beside herself with worry for her family. Perhaps the king had a difficult episode, as has been rumored. It stands to reason she would seek some pleasant distraction."

Pleasant distraction.

Elizabeth inhaled slowly.

She knew better. Her father's theories were reasonable, but they were wrong. She had stood before the Queen only hours ago.

She had seen the calculation behind those dark eyes, the way the Queen had given nothing away—and yet had already determined a course of action. And now, Elizabeth was being summoned again.

This was no idle whim.

Should she tell her father?

She could say it now—tell him why the Queen was calling for her, why she had already had an audience earlier that day, why this had nothing to do with courtly amusements and royal melancholy.

But she knew what he would say. She could hear it now.

"*I believe that you believe what you saw.*"

"*I am sure whatever you thought you witnessed was very serious indeed.*"

"*Let the ministers handle it.*"

He had already dismissed her once. She could not bear to hear it again.

Her father clapped his hands together.

"Well, petal," he said, smiling broadly, "you had best be on your way."

Elizabeth blinked. "What?"

"I have already called for the carriage and it is at the door." He grinned. "Her Majesty has called, and we cannot keep her waiting, can we?"

Elizabeth's breath caught.

No warning. No time to prepare. No time to even change into a gown fit for court. The Queen had summoned her, and now she had no choice but to obey.

She lifted her chin, suppressing the flicker of unease curling in her stomach. "Of course not."

DARCY HAD NO TIME to adjust his cuffs, steel his thoughts, or even register his irritation before he was ushered through a set of double doors and directly into the presence of the Prince Regent.

The room reeked of excess.

Candelabras dripped wax onto polished tables, their flames casting flickering light over brocade-covered chairs and gilded mirrors. The air was thick with the scent of expensive cologne and tobacco, mingling unpleasantly with the remnants of a half-eaten meal left to congeal on a sideboard.

In the center of it all, the Prince paced.

His coat was too elaborate, his waistcoat over-embroidered, his lace cuffs too frilled for a man of his age and physique—but it was the restlessness in his movements that caught Darcy's attention.

An attendant hovered anxiously behind him, a delicate glass of brandy in one hand, a jeweled snuffbox in the other, scrambling to keep up as the Prince paced, muttering to himself.

"Ah, Darcy," the Prince declared abruptly, not pausing in his stride.

Darcy bowed sharply. "Your Royal Highness."

The Prince waved a hand vaguely, as if brushing aside formalities. "I have a witness now."

Darcy stilled. A witness?

His own skepticism regarding the rumors had been swiftly losing ground—but this, *this* was something tangible.

"I assume," Darcy said carefully, "Your Highness finds this witness credible?"

"Credible?" The Prince snorted, finally stopping to pluck the snuffbox from his attendant's fingers. He flicked it open with a well-practiced motion, inhaling a pinch before exhaling sharply. "My dear fellow, she saw the blasted thing happen."

Darcy's pulse quickened. *She?* What the devil?

He cleared his throat, affecting his most professional manner. "Then I should like to hear the account in full."

The Prince huffed and resumed pacing, waving the snuffbox about as he spoke.

"'Twas a young lady—strayed from her companions, found herself in a bad spot. Right place, wrong time, that sort of thing. The Queen heard her story and passed the account to me."

Darcy nodded. "If Your Highness permits, I should like to take notes."

The Prince gestured lazily toward a nearby writing desk. A footman materialized at Darcy's side, setting out ink, paper, and a fine-pointed quill.

Darcy took his seat, dipped the pen, and glanced up expectantly. "Continue, if you please, Your Highness."

The Prince stared at him. "Continue what?"

Darcy blinked. "The account," he said slowly. "The witness's description of the man she saw, his physical characteristics—was he tall or short? Did he limp? The sort of gun he used—did she note it? His position in the chamber—where exactly was he standing?"

The Prince arched a brow, looking almost bored. "I expect *you* to glean that information," he said, flicking his fingers. "That is *your* duty, after all."

Darcy set the quill down, resisting the urge to pinch the bridge of his nose. "With all due respect, Your Highness," he said, keeping his tone painfully even, "how am I to glean such information if I have never spoken with the witness?"

The Prince waved airily. "No bother. You will have your answers momentarily."

Oh. So he had been summoned here with no briefing, no details—nothing but a royal whim and the expectation that he would, somehow, pluck answers from thin air. It took several measured breaths to keep his irritation in check.

A noise from the hall broke the charged silence. The thud of boots on marble echoed down the corridor, steady and deliberate. Too many footsteps for a single visitor. A sharp command was issued—low, authoritative. A rustle of fabric followed, the whisper of skirts brushing against the floor.

Servants darted out of the way, moving with the quick, trained efficiency of those who knew better than to impede royal business. One footman hesitated before scurrying to adjust a candelabrum, as if suddenly aware that the lighting should be just so.

Darcy straightened slightly, instinct sharpening.

Two guards arrived first, their gold-trimmed coats pristine, each positioning himself at either side of the door. One reached for the handle, but instead of opening it immediately, he hesitated—listening, waiting for some unseen signal.

Darcy glanced toward the Prince.

The man was grinning.

Not in amusement, but in pleasure—the look of a man who had orchestrated some great revelation and was now delighting in the moment before the curtain lifted.

With great theatricality, he adjusted his cuffs, took a slow sip of brandy, and exhaled in satisfaction.

"Ah," he said smoothly, his voice silken with amusement, "here she is."

E LIZABETH EXPECTED TO BE taken to the Queen's private chambers.

That was where she had been before, when she had been summoned that afternoon with the Duchess. The corridors of Buckingham House were labyrinthine, but she had taken note of her surroundings as she walked, cataloging the turns, the rooms, the adornments, the lighting, the rugs... all of it.

Now, however—they were going in the opposite direction.

She hesitated slightly, her silk skirts almost tangling around her ankles as she tried to conceal a glance at her surroundings.

Perhaps the Queen simply spent the evening in a different part of the house? That would make sense. Yes. That would—

Her thoughts cut short as she realized the guards escorting her had suddenly... multiplied. Two had walked with her from the carriage, but now more men closed in behind them, moving with the crisp efficiency of soldiers accustomed to forming a perimeter.

Elizabeth glanced at them sharply. They did not meet her gaze.

She swallowed. Was this still a royal summons, or was she being taken into custody? Had she inadvertently confessed to some crime? Surely, it was not against the law for a lady to be in the House of Commons. So, what...?

She forced herself to breathe evenly, to keep her head high, though her pulse had begun to pound in her throat. She had no choice but to keep walking.

The doors ahead swung open, and she was ushered inside. Elizabeth stepped forward—and stopped short.

The Queen was not here.

Instead, leaning against a gilded chair, dressed in far too much embroidery, a brandy glass in one hand and a jeweled snuffbox near the other, was—

The Prince Regent.

Elizabeth's pulse skipped. She immediately dropped into a curtsy, so abruptly that her feet might have been knocked from under her.

She had never been formally presented to the Prince Regent—she had seen him at court, certainly, but this was... intimate.

Uncomfortably so.

The Prince made no immediate acknowledgment of her bow. He simply exhaled lazily, adjusting the cuffs of his too-elaborate coat before gesturing vaguely in her direction. Then, to her continued astonishment, he turned—not to a lord or a minister, but to a man seated at a writing desk. A man with a questioning look on his face.

Elizabeth could not see much of him, only the sharp set of his shoulders, the marked widening of his eyes, the faint gasp he emitted before he turned back to the Prince with studied patience.

The Prince waved his hand vaguely in her direction. "This is the lady, Darcy." He leaned forward, as if trying to recall something. "Lady Elizabeth Mont..." He trailed off, then turned to her with a flick of his fingers. "Go on, pronounce it for me, if you please."

Elizabeth's throat refused to work.

Something in the stiffness of the man at the desk—this Mr. Darcy, apparently—made her think he was annoyed by the delay.

She kept her gaze low, fixing her eyes on the marble just near the Prince's feet. "Lady Elizabeth Montclair, Your Royal Highness."

The Prince smirked in satisfaction and repeated her name as if tasting a rare delicacy. Then he waved a lazy hand. "Ask her your questions, Darcy."

There was a brief, charged silence. Then—a chair scraped against the floor as Mr. Darcy rose. Elizabeth had barely composed herself before he stepped forward, standing fully within view for the first time.

He was younger than she had expected. Not *young*, exactly, but certainly not some stuffy royal secretary, either. His dark hair was severe, neatly styled, his black coat cut with precision, entirely free of the garish embellishments that adorned the Prince.

His expression was controlled, his features marked by sharp angles and sharper intelligence. He studied her for a moment, then motioned for her to come closer as he returned to his desk and reached for a sheet of paper.

Elizabeth swallowed and did as he invited.

"Lady Elizabeth," he said, his voice deliberate and slow, the kind of tone one used when trying to extract the most accurate response possible.

She nodded slightly, gripping her hands tightly together.

"You saw a second man in the lobby," Darcy stated. "Describe him."

Elizabeth inhaled slowly. "He was... he was tall, I think."

Darcy's quill hovered over the paper. "You think?" he echoed.

She flushed slightly. "I was standing at a distance."

"Then describe his shape."

Elizabeth frowned slightly. "Broad-shouldered, I believe. But not as large as the guards. He was well-dressed, though not ostentatiously so."

Darcy nodded slightly, jotting something down. "What color was his coat?"

Elizabeth paused. "It was dark," she said, then hesitated. "I... I think it was brown?"

Darcy's eyes narrowed slightly. "You are uncertain?"

"There was a great deal of commotion at the time, Mr. Darcy."

"Indeed." He turned the paper slightly. "And what of his hair?"

Elizabeth blinked. "His hair?"

"Yes," Darcy said, voice cool. "What color was it?"

Elizabeth felt heat creeping up her neck. "I... I do not know. He was wearing a hat that looked like every other man's hat."

Darcy tilted his head slightly but said nothing.

The Prince, meanwhile, popped open his snuffbox and inhaled a pinch, looking thoroughly unconcerned.

"What sort of pistol did he carry?"

Elizabeth pressed her lips together. "A small one."

"Of what make?"

Elizabeth's stomach twisted. "I... do not know."

"Engraving? Silver accents?"

"I did not see."

Darcy exhaled loudly, clearly irritated.

Elizabeth stiffened. "You are asking questions that require a level of knowledge I do not possess, sir."

Darcy looked back at her sharply. "Then what, exactly, *did* you see?"

"The second most powerful man in England falling to the floor, covered in his own blood."

Darcy's quill paused over the page. He stared at the page before him for several seconds. Then, after a moment—he nodded.

"That," he said, voice quieter, "is useful."

T HE PRINCE HAD GONE mad. Darcy was sure of it now. But there was nothing to do but carry on with his inquisition, though his pulse was about to burn through his temples and his stomach threatened at any moment to give up its contents.

"The exact moment he fell," Darcy said, keeping his voice level, precise. "Do you recall when the shot struck him? Was there a delay?"

Lady Elizabeth's brow furrowed. "A delay?"

"Yes." Darcy dipped his pen into the ink, the scratch of the quill filling the brief silence. "Did he collapse the instant the shot was fired, or was there a moment—even a breath's hesitation—before he fell?"

She hesitated. "I—"

Darcy pressed. "Did he turn toward the shooter? Did he clutch his wound? Did he attempt to speak?"

Her lips parted, then pressed together in frustration. "He staggered," she said, as if testing the memory against itself. "I think."

Darcy nodded sharply.

"Which way?" he asked.

She blinked. "Which—way?"

"When he staggered," Darcy clarified, his pen poised, "did he reel backward? Forward? To his left or right?"

Lady Elizabeth inhaled, her dark eyes shifting up and to the right... or, rather, to *her* left. Darcy watched carefully—that, in itself, was a good sign. At least she seemed to be remembering something rather than inventing something.

"Backward, I believe," she said at last.

"You *believe*."

Her chin lifted slightly at the coolness of his tone. "Yes."

Darcy narrowed his eyes slightly but nodded, his mind already calculating.

The angle of the body, the reaction time—these things mattered. They could determine the position of the shooter, verify whether a single bullet had struck or if—

The Prince sighed loudly from his chair.

Darcy paused, glancing up.

"Oh, do settle all this later, will you?" The Prince waved a lazy hand, reaching for his brandy glass.

Darcy blinked. *Settle it later?* The Prime Minister had been murdered, and he had been summoned here for answers. The very idea of—

Steady, Darcy, his own thoughts interrupted him. He could hardly afford to make a hash of this.

Very politely, he asked, "How does Your Highness desire for me to carry on?"

The Prince sighed again, as if Darcy were a particularly slow pupil. "Well, obviously, the lady cannot go home," he said, as if this were the most self-evident thing in the world. "We must detain her."

Darcy's head snapped toward Lady Elizabeth—

And immediately regretted it.

She had gone pale as bone, her pupils wide and dark, the whites of her eyes stark against them. Her breath had quickened, the rise and fall of her bodice subtly unsteady.

Darcy swallowed.

Turning back deliberately, he said, "I hardly think it necessary to detain the lady like a common thief. She has done nothing to merit such treatment."

The Prince shook his head, tutting. "Darcy, Darcy—you quite do not comprehend the matter."

"And how, Your Highness, ought I to comprehend it?"

The Prince leaned forward, swirling the amber liquid in his glass. "She cannot return home because she was seen." His voice was light, careless, as though discussing a matter of mere inconvenience. "And I do not relish the notion of losing my only witness before the true murderer has been caught."

He took a sip, as if that settled things. Then, with a lazy flick of his fingers, he added, "Besides, I imagine the Marquess would be dismayed to be deprived of his daughter."

Darcy's stomach tightened. Something in the air shifted, and he glanced at Lady Elizabeth again—

And nearly had to dash his eyes down before his own reaction gave him away.

The color had returned to her face—but not in relief. Her breath had quickened for an entirely different reason. Her fingers knotted at her sides, knuckles white, her gaze darting not to the Prince but wildly around the room, as though she were seeking an exit.

She was furious. Barely restraining herself.

In seconds, she was like to do something rather... irreverent, and then all would be lost.

Darcy turned sharply back to the Prince. Between clenched teeth, he asked, "What, precisely, does Your Highness mean to do with her?"

The Prince frowned. "*Do* with her?"

Darcy's jaw locked. "It is a matter of some pertinence."

The Prince sighed as if the matter were tedious and gestured vaguely. "*You* will take her, of course."

A beat of silence.

Darcy's jaw dropped. For a long, heavy second, he could only stare.

Then—he felt it.

A heat on his cheek. Not a flush, but the distinct weight of someone's eyes on him.

Lady Elizabeth was staring at him.

Slowly, very slowly, he turned his head.

Her lips had parted, her chest rising and falling rapidly. She looked betrayed.

Darcy quickly turned back to the Prince.

"Your Highness," he said carefully, "where, pray, do you expect me to take her? I can hardly put her in my closet at The Albany. No ladies are permitted, and besides—"

The Prince scoffed. "Do you take me for a fool? The lady must be hidden. You must take her somewhere to that effect."

Darcy's blood—what remained of it—rushed to his head. *No.* No, no, no... Anything but—

"Another name," the Prince went on, "another place of residence. I trust no one but you, Darcy—you owe no man anything."

Darcy's tongue clove to the roof of his mouth. "Your Highness, I am... I am a bachelor."

"You are a gentleman by reputation," the Prince continued as he drew another pinch of snuff, "so I expect the lady will remain intact in your keeping."

Darcy's breath hissed in through his teeth. *Intact...* how very delicate. And entirely out of character for the Prince to even care about.

"And the fewer who know her whereabouts, the better. *I* do not even wish to know where you take her."

A sharp inhalation.

Darcy felt it rather than heard it, and Lady Elizabeth Montclair's voice cut through the air like a knife. "What am I to tell my father? Does His Highness expect I will not be missed?"

She had spoken out of turn, her voice sharp with disbelief.

Darcy glanced at her in alarm, but she did not look at him. Her eyes were fixed on the Prince. She lifted her chin defiantly, waiting for an answer.

The Prince blinked. "Well, by Jove, she is a sprightly creature! I could have you hanged, dear thing."

Darcy rose from the desk, his paper and quill abandoned. "She asks a reasonable question, Your Highness. One cannot simply 'disappear' with the daughter of a peer."

"Oh, Her Majesty will manage the affair." He waved a bored hand. "It will probably be reported that you have been invited on a pleasure tour with some of the Queen's ladies-in-waiting—one of those dreadful little excursions to the countryside. I know nothing of such matters, but my mother is very clever in these things. Your father will think nothing amiss—will likely be terribly flattered, in fact. And of course, we shall see to it that he receives regular 'letters' from 'you' while you are away."

Darcy winced.

Lady Elizabeth's mouth fell open. Slowly, stiffly, she turned her head and stared at him.

Darcy was not a coward. But at that moment, he rather wished he were *anywhere* but here. Dead would be easiest.

The Prince yawned and motioned away the servant who was offering to refill his glass. "Well, then," he said brightly. "That is all settled." He flicked his fingers at his guards. "Escort them out."

Darcy's stomach clenched.

The guards immediately stepped forward, gesturing toward the doors.

"I expect your reports in the usual way," the Prince called.

Darcy barely heard him. He was too busy considering the many, many ways this was about to become a disaster.

"Oh, and I shall have satisfaction within a fortnight, Darcy. No show of it this time—just a body. Am I quite understood?"

Darcy clenched his jaw, inclining his head. Then—before Lady Elizabeth could unleash the treasonous outrage he could see simmering on the tip of her tongue—he turned, grabbed her hand, and dragged her out of the Prince's sight.

Chapter Five

Lady Elizabeth Montclair had never been forcibly removed from a royal residence before.

There was a first time for everything.

The moment the doors shut behind them, she yanked hard against the grip on her arm. "Unhand me!" she snapped, breathless with fury, twisting against the unforgiving hold of the man dragging her down the marble steps of Buckingham House.

He did not let go.

"Keep your voice down," the man—Darcy, the prince had called him—hissed, barely glancing at her. He moved quickly, efficiently, his grip firm but not cruel. He was not manhandling her, exactly—but neither was he giving her a choice.

Elizabeth dug her heels into the stone. "This is madness—"

"Yes," he bit out. "It is."

Her head spun. She had barely had time to process the absurdity of what had just happened. She had been summoned for a second audience, ushered into a room where—instead of the Queen—she found herself face-to-face with the Prince Regent, and then tossed like a parcel into the hands of a man she did not know.

And now she was being marched into the London streets in the dead of night, while her own carriage—her own attendants—were nowhere to be seen.

"Where is my carriage?" she demanded.

"Dismissed," he said shortly, never breaking stride.

Elizabeth stumbled in shock. "Dis*missed*? You cannot mean—you had no right to dismiss it!"

"*I* did not dismiss it," he ground out. "Your royal summons did. It probably left as soon as you entered the house."

Her stomach dropped. She twisted again, trying to wrench free, but he only tightened his grip and half-led, half-dragged her past the iron gates of the palace grounds.

Elizabeth scanned the street wildly. She would find a way to set this right. *Someone* would mend this nonsense.

"I must speak to the Queen," she said breathlessly. "Or the duchess—yes, the duchess will—"

Darcy suddenly stopped short, whirling toward her so fast she nearly collided with his chest. She gasped, startled, and staggered back a step.

His dark eyes burned with frustration. "The Prince Regent," he enunciated slowly, "has issued a command."

Elizabeth's breath came fast and unsteady. "Then I shall appeal to my father! He will—"

"Your father," he cut in, "can know nothing of this."

Elizabeth's hands curled into fists. "Then I shall tell him!"

Darcy exhaled sharply, pinching the bridge of his nose. "Lady Elizabeth, you do not seem to comprehend the nature of what has happened."

"I comprehend quite well," she retorted, lifting her chin defiantly. "You are abducting me—"

"I am saving your life."

She froze. *That* certainly sounded melodramatic.

Darcy did not *look* like a man prone to histrionics. It must be a joke!

And yet, there was no jest in his voice. Only tightly contained anger.

Only a warning.

A cold shiver trickled down her spine. Somewhere in the distance, a carriage rumbled down the street, and the faint sound of London's evening revelers drifted in from the squares.

Elizabeth swallowed. She could not stay here arguing. She had no carriage. No escort. And whether she liked it or not—this strange, impossible man was the only thing standing between her and the darkened city.

She took a shaky breath, forcing her voice steady. "And where," she asked, lifting her chin once more, "do you propose to take me?"

Darcy's jaw tightened. He exhaled slowly, as though only now realizing he had no answer.

Elizabeth's heart pounded. For the first time since she had entered that royal room—since her world had been so unceremoniously upended—she saw something in him besides frustration. She saw uncertainty.

He had no plan.

Lord help them both.

D ARCY WAS FURIOUS.

Not just irritated. Not merely inconvenienced.

Livid—shaking and speechless and seeing a reddish haze around all his eyes took in.

The night air was thick with damp and coal smoke, the sounds of late-evening revelers drifting from the squares. The streets gleamed beneath the gas lamps, reflecting the flicker of carriage lanterns and the slosh of horse hooves through the filth of the road.

And here he was—standing in the middle of it with an infuriatingly stubborn heiress, no plan, and the single most absurd command he had ever received. His jaw ached from clenching it too tightly.

The Prince had given him nothing.

No details. No leads. No clue how he was supposed to find whatever was missing from this case.

And now—*now*—he was saddled with a witness who was not only entirely useless, but also an absolute menace to his already limited patience in every possible way.

The lady had not stopped talking. She had twisted, argued, and stared daggers into his very soul as though *he* were the one responsible for her predicament.

He was not! By her own admission, she had strayed from her companions and been in the wrong place at the wrong time. This was *not* his doing!

He had spent the last ten years carving out a life of solitude and competence. He had learned to be quick-witted, sharp, decisive—he had navigated London's most dangerous circles and survived.

And yet—

And yet...

Somehow, this woman had rendered him incapable of remembering which way was north.

She was pacing beside him now, her arms wrapped tightly around herself as though she were freezing, even in the heavy cloak she wore. Her breath came fast, her eyes wild with barely restrained outrage.

And blast it all—he could not think a single coherent thought with her standing there looking as though she might set something on fire at any moment.

He *had* to get them off the street. Darcy's hands curled into fists, his mind working rapidly.

He could not take her to Albany.

He could not take her to *any* reputable household where she might be recognized.

Which left... nothing.

No, not nothing.

A terrible idea.

An idea that would make his skin crawl, his pride wither, and his temper snap. But it would have to do.

Darcy exhaled sharply, lifting his hand to hail a carriage. One rattled toward them almost instantly, the driver leaning forward with an eager expression.

"Where to, sir?"

Darcy hesitated. Just for a single, fatal second.

Because the moment the words left his lips, he knew he would regret them.

"...Take us to cheap lodgings. In Southwark."

The driver grinned, tipping his hat. "Aye, sir."

Darcy turned back just in time to see Lady Elizabeth stare at him in sheer horror.

"*Southwark?*" she repeated, as though she had never heard the word before.

Darcy ignored her. Instead, he opened the carriage door, placed a firm hand against her back, and—as gently as his patience allowed—guided her inside.

Then, before she could argue further, he followed her in, shut the door, and let the carriage plunge into the London night.

"THIS IS ENTIRELY UNNECESSARY," Elizabeth said for the third time, her arms folded tightly as the carriage rattled through the darkened streets of London. Darcy said nothing.

The man had barely looked at her since forcing her into the carriage, his expression set in stone, his posture stiff as he watched the city blur past the filthy glass window.

Elizabeth scowled.

"I need only send word to someone," she insisted. "Lady Charlotte would take me in—her mother is a duchess, for heaven's sake, do you truly think—"

"No."

Elizabeth gasped, affronted. "*No?*"

He dragged a hand over his face, clearly suppressing his temper. "You still do not comprehend," he muttered. "You cannot go *anywhere* you are known!"

Her lips parted in protest. "That is—"

"You were seen, Lady Elizabeth! Your life is now nearly forfeit! And for some unknown reason, the prince wishes to *keep* you alive, so the places you might have gone before are no longer options."

"But how could anyone know who I—"

"It would be the work of a moment to identify a woman as striking as you!" he cut in, dark eyes flashing in the dim carriage. "Are you truly so naïve that you think the questions have not already been asked and answered? Everyone within five miles of London can identify the Marquess of Ashwick's daughter!"

Elizabeth's mouth snapped shut. Then, she blinked. "You think me striking?"

"Heaven help me." He covered his eyes and groaned out a heavy sigh. "And now that I am stuck with you, I cannot even go back to my own flat for a change of clothing! What the devil am I to do with a spoilt, contrary, ignorant—"

"I will have you know, I speak Latin, French, German, *and* Portuguese. I am better with figures than most gentlemen, I can argue Plato and Socrates, I play chess and whist—"

"And you are also a liar," Darcy growled. "Or seriously deluded about your own abilities, which is worse."

Elizabeth curled her lip and huffed, crossing her arms and turning her gaze toward the window.

The streets had changed. They were no longer in Mayfair or St. James's—no longer among the grand terraces and townhouses she recognized.

These streets were narrow, winding, with buildings pressed close together, their second stories jutting out over the road. The people they passed were roughly dressed, the inn signs dirtied with soot, the air heavy with the smell of stale ale, damp wood, and unwashed bodies.

Elizabeth stiffened. "Where, in the name of all that is holy *are* we?"

Darcy did not answer.

A moment later, the carriage jerked to a halt. The driver twisted in his seat and called down to them. "Lodgings, sir."

Elizabeth's stomach sank.

Darcy opened the door, stepped down without hesitation, and held out his hand.

She did not take it.

Instead, she stared at the crooked sign swinging over the door of a dingy, low-roofed inn, its windows thick with grime, the doorway uneven.

Her breath came fast. "You expect me to—"

"Yes," he said shortly. "Out."

E LIZABETH'S TEETH CHATTERED AS they stepped inside.

The common room was dimly lit, the walls stained with tobacco smoke and splattered ale. A few patrons sat at rough wooden tables, hunched over their drinks, casting furtive glances at the newcomers.

Darcy paid them no mind. He strode toward the counter, where a bored-looking innkeeper wiped a tankard with a rag that looked dirtier than the floorboards.

Elizabeth wrapped her cloak more tightly around herself.

This was indecent.

This was unacceptable.

"I need a room," Darcy said, tossing a coin onto the counter.

The innkeeper squinted at it, then at Darcy... then at her. "One?"

Darcy exhaled slowly. "One."

Elizabeth's head snapped toward him.

"*One?*" she hissed in horrified disbelief.

Darcy turned to her, his jaw tight. "Yes," he said shortly.

The innkeeper dropped a key on the counter and pointed. "Upstairs. Second door."

Mr. Darcy sighed and took the key. "Thank you."

Elizabeth's face burned. "You cannot mean to—"

He placed a firm hand against the small of her back and steered her toward the stairs.

She bristled. "Do not put your hands on me!"

"I assure you, my lady," he muttered darkly, "it is not my preference, either."

She gasped in fresh outrage.

There was no kindly maid waiting with a lantern, no polite footman to guide them. Just a narrow, uneven staircase, a creaking banister, and Darcy push-dragging her up the steps before she could gather herself enough to scream.

The room was small, cold, and utterly wretched. A narrow bed, a rickety table, a single window with a threadbare curtain. It smelled of old wood, damp wool, and the ghost of tobacco smoke.

Elizabeth whirled toward him, seething. "You mean to leave me here *alone?*"

Darcy closed the door behind them, exhaling heavily and bolting the door. "No."

She reeled back. "Then—"

Darcy shrugged off his overcoat.

Elizabeth's heart dropped into her feet, and her back pressed against the wall. *"What,"* she demanded, voice high and sharp, "are you *doing?"*

Darcy tossed the coat onto the back of the chair, utterly ignoring her distress.

Elizabeth's heart pounded.

She had heard of men like him—men who thought they could take what they wanted—

"I will scream!" she warned.

Darcy let out an exhausted breath, rubbing a hand over his face. "For the love of—" He turned toward her, exasperation burning in his dark eyes. "We are in Southwark! I cannot very well put you in a room alone like a fine lady with no attendant."

Elizabeth's mouth parted. "Then you mean—"

"To make you appear as anything *but* a fine lady," he cut in.

A terrible silence stretched between them.

Darcy lifted his chin, eyes flashing in warning. "We must either appear as man and wife, or—" His jaw worked, and he fell into a stubborn mute glare.

"Or?" she prompted with suspicion.

"Or, the more likely supposition, as a man and his mistress."

Elizabeth recoiled. She opened her mouth—then snapped it shut.

Then opened it again.

Then—

Her breath hitched, and she whirled toward the door. "No. Absolutely not."

Darcy caught her wrist before she could reach for the handle. "Would you rather be seen as an heiress eloping with her amour?"

Elizabeth gaped.

He stalked close and lowered his mouth to her ear, his breath creating little tickles in the hair at her temple. "Because that is the only other conclusion they will draw! And the more you are seen, the more they get a look at your fine gown or hear your noble protests, that is *precisely* the conclusion that will be drawn."

She yanked her arm free. "You would be the last man in the world I would elope with!"

Darcy's expression did not change. "The feeling," he said dryly, "is mutual."

"At least we agree on *something!*"

"You do not understand. A man and his mistress—that is so common as to be *de rigueur*. These establishments would hardly exist without such custom. But a noble heiress, dragged to a shabby rooming house by night? Particularly one who sounds like the veriest snob and keeps raising her voice in protest? That, my dear Elizabeth, is rather suspect."

She straightened. "That is *Lady* Elizabeth to you, you cretin."

"Not here, it is not, and you had best accustom yourself to somewhat less genuflection than you are acquainted with. A protesting heiress draws attention. That innkeeper below cares nothing for your virtue, but he likes coin well enough, particularly in the form of a reward given by a grateful father. If he hears a scuffle, the sounds of an outraged young lady, and pieces together your looks with your snobbish manner of speaking—why, there will be a constable below within an hour."

"Perfect!"

"Not if you like breathing," he shot back. "The same men with the power to execute a scapegoat for murdering a Prime Minister would think nothing of making an annoying heiress 'vanish.'"

She blinked. And she hated how small her voice sounded when it finally emerged. "Then... what do I do?"

Darcy turned, crossing the small room to glance out the window.

Elizabeth huffed. He was always looking at something. Always watching, always calculating. As if he were some cloaked figure in those novels Charlotte read! It was most vexing.

She folded her arms tightly. "And *what,*" she asked, voice clipped, "are you looking for now?"

Darcy did not turn. Instead, he reached for the curtain.

And closed it.

D ARCY LIFTED THE EDGE of the curtain once more to steal another glance out the window, his body tense, his thoughts racing.

Elizabeth—*Lady* Elizabeth—stood silent behind him, a miracle in itself. Her question still hung in the air.

"Then... what do I do?"

A fair question.

One he was hardly prepared to answer.

Outside, the street was dimly lit, the glow of a nearby lantern illuminating puddles in the uneven road. A few figures lingered, dark shapes moving through the fog. He could not tell whether they were drunken revelers, pickpockets, or something worse.

The room was small, suffocating, the walls too thin, the locks too flimsy for his liking. But it would do for now. His breath fogged against the windowpane. Behind him, he heard the rustle of skirts, a huff of frustration.

"Are you always this brooding?"

"I prefer 'thoughtful,'" he said dryly.

She huffed again. "I asked you a question. You seem so determined to control this situation—so tell me. *What* do I do?"

He turned, leaning against the sill. His gaze met hers, and for the first time that evening, she was not glaring at him in open defiance.

She was waiting.

She was frightened.

And something in that look made his chest shatter.

He exhaled slowly. "You behave," he said. "You do not draw attention to yourself. You speak as little as possible."

Elizabeth's brows lifted. "I am not a silent person."

"So I gathered." Darcy folded his arms. "I have done what I can to keep suspicions away, but I assure you, it would not take much for you to ruin it."

She squared her shoulders. "I do not make a habit of ruining things."

"The past hour would suggest otherwise."

She glowered. "Only because *you* are impossible."

He pushed off the windowsill. "You are tired. You may take the bed."

Elizabeth blinked in surprise. "*That* thing?"

"I will take the chair."

She glanced at the chair and shivered visibly—a sentiment he shared, for it looked even more worn and rickety than the bed. Darcy was not terribly inclined to allow his clothing to touch it, but he suspected the bed was, in actuality... the worse of the two.

"You expect me to believe you would sit there all night?"

"I have endured worse."

She pressed her lips together, hesitated, then wrinkled her nose slightly.

"Well," she muttered, shifting her weight. "I can only imagine what that bed must be like."

Darcy could hardly blame her disgust. He grabbed his overcoat from the chair, strode over to the bed, and threw it over the bedding. "There. Try not to expire."

Elizabeth blinked. Then scowled.

Darcy turned away before she could find another reason to complain, brushing past her toward the chair.

"You do not look like a man accustomed to discomfort," she muttered.

Darcy huffed a humorless laugh. "*You,*" he murmured, lowering himself stiffly into the chair, "do not look like a woman accustomed to patience."

Her mouth fell open, but instead of speaking she just waited... and finally closed it with a deep glare that would have shot ice into his bones, were he not already so blasted weary.

Darcy sat down with finality, stretching his legs out before him, his body exhausted but his mind still racing.

She muttered something about arrogant, impossible men, but at last—at long, *long* last—

She did not argue. She even gingerly stretched out on top of his coat on the bed.

Darcy let his head fall back against the chair.

He had no idea how the devil he was going to get through the night.

DARCY HAD SPENT NIGHTS in some miserable conditions before.

He had slept in a damp prison cell, disguised as a common pickpocket. He had spent an entire week in a filthy tavern in Liverpool, pretending to be an out-of-work dockhand, while gathering intelligence on a smuggling ring. He had lain on rooftops in the freezing cold, waiting to intercept a courier carrying treasonous letters.

And yet—somehow—

This chair was worse.

The legs wobbled if he shifted even slightly. The seat was too narrow. The back angled just enough to make it impossible to rest his head comfortably.

And the company?

The most trying of all.

A frustrated sigh drifted from the bed. Darcy rolled his head to the side, cracking open an eye.

Elizabeth—*Lady* Elizabeth—was not asleep.

Not for lack of trying, clearly. She had turned onto one side, then the other. She had pushed back the overcoat, then pulled it up again. She had lain on top of it, under it, and inside it, touching every surface of the thing so that he would never get her perfume out of it. She had huffed, sighed, growled under her breath, and shifted so many times that he had lost count.

Darcy sighed, rubbing his forehead. "What," he muttered, eyes half-lidded, "is the matter now?"

She flopped onto her back, glaring at the ceiling. "This *bed*," she hissed. "Is an insult to the word 'bed'."

Darcy huffed a low laugh, more breath than sound. "Welcome," he murmured, voice heavy with exhaustion, "to disreputable lodgings."

A long silence followed.

Then—softly— "This is the worst night of my life."

Darcy snorted, cracking open one eye. "Then you have been extraordinarily fortunate."

Elizabeth made a rude noise, yanking the sleeve of his overcoat higher over her chest.

Another stretch of silence.

Darcy exhaled, tilting his head back, letting his eyes fall closed. For a single, fleeting second, he thought she had finally given up.

Then— "Why are you looking out the window all the time?"

Darcy's eyes snapped open. She had been watching him? He shifted, slowly rolling his head back toward her.

Elizabeth lay still, her face half-hidden in the dim glow of the dying firelight. Her gaze was sharp, keen, waiting for an answer.

He considered his words. "I... do not take unnecessary risks."

Elizabeth scoffed, rolling onto her side, tucking her hands under his overcoat. "Well," she muttered. "You are doing a poor job of that."

Darcy sighed, closing his eyes again.

Tomorrow.

He would deal with her tomorrow.

CHAPTER SIX

Southwark, May 15, 1812

E LIZABETH AWOKE COLD, MISERABLE, and vaguely furious at existence.

For a single, blissful moment, she did not remember where she was. The scent of her familiar rosewater perfume still clung faintly to the fabric twisted around her, and there was warmth against her cheek from where she had pressed into the folds.

A sharp ache throbbed at the base of her skull, her back protesting violently as she tried to shift her position. The mattress beneath her had been stuffed with something far less forgiving than feathers—straw and wood shavings, perhaps, or scraps of fabric stolen from a tailor's floor. She had been uncomfortably cold all night, and yet she was overheated now, tangled in the heavy folds of some wool thing that was both too heavy to be a proper blanket and too misshapen to cover her evenly.

That would be why the draft hit her when she tried to roll over.

She inhaled sharply, eyes blinking open to a ceiling that was not familiar, not elegant, and not remotely respectable. The scent of moldering wood, unwashed linens, and something musty and unpleasant filled her nose. The muffled sounds of a raucous argument from downstairs drifted up, accompanied by the occasional thud of something hitting a table—or a person.

It all came back in a rush.

She sat up too quickly and winced. Her back protested.

The bed—if one could call it that—would have made a passable torture device, the thin mattress barely disguising the hard slats beneath. Her legs were tangled in something thick and heavy, and she realized with a fresh wave of horror that it was that strange man's coat.

Or at least, it *had* been his coat.

Now, it was something far worse—a casualty of her restless sleep, wrinkled, twisted, hopelessly rumpled and probably soiled from whatever was on that mattress. And worst of all, as she shifted beneath the overcoat, she felt the grainy stickiness on her palm where it had brushed against the bedsheets.

She inhaled sharply and shoved the overcoat to the floor. Darcy could hardly complain—it was not as if that would make it any more soiled than it already was.

Pushing the coat away only served to remind her of how freezing the room was, and she shuddered. She sat up with a groan, rubbing her hands up and down her arms, attempting to restore some feeling to her chilled body.

What she would not give for a proper fire, for a warm bath, for a breakfast served on a tray rather than whatever stale bread and weak ale the downstairs innkeeper would consider a meal.

But it was not the cold, nor the discomfort, that truly set her stomach twisting. It was the fact that she was still here.

Still trapped in this awful, suffocating little room.

Still trapped with *him*.

The chair across the room groaned under the full weight of Mr. Darcy, who was slumped back at an uncomfortable angle, his arms crossed, his head tipped back against the wall. The sight of him—a tall, immovable force, both brooding and disheveled—reminded her of the fact that she could not go home. That her father had no idea where she was.

Her father! Surely by now someone had come for her. Her father would have sent men searching. The duchess would have been appalled, no doubt asking the duke to storm the palace for answers. The Queen—surely—had seen fit to clarify whatever absurd mistake had landed Elizabeth in this predicament.

Yes, surely someone had sorted this out.

All she needed was to compose herself, smooth her hair, and—

Her gaze caught the cracked mirror above the rickety dresser, and her mouth fell open in horror.

Elizabeth scrambled to her feet, crossing the room in two strides, eyes widening in abject horror at her reflection.

Her normally smooth waves had transformed into a disaster, tangles escaping from her pins, loose strands sticking up at angles that defied nature. Her face was pale, smudged with fatigue, her gown wrinkled beyond repair.

She looked—dear heaven—she looked *common*. And she did the only thing she could possibly do.

She screamed.

DARCY AWOKE IN A state of pure instinct. His body jerked upright, muscles snapping tense as a rush of blood kicked into his muscles and propelled him into immediate alertness.

His mind instantly leapt to the worst possible conclusion—someone had broken in, they had been followed, they were in danger—his hand shot to his boot, fingers closing around the hidden blade tucked beneath the worn leather.

But instead of an attacker, instead of an intruder, instead of the reasonable cause for alarm that his instincts had anticipated...

He found Lady Elizabeth Montclair standing before the mirror, her hands in her hair, her face frozen in absolute horror.

"What is it?" he barked.

She whipped around, pointing at herself in the cracked mirror like she had just seen an actual demon. "*That!*"

Darcy blinked. And then dragged a slow, exhausted hand down his face. "You are screaming," he muttered, voice hoarse from sleep, "at your own reflection."

She whirled toward him again, her expression a mixture of indignation, disbelief, and distress. "Look at me!" she cried, flinging a hand toward the mirror.

His head fell back against the chair, and he closed his eyes again. "I *am* looking," he said flatly. "And yet, I see no crisis."

"No crisis? My hair looks as though I woke in a ditch and rolled the rest of the way here!"

Darcy opened one eye, surveying her for a long moment before allowing a slow smirk to curl at the corner of his mouth. "Well," he mused, "in that you are correct. That is *precisely* what you look like."

Elizabeth spun back to the mirror, gesturing violently at her head. "You do not understand. *You* do not have waist-long hair that kinks into fist-sized snarls at the slightest provocation. *You* have not had to sit by the hour letting someone work out the knots with tears in your eyes and praying you have hair left when she is done!"

Darcy sighed again, deeper this time, rubbing his temples. "I fail to see the problem," he said, not bothering to hide his exasperation. "No one expects you to look like a marquess's daughter today. You are in hiding. Perhaps you should refrain from screaming your distress for all of Southwark to hear."

Elizabeth scowled. "Forgive me for not wishing to look like a street beggar."

Darcy let his head thud back against the chair. "Your vanity," he muttered, "is the only thing untouched by the night's trials."

She whirled on him. "My *vanity?* You think this is about vanity? I am talking about hours of pain and forced idleness!"

He gestured vaguely toward her undone curls. "Be that as it may, I can assure you, the greater danger this morning is not your hair."

She shot him a venomous glare, muttering something about arrogant, impossible men, then whipped the overcoat off the floor and flung it in his direction.

He caught it without blinking.

It was wrinkled beyond repair, the fabric still warm from her body, and, just as he had feared, the scent of her perfume clung to it like it had been deliberately seared into the wool.

His fingers flexed involuntarily over the fabric, and for an instant—only an instant—he lifted it to his nose.

Then he jerked it away. What a silly reflex! It was not as if he needed to confirm what he already knew. She had spent all night burrowing into the coat, rolling over it, wrapping herself in it like a blasted cocoon.

And now—it smelled like her.

His shoulders stiffened as he shook it out and threw it over the back of the chair with a bit too much force.

Elizabeth, thankfully, had already turned back toward the mirror, sighing in gloomy despair as she attempted to restore some order to her tangled curls.

Good.

He did not want to discuss it.

"**T**HIS IS INTOLERABLE. WE *must* send word to my father."

Darcy did not look up from fastening his coat. The insufferable man. "No."

Elizabeth's brows drew together. "*No?*"

"The last thing we need is to tell the Marquess of Ashwick where to send an armed retrieval."

She opened her mouth, indignant, then shut it. "Then the Duchess of Wrexham—only a letter! Enough to tell them—"

"Still no. I thought we settled this last night."

Her nostrils flared as she turned away, pacing toward the window. "My father will be looking for me," she insisted. "I was only summoned for an audience with the Queen. I ought to have been home! The palace—surely they sent word?"

"Naturally. You heard His Highness. Her Majesty has already seen to it. You are invited on a 'pleasure tour' with some of the Queen's favorites, and your father will receive 'letters from you.'"

She turned fully toward him. "And you know this for certain?"

He hesitated. It was only for an instant, but the crack in his veneer shone through. "Yes."

Elizabeth's lips parted slightly, as though tasting the words. "And who, do you suppose, will they get to write these letters?"

Darcy stopped to peer out the window again, so he was not facing her when she heard him say, "Her Majesty employs skilled people. They have your handwriting from invitations and acceptances..."

"They cannot."

He let the curtain fall and turned toward her. "Very well. Think that if you will."

"No, I..." She shook her head. "Perhaps my *hand* might be copied convincingly, but what of my words? Anyone who knows me would know *I* was not the one writing."

He collected his hat with a quiet, humorless laugh. "Every young lady thinks she is so unique that her friends would discover the same at the slightest whiff of oddity. Do not flatter yourself, Miss Elizabeth. No one knows you as well as you think or cares as much as you believe. And do not sneer at me when I call you that. Far better that I should call you 'Miss Elizabeth' than 'Lizzy' like some doxy."

She lifted her chin. "You would not *dare*."

"No, what I 'would not dare' is to let a lead ball puncture that pretty satin bodice on your gown. I should think His Highness would be rather put out with me. I might even lose my place at the Home Office. So, until further notice, you are my cousin, 'Miss Elizabeth'—dash it all, I suppose we shall have to invent a surname for you—or you shall be my mistress, 'Lizzy' from Rotten Row. Which do you prefer?"

She puckered her mouth into a scornful pout that she hoped would scald whatever conscience this wretched man possessed. "Neither."

"Just as well. A proper mistress is much friendlier, and as for a respectable maiden..." He squinted one eye at her. "I would be ashamed to confess a relation to someone so haughty."

Elizabeth bent and threw the chamber pot at him. A pity it was empty.

He caught it easily, but his expression turned from mocking to grave. "Fool," he growled. "You almost broke the window! Do you *want* to be discovered?"

"What I *want* seems to be irrelevant, does it not?" she snapped.

He sighed and set the empty pot back on the floor. "You will get used to it. We all do."

Elizabeth crossed her arms. Silence. And glares—he was rather skilled at glaring back at her, much to her dismay. Better than her father, which was unfortunate.

Then, she gave a short, bitter laugh. "They really told my father I was on a royal pleasure tour?"

Darcy remained silent.

She let out a slow breath, turning toward the mirror again. Her cheeks were sallow, her hair only slightly less shocking than it had been.

"How long," she asked, glancing at his reflection, "do you suppose this pleasant excursion shall last?"

Darcy looked down. He had no answer. And she knew it.

She exhaled sharply, shaking her head. "This is absurd."

Darcy did not disagree. But it did not matter.

Because it was happening anyway.

D ARCY HAD A HEADACHE.

Not a faint one. A real, pounding, behind-the-eyes sort of headache that he normally associated with weeks of little sleep, too much responsibility, and Home Office reports that ran in circles and told him nothing.

Except this headache had nothing to do with reports.

It had everything to do with the infuriating woman pacing a hole in the floor of their rented room.

Elizabeth Montclair had been fuming in silence since he had all but dragged her from the lodging house and bundled her into a hired carriage. Now that she had been fed, slightly rested, and was somewhat less horrified by her own reflection, she had apparently rediscovered the energy to be difficult.

Darcy had no time for it.

He had already sent a coded message to Fitzwilliam, arranged for a private room, and given explicit instructions that they were to receive no visitors save the one he was waiting for. Lady Elizabeth Montclair had not taken well to the arrangements.

"This is indecent!" she declared, for what had to be the twentieth time. She crossed her arms, turning to him with a scathing glare. "You mean to leave me here alone?"

Darcy did not look up from double-checking the locks on the window. "You will not be alone," he said shortly. "The innkeeper and his wife are here."

"Yes, and I am sure they will be absolutely heroic should anyone attempt to drag me out of here at gunpoint."

He turned to her then, arms folded, expression unimpressed. "And who, precisely, do you imagine will be dragging you anywhere? They would have to find you first."

She lifted her chin. "I do not know, Mr. Darcy. You have made it quite clear that someone might."

Darcy exhaled through his nose, pinching the bridge of it between his fingers. "I will not be long," he said tightly. "And you will be safer here than anywhere else."

She scoffed. "A coaching inn? Hardly. And why must *I* stay behind while *you* go off unattended?"

"Because *your* input is not helpful at this present juncture. And because *I* am not the one being hunted."

That stopped her. For just a moment, she seemed to process his words, but instead of accepting them, she sniffed and turned away, pretending to study the ragged curtain over the window.

"I *could* be of use," she muttered. "You do not know that I would not be."

Darcy huffed a laugh, rubbing his temple. "Oh yes," he said dryly, "I cannot imagine a finer asset to a covert investigation than an heiress with a penchant for throwing chamber pots at her captor."

She whirled back to him, eyes flashing. "Captor?"

He should have chosen a different word. But it was too late now.

Elizabeth Montclair, rightful heiress, only pride of the Montclair lineage, and notorious thorn in his side, pursed her lips in scandalized offense. She was about to unleash hell.

And that was when the coded knock came at the door—two short, one long, and two short.

Darcy opened the door without preamble, letting Fitzwilliam stride into the room with all the casual confidence of a man who was only half-surprised to be summoned to a questionable inn.

"You had better have a bloody good reason for this," Fitzwilliam said, shaking his head as he stepped inside. "You know how I feel about unplanned excursions to Southw—*oh.*"

He froze in his tracks as he caught sight of Elizabeth.

She stared at him, arms still crossed in defiance, her expression the perfect mix of indignation, hauteur, and deep, unconcealed skepticism.

Fitzwilliam turned slowly back to Darcy.

Darcy braced himself.

"Well," Fitzwilliam drawled. "This is new."

Darcy sighed.

Elizabeth lifted her chin. "What manner of fresh cretinery is this?"

"My cousin," Darcy said stiffly. "And 'cretinery' is not a word."

"It is now," she decided. "Language adapts to life. There was never a need for such a word until now."

Fitzwilliam grinned, stepping forward with a flourishing bow. "Colonel Richard Fitzwilliam, at your service."

Elizabeth did not curtsy. She merely narrowed her eyes, looking Fitzwilliam up and down with clear disapproval.

"And you," Fitzwilliam continued, straightening, "must be the reason my dear cousin looks as though he's just spent a month marching through the gutters of Whitechapel."

Elizabeth tilted her head. "I was rather under the impression he always looked like that."

Darcy exhaled sharply, looking at the ceiling.

"Excellent," Fitzwilliam said, clapping his hands together. "You do have a sense of humor. That should serve you well. Now then—" He turned back to Darcy, stepping closer and lowering his voice. "I assume you've not gone completely mad. What the devil is going on?"

Darcy's jaw tightened. "I will explain everything," he said, avoiding Elizabeth's gaze. "But first—"

"Wait." Fitzwilliam held up a hand and sniffed.

Darcy stiffened.

Fitzwilliam's brows lifted. "Do you smell that?"

Darcy exhaled. "I am well aware I have not bathed. We have not been afforded such a—"

Fitzwilliam waved a hand. "No, no, you—" He sniffed again. "You actually smell quite nice."

Darcy blinked.

Fitzwilliam grinned. "Rosewater," he declared. "It's distinctly rosewater."

There was a silence. Darcy did not move. From the corner of his vision, he could see Elizabeth still as a statue, her arms folding just a bit tighter over herself.

Fitzwilliam's grin widened.

Darcy cleared his throat, brushing past him toward the window. "That is irrelevant."

Fitzwilliam laughed. "Is it, now? Well, then, I am all anticipation to learn what you do consider 'relevant.'"

Elizabeth sniffed and turned away.

Darcy pointed at her. "Lock the door behind us. Am I quite understood?"

She tilted her head just enough to show him the tip of her pointed chin and the slit of one half-lidded eye. Well. That would have to do—she was not going to offer any better promises.

He gestured to his cousin. "Let us have a private word downstairs."

D ARCY HAD NEVER REGRETTED anything more than answering the Prince Regent's summons.

That was saying something, considering he had once voluntarily set foot in Whitechapel on a rumor and spent a full night in an alley pretending to be unconscious just to hear the right conversation.

But this—this was worse.

This was playing nursemaid to a nobleman's daughter—a woman who had no useful information—while unraveling a conspiracy—again, with no useful information, while actively resisting the urge to strangle everyone in sight.

Including his own cousin.

"So let me see if I comprehend this," Fitzwilliam said, stretching his legs out beneath the small, rough-hewn table in the dim alcove where they had found some measure of privacy. "The Prince has sent you to unravel a potential conspiracy—on nothing but a whisper—because a young lady claims she saw a second shooter?"

"She *did* see a second shooter."

Fitzwilliam arched a brow. "Did she? And you know this for certain?"

Darcy made a face. "To the best of my discernment. She was hiding, out of sight. No one else had the vantage point she did," he said, choosing his words carefully. "She saw something that does not align with what everyone else believes."

Fitzwilliam rubbed his jaw thoughtfully, nodding. "Well. If the Prince believes it, it must be true."

Darcy shot him a scathing look.

Fitzwilliam grinned. "I do have some news, cousin," he said, leaning back. "Bellingham was convicted not two hours ago."

Darcy had expected that, but his stomach still sank. "I see."

Fitzwilliam looked grim now. "It was quick. Too quick. The evidence was presented, the witnesses all aligned, and the jury did not even leave the box before delivering their verdict. He will hang within the week. A pity, the poor soul."

"Why do you say that?"

"Well, if your... lady... whatever she is... is to be believed, Bellingham is not the murderer."

"No, he was guilty," Darcy muttered. "She saw him fire. Everyone saw him fire. His may not have been the fatal shot, but he is not an innocent man."

"Yes, but was he guilty alone?" Fitzwilliam asked.

"That is the very thing the Prince has asked me to determine."

Fitzwilliam took another sip of ale, then eyed him over the rim of his glass. "And what in blazes do you mean to do with *her?*"

"She cannot stay in London," Darcy said shortly. "And I cannot keep her."

Fitzwilliam's lips twitched. "Oh? You mean to say you do not wish to install an heiress in your Albany flat? What a waste."

Darcy leveled him with a dark glare.

Fitzwilliam grinned wider. "You could always bring her home to Matlock. I am sure my mother would adore—"

"I would rather put my head through that wall."

Fitzwilliam laughed, but Darcy ignored him, muttering half to himself as he mentally eliminated the few, terrible options before him.

"I cannot take her to Netherfield. No plausible reason for her to be there. Bingley has his sisters with him, and they would talk."

Fitzwilliam hummed in amusement. "I would pay to see Caroline Bingley's face."

Darcy did not dignify that with a response.

"She cannot go to Matlock. Or to Pem—" He cut himself off. Pemberley was not his to take her to. He exhaled. "Well. She cannot remain in London."

"Yes, you have said that twice now," Fitzwilliam pointed out helpfully.

Darcy scowled. Blasted, bloody nonsense, all this! Had he not answered that summons, he could have been comfortably settled by a roaring fire with Bingley last night. Might be out after the hounds this morning, possibly with a stimulating game of chess to look forward to with Bennet. But no, he had gone to White's, like a blighted fool, and been dragged into the thick of it.

He sighed. "She needs to be hidden somewhere no one would think to look."

"That much is obvious," Richard replied.

Darcy plucked at his chin as his eyes glazed over in thought. Somewhere discreet. Somewhere no one would question an unknown "relation" suddenly appearing in the household. Somewhere—

His thoughts stuttered.

Hertfordshire.

Netherfield.

Longbourn.

Darcy's thoughts lurched, catching on a thread of something—something that might actually make sense. His spine stiffened.

Mr. Bennet.

It was preposterous.

It was *perfect*.

The Bennets had a cousin no one had ever met. A connection already whispered about among the neighbors, an expectation of someone appearing someday to claim the estate. No one would think twice if *another* relative—distant, forgotten, unimportant—also surfaced from obscurity.

The Bennets were loud, chaotic, impossible to ignore, yet utterly unremarkable to those in high society. Who would suspect them? Who would believe them capable of harboring a fugitive?

No one.

No one would ever look for a missing heiress there.

Darcy rubbed a hand over his mouth, mind racing.

Would Bennet agree?

Darcy huffed. Of course, he would. He would find it amusing. A lark. A secret to keep from his wife, a joke to play with himself as the only audience.

But there would need to be compensation.

That, too, could be arranged. The Prince owed him. And Bennet was practical—he would not turn down a financial incentive, not when it meant an easy favor.

Darcy's fingers twitched at his side, tapping his thigh as he ticked off the ideas.

If he took residence at Netherfield again, he could keep watch. He would be close. He could—

It could *work*.

God help him, it *could* actually work.

His thoughts spun, momentum building, one possibility tumbling into the next, barely aware that Fitzwilliam was staring at him with increasing alarm.

"What the devil are you doing?" Fitzwilliam asked, voice slow with suspicion.

Darcy did not respond.

"You're doing it again," Fitzwilliam muttered. "That thing where you start speaking in half-sentences and your eyes dart around like you're reading invisible reports in the air."

"I need to write to Mr. Bennet," Darcy muttered. Then, before the thought even finished forming, he shook his head. "No. I need to speak with him."

Fitzwilliam blinked. "Who? Where?"

"Hertfordshire."

A pause.

Fitzwilliam's expression edged toward genuine concern. "Are you well?"

Darcy barely heard him.

"Longbourn," he muttered, the plan assembling itself faster than he could articulate it. "A family of daughters—quite respectable. A cousin no one has met. If she takes the name..."

Fitzwilliam's brows pulled together, deeply, profoundly concerned now. "Darcy," he said slowly. "Do try to form a coherent—"

A noise.

Faint, at first—just the low murmur of voices from above, indistinct, blending with the general hum of the inn.

Fitzwilliam stopped speaking and rolled his eyes upward, toward the sound, but Darcy barely registered it. His mind was still spinning, assembling, caught between the details of Hertfordshire, Longbourn, and how precisely he was going to convince Mr. Bennet to take in a fugitive.

Then something shifted.

A different tone. A shuffle of movement on the stairs. A disturbance.

Darcy's brow furrowed, his mind stumbling, trying to process it before it could fully break through.

Then— that voice.

Sharp. Cutting. *Familiar.*

Darcy's entire body snapped to attention.

"Mind your hands, sir!" came Elizabeth's unmistakable tone, cool and clipped despite the fire beneath it. "*And* your eyes! I will thank you to put them back in your head where they belong!"

The words hit Darcy like a trigger pulled.

He was on his feet before he fully knew why, the chair scraping back with a harsh clatter. Fitzwilliam's voice reached him—something questioning, something alarmed—but Darcy was already moving. Shoving past the table. Striding toward the door.

The words replayed in his mind—a warning, not a scream—but his pulse was already pounding violently, drowning out thought.

The stairs were before him.

He rounded the corner.

And there they were.

Two men.

Both staggering slightly, the stench of cheap spirits thick in the air around them. Their postures were too close, too familiar, their weight tipped slightly forward, that telltale lazy confidence of men accustomed to women tolerating their presence whether they wished to or not.

Elizabeth's expression was carved from stone—her chin lifted, her dark eyes blazing with a quiet, deadly fury—but there was a slight tension in her shoulders, the kind that spoke of bracing for impact.

One of them had his hand on her sleeve, despite the fact that she had hooked her arm in an attempt to pull away.

The moment registered. And Darcy saw red.

The next second happened on instinct. His stride never faltered—his arm shot forward, his hand closing into a fist before he fully thought to do so—

Contact.

A satisfying crunch.

The shorter of the two men reeled back, a sharp grunt of pain tearing from his throat as he stumbled, clutching his jaw.

The taller man turned, blinking blearily, as if his ale-soaked mind was struggling to process what had just occurred. Darcy had no intention of waiting for him to catch up.

Behind him, Fitzwilliam had reached the scene. He was already moving, his hand clamping onto the second man's shoulder with a casual sort of strength that belied its iron grip.

"You might leave now," Fitzwilliam said, voice dangerously light, as though offering a pleasant suggestion rather than a command.

The man, still sluggish, frowned. "We meant no harm—"

Darcy turned fully toward him, deliberately stepping closer.

The drunken man finally registered the look on Darcy's face. And turned pale.

"*Out.*" Darcy's voice was low, controlled, but there was murder in it.

The two men hesitated for the briefest moment, as if debating whether the appeal of the lady before them was worth risking a broken jaw—but with one final glance at Darcy and Fitzwilliam, their resolve crumbled.

The shorter man muttered something under his breath, rubbing his jaw as he stumbled toward the door. The second man followed, shoulders hunched, eyes avoiding theirs.

Silence.

Darcy turned. Elizabeth was still standing in the doorway where she had been, her arms crossed tightly over her chest, her lips pressed into a thin line of defiance.

She looked him straight in the eye.

And he could see it—

The stubborn tilt of her chin. The fury still simmering beneath the surface. The refusal to look even slightly shaken.

She was furious. And she was not backing down.

"You opened the door?" he barked. "After I explicitly told you not to? To keep it locked? What the devil were you *thinking?*"

She arched her brows, utterly unrepentant. "I was *thinking* that you two cads were talking over what to do with me while I sat up here like some porcelain doll. I was *thinking* I would much rather have a hand in my own fate, thank you very much."

Darcy dragged a hand through his hair, exhaling sharply. "Only daughters," he muttered, more to himself than to her. "Too often indulged, thinking the world operates according to their whims."

Elizabeth lifted her chin. "We do not *think* that, Mr. Darcy. We *know* it."

Darcy growled something incoherent, pushed both of them back inside the room, and bolted the door.

CHAPTER SEVEN

D ARCY HAD ENDURED MANY unpleasant things in the past few days.

Being summoned by the Prince Regent. Being saddled with an impossible woman. Navigating London's underbelly with no clear plan, no solid leads, and the distinct possibility of failure.

He had faced them all with steadfast resignation—irritation, certainly, but nothing he could not bear. But this— this particular moment— was the first time in days that he felt truly unprepared.

He stepped into the small, dim room of the coaching inn, his grip tightening around the modest bundle in his hands. Lady Elizabeth Montclair stood by the window, her back rigid, hands braced at her hips, her fingers drumming impatiently against the fabric of her rumpled silk gown. The sharp frown etched between her brows made it clear that she had spent the time alone thinking, no doubt concocting a fresh barrage of arguments against their situation.

At the sound of the door, she turned. Her eyes flickered toward him, then lower, landing on the parcel in his hands.

She did not look relieved.

Darcy was not sure what reaction he had expected—resignation, perhaps, or some shred of reluctant understanding—but it certainly was not this.

Her expression twisted. Not suspicion. Not skepticism.

Pure, unfiltered horror.

His steps slowed as he crossed the room, tossing the bundle onto the bed with a quiet thud. She did not move toward it. Did not even blink. Instead, her gaze darted between the offending object and the man who had brought it into her presence, as if struggling to decide which was more repulsive.

She remained where she stood, arms still folded, posture a fortress of resistance.

"...What," she said at last, her voice slow and deliberate, as though the very notion defied comprehension, "is that?"

"Your new wardrobe."

A long pause.

Then—flatly, with the cool, clipped precision of a woman genuinely insulted— "You cannot be serious."

"Entirely so."

He had spent the last two hours securing the most reasonable, respectable, and utterly unremarkable garments he could find. No rich silks, no bright colors, nothing that would catch the eye. They were plain, simple, practical—clothing meant for a gentleman's poor relation, not an heiress accustomed to fine gowns embroidered by the most skilled hands in Paris.

It had cost him more than he could afford. But that was not the point.

The point was getting her out of London alive.

And yet, she still had not moved. Her fingers twitched slightly, curling and uncurling at her sides, as though considering whether the bundle might be contaminated.

"Lady Elizabeth," he said tightly, "we cannot travel with you dressed as a missing heiress."

"I rather think I should prefer to travel dressed as myself."

"You would prefer to be recognized?"

"I would *prefer*," she shot back, eyes flashing, "to wear something that does not look as though it was stolen from a retired governess."

Darcy exhaled. It was going about as well as expected.

"You are to be a gentleman's poor relation," he said. "No one must question your presence. No one must look at you twice. That means no silks, no jewels, no embroidered hems, no French lace—"

"I like French lace."

"I do not care."

Elizabeth had not moved. She was still staring at the bundle on the bed as though it were a rotting carcass, her arms crossed in uncompromising disapproval. Her gaze flicked toward him, eyes narrowing.

"Where did you find these?" she asked at last.

Darcy hesitated. The question was inevitable, but he had rather hoped she would not ask it. Or at the very least, that he could avoid this particular conversation until they were already on the road.

But of course, Lady Elizabeth Montclair never let a thing go unexamined.

He exhaled, knowing there was no use avoiding it. "I have a sister."

Elizabeth blinked. Then—her chin lifted, and her lips curved into a slow, knowing smirk.

"*You* have a sister?"

Darcy gritted his teeth. "Yes."

"Well," she mused, tilting her head as though this revelation had confirmed some great personal theory, "that does explain a great deal."

Darcy's scowl deepened. "I fail to see how."

She did not answer. Instead, her gaze swept toward the bundle of fabric once more, her expression turning speculative.

"These were hers, then?" she asked, lips quirking slightly. "Your sister's? They must not pay well at the Home Office."

His scowl darkened into something almost dangerous. "Not hers," he bit out. "Her companion's."

That, at least, broke her amusement. The smirk faltered, her brow furrowing slightly. She looked at him, then the bundle, then back at him again.

"You wish me," she said at last, deliberate and slow, "to dress as a paid companion?"

Darcy rolled his shoulders, already exasperated. "I wish you to dress as someone entirely unremarkable."

Elizabeth bristled. "I will look dowdy!" she accused.

"That," Darcy said shortly, "is the point."

Elizabeth let out a quiet, irritated noise, reaching reluctantly for the bundle. She turned it over, inspecting the plain fabric. "Awful," she muttered.

"It is practical."

"It is hideous."

Darcy rubbed his temple. "Elizabeth…"

She looked up, and—Heaven help him—there was actual hurt and disappointment in her eyes. "It is dull," she tried again, as though this would change his mind.

"Good."

Elizabeth huffed.

Darcy crossed his arms.

"You have two choices," he said, tone firm. "You may wear those clothes, or you may wear your current gown and inform every highwayman, footpad, and bounty hunter in England that Lady Elizabeth Montclair is out for a countryside tour."

Elizabeth's mouth snapped shut. Darcy could see her mind working furiously, trying to conjure up some way to win this battle.

But there was none.

Finally, with an exaggerated sigh, she snatched the bundle from the bed. "I shall keep my own stays," she said, tossing him a sharp look. "And my petticoats."

"No."

Her eyes narrowed. *"No?"*

Darcy straightened, bracing himself. "No."

Elizabeth's expression darkened. "Why not?"

"Because you cannot carry a wardrobe fit for a marchioness into a household of modest means without someone noticing. Unless you mean to do your own washing."

Her gaze sharpened. "A *household?* Where, oh wise one, are we going?"

Darcy ignored that, pressing on. "The maids would see them. They would be hung on the line. They would be remarked upon. That is precisely the sort of attention we cannot afford."

Elizabeth crossed her arms, still unconvinced. "And what, pray, am I to wear instead?"

Wordlessly, he gestured toward the bundle.

She hesitated. Then, with exaggerated care, she plucked up the stays from Mrs. Annesley's collection and held it aloft, inspecting it like a fine lady judging an inferior cut of silk.

Darcy felt his face heat.

The stays were not scandalous—certainly not by themselves—but something about the sight of them in her hands made his collar feel unreasonably tight.

Elizabeth turned a slow, deliberate gaze toward him. "I think," she said sweetly, her voice all honeyed innocence, "that the bust will be too small for me."

Darcy's entire body locked.

A muscle in his jaw ticked.

Elizabeth's lips curved.

That—*that*—was entirely deliberate.

Darcy turned sharply on his heel and strode toward the door. "I shall be downstairs," he bit out.

Elizabeth hummed sweetly. "I should think so."

ELIZABETH WAS GOING MAD.

She could feel it—a slow, crawling frustration beneath her skin, an unbearable restlessness that made the walls of this room feel smaller by the minute. She had paced the floor so many times that she was surprised she had not worn a path in the wooden planks.

It was not just the confinement. It was the helplessness.

For a full day now, she had been dragged from one miserable hiding place to another, her entire life stolen from her without consent or reason. She had been told where to sit, when to move, what to wear, and all by a man she had never met until yesterday—an infuriating, high-handed, impossible man who, for some reason, had been appointed as her keeper.

And yet, he was not "keeping" her at all. He had abandoned her upstairs in this inn, left her to wait while he did—what? Made arrangements? Secured transport? Set the terms of her exile?

She had been forced into this situation without say, without question.

But she could make *one* decision for herself.

She could go home.

A sharp breath pushed past her lips as she turned toward the window, watching the movement on the street below. Mayfair was not far. Her home was not far. If she left now, she could be there before Darcy even realized she was gone.

She would explain everything to her father, make him understand. Once he knew the full extent of it—the truth of what she had seen—he would handle it, as he always did. No one would dare threaten or endanger her while she was in her father's house.

Elizabeth pressed her fingers against the cool glass, taking one last look down at the street.

It was foolish. It was reckless.

But it was necessary.

She pulled up her borrowed hood, squared her shoulders, and slipped out the door.

It was far too easy.

No guards. No obstacles. Just a busy inn, a crowded street, and a steady stream of coaches rolling past, bound for the heart of the city.

She barely hesitated before hailing one. The pulled up and sprang down at once to get the door for her.

"Mayfair," she said. "Quickly, if you please."

The driver tipped his hat, flicked the reins, and she was off.

She leaned back against the seat, heart pounding in her ears. It was done.

She was going home.

T HE RIDE TOOK LONGER than she expected.

The streets were thick with traffic, and the air had grown warmer, stifling from too many bodies moving through the city. Elizabeth barely noticed. She was too focused on what she would say. Her father must be made to understand the urgency, yes, but she fancied that her first duty would be to reassure him that she was well and safe. She did not believe for a moment that he could have been convinced by whatever message His Highness had sent.

She imagined stepping through the front door, the shock on the servants' faces, the relief. Her father would be in his study, buried in his work, too busy to notice the lingering soot on his jacket from the House of Lords. She would sit before him, calm, respectable, explaining everything in crisp, logical terms.

And then—he would make it right.

That thought comforted her.

And then, quite suddenly, it did not.

A strange acrid smell burned in her nose, something sharp and bitter.

Smoke.

She barely had time to register it before the coach slowed, then stopped altogether.

A crowd had gathered on the street. The driver turned toward her, adjusting his cap. "Might be a delay, miss. Something happened just up ahead."

Elizabeth frowned. "What sort of something?"

The man gave a one-shouldered shrug. "Fire brigade's still there. House caught flame, sounds like. Not much damage, though. Lucky that."

Her fingers sank into the fabric of her borrowed skirt, lifting the hem out of her way. She reached for the carriage door, ignoring the driver's call of, "Wait, miss!" and stepped down onto the street, pushing past the crowd until she could see it.

Her home.

Or what remained of it.

The front of the house stood untouched, pristine white stone, a perfect facade of normalcy. But above—

The windows were blackened. *Her* windows.

Smoke curled from the upper floor, the sharp scent of charred wood still thick in the air.

Elizabeth barely registered moving forward, pushing through the mass of onlookers, her body numb, her mind struggling to make sense of what she was seeing.

The voices came in scattered fragments, bits of conversation floating through the thick, acrid air.

"...Marquess of Ashwick's house..."

"...Lord above, look at the damage..."

"...Heard it started in the bedchamber—a coal bucket too close to the embers..."

Elizabeth's feet slowed. Her stomach clenched. She did not know what to think, but she knew enough to sense that was a lie. The hearth in her room had not even been lit when she left.

"...A maid's mistake, sure enough..."

"...I heard it was the daughter's room..."

"...Young miss is like enough dead from the smoke."

A chill crawled over her skin.

She turned sharply, her gaze darting over the crowd, seeking a face, a familiar presence, something—anything—to tell her this was all some terrible mistake.

"...No, no, I tell you, she was not home..."

Elizabeth's breath hitched.

"...Fire brigade came right quick—his lordship said she was quite safe."

"...Off with the Queen's ladies, I heard. Nothing harmed. Lord Ashwick said it himself."

Her vision blurred.

Nothing harmed.

Nothing harmed.

She almost laughed. If she had been home, asleep in her own bed, as she was meant to be—

Her hands trembled.

She would have never woken up.

A hand clamped around her wrist, firm and unyielding.

Elizabeth gasped, twisting instinctively, but the grip did not loosen. *No, no, no!* She could fight them off this time, could kick and scream...

The crowd blurred around her, voices fading into the rush of blood pounding in her ears. Oh, *where* was her father? She swung around, preparing to claw the face of her attacker, but pulled up short at that familiar stern glare.

Darcy.

He was breathing hard, his chest rising and falling with controlled effort, his entire frame tense as though restraining something more volatile than anger alone. His grip was strong, but not cruel. His expression—harsh, furious—shifted ever so slightly as he took in the wreckage before them.

For a fleeting second, his gaze lingered on the smoldering remains of her bedroom, tracking the soot-streaked stone, the shattered glass, the beams blackened by flame.

His fingers loosened against her skin.

She felt it—a fraction of hesitation, a flicker of something she had never seen from him before. Not impatience. Not frustration.

Understanding.

His mouth pressed into a narrow thread, his jaw locking tight, but the crack in his composure was already exposed. He saw what she saw. He knew what this meant.

The moment did not last. It was gone as swiftly as it came.

His fingers tightened once more around her wrist, this time with clear intent. "What," he demanded, voice low and dangerous, "do you think you are doing?"

Elizabeth opened her mouth, but nothing came out.

She had argued against him at every turn. She had dismissed his warnings, refused to believe that she was truly in danger. But now, staring at the wreckage of her home, with soot still clinging to the broken window frame, she could no longer deny the truth.

If she had been here last night—if she had gone home as planned—she would have been dead.

Her throat was too tight to speak.

Darcy's expression darkened further when she failed to respond, but instead of snapping at her, he exhaled sharply and pulled her toward the waiting carriage.

"Inside," he said, his voice clipped, brooking no argument.

She dug in her heels, turning sharply. "My father—"

"Is not here," he bit out, hauling her forward as her skirts tangled against her feet. "And neither should you be."

Elizabeth stumbled as he all but lifted her into the carriage, her thoughts sluggish, her body moving without her mind's permission. The door slammed shut behind her, sealing her inside with the most infuriating man in all of England, but all she could do was sit there, staring numbly out the window.

The carriage lurched forward. The crowd blurred behind them.

She barely felt the movement.

Her hands were trembling in her lap, the fabric of her borrowed skirts twisting between her fingers. She could still hear the gossip of the onlookers, still smell the acrid smoke.

Her bedroom was gone.

And if she had been there last night, she would have been gone, too.

THE CARRIAGE RATTLED OVER the uneven road, the sound of hooves and wheels blending into a dull, ceaseless rhythm. Darcy sat stiffly, arms crossed, eyes fixed on the scenery beyond the window. He was *not* staring at her.

Except he was.

Lady Elizabeth Montclair sat across from him, unnaturally still. She had been rigid as stone when they left Mayfair, jaw tight, hands clenched in her lap. But now, as the city faded behind them and the open countryside stretched ahead, her posture had softened.

She was not weeping. Not in any grand, dramatic display. No heaving sobs, no shaking shoulders. But a single tear tracked slowly down her cheek.

Darcy exhaled and dug into his coat pocket. He extended the handkerchief across the small space between them.

She glanced at it, blinked once, then hesitated before taking it. And then she blew her nose. Loudly.

Darcy cringed. His fingers twitched slightly where they rested on his knee. He could not decide if she was testing him or if she was truly that done in. And he could not decide which possibility unsettled him more.

A moment passed before she finally spoke.

"I hope my maid does not take the blame for this."

Darcy blinked, surprised.

Not a demand. Not an accusation. Not another ill-conceived plan for fixing things herself.

She was thinking of a servant. How... peculiar.

He watched her carefully, but she was not speaking for effect. Her gaze was fixed on the countryside, lost in thought.

"She was only supposed to tend my dressing room," Elizabeth continued quietly. "But she often tidied my chamber as well. If they think she left something near the fire..." Her brow furrowed. "I have never seen her careless, but I doubt that would matter."

Darcy folded his arms, studying her a moment longer before replying. "They will not need a scapegoat if they believe it was an accident."

She sniffed, dabbing at her nose with the handkerchief. "And how do you think it truly started?"

He took a slow breath. "Likely something incendiary thrown through the window."

Her head snapped toward him. "You say that so easily."

Darcy shrugged. "It would not have been difficult. A man could have climbed the tree that leans over from the street, slipped the latch, and shut the window again. The room would have smoldered before the flames caught. By the time anyone noticed, all evidence of how the fire started would have been destroyed."

Elizabeth sat back, staring out the window once more.

Darcy waited for another question, another argument, but instead, her expression shifted—her gaze turned inward, as if something else was occupying her mind. A crease formed between her brows.

Then, without looking at him, she murmured, "Georgiana. Georgiana Darcy."

It was as if a bolt of lightning shot through his spine. He stiffened, sitting straighter. "I beg your pardon?"

She turned her head, watching him with open curiosity. "That is your sister's name, is it not?"

His entire body went still. He had not spoken of Georgiana. Not to her. Not to anyone outside his own family.

"Yes," he said carefully. "How do you know that?"

Elizabeth lifted a shoulder. "I am acquainted with Lady Julia, Lord Matlock's daughter."

Darcy sat forward slightly. That, at least, was not surprising. Lady Matlock certainly knew who Lady Elizabeth Montclair was—had she not told him so... too many times? She had even invited her to a ball, and... Well, it stood to reason that her daughter would know Lady Elizabeth, as well.

"Are you a relation of theirs?"

Darcy hesitated before giving a short nod. "Yes. Lady Matlock is my aunt. Her daughter, Julia, is my cousin. Naturally." He paused. "As is Colonel Fitzwilliam, whom you have already met."

"Ah," she hummed in acknowledgment, then said flippantly, "I see the resemblance now. I like him better than his sister."

Darcy let out a short, startled laugh.

He did not mean to. But it had been so long since someone had spoken plainly of his relations, without expectation or pretense, that the sheer unexpectedness of it disarmed him.

He quickly schooled his expression. "You are not alone in that opinion."

Elizabeth's lips curved slightly, but the moment passed too quickly to examine.

Instead, she looked out the window again. "Lady Julia invited me for tea a handful of times last autumn. She had a cousin living with her," she said after a moment. "She took a rather perverse pleasure in trotting her out like some kind of pet."

Darcy's jaw slackened.

"She would make a great show of it," Elizabeth continued, still speaking as though recounting some trivial social offense. "Making her play the piano for us and so on. A prodigious talent, I must say—that is why it caught in my mind. The girl did not seem to enjoy the attention, but Lady Julia found it amusing. I thought it was not quite the thing—I said as much to her face."

Darcy's stomach turned.

"She has not invited me back for tea since," Elizabeth mused. "I am not sorry."

Darcy's jaw clenched, and his fists balled. Blast Julia! Parading Georgiana about like a spectacle.

He had left his sister in his aunt's care because he had no other choice—but he had never imagined spoiled Julia would treat his own flesh and blood as some curiosity for her amusement.

Elizabeth glanced at him then, her expression softer. "She had a sweet countenance, your sister."

He blinked, forcing his shoulders to relax. "She does," he agreed softly.

He had heard from Georgiana just that morning. It was Richard who had gone to Matlock House to retrieve the clothes from Mrs. Annesley, and he had brought back word that Georgiana was well enough for now. And Lady Matlock was hardly cruel—her daughter might be spoiled, but she would not let matters carry too far, surely. Besides, now that he knew, he would say something to Richard, who would speak to his father on the matter.

And hopefully, if he resolved this affair to the prince's liking, he could finally offer her something better. A home of her own again. As she should have had all along.

That had become his sole purpose, and perhaps, the possibility had fallen into his hands, in the form of a stubborn heiress with a penchant for trying to get herself killed.

Elizabeth had fallen silent again. Just as well, for he had a number of thoughts to mull over, things to consider, and somehow, whenever she spoke, any form of logic or reasoning went clean out of his head.

The road stretched ahead of them, fields rolling past, trees arching overhead as the sun dipped lower toward the horizon. At length, she asked, "Where are we going?"

Darcy straightened and adjusted his cuffs. "To a house in Hertfordshire."

Elizabeth's brow furrowed.

"To inquire about gaining some sisters for you," he added.

She gave him a long, puzzled look.

He only smiled.

And for the first time in a very long time, Darcy was looking forward to someone else's confusion.

CHAPTER EIGHT

THE COACHING INN AT Meryton was not ideal.

Darcy surveyed the bustling interior, the air thick with the scent of roasting meat, spilled ale, and the faintest trace of horse dung clinging to boots. The noise was nearly as bad—traders, farmers, and travelers alike packed the common room, their voices carrying over the clatter of tankards and heavy boots against the floorboards.

Elizabeth stood beside him, silent but watchful. For once, she was not arguing.

That, more than anything, put him on edge.

He turned sharply to the innkeeper. "A private dining room."

The man gave a weary shake of his head. "All taken, sir. Had a large party pass through just this morning. We're full up."

Darcy bit back a curse. He turned to Elizabeth. "Well, that settles it. You can hardly come with me until I have... made certain arrangements. You will have to remain in the carriage."

"I will not."

He pinched the bridge of his nose. Of course. "This is hardly a place for a lady of your station," he hissed.

She lifted a brow. "That is precisely the point, is it not?"

He narrowed his eyes and leaned closer, dropping his voice. "You are in danger, or have you already forgot the state of your home?"

She stiffened, but held his gaze. "I have not forgot."

"Then you—"

"I have no intention of making trouble," she cut in, voice deliberately even. "I will remain seated. I will eat. I will not draw attention." Her jaw set. "I am sensible of the danger, Mr. Darcy."

Darcy almost laughed. That was the most blatant falsehood he had heard in weeks. She had no idea what it meant to be truly sensible.

But the alternative was leaving her unsupervised in the carriage while his driver loitered about with the other grooms. Hot. Thirsty. Hungry, and, more concerningly, growing more impatient by the second.

Darcy ground his teeth and turned back to the innkeeper. "A quiet corner, then. One with some privacy."

The innkeeper hesitated, then gestured toward the far end of the room. "We have a space near the back. Bit more removed. There's a curtain that can be drawn if you want."

Darcy exhaled. It would have to do.

Elizabeth gave a small, satisfied nod before moving past him, making her way toward the seat before he could change his mind.

Darcy turned to the innkeeper and placed a few coins on the counter. "See that she eats," he said quietly. "Something warm and filling. And give her a bit of ale, too, if she will drink it." It might make her more... amenable to his plans.

The innkeeper pocketed the money without question.

Darcy glanced toward Elizabeth, who had already settled into her corner seat. She was watching the room but making no spectacle of herself, hands folded neatly on the table, chin lifted at a practiced, indifferent angle.

She looked... composed.

For once.

It was probably an act.

She met his eye casually, as if she were only lightly scanning the room, and he made a motion with his hand. She puckered her lips and pulled the curtain closed, but she looked away as she did so, as if to make certain he knew it was not *his* suggestion but her own decision that caused her to do so. Well, whatever it took.

Without another word, he turned toward the door.

He had a most unusual proposition to make at Longbourn.

T HE ALE SMELLED VILE.

Elizabeth eyed the mug before her, nose wrinkling slightly as she lifted it for a tentative sniff. The scent was sharp and yeasty, nothing like the wine and cordials she was accustomed to.

She cast a glance toward the innkeeper, who had delivered it with an odd sort of grin, as if he knew something she did not.

Elizabeth huffed. Typical. Another one of Mr. Darcy's little tricks, no doubt. She imagined him issuing his tight-lipped instructions before leaving, muttering something about keeping her docile.

As if she could be so easily managed.

She scoffed under her breath and took a sip, fully prepared to hate every drop.

She did not.

It was thicker than she expected—smoother, the flavor settling on her tongue in a way that was almost... pleasant.

She took another sip.

Then a longer one.

After two mugs, she was warm. A bit too warm, but not in a stuffy sort of way. Rather a muzzy, pleasant warmth that came from her belly.

She had stopped clutching her cloak around herself, had even—hesitantly, deliberately—tugged at the curtain, pulling it open slightly. She needed just a breath more of air, and what harm could it do? They were miles from London, along no path where anyone would be looking for her.

She exhaled slowly and settled back, fingers tracing the rim of her mug, eyes drifting toward the small window on the far side of the inn.

The leaded glass was streaked with dust, but she could just make out the view beyond—the narrow side street, the small garden beside the inn, the group of young ladies gathered there.

Elizabeth tilted her head, watching them.

There were four of them, all with the same noses and eyes, but there, the resemblances diverged.

Two were loud, talking over each other in a flurry of animated gestures and shared laughter. The third, a plain, solemn girl, kept attempting to steer the conversation back to something more serious, but the others paid her little mind.

The fourth, however—she was different.

She stood slightly apart, listening more than she spoke, her smile faint but genuine. She was not commanding the conversation, not competing for attention, but her presence was felt, nonetheless.

Elizabeth found herself leaning forward, studying them more intently. Their ease with one another was something unfamiliar, yet oddly compelling.

Something Elizabeth had never quite known for herself.

Before she realized it, she had risen from her seat and moved to another table, closer to the window.

Better view.

Better light.

And if she breathed very, very quietly, she could hear what they were saying.

She had not meant to order another ale, but when the innkeeper passed by, raising a brow toward her nearly empty mug, she had inclined her head without thinking.

And now—well.

The warmth in her limbs had spread, her head light but pleasantly so, her usual restlessness gentling into something looser, more languid. Her cloak had been discarded over the back of the chair. Her posture, normally poised and proper, as it had been schooled to be, was decidedly less rigid.

She should probably stop.

But the ale was quite good. And the girls outside were too interesting to ignore.

She had decided they must be sisters, and she had a fair guess at their ages. The quiet one, now she was the tallest, her features the most womanly—she was surely the oldest. Elizabeth fancied they were rather close to the same age. The one who liked to hear herself talk when no one else did, now that one might be about eighteen.

She could not be entirely certain about the remaining two. They might be twins, but one was decidedly taller than the other. They looked somewhere between fifteen and seventeen, both lively and silly. Ridiculous, really. And far too young to be out in public without a governess to keep them in check, since they clearly needed one.

But still... very entertaining.

The taller of the two younger ones, a round-cheeked girl with a ribbon slipping loose from her curls—clutched at the sleeve of the more serious one, shaking her head emphatically. "You did *not* say that to Mr. Hodge, Mary. Tell me you did not."

"Mary" lifted her shoulders and sniffed primly. "I did. It was an illogical argument, and I would not let it stand."

The dark-haired one groaned. "Mary, a man does not like to be told that his thoughts on the French war are 'founded on a fundamental misunderstanding of economic prin ciples.'"

"Well, they are."

"You are ridiculous!" the younger one cried.

The quiet one—the one with the faint smile and keen eyes—laughed softly. "She is probably right, Kitty."

Mary lifted her chin. "I *am* right."

The first girl huffed. "You will never marry, you know."

Mary did not look remotely concerned.

The dark-haired one grinned. "And if she does, her husband will spend his days crushed beneath the weight of his own poor arguments."

The quiet one chuckled. "You are all dreadful."

"But you love us anyway, Jane."

Ah, so now Elizabeth knew the name of the girl who fascinated her the most. Jane sighed, smiling more fully now. "I do."

Elizabeth blinked.

The exchange had been nothing. A silly, meaningless conversation between sisters. But something about it... unsettled her.

No, not unsettled.

Itched.

Like something out of reach, like a word on the tip of one's tongue, a memory that almost surfaced but slipped away before it could be grasped.

She fingered the handle of her mug, watching as they moved down the street, their voices fading into the hum of village life.

Her feet shifted beneath the table.

She hesitated.

She was *supposed* to stay here. She had agreed—more or less. Darcy would have a fit if he found her wandering.

Then again, Darcy was not here. Might not be for another hour or two.

She stood.

Her cloak was still draped over the other chair, but she made no move to take it. The spring air outside would be better. Fresher.

She moved through the common room, head tilted just slightly downward, watching the odd shadows swirling around her as the floor seemed to sway and shift, until finally she reached the door.

Then, with the ease of someone who had never once been told no in her life, she slipped out into the street.

T HE AIR IN HERTFORDSHIRE was distinctly fresher than the thick, soot-laden streets of London. But Darcy did not have time to stop and appreciate it.

He rode to Longbourn with his mind still tangled in plans and contingencies, mentally fortifying himself for a conversation that could go any one of a hundred different directions. He had always found Mr. Bennet to be an intelligent, if maddening, conversationalist. Unlike most country gentlemen, Bennet had a sharp mind and a sharp tongue, and while he rarely left his estate, he was well-informed, well-read, and, above all, amused by nearly everything.

Including, most often, Darcy himself.

Darcy reined in his hired horse at the entrance to the modest but well-kept estate. He barely had time to dismount before a servant greeted him at the door, looking mildly surprised at the unannounced visitor. Darcy had called at Longbourn before, but never unexpectedly, and never alone.

The servant led him through the hall and into Bennet's study, where the master of the house sat comfortably ensconced in his chair, surrounded by books and papers, a glass of brandy within easy reach.

Mr. Bennet looked up from his reading, his spectacles sliding ever so slightly down the bridge of his nose as he took in the sight before him. He blinked, then slowly closed his book with a measured deliberation, tapping the cover lightly with his fingers.

"Mr. Darcy," he said at last, with all the enthusiasm of a man remarking on the arrival of a particularly unusual species of bird in his garden. "Well, well. What an... unexpected pleasure. I thought you had gone back to London suddenly."

Darcy bowed briefly. "A simple matter, quickly resolved, sir."

Bennet did not immediately offer him a seat. Instead, he simply sat there, his expression one of idle curiosity, as though determining whether Darcy's presence was the result of some strange celestial accident.

After a long pause, he sighed, gesturing vaguely toward the chair opposite his own. "Well, do sit down, sir. You are making the room look unbalanced."

Darcy took the offered seat, adjusting his coat as he did so. "Thank you."

Bennet regarded him with his usual air of mild amusement. "I presume you are not here to check my King's Gambit from our last match? If so, I warn you, I shall take it as a grievous insult to my honor."

Darcy grunted a negative. It had been some time since their last game of chess, but clearly, Bennet had not forgot.

"I am afraid I am not here for chess, Mr. Bennet," he said. "I have a rather curious proposition to put before you."

Bennet leaned back, swirling his brandy. "Oh, how delightful. It is not every day a man receives a proposition from Fitzwilliam Darcy. Tell me, is it legal?"

Darcy's jaw tightened ever so slightly. "That depends on who knows about it."

Mr. Bennet's grin widened.

Darcy took a slow breath. *Patience.*

"I require a place of safety for a young lady," he said carefully. "A respectable household where she can remain undisturbed while certain matters are... sorted out."

Bennet's brows lifted. "A young lady? My dear fellow, if you have ruined someone, I am afraid my household is quite full. You must do the honorable thing and offer for her at once."

Darcy gritted his teeth. "She is not my mistress."

Bennet chuckled. "Ah. So she is someone else's mistress, then. My dear sir, I am flattered, but I really must decline."

Darcy's hands clenched over his knees. "Mr. Bennet," he said, voice perfectly level, "the lady in question is quite respectable, and in some... straits, not of her own making. She requires temporary lodging under an assumed name. I am prepared to compensate you for your trouble."

Bennet tilted his head, considering. "I am to take in an unknown young woman, under a false identity, for an unspecified length of time, with only your vague assurances of decency and payment?"

"...Yes."

Bennet took a sip of brandy. "Well. You are in luck, sir. My wife and daughters are in Meryton at present, so we shall have no one listening from the hall. Now, tell me—who is this mysterious young woman, and what kind of trouble does she bring to my door?"

Darcy hesitated. He could not tell Bennet the full truth.

He could not mention the Prince, the Home Office, or that this was a matter of national importance.

So he chose his words carefully.

"She is twenty as of last month," he said slowly—a curse on his soul that he even knew that about her without having to be told. "She is of a good family and well-educated. She speaks multiple languages, claims to play chess as well as whist, and is—"

Bennet held up a hand. "My dear Darcy, I do not need her qualifications for a governess. I need to know if she is tolerable company."

Darcy stopped short.

Tolerable company.

A question for which he had no ready answer.

"I—" He cleared his throat. "She is... independent-minded."

Bennet looked delighted. "That is to say, impossible."

Darcy scowled. "She is well-bred, if occasionally prone to—" He hesitated. "Vexation."

Bennet grinned. "Ah. A young lady with opinions. You know, I have an entire household of those."

"I had noticed."

"Well..." Bennet mused, tapping his fingers against the arm of his chair. "I suppose my Jane could do with a companion. If the lady is amiable."

Darcy hesitated. "I—"

He considered Lady Elizabeth Montclair's quick temper, her stubbornness, her ability to argue in three languages.

And yet—he had seen flashes of warmth in her. More than he cared to recall at this moment. He had seen the way she worried for her maid, how she had taken note of Georgiana's discomfort.

It was not amiability... exactly. But it was something.

"She will make do," he said at last.

"And her name?"

Darcy swallowed. "I am afraid, sir, the only name I can give you by which you may call her is 'Elizabeth.'"

"Elizabeth. Hmm." Bennet shrugged. "Very well, then. I shall inform my household that we are expecting my uncle Daniel Bennet's daughter for the summer."

Darcy narrowed his eyes. "And is this Daniel Bennet a real person?"

"Oh, yes." Bennet waved a hand airily. "A distant cousin, several times removed. *His* son might have been my heir, if he had one—alas, he did not. The last I heard, he was in America growing tobacco."

Darcy's jaw clenched. "And your wife is unaware of this fact?"

"She is unaware of many things, sir, and I prefer it that way."

Darcy exhaled slowly. It would have to do.

He stood. "The lady is waiting for me in Meryton. I shall retrieve her at once."

Bennet gave him a pleasant smile. "Do be careful. You look rather peevish today, and I do hate when people frighten my carriage horses."

Darcy ignored him and left.

THE VILLAGE OF MERYTON was a most charming place indeed.

Elizabeth swayed slightly as she took another handful of warm, salted nuts from the paper cone in her hands, nibbling thoughtfully as she peered into the window of a milliner's shop. Inside, an array of modest but well-made bonnets sat prettily on display.

She rather liked bonnets.

Perhaps she should buy one.

She squinted down at the few remaining coins in her palm, trying to remember exactly how much money she had promised to the street vendor in exchange for the nuts.

Surely not all of it.

Ah, well. Darcy could sort it out.

At that precise moment, she heard her name—or at least, something suspiciously like it, spoken in a rather strangled, despairing tone.

She turned lazily.

Ah. There he was.

Darcy was cutting through the street toward her, his coat flaring slightly behind him, his expression tight, his jaw locked. He looked almost feverish with frustration, his entire frame tensed as though bracing for battle.

Elizabeth beamed. "Mr. Darcy!" she called out cheerfully, lifting a hand and waving at him. Then, in a spirit of generosity, she turned and waved at a few other passersby as well. "Capital afternoon!"

Darcy reached her far too quickly for her liking.

"Inside," he bit out.

She blinked up at him. "Inside what?"

"The carriage." He nodded toward a plain black coach waiting nearby.

Elizabeth huffed. "It is perfectly pleasant out here." She tilted her head up toward the sky. "The air is delightful."

"Inside!" he repeated, his voice rather strained.

She popped another nut into her mouth, watching him thoughtfully. "I rather hoped to speak to those young ladies I saw earlier," she said lightly, peering up and down the street for the girls from before. To her dismay, they were nowhere to be seen. "I have been looking for them for... I think some while."

"That is a pity. *Inside.*"

Elizabeth turned to him with an exaggerated sigh. "Must you always be so serious?"

Darcy made an unintelligible sound and took her firmly by the elbow.

"I suppose you will want to know what I have spent," she said breezily as he guided her rather more quickly than necessary toward the carriage.

His lips pressed into a tight grimace.

"I promised the street vendor you would be good for it," she added. "I did not have enough... I think. He said something about charging it to my room at the inn?"

Darcy heaved a sigh that sounded like it came from his boots. "I will leave the money with the innkeeper," he muttered.

"That is most obliging of you," she said magnanimously.

Darcy hauled open the carriage door and turned back to her. "Inside."

Elizabeth placed a hand on her hip. "You are truly dreadful company."

"*Inside.*"

"Oh, very well, very well."

She lifted her foot to step up—miscalculated entirely—and nearly toppled forward.

With a muttered curse, Darcy caught her around the waist, hoisting her up into the carriage with all the ease of a man throwing a sack of grain over his shoulder.

Elizabeth gasped. "That was entirely... Oh, goodness. You *are* rather strong," she declared, clutching at his lapel for balance.

Darcy gritted his teeth and tried to pry her off him.

Her fingers held fast.

The man was warm.

And rather solid.

Her cheek brushed against the crisp fabric of his coat, and she took a deep, soaking-in sort of breath, which—rather unfortunately—filled her senses with the faint scent of sandalwood and leather.

Not entirely unpleasant, which really was quite a pity. She did not quite think she ought to be regarding him as pleasant.

Darcy sounded as if he were choking.

Elizabeth blinked up at him. "Mr. Darcy," she said, entirely serious. "You are gone quite red in the face. Do you have a fever?"

He all but launched her into the opposite seat and fell back against the cushions, rubbing a hand over his face in what she could only assume was silent prayer.

Elizabeth grinned. "Oh, you were *blushing!* Such a prude," she teased, crossing her arms. "It is not as if I were showing you my ankles."

Darcy made a strangled sound.

So naturally, she pulled up her skirts just enough to extend one foot, wiggling her ankle for his viewing pleasure. "See? They were quite covered."

Darcy closed his eyes in sheer agony. "Lord above," he whispered. "You are determined to ruin me."

Elizabeth giggled, dropping her skirts back down. "You are no fun at all."

"And you are intoxicated! What did you drink?"

"Only some of that lovely ale."

His brows arched. He really looked rather funny when he did that. "I cannot believe you would even touch it. How much did you drink?"

She frowned. "Two... no, three... five?"

"*Five?*"

"Is that a lot?" She tapped her chin. "It was probably only four. You were gone for some while, Mr. Darcy."

Darcy dragged his hands down his face, clearly trying to collect himself. "Listen to me," he said tightly, his voice taking on that bossy, tiresome quality she found so irritating. "You are about to be presented to a gentleman's family. You are to live there as a 'cousin' who has come to visit for the summer. Do you under... Elizabeth, wake up."

She shook her head and blinked, sniffing slightly. "I was not asleep."

"You were. Your eyes were closed and you gave a sound rather suspiciously like a snore."

She sucked in a breath and smiled brightly, but his face swam somewhat. "Well, I am awake now. Go on, then. A cousin?"

"Yes, you are to stay at a house called Longbourn. I will be three miles away, at my friend Bingley's home of Netherfield. We are not... Elizabeth!" He snapped his fingers before her face.

"Will you stop acting as if I am falling asleep?" she huffed, swatting his hand away.

"First, you will have to stop *falling* asleep. Now, as I was saying, it will not be generally known that I have brought you, or that we are even acquainted, unless your little scene on the streets of Meryton gave you away. Only Mr. Bennet knows the circumstances, and he knows as little as I could get by with telling him. I am confident in his discretion. Yours, however..." he frowned. "You *do* now comprehend the gravity of your circumstances, I assume?"

She sighed. "Yes, yes. I was quite a lot more upset some while ago. I suppose I shall be again. Do you think I will have a headache tomorrow, Mr. Darcy? I did the first time I sampled French wine."

"I should think you did more than 'sample' it if you had a headache the next day. Look, we have not much longer before we are at Longbourn and you must make yourself presentable. I suppose there is nothing we can do about the reek of ale on your breath, but do try to look..." His face wrinkled. "Alert."

She yawned, fanning her hand over her mouth, and then gave him a confident grin. "Wide awake, sir."

How silly that he did not look in the least reassured. "And you must start learning the name Elizabeth Bennet."

Elizabeth wrinkled her nose. "I am quite certain that is not my name."

"It is now."

She leaned forward, resting her chin in her palm, her fingers idly tracing her cheek. "Elizabeth Bennet," she said, testing the name on her tongue.

Darcy nodded sharply, as though relieved she had not already forgot.

She said it again, more slowly this time, listening to the way the syllables linked together.

El-*i*-za-beth *Ben*-net.

The rhythm was all wrong.

She tried again. "*E*-liz-a-beth Ben-*net*. Are you sure the 't' is pronounced? Perhaps it is silent, like the French. Or is it spelled with two 't's?"

Then—unexpectedly—she laughed. It felt funny in her mouth, like wearing someone else's shoes—a name that did not belong to her, that had never belonged to her.

"No. You are making too much of it. I only want you to remember it—Elizabeth Bennet. Now, say it without laughing," he directed.

"E-lihza-beth Ben-net," she repeated, tilting her head, letting the words roll from her lips as if saying them aloud might make them fit better.

Darcy sighed, running a hand over his face.

But she was not looking at his face.

She was watching his mouth. Why had she never noticed how firm his mouth was? The way it moved around the words, the shape of them pressed between his lips. "Say it again for me," she begged, having some trouble not slurring her words. Watching him talk would be worth a little embarrassment.

He repeated it, slower this time, his voice deep and precise as he touched his pointer finger to his thumb. "Elizabeth Bennet."

Elizabeth murmured it after him, barely paying attention to the name now.

His mouth was—*well*. The sort of mouth she and Charlotte used to giggle about behind their fans. She had never noticed before. Perhaps he would speak some more if she asked him to.

"Are you sure I cannot use the 'Lady Elizabeth' title?"

Darcy tilted his head back against the seat, exhaling sharply, looking as if he were seriously contemplating leaping from the moving carriage. Apparently, she was not going to be able to goad him into saying it again for her.

Elizabeth lifted her shoulders. "That is an awful lot of syllables for my head right now. Perhaps it would be easier if I went by Lizzy."

Darcy visibly recoiled.

She laughed again. Oh, he was becoming delightfully predictable, this man. And predictable people could make for the most delicious entertainment.

The carriage took a turn, and Elizabeth saw a gate post pass the window. They must be approaching Longbourn.

Darcy straightened, taking one final, steadying breath before giving her a pleading look. "Please," he said, voice tight with desperation, "for the love of all things decent, try to act with some dignity. Mr. Bennet shall perform the introductions and hasten you upstairs—hopefully before you make too much of fool of yourself, but you must *try* not to act inebriated when you meet the family."

"I shall not disappoint, sir." Elizabeth tilted her chin, adjusting her fichu with all the composure of a reigning queen, her fingers fumbling only slightly at the delicate fabric.

She barely noticed when Darcy groaned, leaning forward abruptly. Before she could blink, his hands were at her collar, cool fingers brushing against her throat as he tugged the fichu back into place.

Elizabeth froze.

His touch was quick, efficient—practiced, almost—as if he had straightened a thousand fichus before hers.

She doubted that.

Darcy, for his part, looked deeply put out, his mouth pressed into that same pained grimace as he sat back stiffly, eyes fixed firmly ahead, as though hoping he might somehow will himself out of this moment entirely. She could almost hear the internal calculations happening behind those dark eyes—the precise mathematics of his suffering.

"Fear not, my good sir." She waved a hand airily. "After all," she continued, with all the flippant confidence of someone who had never once needed to be competent, "I am the daughter of a marquess. I can handle a little country gentleman's family."

The carriage lurched to a stop. Elizabeth swayed slightly with the motion, the warmth of the ale still sloshing pleasantly in her stomach.

Darcy made a noise that sounded suspiciously like a prayer.

Then, very deliberately—very slowly—he dragged his hands down his face and let them fall limply to his lap.

Elizabeth thought she saw his lips move. She was fairly certain he had just mouthed the words "God help me."

CHAPTER NINE

T HE MOMENT ELIZABETH STEPPED down from the carriage, she was greeted by a flurry of voices.

A large, pleasant-looking woman was already bustling forward, flanked by a cluster of familiar faces—the very same young ladies she had watched in Meryton.

Elizabeth blinked. How... unexpectedly convenient.

She turned her head slightly, glancing back toward the carriage just in time to see the driver set down a modest trunk before stepping away.

Her eyebrows lifted. So, Mr. Darcy had secured some luggage for her? How very thorough of him. She glanced up, meaning to acknowledge the fact with a simple look, but the curtain of the carriage window had already been drawn.

Still, as the carriage lurched forward, disappearing down the lane, she caught the sharp gaze of Mr. Bennet. He was not watching her.

He was watching the retreating carriage.

Elizabeth's brow furrowed slightly. What curious connection must exist between Mr. Darcy and this fellow?

But she had little time to think on it, for the lady of the house was upon her. "Oh, my dear! My dear! You are most welcome!" Mrs. Bennet swept forward, her face alight with excitement. "We have heard ever so much about you!"

"Have you?" She glanced at the gentleman of the house, whose only reply was a faint chuckle.

"Oh, and it is just like Mr. Bennet," she declared, loudly and with great enthusiasm, "to have had your letter for weeks and only now decide to inform me of your visit!"

Elizabeth's lips parted slightly. A letter?

She flicked another glance toward Mr. Bennet, who was watching the scene unfold with a distinct air of amusement. Elizabeth had no time to form a response before Mrs. Bennet carried on.

"I declare, when I arrived home from town not half an hour ago and he said I had best have done well at market, as we were to have a guest, I feared it might be quite another cousin coming to stay altogether!"

Elizabeth blinked slowly at Mrs. Bennet, her mind sluggishly trying to keep pace with the conversation.

Another cousin?

Her head still felt uncomfortably warm, and everything was happening far too fast for her to process. Had they been expecting someone else? Or was this about her?

She did not have time to figure it out before Mrs. Bennet beamed and clasped Elizabeth's hands with a warmth that was nearly overwhelming. "But another young lady in the house—well, that is quite agreeable, is it not, girls?"

The four Miss Bennets stood behind their mother, watching her with open curiosity. Elizabeth stared back rather boldly. These were the Bennets. Four daughters. Which meant she was supposed to be one of them now. A cousin.

Right.

She barely had time to absorb this notion before Mrs. Bennet pressed on, her voice as bright as ever. "Oh, you must tell us all about your family in Shropshire! I have not seen them in... oh, ages, I declare!"

Elizabeth felt her stomach drop.

Shropshire?

She had never been to Shropshire.

She knew nothing about Shropshire.

And her accent—it would be all wrong.

Think. *Think.*

Her breath faltered slightly, but she forced a composed expression, flicking a glance toward Mr. Bennet. He raised an eyebrow, his expression curious, as if to say: "Well, go on then."

Elizabeth's pulse fluttered violently in her throat. She needed to answer. She needed to not ruin everything within the first five minutes.

Her lips parted— "Well—of course," she said, keeping her tone as even as possible.

That was a start.

She swallowed, scrambling for something plausible. "...But I have been in Hampshire these last three years, so I have seen... most of them... but seldom. In fact, I... expect I even sound rather different from the rest of the family."

Good. That was believable.

Mrs. Bennet beamed. "Oh, how lovely! And your dear parents—how do they do?"

Elizabeth's mouth went dry.

She did not have parents in Shropshire. A mother in Devonshire whom she had not seen in two years or better and a father who... She swallowed.

Her heartbeat drummed in her ears. But she had to answer. Quickly.

"Mama sends her love," she said, watching Mr. Bennet closely for any sign of disapproval.

He gave none.

Encouraged, she pressed on. "Papa is ever busy with... his... fishing."

A pause.

A long one.

"Trout fishing," she clarified. "He... ties his own lures."

Mr. Bennet's lips twitched.

Oh.

This was a game to him.

Elizabeth wanted to scowl, but instead, she smoothed her expression into a demure smile.

Mrs. Bennet, happily oblivious, beamed. "Well! That is charming, is it not, girls?" she said, gesturing to her daughters. "Come now, let us have the proper introductions. This is my eldest, Jane."

Elizabeth focused on that name, trying to anchor herself.

The quiet one—the one she had liked in Meryton—stepped forward, offering a smile so serene and warm that Elizabeth felt some of her tension ease.

Jane curtsied, and Elizabeth did the same.

"And here we have Mary, and then Kitty and Lydia." The serious one, the excitable one, and the impossibly young, impishly grinning one.

Elizabeth murmured her greetings, still trying to regain her footing.

She was here.

She was Elizabeth Bennet now.

And she had absolutely no idea how she was going to keep that up.

Mrs. Bennet clapped her hands together. "Well! You must be exhausted, dear. Jane, why don't you take our guest upstairs to refresh herself before supper?"

Jane stepped forward immediately. "I would be delighted," she said warmly.

Elizabeth hesitated, still not entirely steady, but followed her inside. The rest of the family dispersed, leaving Jane to lead Elizabeth up the stairs.

The stairs. Which were swaying slightly.

She misjudged a step, her foot catching awkwardly, her weight tilting—but a gentle hand caught her elbow.

Elizabeth exhaled, forcing a sheepish smile. "I must have mis-stepped."

Jane said nothing—just tightened her grip on Elizabeth's elbow, guiding her up the rest of the way. That was... really rather sweet. Elizabeth was touched.

Her pride ached, but her heart did not.

Once inside the room, Jane gestured to the modest but tidy space. "Your trunk is already here, and Mrs. Hill will be up soon with a basin for you to refresh yourself. Is there anything else you would like for now?"

Elizabeth sighed. "I should like a nice lie-down before it is time to dress for dinner," she admitted. "A long one."

Jane paused, looking slightly uncomfortable. "We do not usually dress for formal dinners," she said apologetically. "We take supper earlier than is done in Town—usually around six o'clock."

Elizabeth blinked. *Six?* That was positively barbaric.

Still, she supposed she had no choice. She nodded tiredly. "Then a short rest will do," she said.

Jane smiled. "I will tell Mrs. Hill," she said, stepping back toward the door.

Elizabeth sank onto the bed. She barely heard the door click shut as she closed her eyes.

So far, she was alive.

So far, she was Elizabeth Bennet.

T HE CARRIAGE ROCKED SHARPLY as it turned into the familiar drive of Netherfield Park. Darcy, bracing one hand against the window frame, exhaled slowly.

Too soon.

He had barely had a single night at this place before being summoned back to London, spent three days away before being thrown into a mess far more complicated than his superiors at the Home Office could have imagined. Now, against all odds, he was back.

But this was not a social visit, not this time. This was a cover.

And he was not alone.

Not that Bingley would know that.

The carriage rattled to a stop before the great house, and within seconds, the door swung open. The footman hardly had a chance to step forward before an exclamation of delight met his ears.

"Darcy!"

And then Bingley was there, striding toward him with all the unfettered enthusiasm of a golden retriever, clasping Darcy's hand and shaking it firmly.

"This is a surprise," Bingley declared, grinning. "I half-expected you to be buried under a pile of papers at the Home Office for the rest of your days. What are you doing back here so soon?"

Darcy forced a half-smile, already anticipating the answer Bingley would accept. "I was needed in Town for obvious reasons," he said. "But my business there is concluded for now."

Bingley nodded knowingly. "Understandable, my friend, quite understandable," Bingley said, leading him toward the drawing room. "A sad business, that, poor devil. But I must say, your timing is impeccable! There is to be a garden party at Lucas Lodge tomorrow. You have arrived just in time!"

Darcy groaned. A garden party?

He had spent most of his adult life perfecting the art of avoiding such things. He could almost hear the tedious small talk, see the aimless wandering, smell the over-sweet lemonade served in delicate porcelain cups.

And yet... Wait a minute.

He lifted his chin slightly. "A garden party?"

Bingley grinned. "Indeed! I have just been persuading my sisters to go. I had nearly convinced Louisa, but Caroline is quite against it. Says such parties bring about her sneezing fits."

Darcy's toes wriggled with inspiration inside his boots. Did that mean Caroline Bingley might not be a complication? Better and better.

He kept his expression neutral. "And the entire neighborhood will be in attendance?" he asked carefully.

Bingley tilted his head, thinking. "I suppose so. The Bennets, certainly, and the Gouldings, and—"

Darcy stopped listening. *The Bennets.* Hearing their name confirmed what he had hoped. Elizabeth would be there.

His temporary ward. His responsibility.

Darcy exhaled. "Then I shall attend."

Bingley looked delighted. "Excellent! I knew you could not hide away forever. Go and refresh yourself before dinner. You look half-dead, man."

Darcy was too weary to argue. With a nod, he excused himself.

Tomorrow, he would see exactly how well Lady Elizabeth Montclair was settling into her new life as 'Elizabeth Bennet'.

He doubted very much that she had taken to it quietly.

E LIZABETH HAD NEVER EXPERIENCED anything quite like a Bennet family dinner. It was loud, lively, and utterly chaotic—an entirely different affair from the structured, civilized conversations of her father's London table. No fine crystal or gilded place settings, no footmen silently refilling wine glasses, no painstakingly rehearsed discussions of Parliament and high society.

Instead, there was laughter, overlapping voices, the clatter of serving spoons and passing dishes, and—perhaps most astonishing of all—no one seemed terribly concerned with decorum.

Kitty and Lydia spoke over one another, jostling elbows as they debated the merits of an upcoming garden party.

"I already know it will be a dreadfully dull affair," Lydia declared, scooping a generous portion of pudding onto her plate. "Captain Denny shall not be there."

Kitty sighed. "Nor Mr. Chamberlayne."

Elizabeth blinked. "And... who are they?"

Lydia waved a dismissive hand. "Officers."

"Of the militia," Kitty clarified. "They are stationed in Meryton, and they are terribly charming."

"Well, most of them," Lydia amended, chewing thoughtfully.

Elizabeth hesitated, uncertain of how to respond. Charming officers? Stationed in Meryton? Was this truly the sort of conversation that occupied the minds of young ladies here?

Across the table, Mrs. Bennet sighed wistfully. "Well, there will be some young gentlemen present, as well. Mr. Bingley, for one."

Elizabeth glanced up at the name. That was Darcy's friend, was it not? The memory of his injunctions in the carriage was already hazy, but that sounded like the right name.

Mrs. Bennet was shaking her head, clearly put out. "It is such a puzzle to me. He likes company so well, and yet he has not given any of my girls the proper attention they deserve. And heaven knows, I have given him every opportunity—why, the number of times I have invited him to supper!"

Elizabeth cut into her food carefully, watching as Jane, seated beside her, clasped her hands tightly in her lap.

Interesting.

Elizabeth might not know much about Miss Jane Bennet, but that slight clench of the fingers, the way her gaze did not lift from her plate as her mother spoke—

She was not indifferent to Mr. Bingley's inattention.

Elizabeth turned her focus back to Mrs. Bennet, who was still lamenting.

"And such a fine, handsome young man, too," she continued. "If only he would choose properly! But men are so dreadfully fickle—one never knows where their affections truly lie."

Mr. Bennet, having so far remained silent during this entire lament, took a slow sip of wine and murmured, "Perhaps he is simply terrified of being welcomed into such a... warm and enthusiastic family."

Mrs. Bennet huffed.

Kitty and Lydia snickered.

Jane's hands tightened further.

Elizabeth quietly took another bite of her food.

After dinner, the family retired to the sitting room, where Elizabeth had expected to be left to her own devices. The ale's effects no longer troubled her overmuch, but she could have done with a bit of time to simply sit back and observe this new "family" of which she was suddenly a part. But before she could attempt fading into the furniture, Mr. Bennet cleared his throat.

"I hear from my cousin Daniel that you are quite skilled at chess."

Elizabeth, seated in a small chair near Jane, nearly choked. "Cousin Daniel." Right. Her imaginary father.

How delightful.

Mr. Bennet gestured toward a small table in the corner of the parlor, where a wooden chessboard had already been set up. "Would you favor me with a game, Miss Elizabeth?"

A pause.

The entire room seemed to go still.

Then Mrs. Bennet blinked rapidly, looking rather confused. "Chess? Why, how perfectly unaccountable. My dear, I wish you paid better attention to your daughters' playing and singing than that tedious game."

Kitty and Lydia stifled giggles, as if their father playing chess with a female was the most astonishing thing they had ever heard. Jane, beside her, offered a small, encouraging smile.

Elizabeth hesitated—then, realizing she had little choice, rose from her seat and nodded. "It would be my pleasure, sir."

Mr. Bennet's lips curled faintly, as if amused by something only he understood. Elizabeth had the distinct impression that she had just stepped into a different kind of game entirely.

The chess pieces were worn from years of use, their edges smoothed by countless fingers moving them across the board. Elizabeth traced her fingers lightly over her own set of pieces, considering her first move.

Mr. Bennet made his opening play without preamble. Pawn to e4.

Elizabeth lifted a brow and met his gaze. "You are bold, sir."

"Some would call it recklessness. But I find it rather depends on one's opponent."

"Rather." She advanced her own pawn, feeling his eyes on her as she did so.

"I confess," he murmured, his tone idly conversational as he moved his next piece, "I had wondered what sort of young lady would arrive on my doorstep, sight unseen."

Elizabeth mirrored his move, her eyes flicking up to meet his across the board. "And have I met your expectations, sir?"

He tapped a finger against his rook, considering. "Not in the least." He shifted another pawn forward. "Which is, I expect, the reason I find myself so uncommonly entertained."

Elizabeth bit back a smile. "I shall take that as a compliment."

"As well you should," he said, watching as she made her next move.

The room around them hummed with casual noise—Mrs. Bennet chattered happily to Kitty and Lydia about their new houseguest, while Jane sat quietly with her embroidery, a picture of serene patience as her younger sisters prattled on. The fire crackled, and someone—Mary, perhaps—was leafing through a book with a determined sort of rustling.

In the corner, shielded from easy eavesdropping, Mr. Bennet moved a knight into position. "You strike me as a young lady accustomed to forming her own opinions," he observed.

Elizabeth raised a brow, moving her bishop. "You think less of me for it?"

His lips thinned into a smile, as though suppressing amusement. "On the contrary. A young lady who thinks for herself is a rare and valuable creature."

"Is she?"

He moved another piece, trapping one of her pawns. "Oh, indeed. A mind unclouded by silliness or excessive sentiment—" He cast a glance toward his younger daughters, who were whispering excitedly about something or other. "—is a treasure not easily found."

Elizabeth tilted her head, tapping a finger against her queen. "And what words would you use to describe your own daughters?"

His eyes gleamed. "A great many of them," he smirked, moving his knight deliberately. "Chief among them: exhausting."

Elizabeth huffed a quiet laugh, nudging one of her pawns forward. "And yet, you seem rather fond of them."

"I am," he admitted, watching the board. "Fondness, however, does not negate the need for fortitude."

"Fortitude?" Elizabeth arched a brow.

"To endure their ceaseless chatter."

Across the room, Lydia let out a peal of laughter, something shrill and conspiratorial.

Elizabeth hid her smile as she examined the board, her fingers hovering over the carved pieces as she considered her next move. A knight or a bishop? The move required careful calculation—much like the conversation unfolding across the board.

"And tell me, Miss Elizabeth," he continued, moving another piece forward, his tone deceptively mild. "What is it that brings you to our humble corner of England?"

Elizabeth's fingers paused briefly over her bishop. She knew better than to assume the question was simple curiosity.

She moved her piece. "I was invited."

"A wise response." Mr. Bennet tapped a finger against his chin, examining the board. "And what do you make of our little society? It must be quite different from what you are used to."

Elizabeth glanced at the others—their lively chatter, the warmth of the room, the utter lack of pretense.

"It is," she admitted, moving a rook into position. "But not unpleasantly so."

"Ah." His knight slid forward smoothly, capturing one of her pawns. "Then you are adaptable."

She pressed her lips together, studying the board. "That depends on the circumstances."

Mr. Bennet chuckled quietly, adjusting one of his pieces. "As it should. Those who adapt too easily often find themselves swept along in directions they never intended."

Elizabeth lifted a brow, meeting his gaze once more. "And those who refuse to adapt at all?"

"Miss Elizabeth, I am an old man," he said with a sigh, shifting in his seat. "I have known many a person to hold stubbornly to their course, even when the road has long since turned against them. And I have known others to change too quickly, losing themselves entirely." His fingers hovered over his queen, then tapped it lightly before settling for a different piece instead. "The best players know when to hold, and when to shift."

She took his queen.

He blinked.

A slow smile touched his lips. "I see I shall have to be wary of you."

Elizabeth gave him a sweet, dangerous smile. "I would advise it."

Mr. Bennet exhaled, sitting back in his chair, regarding her with something resembling satisfaction.

"I could do with a female in the house who dabbles in sarcasm," he mused, moving his knight again. "My wife is inclined to dramatics, Kitty and Lydia are frivolous, Mary is too busy sermonizing to engage in proper conversation, and Jane—"

His gaze flicked toward his eldest daughter, still seated quietly, her expression pleasant, her hands folded neatly in her lap.

"Jane is good. To her very heart of hearts, she is good, but I fear, too sweet and bashful to be of any use to me at all."

Elizabeth glanced at Jane thoughtfully.

She already liked her. There was something genuine about Jane Bennet, something kind and steady that Elizabeth found easy to appreciate. But this—this easy dismissal by her own father, however affectionate—was disheartening. Almost tragic.

She moved her next piece carefully, her mind lingering not on the game, but on the quiet, lovely girl seated across the room, who deserved far more than to be labeled 'of no use'.

And Elizabeth, who had never been anyone's cousin before, suddenly felt quite protective of this particular one.

Chapter Ten

May 16, 1812

T HE GARDENS WERE ALREADY swarming with guests, their bright summer attire clashing against the expanse of manicured hedges and gravel paths. A violin played somewhere, mingling with the rise and fall of cheerful conversation. Glasses clinked, voices laughed, and every inch of the lawn seemed occupied by people ambling, gossiping, and generally making a nuisance of themselves.

There had been many poor decisions in his life, but agreeing to attend a garden party voluntarily was swiftly climbing the ranks. As the carriage rolled to a stop, Darcy resisted the urge to sigh.

Beside him, Bingley was already stirring, peering out of the window with an expression of untouched enthusiasm, while across from them, Miss Bingley and Mrs. Hurst looked equally unimpressed. A pity they had decided to risk the summer sneezes, after all.

"Well," Miss Bingley said with a sniff, adjusting her gloves. "If one must endure an afternoon of country society, I suppose a garden party is as tolerable as any other form of drudgery."

Bingley ignored her entirely, turning a broad grin toward Darcy. "Come, man, at least pretend you are not already regretting this."

Darcy arched a brow, but before he could retort, the footman opened the door.

Bingley was the first to alight, stepping onto the drive with unshakable cheer, while his sisters followed, the very image of reluctant civility. Darcy took his time, adjusting his coat before stepping down to join them.

Bingley grinned, stepping back and gesturing to the assembled guests. "What do you think? A fine turnout, is it not? Sir William hosts the best garden parties in the county.

He rather thinks it his solemn duty to do so. I understand his early roses are exceptional this year."

Miss Bingley sighed extravagantly. "Yes, how noble of him to gather so many fine gentlemen and so many… eager young ladies."

Darcy ignored her, his gaze sweeping the crowd absently. He was not here for leisure. A great many respectable families were present—some already seated beneath the white canvas of the refreshments tent, others strolling between rose-laden trellises or pausing to greet acquaintances. The scent of the first summer flowers and lemonade hung thick in the air.

He could already feel a headache forming.

"You look delighted to be here," Bingley teased.

"I do not recall saying I was."

"Then why have you come?"

"Perhaps I merely wished to see how much havoc you have caused in my absence."

Bingley laughed. "Oh, hardly any at all. And if I have, I am certain it has been delightful havoc. Look—Sir William has arranged all manner of amusements—quoits, croquet, and something absurd involving blindfolds, which I refuse to take part in." He lowered his voice again. "Miss Lydia Bennet seems intent on ensuring I do, however. I may need your assistance in fending her off."

Darcy arched a brow. "I will not be rescuing you from Miss Lydia, Bingley."

"Even if it is a matter of life and death?"

"Especially then."

Bingley sighed. "You are a cruel friend, Darcy."

"I have been told as much."

Bingley only grinned before motioning toward the central gathering of guests. "Come. I shall introduce you to some of the new arrivals."

Darcy, against his better judgment, followed.

His gaze swept the crowd absently, noting Sir William Lucas in full enthusiasm, bowing deeply to an elderly woman and launching into an elaborate speech about the virtues of country society. Mrs. Bennet was already at work, fluttering and beaming as she boasted to anyone who would listen about her daughters, and Mr. Goulding was arguing about the merits of spring crops.

Darcy listened without listening, his mind too occupied with duty to engage in more of Bingley's pleasantries. Lady Elizabeth... or, rather, *Miss Elizabeth Bennet* was here somewhere. And today, for the first time, he would be expected to "meet" her.

D ARCY SAW HER THE moment she stepped out of Sir William's little maze. It was impossible not to.

She looked exactly as she should—her gown simple, her hair modestly arranged. She was entirely unremarkable. And yet—he noticed her immediately. Apparently, that was his curse.

She walked beside Jane Bennet, her expression pleasant, her movements comfortable. Not stiff or uncertain, as one might expect of a young lady suddenly deposited into unfamiliar company. No, Elizabeth "Bennet" looked perfectly at ease. As though she had belonged among them her entire life.

That, more than anything, unsettled him.

He had expected... he did not know what. Her usual hauteur? Disgust? A slip, a sign of unease? Instead, she carried herself as though she had never been anything other than the obscure daughter of a distant cousin, welcomed without question into the fold.

The ruse was working. That was all that mattered. He forced his attention elsewhere.

But then, as he was doing his best to admire the daffodils in the garden beds, Mr. Bennet approached. "Mr. Darcy," he said, as if the entire exchange were some fine joke, "I do not believe you have been introduced to my cousin, Miss Elizabeth Bennet from Shropshire."

Darcy turned.

She stood beside Mr. Bennet, the very picture of politeness and composure.

She curtsied. Smooth, graceful. The performance of a young lady who had been executing such movements since infancy.

"Mr. Darcy," she murmured. "A pleasure."

He bowed... unfortunately rather stiffly. "Miss Bennet."

When she straightened, she met his gaze—too directly, too knowingly.

Darcy narrowed his eyes. She was *enjoying* this. As bad as Mr. Bennet, she was. That tiny flicker of amusement, the barely-there quirk at the corner of her mouth—he knew a challenge when he saw one.

"I understand you are just returned from London. I hope you are enjoying Hertford-shire," she said pleasantly.

The words were harmless.

The look in her eyes was not.

Darcy inclined his head. "As much as can be expected."

Her lashes swept downward. A slow blink, deliberately measured. When she looked at him again, there was no mistaking the satisfaction in her eyes.

"Oh, but surely there is much to appreciate in a country setting," she said. "The air is fresh, the company lively—"

"Indeed," he said. "I imagine you have found the company quite... educational."

Her lips parted, just slightly. The barest flicker of amusement. "Oh, exceedingly," she murmured.

Before either of them could push the exchange further, another figure stepped beside them. Bingley, of course. Darcy could feel his friend's presence without looking—could sense the way Bingley's gaze flickered between them, the way his brow creased just slightly in confusion.

"Ah, Miss Bennet, allow me to introduce my friend and neighbor, Mr. Bingley," Mr. Bennet said, his tone still carrying the faintest trace of laughter. "Mr. Bingley, Miss Elizabeth Bennet—a cousin come to grace us with her presence for the summer."

Bingley gave a quick bow. "A pleasure, Miss Bennet."

Elizabeth curtsied smoothly. "And you, sir."

Bingley smiled, but Darcy saw the flicker of hesitation. His friend's gaze darted briefly between them, his brow knitting ever so slightly.

Darcy braced himself.

Bingley was not a man given to suspicion or even quick observation, but could be was attentive in ways that often proved inconvenient. Bingley shifted his weight, clearly expecting someone to offer some kind of explanation. "I must say, it is a surprise to meet a new relation of the Bennet family."

Darcy cleared his throat. "Miss Bennet is visiting from Shropshire."

Elizabeth barely suppressed a smile. "Hampshire, actually."

Bingley looked between them again. "Rather a long way between the two places, I should think."

Darcy swallowed, but Elizabeth only lifted one shoulder. "And yet a person can call more than one place home, sir."

"Of course, of course," Bingley agreed. And then he smiled at her as if she were the prettiest creature he ever beheld.

Darcy would have decked the fool if it would not have caused a scene. Instead, he turned to Mr. Bennet and said, with all the politeness he could muster, "I believe your cousin has already made herself quite at home."

Mr. Bennet gave a slow nod, clearly enjoying himself far too much. "Oh, I imagine she will fit in quite nicely."

Darcy did not respond. He did not need to.

Elizabeth was watching him again, that same knowing glint in her eyes. He resisted the urge to exhale sharply and turned his attention elsewhere.

She was someone else's problem now.

Or at least, that was what he told himself.

D ARCY FOLDED HIS HANDS behind his back, forcing himself to focus.

The conversation had already begun by the time he approached the cluster of gentlemen standing near the terrace, their voices low but firm with opinion. Politics were as divisive as ever, and with a Prime Minister assassinated, there was hardly a topic more suited to a gathering of respectable country gentlemen who had read just enough of the broadsheets to consider themselves well-informed.

"...Dreadful business," Sir William Lucas was saying, shaking his head gravely. "A terrible thing, losing a Prime Minister that way. Never happened until now."

"And a public spectacle, no less," added Mr. Goulding, gesturing broadly with his glass of claret. "The House of Commons! Imagine it. Never has such an act of violence occurred in our very halls of government."

A murmur of agreement passed through the group.

Darcy said nothing. He had read the official statements. He had also read between the lines.

"It is already a settled matter," Mr. Long grunted. "Bellingham's guilt was plain, and his sentence will be swift. He shall be hanged before the week is out."

"Yes, yes," Sir William agreed, though with less certainty. "And yet, some argue there is more to it."

Darcy lifted a brow. "Some?"

Sir William sighed. "Audley, for one."

"Henry Audley?" Mr. Goulding frowned. "The Hertfordshire man?"

"The same."

There was a murmur of interest.

"Audley has been pushing hard for an inquiry," Sir William went on. "He claims the case was closed too quickly."

Mr. Long scoffed. "Nonsense. What else is there to say?"

"Bellingham fired the shot," agreed another gentleman. "Everyone saw it. It is all quite cut and dry."

Sir William looked less convinced. "And yet Audley insists it was too simple. That the investigation was rushed, no due process."

Darcy kept his expression carefully neutral. *Rushed, indeed.*

He reached for his glass, taking a slow sip as he turned the thought over in his mind. Henry Audley was no radical, but he was a man of reform. He had made a name for himself in Parliament as an idealist—a man who spoke of justice and progress in a way that either inspired or infuriated his peers.

He was also, by all accounts, scrupulously honest.

Darcy had not yet spoken with him, but if Audley was insisting that Bellingham had not acted alone...

A small movement caught his eye.

Elizabeth.

She was standing just beyond the group, not so close as to be part of the conversation, but near enough that she could hear.

She had been disinterested a moment ago, laughing with three or four other young ladies. But now?

Now, her entire focus was fixed on the conversation. A conversation she could hardly afford to look interested in. She was trying to be subtle about it.

She was failing.

Her hands were clasped tightly before her, her posture rigid, her expression carefully neutral—but her eyes were sharp, her lips slightly parted.

She knew something.

Darcy was certain of it. And blast him, he had hardly asked her a single question since the Prince passed her off into his keeping. He had been too convinced she saw nothing useful, and too concerned with keeping her alive to stop long enough to inquisite her again. Perhaps he ought to reconsider.

He forced himself to take another sip of his drink, glancing away as though he had not noticed her reaction.

But he had.

And he was going to find out why.

ELIZABETH HAD NOT EXPECTED to enjoy herself.

She had thought—perhaps foolishly—that this garden party would be another ordeal to endure. That she would drift about the hedgerows, making polite conversation with perfect strangers, ever on guard, hoping desperately to avoid missteps and suspicion.

And yet, here she was—walking through a sun-dappled garden, perfectly at ease beside Jane Bennet.

She rather liked Jane.

The eldest Bennet daughter was quiet but warm, her words chosen with care, her presence easy and uncomplicated. Unlike her younger sisters, Jane did not chatter endlessly or demand attention. She simply existed beside Elizabeth, a companion rather than a burden.

A pleasant surprise.

It was in this unhurried state that Elizabeth's attention was caught by a young girl sitting on a stone bench near a garden wall, a sketchbook open across her lap. It was Maria Lucas, Sir William's daughter.

Elizabeth had met her earlier that afternoon, but even in those brief moments, she had learned much of her. For one, she was excellent friends with the younger Bennet sisters. The girl had sharp, bright eyes, a lively way of speaking, and the unmistakable look of someone trying her very hardest to appear more serious than she was. She reminded Elizabeth a little of Charlotte Wrexham in that way.

She was trying—and failing—to sketch a landscape.

At least, that was what she wanted people to *think*.

Lydia Bennet sat beside her, peering over her shoulder, her brows drawn in a dramatic frown.

"I tell you, his chin is sharper than that," Lydia declared, gesturing toward the distant group of red-coated officers standing near the refreshments. "See how it angles just so?"

Maria's pencil hesitated. "You think so?"

Elizabeth stifled a laugh. This was not a landscape.

It was a portrait.

And judging by the number of bold, decisive strokes, Maria had drawn him before.

Jane must have noticed as well, for she giggled, then cleared her throat. "You sketch very well, Maria."

The younger girl sighed. "It is not so bad, I suppose, but—" She made a face and rubbed at the page with her thumb. "I can never seem to get the shape of his face quite right."

Elizabeth watched her for a moment, then—without thinking—she reached for the charcoal.

Maria's eyes widened, but she said nothing as Elizabeth kneeled beside the bench and took the sketchpad into her own hands.

"The problem," Elizabeth murmured, "is that you are drawing what you *think* you see, rather than what is actually there."

Maria leaned in eagerly. "How do you mean?"

Elizabeth tilted the pad slightly. "Look at him now. Do not think about how he looks, how handsome he is or the way he laughs. Think about shapes and shadows. Where does the light strike? Where does the line truly go?"

Maria blinked, considering.

Lydia, however, was far less patient. "Yes, yes, but fix his chin first."

Elizabeth huffed a laugh but obeyed, adjusting the line of the jaw with a few quick strokes.

Maria's mouth fell open. "Oh! That is so much better."

Jane, standing beside them, watched with quiet admiration. "You are very skilled, Cousin."

Elizabeth stiffened.

Cousin.

She had almost forgot that.

She cleared her throat and gave a small, dismissive shrug. "I had some... instruction."

"Some?" Maria gaped. "This is far more than *some.*"

Jane tilted her head. "Your family must have placed great importance on education."

Elizabeth's heart lurched. Indeed... that was her father's fondest indulgence. The finest masters all his money could afford, as often and as long as she pleased. And drawing had been her chief pleasure—a luxury very few in her present circumstances could even dream of.

For a moment, she could not answer.

There was a sharp awareness in Jane's expression—not suspicion, but curiosity. It was a harmless question. An innocent assumption.

And yet, Elizabeth felt a wave of panic.

She forced a careless smile. "Yes, well... I suppose they did."

Jane's expression softened, and she nodded as though the response satisfied her. Then, to Elizabeth's great surprise, she said, "If you like drawing so well, I shall ask Papa to procure you some charcoals."

Elizabeth blinked. She had not expected that.

People had always spoken of her talents in terms of accomplishment—a thing to be shown off, to be praised, to be used for admiration or advantage.

No one had ever thought about it as a thing she might *want.* A thing she might miss or enjoy.

Elizabeth hesitated. "You need not trouble him."

"It is no trouble," Jane said simply. "You have a gift. You ought to have the means to use it."

Elizabeth swallowed. Something warm unraveled in her chest.

A gift.

Not an accomplishment.

A gift.

She exhaled slowly, glancing back down at the sketchbook in her hands.

Maria was still staring at her in open fascination.

Lydia huffed. "Well, if you will not fix his expression, at least let me color in his uniform."

Elizabeth let out a soft laugh and handed the charcoal back.

D ARCY DID NOT COME here to play games.

And yet, it seemed the world conspired against him.

"I insist, old man!" Bingley declared, clapping him heartily on the back. "We cannot have you brooding in a corner all afternoon. It is a party, you know."

Darcy sighed. "Bingley—"

"No excuses," his friend interrupted cheerfully. "Sir William has declared the game, and as you are an esteemed guest, it would be the height of bad manners for you to refuse."

"Bingley," Darcy repeated.

Bingley only smiled. "Come now, it is just a bit of Pall-Mall."

Darcy closed his eyes.

Pall-Mall.

A most undignified game.

But he could already feel the attention of their host—and of several other guests—turning toward him, expectant, eager. A refusal now would be pointedly noticed.

With a slow breath, he nodded.

The group cheered.

Bingley beamed.

Darcy resigned himself to his fate.

Sir William clapped his hands together, beaming at the assembled guests. "Now, my dear friends, I have devised a most delightful variation for our game this afternoon! Rather than each of you competing alone, I propose we engage in a friendly contest of pairs. A gentleman and a lady shall form a team, alternating strokes through the course. This way, we may ensure both lively conversation and a fair chance for all." He winked broadly, clearly pleased with his ingenuity.

"This is most irregular," murmured one of the older gentlemen, though not with any real complaint.

"Indeed!" Sir William said cheerfully. "But we must allow for a bit of amusement in life, must we not?" He gestured to a waiting footman. "The names shall be drawn at random."

The guests assembled as Sir William Lucas enthusiastically read out the game pairings. One by one, names were called, players matched, the crowd bubbling with excitement as friends and flirtations alike were thrown together for the afternoon's sport.

And then—

"Mr. Darcy and Miss Elizabeth Bennet!"

Darcy's stomach dropped.

He turned his head sharply toward Sir William, as though hoping he had misheard.

But no.

There stood Elizabeth, already stepping forward with a sweet, slow smile—one that made something in his chest rip apart and caused his toes to curl in dread.

"Mr. Darcy," she said pleasantly, dipping into a perfectly polite curtsy.

Trapped.

He could feel Bingley's silent laughter beside him, could see Caroline's visible irritation, could sense the general hum of interest among the gathering crowd.

It was a perfectly innocent pairing. A random one. So why did he feel as if Fate were trying to torment him?

THE WOODEN BALL ROLLED across the grass, Darcy adjusting his stance before striking it with his mallet. The crack of impact was sharp, clean, precise—the ball sailing neatly through the metal hoop ahead.

A perfect shot.

Elizabeth, standing beside him, hummed thoughtfully. "A fine start, Mr. Darcy."

Darcy ignored her tone, stepping back as she moved forward for her own turn.

She studied the ball, gripping her mallet lightly, her posture relaxed, almost careless. Then, in one smooth motion, she struck—sending the ball gliding effortlessly through the next hoop.

Darcy's eyes narrowed.

Elizabeth met his gaze, all innocence and mirth.

"Oh dear," she said lightly, swinging her mallet onto her shoulder. "Did I do that correctly? You shall have to forgive me, sir, I am ever so unfamiliar with these country amusements."

"You seem to be managing well enough," Darcy remarked as evenly as he could, lining up his shot.

Elizabeth lifted her mallet, her expression all bright-eyed innocence. "How very reassuring. I would hate to put my partner at a disadvantage."

Partner.

Darcy adjusted his grip on the mallet, trying to hide how his hand flinched. He struck, sending the ball rolling cleanly through the hoop.

She stepped forward, taking her turn, barely sparing a glance at the ball before striking it with casual perfection. Dash it all, she was even good at *this*.

"Miss Bennet," he said, watching her progress, "I trust you are settling in well at Longbourn?"

Elizabeth's mallet paused just slightly before she swung. Not enough for anyone else to notice—but he did.

"Oh, quite well, sir," she replied smoothly, stepping back as her ball cleared the hoop. "Your concern is touching."

"I had no intention of 'touching' anything, I assure you," he muttered under his breath.

She turned, brows lifting. "I beg your pardon?"

Darcy cleared his throat and gestured for her to continue. "It is merely my duty to ensure all matters are proceeding as they should."

She hummed. "Ah, yes. Your duty." She lined up her next shot, giving him a sidelong glance. "And do you make it your duty to concern yourself with all the young ladies of the neighborhood? Or only the ones you so conveniently find in need of shelter?"

Darcy set his jaw. She was enjoying herself entirely too much.

He took his shot, sending his ball rolling smoothly through the next hoop. "There. That is how it is done."

Elizabeth approached, adjusting her grip. "Is it?" she mused, tapping her mallet idly against the ground. "How very enlightening."

She swung.

His ball, not hers, went sailing off-course.

Darcy stopped short. His eyes followed its trajectory into the grass, landing well outside the playing field.

Elizabeth pressed a gloved hand to her chest. "Oh dear," she said, her voice all syrupy innocence. "Was that yours?"

Bingley, watching from a few yards away, gave an inelegant snort of laughter.

Caroline, meanwhile, looked as if she had just swallowed a lemon whole.

Darcy turned, slowly, back to Elizabeth.

She twirled her mallet lazily, gazing up at him with mock concern.

"You did say the goal was to eliminate the competition," she reminded him.

Darcy rubbed a hand over his face. *This woman.*

A few paces away, a group of gentlemen were speaking in low tones. Darcy caught the familiar name Audley and flicked his attention toward them—only to notice that Elizabeth had, too.

She was trying not to look as though she was listening. Failing miserably, of course.

"You seem quite interested in the conversation over there," he observed idly.

Elizabeth did not miss a beat. "Do I? How very fascinating."

Darcy studied her carefully. "Mr. Audley is a reformist, is he not?"

She arched a brow. "Are you concerned I may have political leanings, Mr. Darcy?"

"I am concerned about a great many things."

Her smile deepened, the picture of ease. "How very unfortunate for you."

She stepped past him toward her next shot, entirely unconcerned. He watched as she lined up her mallet, tapped her ball forward with infuriating precision, and sent it sailing exactly where it needed to go.

Effortless. Graceful. Entirely too composed.

Darcy's grip tightened around his own mallet.

It was not just the game. It was *her.* The way she spoke in circles, always just on the edge of saying something significant—before pulling away at the last moment, leaving him grasping for meaning.

He was accustomed to control. To order. To reading a person's intent within moments. That was his entire occupation—that was why the Prince trusted him. And yet—Elizabeth was an enigma. A puzzle he could not quite fit together.

Which made her dangerous.

Darcy inhaled slowly, counting to three. He was going to lose his mind.

And Elizabeth-whatever-her-name-was was having the time of her life watching it happen.

CHAPTER ELEVEN

Longbourn, Monday, May 18, 1812

E LIZABETH AWOKE TO THE unfamiliar sound of laughter drifting through the open window. Birds chirped somewhere beyond the hedgerows, but it was the riotous giggling that drew her attention first. It was a high, unchecked sort of laughter, the kind that belonged to girls who had never once been scolded for being too loud.

She sat up, rubbing her temples. Her head still ached faintly from all that blasted sunshine the day before—and, no doubt, from the sheer effort of playing the part of "Miss Elizabeth Bennet"—but at least she had not slept through half the day. At home—no, not home. Not for now, at least. At her *father's house*, she would have laid abed for at least another hour, then taken breakfast on a tray, her maid attending, the day's itinerary arranged in a quiet, orderly fashion.

Here, life had no such structure. The household had been awake for hours already, the servants in and out, the younger Bennets dashing through the hallways without a care in the world.

It was chaos. And Elizabeth had no choice but to step into it.

She dressed quickly and made her way downstairs, smoothing her skirts as she stepped outside into the morning sun. The laughter had not ceased.

At the far end of the garden, Kitty and Lydia were sprawled on the grass, arms linked as they gasped through fresh peals of mirth. Their bonnets lay discarded beside them, their skirts haphazardly arranged, their ankles completely visible to the world—and worse, they did not seem to care.

Elizabeth smiled thinly. "You are indecent, dear Lydia and Kitty."

Lydia propped herself up on an elbow, utterly unbothered. "We are at home, Cousin."

"That does not make you decent," Elizabeth returned.

Kitty giggled. "She sounds like Mary!"

Elizabeth sighed, pushing a hand through her hair. It was far too early for this.

"Cousin Elizabeth, good morning."

Elizabeth turned. Ah, at least there was still Jane.

Unlike her younger sisters, Jane sat with perfect composure on a garden bench, an embroidery hoop in her lap, her gown untouched by the grass and dust. Sunlight caught the gold in her hair, making her look almost otherworldly.

But Elizabeth had learned something in the last few days—Jane was no angel.

Not in the way people meant, at least.

She was kind, yes, and graceful, and quick to smile. But she was also achingly quiet. Unassuming to the point of being overlooked, and not as indifferent about being ignored as people believed. And, most interestingly, she seemed to spend a good deal of time watching a man who did not notice her at all.

"Miss Bennet," Elizabeth greeted, taking a seat beside her.

Jane reached for the embroidery in her lap, her fingers working with quiet skill. "I hope you slept well."

Elizabeth hesitated. She had slept terribly, actually.

Longbourn's walls were too thin. The air smelled different. The pillows were too soft, and the silence of the countryside was nothing like the quiet of London—it was louder, in a way, full of rustling leaves and the occasional fox's cry.

She gave a polite nod instead. "Well enough."

Jane's needle moved through the fabric. "And you are settling in?"

Elizabeth exhaled, watching as Lydia rolled onto her back in the grass, arms stretched above her head as if she had not a care in the world.

"I am…" She searched for the right word. Not 'comfortable.' Not 'content.'

"…adjusting."

Jane studied her for a moment before giving a small, knowing nod, as if she understood precisely what Elizabeth meant.

Elizabeth frowned. "And what of you?"

Jane blinked. "Me? Why do you ask?"

"Well, I only thought it would be impolite not to. After all, you asked how I was, so I now ask you the same. Are you well?"

Jane's shoulders stiffened—just slightly—but her expression remained neutral. "Oh—yes, of course."

Elizabeth followed her gaze—to the drive. No one was coming—no carriages or horses or even gardeners on foot. But Jane seemed to be looking for someone, nonetheless.

Jane looked back to her embroidery, then looked up at Elizabeth. "I have been meaning to ask... what have you heard from your family?"

Elizabeth narrowed her eyes. "My family?"

"Yes, surely they have written by now to see that you are settled in and content here. Your mother must miss you terribly."

Oh. Yes, the mother in... Shropshire? Was that it? She cleared her throat. "I am sorry to say, I have not received one letter since my arrival, so I do wonder how they are getting on without me."

Jane's brow furrowed slightly. "Well, Papa mentioned that your father is ever so devoted to his fishing."

Fishing. Right. That had been her story. Elizabeth forced a smile. "Yes. Quite devoted."

"And your mother?"

"My mother?" Elizabeth repeated, stalling.

Jane nodded, waiting patiently.

Elizabeth's mind was a blank. Who was her mother supposed to be? She had not the faintest idea what sort of woman she was meant to describe.

"Ah," she said finally, keeping her tone light, "she is much the same. You know how mothers are."

Jane smiled. "Indeed."

Elizabeth made a mental note to speak with Mr. Bennet before the day was out. She would need a great deal more information if she were to continue this charade. Jane Bennet might be quiet and polite, but she was surely not stupid.

Elizabeth studied her face in silhouette, pondering about this girl who was so different from herself. Quiet... no, that was not right. *Reserved*—that was a better word. A riot of feeling was tossing on the stormy seas of Jane Bennet's blue eyes, but it was kept in vicious check—for what reason, she could not say.

Then, unexpectedly, Jane's grip on her embroidery tightened. Elizabeth frowned. "Are you well?" Jane's shoulders tensed, just slightly, but her expression remained neutral. "Oh—yes, of course." Elizabeth followed her gaze—again, to the drive.

Where a certain gentleman was stepping down from his carriage.

Mr. Bingley.

And suddenly, Elizabeth understood.

It was in the way Jane did not move, did not call out to him, did not let even a flicker of anticipation cross her face. It was too careful. Too measured.

Too much like a girl who had long since given up hoping.

Elizabeth turned back to Jane, watching her for a moment longer. Then, ever so casually, said, "Your Mr. Bingley seems to have arrived."

Jane's fingers jerked on the embroidery hoop. A single drop of blood welled up where the needle pricked her skin.

Now, this was interesting.

Jane's mouth parted slightly, then snapped shut. A moment later, she forced a light laugh, dabbing at her fingertip with a lace handkerchief. "It is a funny thing that you should call him *my* Mr. Bingley," she said, too carefully, too deliberately. "We have no particular acquaintance. I believe Papa knows him better than any of the rest of us."

Elizabeth's eyes gleamed, but she smoothed her expression. "I misspoke," she amended swiftly. "I meant—your neighbor."

Jane's lips pressed together, and though she nodded, something in her posture remained stiff. "Yes," she murmured. "Our neighbor."

Elizabeth turned her gaze back to the drive, humming thoughtfully.

How very, very interesting, indeed.

T HE PLAN WAS SIMPLE.

Or at least, it *should* have been.

Darcy had orchestrated this visit with a perfect scheme in mind—convinced Bingley that a call upon the Bennets was due, persuaded him that a walk would be the most amiable of country neighborly gestures, and ensured that Elizabeth would be among those in attendance. It had all been done with the utmost subtlety, of course.

And yet, as they stood in the bright summer sunlight, watching the Bennet sisters retrieve their bonnets and gloves, Darcy had the distinct sense that he had once again miscalculated something.

He could feel it the moment Elizabeth adjusted her hat, a slow, deliberate motion as she glanced down the path. There was nothing remarkable in her posture, nothing obvious in her tone. And yet, something in the air shifted.

"Oh, look at the path ahead," she remarked lightly, barely glancing toward it. "With all the rain last week, I daresay there will be mud in places."

Darcy narrowed his eyes. What the devil was she about?

It was nothing—just an idle remark. And yet, there was something—

"Oh! I shall go ahead and see if it is dreadful," Lydia declared at once, snatching Kitty's arm before anyone could intervene.

"What—? Lydia, wait—" Kitty stumbled after her, protesting faintly but making no real effort to resist. Their voices trailed off, skirts rustling as they hurried ahead.

Darcy sighed, looking after the dismissed sisters. She made that look too easy. Dash it all, how had he never thought of such a devilish clever means of getting rid of them?

"I suppose," Elizabeth went on, "should the path prove troublesome, it is a fine thing that we have steady escorts."

Darcy turned his head sharply. Apparently, she had not yet done.

Bingley straightened slightly, as if only just realizing the merit of the suggestion. "Quite right! Ladies ought to have proper support on uneven ground."

Elizabeth dusted off her skirts with deliberate ease. "Indeed. A gentleman's arm would be most welcome, particularly if the path is treacherous."

Jane Bennet, who had been silent until now, went still, with great round eyes.

Darcy noted the shift—small, but unmistakable. A breath held, a glance flickered, a moment's delay.

Elizabeth, meanwhile, adjusted her glove, deliberately avoiding any chance that Bingley's gaze might blunder into hers. Oh, she was good.

Bingley hesitated for only a second before turning to Jane with an easy smile. "But of course! Miss Bennet, if you would allow me the honor?"

A pause.

Jane Bennet's lips parted, as though a protest was forming—but she swallowed it.

"I... suppose I would not object to the company."

Bingley brightened. "Splendid!"

Darcy kept his expression neutral, but his patience wore thin. Elizabeth merely smoothed her sleeve, not looking at him, not looking at anyone in particular.

And yet, she had done exactly what she meant to do. Without a single misstep.

Mary, who had been hanging reluctantly back, but still making a great show of donning her gloves, cleared her throat and glanced between Elizabeth and Jane. "Oh, well, if you two are together, perhaps I may as well remain at home. I never fancy being an odd number, and I did not finish my reading this morning."

Darcy did not miss the way she clutched her book closer, nor the slight relief in her posture as she took a backward step toward the house.

Mrs. Bennet, who had been standing just inside the threshold, took one look at Mary's stance and sighed. "Well, if you must, you must," she said, though she sounded more exasperated than disappointed. "But do not sit cooped up all day, Mary. It is not healthy for a young lady."

Mary nodded, already turning away, clearly pleased with the outcome.

"So," Elizabeth said brightly as they began their walk, "how do you find the country air, Mr. Darcy? Quite different from London, I expect."

Darcy shot her a sidelong glance. "Indeed. Though I am not unfamiliar with country life."

"Ah, yes." She clasped her hands behind her back, tilting her head slightly. "You did say you had family near Matlock, did you not?"

He hesitated. "I did."

A little too much interest gleamed in her expression. "And are they all so... discreet as yourself?"

He did not dignify that with a response.

Elizabeth only hummed, falling into step beside him.

Bingley and Jane Bennet were ahead, though not far enough for Darcy's comfort. He watched as Bingley leaned slightly toward her, speaking animatedly about something that made her smile.

He turned sharply back to Elizabeth. "You enjoy making sport of your 'cousin,' I see."

Elizabeth blinked, all feigned innocence. "Whatever do you mean, sir?"

He gave her a look. "You orchestrated that pairing."

She sighed, her expression one of exaggerated resignation. "You are entirely too suspicious, Mr. Darcy."

Darcy lifted a brow.

Elizabeth pursed her lips. Then, with a small smirk, she said, "But I am also not denying it."

Darcy sighed heavily. "Of course not."

She clasped her hands, looking ever so pleased with herself. "It is only right that a gentleman should properly escort a lady, is it not? I cannot imagine what you are so put out about."

Darcy did not dignify that with a response, either. Elizabeth Montclair was a menace.

He glanced at her. She was walking easily, idly trailing her fingers along the tall grasses lining the path. Her cheeks were flushed from the sun, and a slight breeze lifted a few wayward tendrils of dark hair from beneath her bonnet.

She was—comfortable.

A pity he had to wreck that.

Darcy cleared his throat. "I have a question for you, Miss Elizabeth."

She glanced at him, arching a brow. "Oh? Is this an interrogation?"

"Hardly." Darcy adjusted his stride, angling slightly toward her. "You have told me before what you saw that night, but I am beginning to suspect I did not ask you all that I should have."

Elizabeth flicked him a glance, wary. "I cannot imagine what else there is to say."

"You might begin by telling me why you were there in the first place."

Her expression did not change. "Oh, you know. The thrill of high-stakes politics. The electric energy of the crowd. I simply could not resist."

Darcy gave her a flat look.

Elizabeth sighed. "Would you believe I was merely sightseeing?"

"No."

"Well, there we are, then." She clasped her hands behind her back, picking her way neatly over a root. "And besides, you seem quite determined to be unimpressed by my explanations, so what is the use?"

Darcy eyed her. "Because, *Miss* Elizabeth, the Home Office does not make it a habit of dealing in absurdities."

She lifted a brow. "A pity, then, for you."

Darcy exhaled sharply, abandoning that line of questioning for now. He would pry it out of her sooner or later.

Instead, he shifted course. "You recall the moment the Prime Minister fell?"

Elizabeth's hand stilled against the tall grass. "Yes."

"Were you watching before the shot was fired?"

A beat.

Then, slowly, she nodded. "I was looking at the crowd in general, not at the Prime Minister specifically, but he was near the center of my view."

His pulse quickened. He had assumed, of course, that she had been a witness after the fact, that the chaos of the event had rendered everything else a muddled haze. But if she had seen the moment before—

"What was his position?" he asked. "Did he turn? Did he see his killer?"

Elizabeth pressed her lips together. "I—" She hesitated.

He did not rush her.

Her brows furrowed. "He... turned slightly. Not toward Bellingham. Toward something else. Someone else. And then—" She cut herself off, shaking her head. "It happened so fast."

Darcy's thoughts spun. This was new. Important. The trajectory mattered—if Perceval had turned toward something else—

Elizabeth was watching him now, her gaze sharp. "Why are you asking me this now?"

"Because, Miss Bennet, I was too busy keeping you alive before."

That was apparently not enough to satisfy her. He felt her gaze warming his cheek and sighed. "And because I am running out of time."

He turned his focus ahead to where Bingley and Miss Bennet were walking, but something still nagged at him. He considered dropping the matter, but no—this was his chance.

He glanced at her again. "And tell me another thing—why were you so interested in what was being said of Mr. Henry Audley at the garden party?"

Elizabeth stumbled.

It was only slight, only for a fraction of a second, but he caught it.

She recovered quickly, glancing at a fluttering tree bough overhead with feigned nonchalance. "I do not recall giving Mr. Audley's name any particular notice."

Darcy folded his hands behind his back. "Indeed?"

"Indeed. Who is he?"

"Nobody, apparently." He watched her, waiting.

She did not meet his gaze. Rather, she stared straight ahead, but her jaw muscles were taut as a bowstring.

Darcy allowed a thoughtful grunt. "Then it must have been my imagination when I saw you loitering at the edges of the conversation."

Elizabeth shot him a sideways glare. "It must have been."

"Curious, though," he mused, as if speaking to himself. "That my imagination should coincide so neatly with your unwavering attention whenever his name arose in conversation."

Elizabeth made a noise of indignation. "Unwavering attention! That is ridiculous."

"Of course."

She huffed. "Very well. If you must know—I find Mr. Audley agreeable."

Darcy arched a brow. "Agreeable?"

Elizabeth waved a hand. "You know. In a sort of... respectable, idealistic, utterly noble sort of way."

"And what exactly are his superior qualifications?"

She sniffed. "He is a gentleman."

"So am I."

She made a scoffing sound. "He is a gentleman with money."

Darcy narrowed his eyes. "Now, see here—"

"Oh, do not look at me like that, sir," she interrupted breezily. "You asked for an honest answer."

He clenched his jaw. "I suppose I did."

Elizabeth clasped her hands in front of her, looking ever so pleased with herself. "And now you have it."

Darcy resisted the urge to pinch the bridge of his nose. "You are insufferable."

"Yes, I know," she said sweetly. "But I am also a key witness in a murder investigation. Which, I believe, is more than some people can say."

Darcy inhaled deeply, forcing himself to return his focus to the path ahead. This woman would drive him to madness.

But at least, now, he had an answer.

E LIZABETH LAY IN THE dark, staring at the ceiling. The house was silent around her, save for the occasional creak of settling wood and the distant sound of a clock ticking in the hallway.

She turned onto her side. Then her other side. Then onto her back again.

Sleep would not come.

Her mind wandered where she did not want it to go—London, her father, Charlotte. The Queen's cool gaze. The Prince's indolent smirk. And most of all—the shot. The acrid burn of the air in that terrible moment. The chaos. The truth she had tried to tell. The details taunting her, just at the edge of memory.

She exhaled sharply and sat up.

Her fingers fumbled for the small writing desk near her bed. A moment later, her hands found what they sought—her sketchbook, the charcoals Mr. Bennet had procured for her at Jane's request. She flipped it open, the paper smooth beneath her fingertips.

For a while, she let her hand move freely, copying down the things that anchored her to the present—to this life she was living for a little while. Anything to help her think of something cheerful and pleasant rather than *that* moment.

Jane, bent over her embroidery, brow furrowed in concentration, needle poised midair.

Mr. Bennet at his desk, pen hovering as though caught between thoughts.

A vague outline of Longbourn's garden, the gentle slope leading toward the fields.

The sketches were rough but familiar. Easy.

Her mind drifted, her strokes fluid, effortless. The repetition of it was calming, the gentle scratching against the page soothing.

Until, without thinking, her hand started sketching something else.

A face.

Her hand stilled when she realized what it was.

The lines were sharper than before, the shape of them forming too quickly, as if her memory had taken over her fingertips.

The jaw, angular and unshaven.

A shadowed cheekbone, gaunt in the dim light.

The thick brows, the narrow lips.

She had *seen* him.

Elizabeth's breath caught.

She had not let herself recall this—not in full. She had spoken of him in vague terms, had told herself she had only glimpsed him for an instant. But her fingers knew better. The memory had been waiting. Lurking.

She had been steps away from him. Had felt his presence in that alcove, had seen his head turn toward her, the recognition flicker in his eyes.

Her stomach twisted.

He had seen her.

And now, here he was again, staring up at her from the page, his outline unmistakable, the sharp intensity of that gaze, piercing straight through her like a needle through silk.

Her pulse thudded loudly in her ears.

What if Darcy could use this?

She stared at the sketch, a prickle of unease running down her spine. But she did not allow herself to hesitate. Carefully, deliberately, she tore the page free and smoothed out the edges.

She folded it once, then again, tucking it beneath her pillow.

Tomorrow, she would give it to him.

Chapter Twelve

May 19, 1812

D ARCY'S ROOM AT NETHERFIELD was suffocating.

He had spent the better part of the morning pacing, hands clasped behind his back, staring out of the window, then back at the desk, then at the neatly folded correspondence he had prepared for London. The Prince's deadline loomed ever closer, and he had done nothing.

No new leads. No progress. No evidence beyond the word of a woman he had assumed saw nothing of consequence.

He would leave for London within the hour. He had convinced Bingley that he had business with the Home Office, though that had only prompted a string of questions about when he would return. Darcy had not answered. The truth was, he did not know.

Nor did he know what he expected to find.

He exhaled sharply and pressed his palms against the desk, bowing his head for a brief moment, forcing himself to think. A week had passed since Perceval fell, since the country was thrown into disarray, since Darcy had become entangled in this wretched affair. A week.

And now, the man convicted for the crime was dead. Executed yesterday.

The news had spread like wildfire through the town. Meryton was buzzing with the details, the certainty of Bellingham's guilt, the finality of justice being served. The people were content to close the matter.

Darcy, however, was not.

The true murderer remained free. The Prince had given him a task, and he had nothing—nothing but the sinking realization that time was slipping away, and the illusion of safety in Hertfordshire was precisely that.

An illusion.

He needed to return to London. He had wasted too many days already. His plan had been simple—take breakfast, settle his affairs with Bingley, and be on his way before noon.

He had not accounted for distractions.

Darcy reached for his coat, prepared to take his leave, when he heard the unmistakable music of female voices from downstairs. A rising and falling of pleasantries, the occasional exclamation—too distant to make out the words, but distinct enough to mark them as visitors.

His brow furrowed. It was morning, the customary hour for calls. But that should not concern him in any way. He planned to leave quietly—he had already made his intentions known.

A sharp rap on the door interrupted that plan.

Before Darcy could respond, the door cracked open and Bingley poked his head inside, beaming in that boyishly eager way that made it impossible to predict whether he was about to say something innocuous or entirely exasperating.

"Darcy! There you are—still here. You are in luck, man."

"Am I?"

"Indeed! You see, the Bennets have come to call." Bingley stepped fully into the room, closing the door behind him with a casual flick of his hand. "I know you were planning to leave today," he continued, "but I cannot in good conscience let you slip away like some fugitive before you have greeted them." His grin widened. "Come, be sociable."

Darcy crossed his arms. "I fail to see why my presence is required."

Bingley waved a hand. "Oh, come now. It is only polite. Besides, you and Mr. Bennet get on famously—you can speak of all your dreadful books and strategy games while the ladies chatter about ribbons and bonnets."

Darcy arched a brow.

Bingley laughed. "Very well, I take it back. Miss Elizabeth, at least, is rather sharp in conversation. You should quite enjoy yourself."

Darcy schooled his features into neutrality, refusing to rise to whatever bait Bingley was dangling before him.

Bingley, naturally, noticed. His expression turned shrewd. "You must come, Darcy. Caroline will take it as a personal triumph if you hide in here all morning."

That, at least, gave him pause.

Bingley was already seizing the moment, stepping aside and gesturing toward the hall. "Come along, man. It is only a few minutes of pleasantries. Then you can run off to London to your heart's content."

Darcy clenched his jaw. It was foolish to risk unnecessary attention by being seen speaking with Elizabeth. And yet—refusing outright would raise questions. And it was just a morning call.

A few minutes of pleasantries.

Nothing more.

He straightened his coat and strode past Bingley into the hall.

By the time Darcy entered the drawing room alongside Bingley, the Bennet women had already settled. The Bingley sisters were seated with stiff politeness, their smiles brittle as they exchanged the customary pleasantries with their guests.

Darcy barely registered any of it.

Because Elizabeth was there.

She was seated near Jane Bennet, gloved hands folded neatly in her lap, her posture composed like she was sitting in her father's drawing room. When she glanced up, her gaze brushed his—just briefly, just enough.

She rose with the others as decorum dictated, offering a graceful curtsy. "Mr. Darcy." But there was something in the way she carried herself—too deliberate, too measured. A slight stiffness in her posture, as though she were bracing for something. That in itself was a message to him.

He frowned. Darcy inclined his head, forcing himself to look away before he revealed anything he should not.

The call unfolded as it ought. Mrs. Bennet exclaimed—again—over Netherfield's fine appointments. Caroline Bingley offered her usual false smiles. Bingley played the perfect host, offering refreshments and easy conversation.

Darcy moved to the far side of the room, hands clasped behind his back, determined to let the visit pass without complication.

Then Elizabeth shifted closer.

A flick of her wrist. A slip of paper.

She let it fall onto the small table beside him as she turned toward Jane Bennet, as though adjusting the folds of her gown.

Darcy squinted at it.

The motion had been fluid, practiced—he would not have noticed had he not been watching her so carefully.

His eyes flicked to the paper. The edges were smudged faintly with charcoal.

Elizabeth was still speaking to the eldest Bennet sister, her expression pleasant, her laughter ready. Not looking at him.

Darcy hesitated, then slowly, carefully, unfolded the paper.

A face stared back at him. Dark brows. Hollow cheeks. A cruel, assessing gaze.

Drawn in clean, deliberate strokes, the sketch was stark—impossible to ignore.

Was this... what he thought it was?

He glanced up at her, and she slid one eye in his direction. So... Elizabeth *had* seen his face. Not as a shadow in the chaos. Not as a half-formed figure lost in the crowd.

She had *seen* him.

Memorized him.

Darcy swallowed, his grip tightening around the edges of the page.

The visit concluded as all such visits did—polite words, curtsies exchanged, murmurs of farewell. The Bennet women rose, adjusting gloves and gathering their things.

Bingley, ever the courteous host, stepped forward. "Ladies, may I escort you to your carriage?"

A chorus of polite assent followed. The Bingley sisters remained behind, relieved, no doubt, to see the visit draw to a close.

Darcy hesitated only a moment before following.

The hallway was cooler than the drawing room, and the footsteps of their small group echoed against the polished floors. Elizabeth walked just ahead of him, her posture straight, composed. She had orchestrated this meeting—of that, he was certain. Just as surely as yesterday's call had been *his* idea rather than Bingley's.

Outside, the Bennet carriage waited. Mrs. Bennet, and then Jane Bennet accepted Bingley's elbow to escort them down the steps to the drive. Kitty and Lydia were just behind, laughing over something.

Elizabeth lingered more slowly.

Darcy moved closer, lowering his voice. "Is this the man?"

She glanced at the page still clutched in his hand, then up at him. "Yes."

The single word sent a chill down his spine.

Ahead of them, the groom opened the carriage door. Not much time...

"You saw him clearly," he murmured. "You drew this last night—a week after the fact. Are you sure this is accurate?"

Elizabeth's lips pressed together in confirmation.

Mrs. Bennet was already settling herself inside. The coachman had climbed into his seat. Darcy studied the sketch again, then turned his gaze back to her. "Why have you never mentioned that you saw his face this clearly?"

Her chin lifted slightly. "I told you what I saw. You never asked for more."

"No, you told me you saw the assassination."

"That is the same thing."

Darcy exhaled sharply. "No, it is not. You saw *him*. You remember him perfectly, if this is a true rendering and not a product of your imagination." He tapped the sketch lightly. "This is not the work of someone with a vague recollection."

A flicker of movement—Bingley now helping a second Bennet sister into the carriage, smiling as he bid the lady farewell.

Elizabeth flicked her gaze at him. "It is. Why do you sound so surprised, sir?"

"Because... I thought you... well, you are not a trained observer."

Her brows drew together in some hurt. "Oh. You thought I was useless to you."

"I..." Darcy exhaled sharply, biting back the rest of the regrettable sentiment.

I thought you were a foolish, reckless, spoiled heiress who had wandered into the wrong place at the wrong time and needed rescuing.

Because I did not realize—

He looked down at the sketch once more. At the crisp lines. The deliberate strokes. The undeniable skill.

Kitty Bennet was now stepping into the carriage, and the horses were beginning to stir impatiently.

"You are talented," he said, his voice quieter now, thoughtful. "Surprisingly so."

Elizabeth blinked, caught off guard. "You sound astonished."

"I suppose I am."

"So? Will it be useful to you?"

The driver adjusted the reins, and Bingley was now handing the last Bennet sister in. The carriage was about to depart.

"Very much so," he murmured, scanning the lines again. "I think you saw more than I realized."

Darcy flicked his gaze toward the carriage, then back to Elizabeth. Their time was up.

Without another word, he stepped forward and opened the door, offering his hand.

She hesitated—just for a breath—before placing her fingers lightly in his. The touch was fleeting, gone as soon as she settled into the seat beside the others.

The door clicked shut. The driver gave a low call. And Darcy's fingers still burned from hers.

E LIZABETH HAD ALWAYS THOUGHT of night as a time of quiet. A time when the world settled, when worries could be tucked away and left for the morning.

But not here.

At Longbourn, night was loud.

Not the clatter from the streets like there would be in London. Not the voices of twenty maids finishing for the evening. No, in that way, night was quite peaceful.

The old house groaned as the evening chill settled in, floorboards cracked under unseen footsteps, and the restless murmurs of the wind pushed against the windowpanes. Somewhere down the corridor, Lydia's muffled laughter drifted through the walls, followed by a burst of hushed giggles from Kitty. A door creaked, then shut with a dull thud.

Elizabeth pulled the coverlet higher over her shoulders. Sleep evaded her again tonight.

She missed London.

She missed the ease of familiarity—her father's absentminded grumbles, Charlotte's sharp wit, the routine of calling on friends, of reading by lamplight in a place where she belonged.

Here, she was an imposter.

A stranger playing a part in a house full of women who accepted her without question. They were kind—far kinder than they needed to be. Jane in particular. But that kindness only made her feel more like an interloper, a guest overstaying her welcome.

And yet... what choice did she have?

A soft sigh escaped her lips, barely audible beneath the sounds of the night.

She had wanted—*needed*—to get away from the stifling house, so she had offered to take Hill's place in gathering the last of the linens from the line. The air had been crisp, the grass damp from the evening dew, and for a moment, it had been peaceful.

Until she noticed it.

A feeling. A prickle against the back of her neck, the unmistakable sense of being watched.

She had turned sharply, expecting to find a servant or one of the younger girls lingering behind her.

But the yard had been empty.

Nothing but moonlight on the damp grass, the flicker of candlelight from the windows, and the soft rustle of the trees.

Still, she had not lingered.

Now, she sat upright in bed, staring at the closed curtains.

It had been nothing. A flight of fancy. She was not used to country nights, to the sounds of the house settling or the unfamiliar emptiness of the fields beyond the garden. She was being foolish.

And yet—

Her fingers tightened in the coverlet.

Darcy had said she was safe. He had *promised* she was safe.

She forced a slow breath and willed herself to believe it.

But Darcy had left for London that very afternoon. And even Mr. Bennet, who was the only person in Hertfordshire who had any inkling she was not who she was supposed to be, had no idea of the truth of the matter.

As she lay back against the pillows, she could not shake the feeling that someone had been there. Watching. Waiting. Was it merely her imagination? The threads of a guilty conscience weaving together to torment her?

Or had she been recognized?

May 20, 1812

D ARCY HAD BEEN AT this for hours.

His rented rooms at Albany were quiet, save for the faint crackle of the oil lamp and the steady scratch of his pen as he copied numbers from one ledger to another.

Pages of figures, columns of names, payments listed under vague descriptions—it was all maddeningly opaque. The Home Office kept thorough records, but thorough did not mean transparent. Whoever had orchestrated this had been careful, using layers of intermediaries to obscure the movement of funds.

The ledgers stretched before him in neat, unbroken rows of ink, each name and figure meticulously recorded, each column an exercise in bureaucratic monotony. A web of numbers. Transactions. Financial trails that should have led somewhere. But instead, they looped endlessly into nothing.

Bellingham had been executed the day before yesterday, and his trial had done exactly what it was meant to do—close the case. The investigation had ceased the moment the noose tightened around the man's neck. The authorities considered it over. Finished.

But someone had paid Bellingham. Provoked him, stoked his motives... likely black-mailed him, threatened his family, even, to make him kill the Prime Minister. That much, Darcy was certain of. And someone had gone to great lengths to cover it up.

A knock at the door pulled him from his work. He exhaled slowly, rubbing the bridge of his nose before rising to answer.

Colonel Fitzwilliam stepped inside without waiting for an invitation, shrugging off his coat. "You look terrible."

Darcy gave him a flat look and returned to his seat. "You came all this way to tell me that?"

"Of course not." Fitzwilliam pulled up a chair, casting a glance over the spread of ledgers and loose papers. "But I might have expected it. Have you slept?"

Darcy did not dignify that with an answer. Instead, he tapped the open ledger in front of him. "I need you to look at this."

Fitzwilliam leaned in, eyes scanning the pages. After a moment, he frowned. "How did you get this? This is the government's own treasury account."

"It is," Darcy said grimly. "And it is incomplete."

Fitzwilliam's brow creased. "What do you mean?"

Darcy flipped to another set of records, ones he had "borrowed"—perhaps less than legally—from a second department. "These are military expenditures. And these—" he gestured to another book, "—are payments made to known contractors. Now, compare the two."

Fitzwilliam did so, his frown deepening. "These amounts do not match."

"No, they do not," Darcy confirmed. "Certain funds are marked as paid, but there is no corresponding recipient. The money is gone, but there is no record of who received it."

Fitzwilliam let out a slow breath. "So it was diverted."

"And it was done carefully. Not in large sums, but in small, regular increments over months—perhaps years." Darcy tapped his finger against one of the entries. "It was routed through several hands before disappearing entirely."

Fitzwilliam sat back, crossing his arms. "Someone inside the government was moving money into false accounts."

"Or false ventures," Darcy corrected. "Some of these payments were made under the pretense of 'supply costs'—munitions, provisions for regiments, commissions for arms manufacturers. But the final ledgers do not match the purchases."

Fitzwilliam nodded slowly, taking it all in. "You think any of this has to do with Perceval?"

"I do not believe in coincidences," Darcy said darkly. "A man does not embezzle government funds for months on end and then, by sheer happenstance, the Prime Minister—the one man in the cabinet who might have discovered it—ends up assassinated."

Fitzwilliam let out a low whistle. "That is a dangerous theory."

"It is," Darcy agreed.

Fitzwilliam exhaled sharply and rubbed a hand over his face. "You know, when I agreed to look into this with you, I was rather hoping it would be something simple. A man with a grudge, an unfortunate coincidence—something I could ignore in good conscience and go on about my life."

Darcy arched a brow. "And yet you are here."

Fitzwilliam huffed. "Yes, well. My conscience is a great nuisance."

Darcy pushed another sheet toward him. "Then help me make sense of this."

Fitzwilliam took up the page, his expression serious now. "And what of your witness? Have you written to... well, whoever it is you left in charge of her?"

Darcy hesitated—only briefly. "She is safe."

Fitzwilliam gave him a look. "That was not what I asked."

Darcy exhaled. "I will write tomorrow."

Fitzwilliam shook his head but said nothing further.

For now, there was work to do.

CHAPTER THIRTEEN

May 21, 1812

THE BREAKFAST TABLE AT Longbourn was a cacophony of sound.

It always was.

Elizabeth sat with her hands wrapped around her teacup, watching as the Bennet family moved around her in their usual morning chaos.

Kitty and Lydia argued over a bonnet, their voices rising and falling in an endless battle of frills and ribbons. Mary sat somewhat apart from the others, reading aloud from a book no one was listening to, undeterred by the lack of audience.

Mrs. Bennet sat at the head of the table, already deep in conversation—mostly with herself—about the latest gossip from Meryton. "—and I declare, Mr. Bingley is just the nicest young man! I only wish he would take more notice of our dear girls. But no, he is always all smiles and no action. I tell you, Mr. Bennet, he will let all his best years slip away before he realizes what a treasure is right before him!"

Mr. Bennet, safely ensconced behind his broadsheet, turned a page over with deliberate slowness. "How very tragic for him."

Mrs. Bennet pursed her lips. "It *is* tragic, sir. If only he had the good sense God gave a goose, we might already be preparing a trousseau."

Across the table, Jane cleared her throat and reached for the pot of honey, avoiding her mother's pointed glance. "Mama, I believe you were speaking of Lady Lucas's new gown?"

Mrs. Bennet brightened. "Oh! Yes, yes, I do not suppose you saw it, Lizzy—terribly unbecoming, poor woman. The color of boiled spinach."

Elizabeth glanced up, amused. Whether Mr. Darcy liked it or not, it seemed she had become "Lizzy" to the Bennets. "I cannot think of anything more unfortunate."

"Nor I!" Mrs. Bennet agreed, gesturing animatedly with her spoon. "What was she thinking? She ought to have consulted me. I always say, a lady must know what suits her." She turned a critical eye on Kitty and Lydia, who were picking at their toast. "And that is why I say you two must have new bonnets. Yours are dreadful and you know it."

Kitty and Lydia did not seem terribly put out by this observation. Lydia, in particular, beamed. "Then you shall take us shopping, Mama?"

"We shall see," Mrs. Bennet said mysteriously, as if the fate of England depended upon it.

Mr. Bennet turned his broadsheet again, looking at his wife over the top of it. "Mrs. Bennet, I trust you are keeping a tally of all these necessary purchases? If I am to be ruined, I should at least like to know what tipped me over the edge."

Mrs. Bennet scoffed. "Oh, you. I do not know why I bother speaking to you. You never take my concerns seriously."

"My dear, I take them as seriously as they deserve."

Mrs. Hill entered then, setting down another plate of warm biscuits. Jane murmured a polite thank you and reached for one, but Elizabeth noted the way her fingers whitened on the knife as her mother continued to lament Mr. Bingley's inattention.

But whatever thoughts Elizabeth might have spared for Jane Bennet's careful study of her breakfast were cut off by the sloshing of a pitcher of cream mere inches from her plate. Her eyes widened, but Lydia, who had caused the upset, carried on as if nothing at all were amiss.

And so did everyone else. They were the next thing to savages, it seemed. There were no dedicated footmen to bring in the morning meal. No maids standing quietly by to pour out tea and serve plates with cadence and finesse. Hill bustled in and out, bringing fresh dishes and taking away empty ones, but beyond that, the family helped themselves, passing plates and teapots, bickering over the last bit of jam.

Elizabeth had never seen anything like it.

She had thought herself prepared for country living. Had imagined, in those first chaotic days, that she was adjusting well enough. But she had never truly considered what it would mean to live like this.

With no schedule.

No formalities.

No one dedicated to her needs or waiting for her requests.

She was... untethered.

And she hated that it made her feel so inept. As if she could not do for herself—that somehow, these simple country girls were more capable, more confident, and better able to manage than she, the daughter of a marquess.

"Lizzy," Jane said softly, drawing her attention.

Elizabeth blinked. "Sorry?"

Jane smiled gently, passing her the teapot. "Would you like more tea?"

Elizabeth hesitated. She had expected a maid to notice her empty cup. Had not thought to pour it for herself.

She forced a smile. "Yes, thank you."

S HE SPENT THE AFTERNOON watching.

Not intentionally, but she could not help it.

The Bennet sisters moved through the house with an energy that fascinated her.

Lydia and Kitty flitted in and out of rooms like a pair of restless birds, their chatter filling the house with relentless energy. Mary withdrew to the sitting room with a book, positioning herself in the best chair with an air of quiet triumph. Jane sat by the window, needle in hand, the sunlight catching in her golden hair as she worked a careful stitch into a delicate handkerchief.

Elizabeth had never embroidered anything in her life.

The thought struck her suddenly, absurdly.

She had learned Latin and Greek, could recite entire passages of Ovid, and had studied under some of the best painters and musicians in England—but she had never once held a needle for anything other than a perfunctory lesson in childhood.

Her mother had not been there for most of her life to see it done, her governesses were never able to gainsay her, and her father! Father had always said it was unnecessary. That she had no *need* to mend or sew.

And he had been right. It was not as if she needed "arts and allurements" to attract a husband. Her dowry and title would see to that, when she finally found a gentleman worth putting up with for that long.

And she certainly would never appear in public attired in something *she* created or even embellished with her unfinished talents. The very idea! That was what her favorite modiste was for.

But sitting here, in this house, watching these girls move through their day, effortlessly weaving themselves into the rhythm of domestic life—Elizabeth felt like an intruder. Not unwelcome. But... an outsider, peering through a window.

She had never thought of herself that way before.

In her world, she had always known precisely where she belonged. The grand rooms, the structured schedules, the endless stream of lessons and tutors. Every moment of her day had been carefully arranged to shape her into *something*—a lady—countess, marchioness, or even perhaps a duchess—something that would be a credit to her father's name.

But here, in a modest country house, where sisters bickered over ribbons and their mother fretted about bonnets and a father indulged them all with dry wit and mild exasperation... Elizabeth felt like a traveler who had lost her map.

And, for the first time, she wondered—had she ever known where she was going in the first place?

She swallowed, turning away.

She missed her father.

It was not as if they had spent every waking moment together. He had always been busy—meetings, affairs of state, the weight of his title deepening the lines in his face by the day. She had never minded. That was simply the way of things. And yet, sitting here in the Bennets' parlor, where Mr. Bennet played chess with her and teased his daughters and Jane sat quietly sewing beside her...

It unsettled her.

Not because she wanted her father to be more like Mr. Bennet—he was a marquess, after all, not a country gentleman—but because, for the first time, she was beginning to wonder if she had ever truly known him.

And if she did not know him, then what exactly was she longing for?

The thought left an odd taste in her mouth.

He was safe, of course. She knew that. The Queen had seen to that much. And he had no reason to suspect anything was amiss.

But someone *had* tried to kill her.

She had not allowed herself to dwell on it too much—the fire, the ruined bedroom, the implications of it all. But... if they knew where she lived, if they had expected her to be there... how long before they realized she was not?

How long before they decided to pursue her father to get to her?

The idea was absurd. Her father was a marquess, one of the most powerful men in England. He had allies, influence, a reputation that could not be touched.

But ten days ago, she would have said the same about the Prime Minister.

A chill crept up her spine.

No. It was foolish.

No one had ever suggested he might be in danger. Darcy had cared only about keeping *her* safe. The Prince himself had hardly seemed to think the matter worth his concern.

Still.

She could not write to him. He had word from "her" already, did he not? She would only cause confusion, and Darcy... oh, that Darcy fellow's head would spin like a dervish if he heard of it.

But perhaps...

Charlotte?

Yes.

Charlotte was expecting her to be away. It would not be strange for her to receive a letter. It would not raise suspicion. And it might just ease a bit of her homesickness.

T HE NUMBERS BLURRED.

Darcy blinked hard, rubbing his fingers against his temples. He could not afford fatigue. Not now.

A candle guttered beside him, wax pooling at its base. The night had stretched thin, creeping toward morning, but still, he pored over the ledgers. *Something* had to be here.

A connection. A misstep. A name.

Instead, all he saw were numbers—cleverly shifted, redirected, passed through so many hands that they left no discernible trail. But this was not impossible. He had uncovered fraud before, traced careful deceptions to their origin.

This time, however, it felt as if the ground was shifting beneath him faster than he could gain his footing. Darcy exhaled slowly, pinching the bridge of his nose. He had not eaten since—when? Yesterday morning? The thought made his stomach turn.

He was tired. Too tired.

That, at least, explained why his mind kept betraying him, why distractions crept in where they had no business being.

Georgiana. He should have sent word to her by now. She was still safely ensconced at Matlock House under his aunt's watchful eye, but for how much longer? How much longer could he leave her in the hands of others—dependent, unsettled, waiting for a home that no longer existed? His sister should have had a future filled with security, with certainty, with a home of her own at Pemberley. But Pemberley—

He rubbed his jaw.

Pemberley.

His mouth twisted. He had not stepped foot on its land in ten years, had not laid eyes on its sweeping hills or walked its halls since the Crown had deemed his father's line unfit to inherit. But it *was* his. It *ought* to be still his. If the Prince would only—

Darcy's teeth clenched. *If.*

He was a fool to think Prince George could be made to exert himself on his behalf. This was not the first time he had been offered a "consideration" only to be brushed off. To find the rug pulled out, the finish line moved. The Prince liked to say one thing and mean another.

This time, however, Darcy was rather certain of the expectation... of what Prince George *really* wanted of him. It was more than what he said, that much was sure. And it would absolutely cost more than he was willing to pay.

And that led him to—

He exhaled sharply, shaking his head. Now, why the devil had *she* come to mind when he thought of impossible obstacles?

Elizabeth Montclair.

Blast her.

Darcy scowled, pressing his fingers to his temple. Of all the irritations of the past week, none had proven more insidious than Lady Elizabeth Montclair, smugly ensconced in Hertfordshire under the ridiculous name of "Miss Bennet"—as if that flimsy alias could somehow temper her relentless obstinacy.

She was a distraction, a dangerous distraction. Not because she was incapable—no, that would have been far easier to manage—but because she got under his skin. From the moment he first met her, his reactions to her...

He closed his eyes, willing the vision of her upturned face out of his mind. The real problem was that she was reckless. A woman with no understanding of caution, who would almost certainly be discovered not by ill luck but by her own doing. If something was going to betray her, it would not be some slip of fate, but her. Her own imprudence. Her temper. Her inability to sit quietly and let matters run their course.

And yet—even as he told himself so, his thoughts betrayed him.

Sharp brown eyes, holding no fear, only defiance. The haughty tilt of her chin, the way she dared him to match wits with her at every turn. The curve of her mouth when she found something amusing—usually him.

Darcy exhaled hard and pushed back from the desk, shoving his chair away with too much force. He had no time for this. The ledgers... there must be some—

A sharp knock at the door cut through his frustration.

Darcy tensed. At this hour?

The knock came again, insistent.

He stood, rolling his shoulders before striding across the room. When he opened the door, a man in dark livery stood before him, looking neither tired nor apologetic for the lateness of the hour.

Darcy's jaw tightened. Carlton House.

The messenger did not bow, did not hesitate. He merely extended a letter—thick, sealed with the Prince's insignia.

Darcy took it, breaking the wax with his thumb.

Darcy—

Your report is overdue. I trust you will not keep me waiting further. Come at once.

—G.P.R.

Darcy exhaled sharply, jaw clenching.

So. The Prince Regent had either been indulging himself all evening and only just now remembered Darcy's existence, or he had deliberately chosen this hour, when fewer people might note the summons.

Neither possibility pleased him.

He looked up. The messenger was already stepping back into the shadows.

Darcy shut the door. There was nothing for it. He reached for his coat, shaking off his fatigue. He would have to be careful—cautious—but there was no delaying this.

Carlton House awaited.

T HE CANDLE WAVERED, THROWING restless shadows across the small writing desk. Elizabeth sat, her chin propped on one hand, the other gripping a quill she had yet to put to use. Outside, the house was quiet. Peaceful. The only sounds were the occasional creak of the old timbers settling for the night and the distant hush of wind through the trees.

She ought to be asleep.

She wanted to be asleep.

Instead, her thoughts chased themselves in endless circles, refusing to still.

With a sigh, she dipped her quill in ink and began.

Charlotte,

I hope this letter finds you well. You must forgive my silence. I have been terribly—

She paused.

Terribly what?

Not busy. That was a lie. She had done nothing of consequence in days.

Not unwell. That, too, was false. She was perfectly well. Restless, impatient, and irritated beyond measure, but well.

She frowned, tapping the quill against her chin. Careful. She had to be careful. If this letter ever found its way into the wrong hands, it needed to be ordinary. Expected.

> —*terribly occupied with travel. The Queen's ladies have been most gracious, and I find myself enjoying their company immensely.*

That was good.

Vague, but believable. Almost.

Elizabeth pressed her lips together, her quill hovering over the page. She smirked wryly, imagining the Queen's ladies. Surely the Dowager Duchess of Devonshire would be among them, with her sharp, regal bearing and maddeningly impeccable manners. Perhaps Lady Anne Hartington, whose voice alone was enough to send Elizabeth into a stupor. And Lady Sybil Havisham—good Lord, Lady Sybil. That woman had been born to preside over a tea table, offering precisely the correct pleasantries in precisely the correct order, until all involved felt their very souls stiffen into fine china.

The image was nearly enough to make her laugh—nearly. If she were going to make this believable to Charlotte, she should mention... something. A milque-toast correspondence would surely make Charlotte, of all people, take notice. And so, she must take care to sound like herself, and to be sure the letter arrived by some expected means.

She could not send it from Meryton, of course. That would be foolish. But perhaps from London—if she could find some way to get it there. Darcy might be traveling back and forth. Could she tuck it among his letters? Oh, no. He would notice. He noticed everything.

She sighed, tapping a finger against the paper.

Perhaps she should wait.

Then again, was not her very intent to ease suspicion? Charlotte would be concerned if Elizabeth did *not* write. And she could do that convincingly, of that she was certain. What else should she write of to make the ruse sound authentic? Who else who she was supposed to be with?

Lady Henrietta Westwood, who never spoke unless it was to criticize the cut of a gown.

Miss Eleanor Standish, whose greatest ambition in life was to marry well and be silent.

And of course, Lady Edith Montrose, whose conversation rarely extended beyond dogs and weather.

That was where she was meant to be.

And yet, she was here. At Longbourn. Playing chess with Mr. Bennet, watching Mrs. Bennet fret over the price of mutton at the market; where the biggest mysteries of her day were to wager with herself over which of the younger Bennet sisters would disgrace herself the fastest, and to ponder whether Jane Bennet truly pined for Mr. Bingley or if she just wanted someone to talk to.

Trying—failing—to feel like she fit among these people who were warm and welcoming and utterly unlike the world she had always known.

She let out a slow breath, setting the quill down for a moment. The firelight cast strange shadows across the desk, long and thin, flickering with the faintest draft that seeped through the old windowpanes.

She chewed her lip, trying to force her sluggish mind to focus on the one thing it required to slip into slumber. There would certainly be some satisfaction in this, and then she could sleep. Assure Charlotte she was well—even if the specifics were not true, the sentiment would be appreciated. And after that, the nagging blur that had jumbled her thoughts for so many days might clarify.

But what if this letter, this simple thing meant to bring her a shred of comfort, would only serve to reveal her?

She stared at the page.

No, she could be cleverer than that.

There were ways to disguise letters. She could think of a dozen schemes at once. Perhaps she could send it through a different town—Stevenage, perhaps—pay a coachman to carry it and post it from a place she ought to be, rather than where she was. A simple enough diversion.

Yes. That could work.

But...

There was still that feeling.

That creeping, insidious sensation that had followed her through Meryton yesterday. Through the market. Through the churchyard. The whisper of being watched.

Was it all in her mind? Probably.

Or... was she being foolish to ignore it?

She hated this uncertainty. This ridiculous, unnerving helplessness.

And worst of all, she could hear Darcy's voice in her head, forced into unnatural evenness and ringing with infuriating prudence— "You cannot afford to be reckless."

Elizabeth scowled.

Of *course*, he would say something like that. He was careful to a fault, striding about as if the weight of England's safety rested solely on his shoulders. She could almost see the way he would react if he knew she was considering this. The sharp narrowing of his eyes. The subtle flickering of those rather spectacular jaw muscles. The exasperated way he would exhale and rub his forehead before lecturing her about caution.

But even he had to see the necessity of it. Surely, there was no harm in writing to Charlotte.

Surely, one letter could do no damage.

D ARCY WAS SHOWN IN without ceremony.

The Prince Regent lounged in an opulent chair near the fireplace, his usual snifter of brandy dangling between two fingers. His cravat was slightly loosened, and his waistcoat strained against a stomach that had known too many rich meals. A platter of untouched fruit sat on the table beside him, yet another indulgence he would let go to waste.

"Ah, Mr. Darcy," he drawled, not looking up immediately. "How kind of you to heed my summons with such urgency."

Darcy inclined his head. "Your Highness."

The Prince swirled his brandy, watching the amber liquid catch the light. "I trust you have come bearing results?"

Darcy hesitated. The delay was brief, but it was enough.

The Prince's gaze flicked upward, sharp as a blade. "Do not tell me," he said, exhaling in exaggerated disappointment. "You have spent days scurrying about like an industrious little clerk, rifling through ledgers and listening at keyholes, and yet you have nothing to show for it."

Darcy's hands tightened behind his back.

"There are... irregularities in certain financial transactions," he said carefully. "But they are buried beneath layers of false names and convoluted routes. If I had more time—"

"Time?" The Prince cut in, setting down his brandy with a deliberate clink. "Darcy, dear boy, I believe I was quite clear about your timeline."

Darcy's pulse ticked at his temple, but he kept his expression neutral. "Your Highness was explicit, yes. I have still six days, if Your Highness recalls."

"But you have already had eight, and I ought to know something of you by now."

Darcy drew a slow breath. "If I move too quickly, I may flush out our quarry before I have him cornered. I need him unaware that I am closing in."

The Prince made a low sound in his throat, neither agreement nor dissent. He leaned back, tapping a lazy finger against his knee.

"And while you have been floundering about," he mused, "I hear whispers in Parliament—nagging little suggestions that we might need a public inquiry. And if that happens, well—how fascinating it would be to see what else turns up. Such investigations have a way of unearthing all sorts of... complications."

He tilted his head, smiling faintly. "Why, even your dear Pemberley might make for an interesting study, if anyone ever chose to look into it."

A slow, deliberate threat.

Darcy's stomach twisted, but he remained still. Pemberley—his Pemberley—had been caught in legal limbo since his father's disgrace. A technicality, the Prince had once said with an airy wave of his hand. An unfortunate situation that might one day be resolved.

But only if it suited the Crown.

Darcy clenched his jaw. As he expected, the Prince was going to keep dangling this, keep needling him with false hope. But if there was even the slightest chance that he might reclaim it—

The Prince watched him, smug and knowing. "I imagine you understand my predicament," he continued. "I am a patient man—so patient—but eventually, I shall require a resolution."

Darcy forced his hands to unclench. "I will have something soon."

The Prince smirked. "Yes, you will."

A pause.

Then the Prince leaned forward slightly, the light from the fire catching his round face. "And the lady?" he asked, voice deceptively idle. "Lady Elizabeth Montclair. Where have you stashed her?"

Darcy's pulse beat once, twice. He had anticipated this as well. He met the Prince's gaze without flinching.

"Your Highness was quite firm. The lady was to be kept safe. She is safe."

The Prince studied him for a long moment. Then—he chuckled.

"Oh, you are good, Darcy." He sat back again, shaking his head in amusement. "Very well. Keep your secrets. I trust she remains... undamaged?"

Darcy stiffened.

The Prince laughed outright. "Of course, of course," he said, waving a hand. "A gentleman of unimpeachable integrity. A pity. A lesser man would have made better use of the situation."

Darcy's grip tightened behind his back.

The Prince took another slow sip of his brandy, still smiling. "I will allow you a few more days," he said, all magnanimity. "But if you fail me, Darcy, I may grow impatient. And when I grow impatient..." His smile did not reach his eyes. "Well. Let us hope you do not test my good nature."

Darcy bowed, forcing the tension in his shoulders to remain unseen.

"Your Highness."

He turned and strode from the room without haste, without showing his hand.

It was only when he reached the cool night air outside Carlton House that he let out a slow breath, hoping his pounding heart did not echo through the very halls he had just left.

He needed to move faster.

CHAPTER FOURTEEN

May 22, 1812

DARCY HAD NOT BEEN home.

Not to his flat, not to change his clothes, not even to rest.

The dim morning light filtered through the high windows of the Home Office as he sat at his desk, sleeves pushed to his elbows, fingers smudged with ink. A half-eaten biscuit sat forgotten near his elbow. His coat, discarded hours ago, hung over the back of his chair, and his waistcoat had long since been unbuttoned in silent surrender.

He had come straight here after Carlton House, bypassing sleep in favor of burying himself in ledgers, in reports, in anything that might lead to an answer.

And yet—

Nothing.

He dragged a hand through his hair, staring blearily at the open ledger before him. The pages blurred together. Numbers, names, transactions. A maze of financial records designed to conceal rather than reveal.

Whoever had orchestrated this had been careful. Too careful.

A chair scraped against the wooden floor nearby. "You look as if you were dragged backward through a hedge, Darcy."

He did not look up. "Insightful, Hughes."

William Hughes had been a colleague of his at the Home Office for several years. Sharp-minded, competent, and, unfortunately, too observant for Darcy's liking.

Hughes leaned back in his chair, crossing his arms. "Are we to assume you've been poring over these records all night?"

Darcy did not answer.

A silence. Then, the rustling of paper as Hughes picked up one of the ledgers Darcy had abandoned. "I don't suppose you'd like to tell me why you've suddenly taken an interest in... parliamentary stipends?"

Darcy's jaw clenched. Of course, Hughes would notice. He had hoped to work in relative peace, but that was a vain wish in an office where curiosity was currency.

He chose his words carefully. "Just reviewing something for His Highness."

Hughes raised a brow. "Ah, of course. The Prince Regent. Odd timing, would you not say?"

Darcy's quill froze, but he did not look up. "What can possibly be 'odd' in the timing of any request from the Prince?"

"Not from him, no. I should think nothing His Highness requests ought to come as a surprise by now. But you—why, you look like a spectre, and with all these comings and goings, I almost forgot you had a month's leave."

Darcy's jaw flinched. "And I shall resume my leave as soon as I have answered a question or two. The matter concerns no one else."

"Of course. How silly of me to assume you might be wasting your time on something trivial."

Darcy did not flinch. "I do not waste my time."

"Mm. Except on things you cannot—or will not—explain." Hughes tapped a finger against the ledger before setting it down with a sigh. "Look, I care nothing for what game you are playing. But if you are digging for something that does not officially exist, be careful. Some people do not like to have their ledgers scrutinized."

Darcy's fingers tightened around his quill. "Noted."

Hughes gave him a long, considering look before shaking his head and pushing back from the desk. "For mercy's sake, get some sleep, Darcy. You are starting to look like one of those miserable romantics who waste away from consumption."

With that, he strolled off.

Darcy exhaled slowly, rubbing his temple. He did not have time to waste away.

He turned back to the ledger, forcing himself to focus. The numbers told a story—one that someone had gone to great lengths to bury.

And yet—something was shifting. He could feel it.

It came in pieces. A conversation here. A notation there. Nothing definitive, but enough to set his nerves on edge.

Fitzwilliam had mentioned it so offhandedly yesterday that it had barely registered at the time: *Lord Cunningham of Northumberland has funded political endeavors before.*

Not an accusation. Not even a new revelation. But confirmation of something Darcy had long suspected.

The problem was, they had no proof of Cunningham's involvement in Perceval's death. Or even a motive, really. They were rivals, but Perceval had many rivals.

Money was moving. That much was certain. But wherever it was going, the trail vanished too cleanly.

Someone had taken great care to ensure there were no loose ends.

Darcy's fingers tightened on his quill until it bent between them. He hated being two steps behind.

And yet, that was precisely where he was.

T HE MORNING WAS MILD, sunlight filtering through the thin clouds, painting the dusty road to Meryton in shades of gold. Elizabeth took a refreshing gulp of the crisp country air, adjusting the bonnet ribbons beneath her chin as she and Jane strolled into the bustling town.

She had been careful. Careful to suggest the errand casually, careful to ensure that it was Jane who accompanied her and not one of the younger girls, who were too excitable and too likely to pry.

Jane, predictably, had been happy to oblige.

It was only a letter.

A harmless letter.

But as they walked, Elizabeth could not shake the sensation that she was doing something reckless. Not dangerous, exactly—she had taken every precaution—but reckless in a way that pricked at her conscience and thrilled her in equal measure.

The plan was simple. She had slipped away, briefly, to pay a farmer who was driving toward London to post it at a different stop while Jane was distracted with some ribbons or lace. And now she was free of the letter and the gnawing feeling of homesickness that had driven her to write it in the first place.

Perhaps now, she would feel... settled.

As much as she could be.

"Miss Bennet! Miss Elizabeth!"

Elizabeth turned to see Mr. Bingley approaching, his usual warm expression lighting up at the sight of them. Jane, beside her, drew in a sharp breath.

Ah. There it was.

Elizabeth pressed her lips together to keep from smiling.

"Mr. Bingley," she greeted, curtsying as he reached them. Jane followed suit, though her curtsy was stiffer, more hurried.

"What a happy coincidence," Bingley said brightly. "I had been intending to call at Longbourn later today, but now you have saved me the trouble."

Elizabeth tilted her head. "How fortunate for you, sir."

Bingley grinned at her before turning his full attention to Jane. "Miss Bennet, I hope you are well?"

Jane's gloved fingers fumbled with the stitching along the edge of her reticule. "Very well, thank you, Mr. Bingley. And your sisters?"

"Oh, quite well," he said, brightening at the question. "Caroline has been occupied with a great deal of correspondence—friends in London, you know. And Louisa keeps busy helping to manage the household." He gave a small, sheepish shrug. "I believe they find country life a bit... uneventful."

Elizabeth arched a brow. "Do they indeed? And you, sir? Have you found Hertfordshire equally dull?"

Bingley laughed. "Not in the least! I must confess, I have been quite entertained."

Elizabeth inclined her head. "I am glad to hear it."

Jane, on the other hand, only smiled, her fingers still nervously working with her reticule.

Bingley hesitated, as if expecting more, but when nothing came, he continued, "Surely you have heard by now of the Meryton Planting Festival next week. I do hope I shall have the pleasure of seeing you there?"

Elizabeth nearly rolled her eyes. He was looking directly at Jane when he said it, though Jane, as ever, kept her gaze lowered, nodding politely rather than giving him anything like encouragement. She only murmured something about it being a kindness for the Lucases to take on the chief duty of organizing the festivities again.

Bingley beamed. "Yes, quite! It shall be a fine day. I believe there will be games and dancing and more food than we can all eat. I have promised a few kegs of apple cider from Netherfield's cellars."

Jane's cheeks pinked, but her response was simply, "I do love cider."

Elizabeth resisted the urge to groan.

Mr. Bingley lingered a moment longer, but when Jane gave him nothing further, he eventually made his farewells and strolled off down the street.

Elizabeth turned sharply to Jane the moment he was out of earshot. "You are absolutely, maddeningly pathetic!"

Jane blinked at her, startled. "I beg your pardon?"

Elizabeth huffed. "Must I spell it out for you? You have a *tendre* for Mr. Bingley."

Jane's face went entirely pink. "Elizabeth—"

"You need not deny it. I am not blind."

Jane shook her head, hands clasping together tightly. "It is nothing."

"It is certainly *not* nothing." Elizabeth threw her hands up. "You are in love with him, and yet you stand before him like a statue! The poor man probably believes you find him dull and tiresome."

Jane's eyes widened. "No! I would never—"

"And yet, you barely spoke to him just now. He was practically begging for some sign of encouragement, and you gave him none."

Jane looked down at her hands. "I do not know how."

Elizabeth frowned. "What do you mean?"

Jane hesitated before saying, quietly, "I do not know how to... to act in such a way. Lydia and Kitty flirt. Even Mary, in her way, postures for attention. I do not. I do not know how to make my affections known."

Elizabeth softened. She had been most often amused by Jane's restraint, but there was something achingly earnest in her expression now.

"I know..." Jane gulped on a particularly large gasp of air. "I know Mama wishes I would do more to attract his notice. I *try*—not to please her, but because I truly do fancy him. I cannot change who I am, Elizabeth. But I do not wish for him to think that I dislike him."

Elizabeth considered this. "Perhaps you do not need to *change* who you are," she said. "Perhaps you simply need to allow him to *see* who you are."

Jane smiled faintly, but did not look convinced. They began walking again as Jane stared at the ground. After a moment, she turned the question back on Elizabeth. "Have you ever had such feelings?"

Elizabeth blinked, caught off guard.

She parted her lips to reply, but... nothing came.

Henry Audley.

That was the name that ought to come first. The name she had once told herself would be the answer to that question.

Henry Audley. Steady, composed, articulate. He had a way of speaking that made people listen—his words passionate, his arguments rational, never given to mundane compromises or unfeeling decision. He was principled, intelligent, admired. And unlike so many men of politics, he had never seemed condescending when he spoke, never dismissed an opposing view with mere arrogance.

She had respected that about him. Liked that about him.

And yet...

Her thoughts strayed—unbidden, unwelcome—to another man entirely.

A scowl. A pair of disapproving blue eyes. A voice laced with exasperation. And most outrageously of all, the only person she could entirely trust.

Darcy.

She nearly tripped over a loose stone in the path.

She straightened quickly, shaking her head as if to rid herself of the thought.

"Well?" Jane prompted.

Elizabeth cleared her throat, forcing herself to look composed. "Once," she admitted. "Briefly."

Jane's brows lifted. "And what did you do about it?"

Elizabeth let out a breath, staring ahead at the road before them.

What had she done? Got caught witnessing a murder, that was what she had done. Been in the wrong place at the wrong time, that was the great outcome of her romantic conquest.

"Well," she said finally, glancing sidelong at Jane with a wry smile, "it was a dreadful failure, I can tell you that much."

Jane's lips twitched. "Oh?"

"The gentleman in question did not fall at my feet in an insensible stupor of admiration. Can you imagine? The audacity."

Jane laughed. "How tragic for you."

"Quite. I am sure I shall never recover."

They walked in silence for a moment, the wind rustling softly through the trees.

Then, more thoughtfully, Jane asked, "Would you have wished him to?"

Elizabeth blinked at her. "Hmm?"

"Would you have wished for him to... return your affections?"

Elizabeth's throat worked. A week ago, she would have had an answer. A week ago, everything seemed so simple for her.

Now... she did not know.

T HE AIR WAS THICK with the remnants of London's daily filth—coal smoke and damp, the scent of overripe refuse lingering even in the wealthier parts of town. Darcy stepped out from the Home Office, rolling his shoulders, exhaustion clawing at the edges of his thoughts. He had spent the better part of the day poring over ledgers, speaking in carefully neutral tones to men who knew more than they admitted, men who gave him just enough information to be infuriating but never enough to be useful.

His patience had worn thin.

He did not go home. Instead, he walked.

Long, deliberate strides carried him through the streets, past darkened shop windows and flickering gas lamps, his thoughts pacing just as relentlessly.

Someone powerful wanted this buried.

Someone was probably watching him by now.

And despite all his talents, his considerable connections and abilities, he was missing something.

The thought gnawed at him as he crossed into Mayfair, weaving through the last of the evening's carriages and the occasional late-night reveler. Somewhere in the city, the truth was lying in plain sight, obscured only by the careful placement of numbers in ledgers and names hidden behind layers of financial obfuscation.

His estate. His name. His family's honor.

He should have been thinking of that.

Instead—

"Well, well," came a lazy drawl from just ahead. "Now here is a sight I never thought to see again."

Darcy stilled.

He did not need to look up to know who it was.

George Wickham was leaning against the rail outside White's, the remnants of an expensive Havana dangling from his fingers, his coat slightly askew in a manner that might have been fashionable if it had not been so careless. His hair was a touch too long, his smirk a touch too smug, and every inch of him radiated the kind of easy, indolent confidence that made Darcy's teeth clench.

"Lord Darcy," Wickham greeted, inclining his head ever so slightly. "Or is it simply 'Mister Darcy,' these days? What is your proper title now? Or has the crown finally seen fit to return you to your former glory?"

Darcy's jaw tightened. He should have walked away. Wickham was not worth the effort, and Darcy had long since sworn to himself that he would not waste breath on a man who had profited so handsomely from his family's ruin.

And yet—

The smirk. The drawl. The sheer gall of the man standing there, dressed in the finest of his stolen wealth, leaning against the railing as though he owned the world.

Darcy's fingers curled into fists. "How fortunate," he said coldly, "that you have taken such an interest in my affairs."

Wickham's smirk deepened. "Oh, but I always have, Darcy. It is something of a habit, you see—taking an interest in things that used to be yours. Or rather, things that *ought* to have been mine from the start. Strange, is it not, how the world sees fit to balance itself?"

Darcy inhaled slowly through his nose. He refused to give Wickham the satisfaction of a reaction.

"How is Pemberley?" he asked instead. As if he did not already know the answer.

"Ah, Pemberley." Wickham exhaled dramatically, as if indulging in the mere idea of the estate. "She is as lovely as ever, though I confess, I have not been giving her the... attention she deserves." His gaze flickered to Darcy, deliberate and taunting. "I am sure you understand. Busy men, and all that."

Darcy's pulse drummed against his temples. He had known, of course, that Pemberley was being mismanaged. It had been plain in the letters his former neighbors had sent him, in the carefully diplomatic phrasing of the housekeeper who still reported to him in secret.

But hearing it from Wickham himself—seeing the satisfaction in his face—was another matter entirely.

"One ought to be careful with such treasures," Darcy said evenly. "Neglect has consequences."

Wickham only laughed. "Indeed it does. But I suppose we all must learn that lesson in our own way, must we not?"

Darcy stared at him, at the careless slant of his posture, at the lazy curl of smoke wafting from the stub of his cigar, at the way he had built his entire fortune upon the ruin of another man's legacy.

He had wasted enough time. Without another word, Darcy turned sharply on his heel, walking away before he did something regrettable.

Behind him, Wickham chuckled. "No parting words? No high-handed lectures?" He raised his glass in mock salute. "Pity. You used to be much more entertaining, Darcy."

Darcy did not look back.

Let him drink himself into oblivion. Let him squander what he had stolen. Pemberley would fall into ruin under his care. That much was inevitable.

But Darcy would see it restored.

And Wickham—

Wickham would not be the one to stop him.

May 23, 1812

THE LATE SPRING AIR was warm, humming with the lazy drone of bees and the occasional rustle of a light breeze through the trees. On the swing beneath the old oak, Kitty and Lydia giggled breathlessly over some whispered absurdity, while further down the lawn, Elizabeth sat beside Jane on a blanket, their bonnets abandoned beside them in the grass.

Elizabeth had been teasing her for the better part of a quarter-hour now, and at last—at last—she had wrung from Jane a proper laugh.

A real one. Not the polite, reserved chuckle she was so practiced at offering in company, but a full, unguarded laugh.

Elizabeth grinned. "You see? That is much better."

Jane pressed a hand over her mouth, as though to recapture the sound and shove it back into its proper confines. "I do not—" Another breathless chuckle escaped. "I do not know what you expect me to do, Elizabeth. I simply cannot be as obvious as Lydia and Kitty."

"Nor should you be," Elizabeth assured her. "But you are not doomed to stand at the edge of the room like a marble statue, waiting for Mr. Bingley to come to his senses, either."

Jane huffed a small, reluctant smile.

Elizabeth tapped a finger against her chin. "You must be subtle. Gentle. Unassuming. Thankfully, you have had a lifetime of practice at that."

"Elizabeth!" Jane scolded, though she was smiling.

"You might let your eyes linger on his for a moment longer than necessary. Or tilt your head just so when he speaks. Perhaps even laugh at his jokes—"

"I do laugh at his jokes."

"Yes, but you must laugh as if you think him the wittiest man in England."

Jane gave her a dubious look. "He will think me a simpleton. He does not even pretend to be any such thing."

Elizabeth grinned. "Yes, well. You must at least make him *believe* you believe it."

Another small laugh from Jane, and Elizabeth felt oddly triumphant.

From the swing beneath the old oak, Lydia and Kitty's giggles rang out. "Oh, but I would have died of laughter had you heard Mr. Tyndale talking about Mrs. Purvis's drawing room rugs!" Lydia was exclaiming. "He said it as if he actually believed it."

Kitty, breathless with mirth, clung to the ropes of the swing. "And did you see the way he tripped over his own feet? I nearly fell into a fit!"

Elizabeth shook her head, returning her attention to Jane. "There, you have an example of the sort of... shall I say 'empty words' that you may freely avoid. You must do precisely none of that."

Jane pressed her lips together, stifling another laugh.

Elizabeth tilted her head, studying her. "But you are afraid of Miss Bingley, are you not?"

Jane hesitated. "Afraid of her? She is... well, I think she is a very fine lady."

Elizabeth sighed. "Come now. You think she would eat you if given the chance."

"Do not be ridiculous."

Elizabeth arched a brow.

A pause.

Then Jane muttered, "...Perhaps only a little."

Elizabeth grinned. "Then it is a fortunate thing that Miss Bingley is not the one you are trying to impress." She leaned forward conspiratorially. "You need not be obvious, Jane. You need not drop your lace handkerchief or sigh his name at inopportune moments."

Jane gave her an exasperated look.

"But," Elizabeth continued, "you might consider a *little* flutter of the lashes when he next takes your hand for a dance."

Jane's blush deepened. "But he almost never asks—"

"A brief brush of your glove against his sleeve—"

"Elizabeth, stop."

Elizabeth grinned. "A slight, breathless sigh whenever he enters a room—"

Jane was laughing again, shaking her head. "You are impossible!"

"Yes, well. Someone must guide you in these things, Jane."

Jane shook her head, still smiling.

And then— the sound of carriage wheels. Both girls turned as a dark, unfamiliar carriage rolled into the drive, its well-kept horses coming to a slow halt before the house.

Elizabeth's mirth faded instantly. Her stomach clenched, her heart tightening into something uneasy. *Was it...?*

She was being foolish. It was likely nothing. But her eyes darted to Jane, searching for confirmation that this was unexpected.

Jane frowned. "I do not know who that could be."

Elizabeth released a breath. Not Darcy, probably. Not yet. Surely, he was still in London, and up to his rather nice shoulders in paperwork.

Mr. Bennet stepped outside now, hands in his pockets, his expression one of mild resignation. He barely spared the carriage a glance before shifting his attention toward his daughters.

"Well, my dears," he said dryly. "It seems we are to have a guest."

The carriage door opened. A tall, rather solemn-looking man stepped down, his movements stiff and deliberate. He took in Longbourn's façade, then turned to Mr. Bennet with a deep bow.

Elizabeth blinked.

Jane did, too. Then she glanced toward her.

"Oh dear," Jane murmured. "I believe that must be Mr. Collins."

Elizabeth's brow furrowed. "Who?"

Jane's voice dropped to a whisper. "Papa's cousin, Elizabeth. The one who is to inherit Longbourn."

Elizabeth glanced back at the stranger, watching as he straightened and adjusted his cuffs with an air of importance. "You have never met him?"

Jane shook her head. "No. Nor have my sisters." A slight sigh. "Papa must have known he was coming, but he said nothing to Mama."

Elizabeth winced. "I imagine that was a strategic choice."

Jane pressed her lips together, her blue eyes holding a tinge of sympathy. "Mama will set up a real fuss now."

Elizabeth sighed.

Then Jane's expression shifted. Her brow pinched slightly. "Oh dear."

Elizabeth arched a brow. "What?"

Jane's gaze flickered toward the house, then back to Elizabeth. "Where is he to stay?"

Elizabeth hesitated. The thought had not even occurred to her. There were always rooms. Spare chambers, guest apartments, places tucked away for when company arrived. At Ashwick's London residence, Elizabeth had never once needed to consider the logistics of accommodating a visitor.

She turned her gaze toward Longbourn.

Jane cleared her throat softly. "It... might become necessary for us to share."

Elizabeth blinked.

Then, turning back to Mr. Collins—who was presently bowing a second time to Mr. Bennet—she smiled faintly.

"I can think of worse fates," she murmured.

Jane laughed softly.

And just like that, she—Lady Elizabeth Montclair, who had never had to share anything in her life—was to have a roommate.

CHAPTER FIFTEEN

D ARCY WAS ACCUSTOMED TO waiting. His entire life had been a careful exercise in patience, in restraint, in knowing when to act and when to observe.

But tonight, he had the distinct and unwelcome sensation that he was already too late.

The boy shifted on his feet, glancing around the dimly lit alley as though expecting someone to drag him back to the Ashwick household at any moment. He was young—ten at most—with a nervous energy that did not suit his somewhat husky frame. He smelled of hay and horses, and his cap was pulled low over his forehead.

Darcy did not waste time on pleasantries. "Are you sure of this, Kenny?"

The boy swallowed with an anxious nod. "She's gone, sir. Alice."

"When?"

"Ain't sure, exactly. No one is. One day she was there, next she weren't." He sniffed, rubbing a sleeve over his nose. "Mrs. Graves—the housekeeper—she was in a right temper over it. Told the other maids Alice ran off with a man." His mouth twisted skeptically. "But no one ever heard Alice talk of no sweethearts before. Not even once."

Darcy inhaled slowly. A chambermaid running off with a lover would hardly make a ripple in a great house like Ashwick's. But this? This was not an elopement.

Alice had been Lady Elizabeth's personal maid. She had dressed her, attended her, known her habits. If anyone had guessed that Elizabeth was not on a pleasure tour with the Queen's ladies...

"She never took her things," the boy added. "Clothes, bonnet, all still there. They're sayin' she left in a hurry. Like 'nough 'cause of that fire in the house."

Left in hurry. Or under duress.

Darcy exhaled sharply and reached into his pocket, pressing a few coins into the boy's hand. The stable lad looked at them wide-eyed.

"If you hear anything else," Darcy said, "I expect to be informed."

The boy nodded quickly. "Aye, sir." Then, after a pause, he whispered, "You don't think she ran off, do you?"

Darcy met his gaze. "No."

The boy nodded once, shoved the coins into his coat, and slipped back into the dark.

F ITZWILLIAM WAS STILL PULLING on his shirt in response to Darcy's knock when he opened the door. He blinked blearily at Darcy, then snorted, rolling his eyes as he stepped aside.

"Of course. I could not be set upon by a proper burglar at one in the morning. No, no, it must be my wretched cousin. Why not?"

Darcy pushed past him without preamble, stepping into the sitting room. "I need you to take over the investigation."

Scratching the back of his head, Fitzwilliam gave a long-suffering sigh. "And good evening to you as well."

Darcy turned, his expression like flint. "Alice is missing."

Richard had been fumbling with his dangling cravat but paused mid-motion. "Who?"

"Lady Elizabeth's maid."

His brows drew together, confusion flickering across his face. "Ah, yes. No doubt dismissed over that unfortunate fire in the chambers."

"No. I was told she ran off."

Fitzwilliam's head tilted slightly, curiosity sharpening. "Oh?"

"She left without her belongings. No farewells. The servants are being given the report that she eloped, but no one believes it."

That got his full attention. Fitzwilliam straightened fully, fatigue vanishing. "How do you know this?"

Darcy did not immediately answer.

Suspicion narrowed Fitzwilliam's gaze. "Do not tell me you have been paying off the kitchen maids for gossip."

"A stable boy."

A quiet curse slipped from Fitzwilliam's lips. "Of course you have." He ran a hand over his face, shaking his head. "So, you have been keeping tabs on her household?"

"Would you not?"

Grumbling under his breath, Fitzwilliam gestured vaguely. "Not through a bloody stable boy. You need someone who works in the house."

"Best I could get."

Fitzwilliam grunted. "This does not mean she has been silenced."

Darcy's gaze darkened. "No, but it is the likeliest explanation."

The timing was too perfect—too convenient. The execution had come and gone. The dust was beginning to settle. Loose ends would need tying.

Fitzwilliam let out a heavy breath. "Blast it." He grabbed his coat. "You are leaving, then?"

"At first light."

One arm through his sleeve, Fitzwilliam hesitated. "You have not told me where you put her. Something about Hertfordshire, but that was the best I got from your mutterings."

Darcy said nothing.

A dry laugh. "Naturally. I imagine His Highness himself asked you outright, and yet you still managed not to answer him. Why should I expect any better?"

Darcy merely lifted his coat from the chair and shrugged into it.

"You have kept her safe, I assume? Her person *and* her reputation?"

The mildly affronted look Darcy leveled at him was answer enough.

Nodding once, Fitzwilliam looked satisfied. "Then I shall not ask again. But when you return, I want a full account of what you find."

Darcy inclined his head. "Agreed."

Sinking into a chair, Fitzwilliam scrubbed a hand over his jaw. "This means I will be stuck in London, a soldier pretending to be a bureaucrat—poring over ledgers, talking to slippery men, and trying to find a money trail that does not want to be found. In short, trying to do your job, but without your... shall I say 'duller' personality traits to help me in the quest."

"I prefer 'careful'."

Fitzwilliam exhaled slowly, shaking his head. "I hate you."

"You will live."

A smirk twitched at Fitzwilliam's lips. "Well, at least this confirms one thing."

Darcy arched a brow.

"You are thoroughly, irretrievably entangled with that woman."

Darcy's jaw locked.

The smirk turned into a grin. "Mother will be delighted to hear of this. I recall her going on about—"

Without missing a beat, Darcy turned on his heel. "Go hang yourself."

His cousin laughed. "Enjoy your little country retreat."

Darcy did not dignify that with a response.

May 24, 1812

THE FIRST MORNING OF sharing a room with Jane had proved surprisingly tolerable. Elizabeth had expected some measure of awkwardness, but Jane, good and decent soul that she was, had made the transition easy.

What was *not* tolerable, however, was Mr. Collins.

Elizabeth had suspected, upon first seeing the man lumber out of his carriage with all the grace of a collapsing wardrobe, that he would be a source of considerable amusement. And in that, she had been correct. He was a fool of the highest order, with a voice like a pompous old toad and the confidence of a man wholly unaware of his own absurdity.

He was also, she suspected, a problem.

Jane had barely said a word all through breakfast, her face carefully schooled into abashed neutrality, but Elizabeth knew her well enough now to recognize the signs of distress. A few rapid blinks. A stiffness in her posture. A deep breath taken and released too slowly, as if to calm herself.

Elizabeth had seen Jane like this at the garden party when she had looked upon Mr. Bingley and his sisters. And now, here she was again, quiet and inwardly troubled.

Collins, of course, noticed none of it. He had spent the better part of breakfast explaining, at great and unnecessary length, the supreme honor of serving under his patroness, one Lady Catherine de Bourgh—a woman apparently so lofty the stars themselves could not aspire to her brilliance, but whose name Elizabeth had never heard. Now, he had turned his attentions to Elizabeth.

"I must admit, Cousin," he said, swallowing a large mouthful of ham before dabbing primly at his lips with a napkin, "I was rather surprised to learn of your connection to the family. My late father, Mr. Bennet's third cousin, spoke often of our extended relations. I was under the impression that Daniel Bennet of Shropshire had no children."

Elizabeth froze. Her hand, poised over her plate, remained motionless as she forced her expression into polite curiosity. She did not dare glance at Mr. Bennet.

"Oh," she murmured, reaching for her teacup to steady herself, "how interesting."

Collins nodded, chewing his next bite with great relish. "Indeed, quite interesting! I had always thought myself well acquainted with our family's lineage. It is most intriguing, is it not, how one can be mistaken about such things?"

There was a pause—too long, too weighted.

Elizabeth swallowed. If he pressed further, what was she to say? She had constructed no backstory, no details beyond what had been hastily thrown together on the day of her arrival.

But Mr. Bennet—bless the man—only chuckled.

"Well, you must not be too hard on yourself, Mr. Collins," he said mildly, cutting into his eggs. "Daniel Bennet was always rather a private sort, and his ventures in trade would have rendered him somewhat forgetful of his own affairs. But then, business has a way of making men rather loose with their recollections."

Collins blinked. "Oh?"

"Indeed," Mr. Bennet continued, his tone smooth, almost careless. "I remember some business about a venture in fishing tackle, of all things. Or was it tobacco? Something dreadful and tedious, I am sure. The last I heard, he had grown quite occupied with it."

Elizabeth quickly took a sip of tea to hide her smirk.

Collins, as expected, took the answer at face value and nodded with great solemnity. "Ah, well. Such enterprises often consume one's time. I have often thought that even I should not be half so devoted to my duties at Hunsford if not for Lady Catherine's excellent guidance."

Mr. Bennet hummed noncommittally, returning to his meal.

Elizabeth allowed herself to breathe again.

She shot a quick glance at Jane, only to find her friend's brows drawn ever so slightly together, her gaze flickering between Elizabeth and her father. She knew something had just happened.

Elizabeth merely lifted her teacup to her lips and smiled.

Collins, wholly oblivious, continued to prattle on.

Elizabeth turned her attention back to her plate, carefully concealing her amusement behind a sip of tea. Mr. Bennet had done his part. She had no doubt he could spin an entire lineage for her if pressed, but she would rather not endure more of Collins' questions before breakfast had even settled.

Unfortunately, the man seemed inclined to linger, all but preening as he ladled preserves onto his toast. Jane, meanwhile, sat with her hands neatly folded in her lap, her posture stiff, her expression carefully composed. But Elizabeth saw it. The slight line beside her mouth. The way she had hardly touched her tea. The faint crease of discomfort between her brows whenever Collins addressed her directly.

And then, there was Mrs. Bennet—Mrs. Bennet, who was dabbing her mouth with her napkin and staring wide-eyed at Mr. Collins, then glancing, all too frequently, at her eldest daughter.

Elizabeth frowned.

That would not do.

She set her teacup down with a delicate clink, then turned to Jane with a bright, conspiratorial smile. "Jane, would you not agree that the day is far too fine to be spent indoors?"

Jane blinked, startled. "I—well, yes, I suppose—"

"Excellent." Elizabeth turned to Mrs. Bennet, adopting her most innocent expression. "I was thinking of walking into Meryton this afternoon, ma'am. Would it not be lovely if we called on your sister Mrs. Philips? I am certain she would be delighted to see us."

Mrs. Bennet, who had been more occupied with watching Mr. Collins enjoy his breakfast than listening to the conversation, blinked at the mention of her sister. "Oh, well! Yes, of course, my dear! You must give her my regards. I am sure she will be most pleased. And while you are there, see if the milliner has received any new ribbons. Lydia will want them."

Elizabeth beamed, ignoring the way Lydia perked up at the mention of ribbons. She turned back to Jane. "You will accompany me? I intend to walk very fast—good for the constitution, you see. I am afraid few can keep up comfortably."

Jane hesitated, casting a fleeting glance at Collins. Elizabeth had to bite back a triumphant smirk.

"I... suppose there is no harm in it," Jane murmured.

Elizabeth took her hand, squeezing lightly before rising from the table. "Excellent. I shall tell Mrs. Hill to pack us a bit of bread and cheese, in case we are delayed."

Jane stood more slowly, fumbling with her chair. "Should we not return before supper?"

"Oh, certainly," Elizabeth said breezily. "But who can say when we may wish to take refreshment? It might seem silly, for Mrs. Philips is never one to let guests leave on an empty stomach. I daresay we shall be well-fed before our return."

Jane looked unconvinced, but Elizabeth had already turned to the housekeeper, murmuring a request for a small bundle of provisions. Mrs. Hill, probably accustomed to the younger Bennet girls taking such liberties, hardly batted an eye.

Half an hour later, Elizabeth and Jane stepped out into the bright new day, the warmth of the sun kissing their faces.

Of course, Meryton was not their true destination.

Elizabeth slung the small bundle of bread and cheese over her arm and cast a sideways glance at Jane. "Tell me, dearest cousin, have you ever walked the pasturelands beyond Lucas Lodge?"

Jane arched a brow. "Not in some time."

Elizabeth's grin turned impish. "Then let us remedy that at once."

She linked her arm with Jane's and set off across the fields, away from the house, away from Collins, away from anyone who might reasonably track them.

It was only as they crossed the first stile that she considered, somewhat absently, that she had neglected to tell anyone where they were going.

D ARCY HAD SCARCELY SET foot on Longbourn's gravel drive before Mr. Bennet was stepping out, propping his thumbs in the corner of his waistcoat. "Mr. Darcy," he greeted, squinting a bit against the sunlight. "You honor us with another visit. I do hope this does not mean my cousin has managed to offend you already."

Darcy barely heard him.

He had ridden hard from London, only pausing long enough to send word ahead to Bingley that he would be returning. He had not bothered with sleep, nor with a proper meal, and he was quite certain he looked as harried as he felt. But none of that mattered. His mind was focused on one thing only.

Elizabeth.

She was here—she was *supposed* to be here.

And she was not safe.

He forced himself to bow in greeting, to respond with some semblance of civility. "I apologize for calling unannounced, sir. I was hoping to speak with you."

"Ah, well. That is most gentlemanly of you." Mr. Bennet stepped aside, motioning toward the house. "By all means, come in. Mrs. Bennet shall be pleased to boast of the company we are keeping."

Darcy hesitated, scanning the grounds. "Is Miss Elizabeth within?"

"I believe she and Jane have gone to Meryton. But I should not expect them to be long. I believe they have gone to call on Mrs. Philips, and her company is best enjoyed in small doses."

Darcy exhaled slowly, clenching his jaw. That was... acceptable. Somewhat. She was in a populated area. She was not alone.

But it was still a risk.

And he could not ignore the gnawing unease creeping through him.

"I do not wish to trouble you," he said carefully. "If the ladies mean to walk back soon, I might take the opportunity to escort them home myself."

Mr. Bennet's eyes flickered with something sharp—something knowing. For a moment, Darcy feared the older man might press him for an explanation.

But then, to his relief, Mr. Bennet only shrugged. "As you like. Though if you mean to play the role of country neighbor, you may as well take tea before you go."

Darcy forced a tight smile. "Perhaps another time."

He turned sharply on his heel, remounting his horse before his tension could betray him further.

Meryton.

If Elizabeth was there, he would see her with his own eyes and make sure she got home in one piece.

And if she was not—

He was not yet prepared to consider that possibility.

T HE TOWN BUSTLED WITH its usual midday activity—merchants calling out their wares, ladies clustered at milliners' windows, a few officers in their bright regimentals tipping their hats as they passed.

Darcy ignored all of it.

He scanned the faces, searching for a bonneted figure in a pale blue walking gown, for a flash of dark curls, for that particular lift of the chin that always—*always*—gave her away.

Nothing.

His unease deepened, though he could not say why. It was not as if he preferred that she should be on the street, was it? She ought to be at the home of the Mrs. Bennet's sister. He turned his horse sharply and directed it toward High Street, scanning the bustling crowd with increasing agitation.

The Philips house stood comfortably on the corner, its windows flung open to the early summer air. As Darcy dismounted and strode up the steps, the door was already opening to reveal Mrs. Philips herself, her expression shifting from mild surprise to sheer delight.

"Mr. Darcy! How very unexpected! We were just speaking of you."

Darcy bowed stiffly, his pulse hammering. "Mrs. Philips, Mr. Bennet sent me to escort your nieces back to Longbourn. I was told they were here."

"Oh! Well, how very neighborly of you to inquire." She laughed, pressing a hand to her chest as if flattered by the attention. "But I am afraid you have been misinformed. My nieces have not been here at all today."

Darcy's stomach twisted. "You are quite certain?"

"Oh yes, quite. I have been in all morning, and had they called, I should have failed to remark upon it." She peered at him curiously, her brow creasing. "Is something amiss, sir? Some emergency at Longbourn?"

Darcy forced a tight smile. "Not at all. It was only a… convenience of the moment, ma'am."

She did not look convinced. "You have been much away from Hertfordshire, have you not? I heard only yesterday that you were still in London."

"Yes," he said curtly.

"And Mr. Bingley was to come to Sir William's for dinner this week. I expect you shall come with him? Oh, but we have all been most curious about you both. Will you be staying longer this time?"

"I cannot say."

Mrs. Philips tutted, shaking her head with a knowing smile. "Well, I am sure the young ladies will be delighted by your return, particularly sweet Lydia. She is always so lively and delightful in company, would you not agree?"

Darcy barely heard her. His mind was whirring too quickly, his frustration mounting. He tipped his hat as soon as her good graces would allow, then mounted again and turned his horse toward the home of the Lucases. Elizabeth had come to town with a Bennet sister, so they might have stopped to pay a call on Maria Lucas, one of their particular friends.

It was Sir William himself who came to the door, beaming as always. "Mr. Darcy! What a surprise. A fine day, is it not?"

Darcy did not waste time. "I am looking for Miss Bennet. Has she been here?"

Sir William's brow furrowed. "Miss Bennet?"

"Yes," Darcy said, struggling to temper his impatience. "Miss *Elizabeth* Bennet."

Understanding dawned, and Sir William let out a hearty chuckle. "Ah, I see! My dear Maria did say she had hoped to see the young ladies in town today, but alas, I do not believe they have met."

Darcy barely muttered a farewell before wheeling his horse back toward the town. The moment Sir William's cheerful voice faded behind him, the world seemed to sharpen—every sound, every movement, every face in Meryton now a potential clue.

He guided his horse back onto the high street, his gaze darting to the usual gathering places—the haberdasher, the bookseller, the confectioner's, all the places where ladies might while away an hour in pleasant distraction. He scrutinized every feminine figure, every dark head in the crowd.

No sign of her.

Damnation.

Jaw clenched, he dismounted and strode into the post office. A line of customers shuffled forward, an elderly gentleman peering at his letter through thick spectacles, a shop boy balancing a parcel on his hip. The clerk behind the counter—a wiry man with an ink-stained cuff—looked up at Darcy's approach.

"Ah, sir. How may I assist you?"

Darcy set his gloves on the counter. "I am seeking the Bennet ladies... at the request of their father. They were meant to be in town today."

The man blinked, his gaze flickering toward the queue behind Darcy before offering a polite smile. "Goodness me! Something amiss at Longbourn, sir?"

Darcy closed his eyes. He ought to have known his request sounded suspicious, but dash it all, he needed answers. "Nothing important, sir. I was to escort the ladies home, preferably sooner rather than later."

The man hesitated, shifting uncomfortably as he looked at the people waiting behind Darcy once more. "Ah, well. I do recall a cluster of young ladies standing outside the window earlier, but I did not examine their faces."

That was useless. Darcy exhaled sharply, turning on his heel and striding back into the street.

The market was next. If Elizabeth had been here at all, surely someone had seen her.

He moved swiftly through the throng of merchants and customers, scanning for a familiar face. The fruit seller was haggling over the price of apples with a stout woman in a straw bonnet. The fishmonger called out his wares, waving a fat trout in demonstration.

Darcy stopped at a butcher's stall where a pair of elderly matrons were inspecting a haunch of mutton. The butcher, a broad-shouldered man with a cleaver at his belt, straightened at Darcy's approach.

"Sir," he greeted. "Good day to you."

Darcy inclined his head. "I am looking for Miss Elizabeth Bennet. She was expected in town today. Have you seen her?"

The butcher frowned, glancing toward the women beside him, as if for confirmation. "Miss Bennet? Can't say I have. We've had a fair number of ladies through today, but none by that name that I recall."

One of the matrons piped up, adjusting the ribbons of her bonnet. "Oh! I did see the younger Miss Bennets earlier. Laughing and chattering about, as they always do."

"Yes, but not Miss Elizabeth," the other woman added, peering at Darcy with keen interest. "She is the cousin, is she not? A very striking girl, with dark curls?"

Darcy's jaw ticked. "Yes."

"No, sir, I have not seen her."

The weight in his chest grew heavier. He gave a terse nod of thanks and moved on. He stopped at the bookseller next, then the milliner, then even the apothecary. Each time, the answer was the same.

No one had seen Elizabeth Bennet.

Darcy was no longer panicked. Now, he was furious.

The pieces fell into place with slow, excruciating certainty. Either he was too late, and someone had got to her first...

Or she had lied. Blatantly. Boldly.

She had walked out of Longbourn that morning with Jane Bennet, claiming to be headed for Meryton, and then... vanished.

A reasonable person would assume the best. His mind spun with every possible explanation, every possible excuse. She would not be so reckless.

She would not be so stupid.

And yet, there was no mistaking the truth.

She had vanished... again.

And by Heaven, he was going to find her.

CHAPTER SIXTEEN

THE AFTERNOON SUN HUNG high in the sky, gilding the rolling fields with gold as Elizabeth and Jane climbed a gentle slope. The scent of fresh earth and wildflowers filled the air, a soft breeze tugging at their bonnets and loosening stray curls from their pins. It was the kind of afternoon that begged for idleness.

Which was precisely what they intended.

Jane spread out their provisions—a bit of bread, some cheese, and a few apples—on a cloth laid over a clean patch of grass while Elizabeth flopped down unceremoniously beside her, stretching her legs in the sunlight.

"Well," she sighed contentedly, lacing her fingers behind her head, "I think we have made our escape most admirably."

Jane gave her a knowing look. "You mean you have spirited me away to avoid Mr. Collins."

Elizabeth cracked one eye open. "I consider it a service to my dearest friend."

Jane laughed, shaking her head as she tore a piece of bread in half. "He is... an odd sort of man, is he not?"

"He is a plague upon the good name of cousinhood."

"That is unkind."

"That is entirely accurate." Elizabeth rolled onto her side, propping herself up on one elbow. "I can see already what the man wants, and it is not tea in the sitting room."

Jane chewed her lower lip and looked away. "It... it would make sense, Mama says. After all, I have no other prospects at hand, and he is eligible..."

"Tell me truly, Jane—do you think you could ever tolerate a man like that?"

Jane fiddled with the edge of their picnic blanket. "It is not a question of tolerating, I think, but of what must be done."

Elizabeth frowned. "That is a most troubling answer."

Jane merely smiled. "I am practical, Lizzy."

Elizabeth huffed. "You are too gentle-hearted by half." She plucked at a stray blade of grass, twirling it between her fingers. "You deserve a man who will admire you properly. Who will see you for the treasure you are."

Jane gave a small laugh, shaking her head. "And where, pray, is such a man to be found?"

Elizabeth smirked. "Well, if I had to wager a guess... I believe we both know a certain gentleman who has been utterly charmed by your presence, whether or not you choose to acknowledge it."

Jane stiffened slightly. "Elizabeth—"

"Oh, Jane, do not try to deny it." Elizabeth sat up, brushing a stray curl from her cheek. "You are quite certain that Mr. Bingley has no intention of marrying at all, but I have seen the man in company. And I tell you now, he is precisely the sort of man who wishes for a wife."

Jane let out a small, skeptical laugh. "And how would you know such a thing?"

Elizabeth raised a brow. "Because men like him are never content on their own. He is too affable, too eager to please. The sort of man who delights in pleasing others generally wishes for someone special to please."

Jane blushed deeply.

Elizabeth grinned. "You see? I am right, am I not?"

Jane looked down, smoothing the folds of her gown with unnecessary focus. "It does not matter if you are right. I do not think he sees *me* that way."

Elizabeth scoffed. "You hide it too well."

Jane looked up, confused. "Hide what?"

Elizabeth leaned forward conspiratorially. "Your heart, Jane. If a man has any inclination toward you, he must first be assured that you return it—or else he will turn away in doubt. A little encouragement does no harm."

Jane bit her lip. "But I have told you, I do not know how."

Elizabeth considered this. "Well, if none of our other ideas seem workable, then you must take inspiration from your sisters."

Jane's expression turned faintly horrified. "Lydia and Kitty? But you said I might not... I... do not think I could."

"You *could*." Elizabeth nudged her playfully. "You simply need a bit of practice."

Jane gave her a sidelong glance. "And tell me, Lizzy, are you in the habit of practicing such things yourself?"

She shrugged, feigning ease. "Certainly not. I have no use for such artifice."

"No use? Not even for a certain gentleman with striking blue eyes and a rather unfortunate tendency toward brooding?"

"Who... you cannot mean Mr. Darcy?"

Jane laughed. "Do not pretend you have not noticed him."

"Oh, I have noticed him, I assure you. But not, I think, in the way you mean."

Jane tilted her head. "He is rather handsome, though, is he not?"

Elizabeth pulled a face. "Terribly, almost painfully so. A pity he can hardly afford to feed himself, let alone a wife."

Jane swatted her arm. "Elizabeth!"

"Well, it is true."

Jane sighed. "He seems... honorable."

Elizabeth hesitated.

That was... true, was it not? For all his frustrating ways, for all his cold, infuriating arrogance, he was—undeniably—principled.

Steady.

A man of unwavering conviction.

And dreadfully, excruciatingly handsome.

Elizabeth scowled at herself.

Jane watched her curiously. "What are you thinking?"

Elizabeth shook herself from her thoughts. "That we have wasted quite enough breath on Mr. Darcy. Let us find a more pleasant subject, shall we?"

Jane smiled softly. "Like how I am to ensnare Mr. Bingley?"

Elizabeth grinned. "Precisely."

The laughter between them came easily after that, their worries momentarily forgotten in the golden warmth of the afternoon.

THE MIDDAY SUN GLARED down over Meryton, though it did little to ease the chill that had settled deep in Darcy's chest. He was barely aware of his surroundings as his horse pounded over the dirt road, hooves kicking up dust in his desperate haste.

Elizabeth was not in Meryton.

Elizabeth was not with the Bennets.

Elizabeth was not anywhere she was meant to be.

He had been ready to believe she had simply deceived everyone—that she had gone somewhere else entirely, careless as ever—but now... now he was back to believing something far worse.

Had someone got to her first?

The thought sent a bolt of fear through him, sharp and searing. His grip tightened around the reins, knuckles pale. *No.* It could not be. She was too clever, too blasted independent, too—

Well. If anyone took her, they would return her rather promptly. Of that, he was... at least somewhat confident.

Darcy pulled his horse up sharply beside the coaching inn, barely allowing the beast to settle before swinging himself down. His coat was still dusted from the road, his gloves dirty from the reins, but he barely noticed.

Inside the small post office, two men stood talking. One was the innkeeper, an elderly man with thin gray hair and spectacles perched on the end of his nose. The other was a footman in faded livery, a parcel tucked under his arm.

"...wouldn't have believed it, but I saw it with my own eyes," the footman was saying. "Three men, just standing there by the corner, watching. Not speaking. Just... waiting."

Darcy's pulse kicked up. "Excuse me, but... who?"

Both men turned, startled by his sudden presence.

The footman hesitated. "Sir?"

"Who were they watching?" Darcy demanded, stepping forward.

The innkeeper gave him a bemused glance. "Mr. Darcy, I am sure it was—"

"Tell me."

The footman shifted his weight, glancing at the innkeeper before returning his gaze to Darcy. "Well, sir... I do not know exactly. But it seemed to me they were paying particular attention to the ladies out shopping this morning."

A cold dread settled in Darcy's stomach.

Elizabeth.

"Describe them," he ordered.

The footman blinked. "Dark coats, looked like London men. Not officers—no regimentals—but they didn't belong here. Too quiet, too still. I only saw them for a moment before they disappeared down an alley, but I could not shake the feeling that they were... looking for something. Or someone."

Darcy's mind reeled. If men had been in town watching… had they followed her? Had she been taken before he even knew to look? His body was rigid, his stomach twisting violently.

No. No, he would not let himself believe it.

His voice was tight when he spoke. "Where did you last see them?"

The footman hesitated before nodding toward the northern road. "Headed that way."

Toward Longbourn.

Darcy did not wait. He was out the door in an instant, swinging himself atop his horse with a forceful motion. The beast, sensing his urgency, barely needed a nudge before launching forward, tearing down the lane in a blur of dust.

His heart pounded in his ears.

Let her be there. Let her be safe.

He had been too slow in everything—too slow to uncover the plot, too slow to find Alice, too slow to realize the danger Elizabeth still faced.

He would not be too slow this time.

The road between Meryton and Longbourn was mercifully quiet, save for a few farm carts making their sluggish way back from market. Darcy scanned every face, every movement. If someone had taken her—if someone had so much as touched her—

He gritted his teeth, forcing the thought away.

Just as he was coming over a ridge, he spotted an older man trudging along the side of the road. One of Longbourn's tenants, judging by his well-worn clothes and slow, steady gait.

Darcy pulled up alongside him without hesitation.

"Sir." His voice was rough, urgent. "Have you seen Miss Bennet?"

The man looked up, squinting against the sunlight. "Eh?"

"Miss Elizabeth Bennet," Darcy ground out. "Or her cousin, Miss Jane. Did you see them in Meryton today?"

The man frowned, scratching his head. "No, sir, not in Meryton."

Blast.

"But I did see them walkin' t'other way this mornin'," the farmer added. "Took a parcel with 'em, looked like they meant to spend the day in the fields."

Darcy's breath stilled.

The fields? Not Meryton. Not taken?

A rush of something—something overwhelming, something fierce—rose in his chest, nearly knocking the air from his lungs. He had gone from cold terror to relief so quickly that he felt almost ill from it.

He had not lost her.

Not yet.

He could barely trust himself to nod his thanks to the man before spurring his horse forward once more, now tearing toward the pastures.

THE LAST OF THEIR apples had been eaten, the crumbs of their meager luncheon scattered by the wind. The sun was pleasantly warm, the breeze cool, and Elizabeth was feeling, for the first time in days, a sense of peace. Jane was finally laughing at all the funny ways she had conjured up to flirt with Mr. Bingley, finally letting herself hope. The world felt wide and open, stretching out before them with golden fields and endless sky.

And then—

A sharp movement at the crest of the hill.

Elizabeth twisted in the grass, shading her eyes against the sun. A lone rider had come upon them, his dark coat unmistakable even at a distance.

She blinked as her mouth dropped open.

Oh, surely not.

But yes, yes, there he was. Darcy dismounted in one swift, fluid motion, his boots hitting the grass hard enough to make an audible thump, even at this distance. His movements were tightly controlled, but she could see it—the wrath boiling in his frame, the rigidity of his shoulders.

Something was wrong.

Beside her, Jane sat up. "Is that Mr. Darcy? What is he doing here?"

Darcy's head snapped toward Jane as he closed the distance to them, as if only just registering her presence. He inclined his head in something resembling civility, but his gaze cut sharply back to Elizabeth almost immediately.

Her stomach twisted.

That look.

She knew that look.

Oh dear.

Darcy drew a breath as he halted before them, his skin mottled with barely restrained feeling. His words were clipped, each syllable deliberate. "Miss Bennet. Miss Elizabeth."

Elizabeth rose to her feet, brushing stray grass from her skirts. "Mr. Darcy," she said, affecting lightness, though her heart had begun to hammer. "What an unexpected surprise. We heard you had gone back to London. Have you come to join our afternoon's excursion?"

He did not answer.

Instead, he took another step forward, looking as though he were fighting the urge to grab her by the arm and haul her bodily back toward Longbourn.

Elizabeth arched a brow.

Well, then.

Jane, dear, oblivious Jane, looked between them, her brow creased with worry. "Is everything quite well, sir?"

Darcy's jaw tightened. He bowed his head briefly. "Forgive me for being the bearer of unpleasant tidings. You are wanted at Longbourn."

Elizabeth folded her arms. "For what purpose?"

The muscle in his jaw jumped. "Because you were expected elsewhere."

Something cold dripped down Elizabeth's spine.

Expected.

As in, people had been looking for her.

She shot Jane a quick glance, but Jane, if she noticed anything amiss, only looked politely concerned.

Elizabeth turned back to Darcy, tilting her head. "I do believe we told Mrs. Bennet of our plans."

Darcy's nostrils flared ever so slightly.

Yes, he was livid.

Jane straightened. "We were only taking advantage of the fine weather," she said gently. "I hope no one was too worried."

Darcy let out a slow, measured breath. "Of course not."

Liar.

Elizabeth lifted her chin, watching him. Whatever had happened, it was *not* nothing. She could see it—feel it. Darcy was not merely irritated. He was disturbed. Deeply so.

And she had the distinct feeling that, once Jane was out of earshot, she would not like what he had to say.

D ARCY HAD WORKED HIS blood to a froth for the last two hours, scouring Meryton, questioning shopkeepers, housemaids, passersby—anyone who might have seen her. And no one had. She had vanished.

And now she was smiling at him.

Darcy fought the urge to catch her by the elbow and drag her somewhere private where he could properly express his thoughts on the matter. But they were not alone. Jane Bennet was still ahead of them, polite, serene, and entirely unaware of the torrent of rage and relief threatening to undo him.

So instead, he fell into step beside Elizabeth "Bennet," forcing calm into his expression, restraint into his posture, and absolute control into his voice.

"You did not go to Meryton."

Elizabeth turned her head toward him with mock surprise. "No."

"You lied."

A small smile. Infuriating. "Yes, I did."

Utterly unrepentant. He ground his teeth. "How do you expect to be protected when I *never* know where to find you?"

She frowned, arching her brows in thought. "Well, I daresay if *you* cannot find me, those who mean to do me harm are likewise inconvenienced."

Darcy stopped walking. He opened his mouth to protest... then closed it. Blast if she did not have a point.

Elizabeth continued another two paces before pausing and glancing back, her brow lifted in challenge. "Had you a pleasant ride from London?"

His muscles coiled so tightly he thought he might snap. Had she any idea what she had just put him through? Did she know he had searched every street, questioned every merchant, every resident, before mounting his horse with the sickening certainty that he had been too late?

That she was gone, taken, *dead*, because he had not acted fast enough?

His voice came out as a snarl—low, brittle, controlled through sheer force of will. "I searched the whole of Meryton. I questioned every shopkeeper, every house, every bloody acquaintance I could find. I probably exposed myself beyond all reason and measure. No one had seen you. No one knew where you had gone."

She rolled her eyes. *Rolled her eyes.* "You are making rather a fuss over nothing."

Nothing.

The rage that boiled in his chest had nowhere to go. He could not bellow at her, could not grasp her arms and shake some sense into her, could not tell her how many times he had relived the moment of arriving in that godforsaken town, asking after her, and hearing nothing but silence in return. And could not wipe from his imagination the image of finding her lifeless body, too late...

So instead, he stepped forward—too close, too sharp, barely lowering his voice to something that would not alarm Jane Bennet.

"Alice is missing."

Elizabeth's teasing demeanor vanished. "Alice?"

That had struck. Finally, something got through.

He pressed the advantage. "She left without her belongings. Without a word. The household is calling it an elopement, but no one believes it."

Elizabeth's hands clenched in her shawl, her lips parting, then pressing together again.

Good. She should be afraid. She should understand.

But instead, she lifted her chin. "You do not *know* that Alice was taken."

"And you do not know that she was not!"

A standoff.

The soft sounds of birdsong. Jane Bennet's easy footfalls ahead of them. The distant murmur of wind through the hedgerows.

Darcy could hear none of it. His blood thundered in his ears, his vision too sharp, his breath too controlled. "Do you not appreciate how unwise it is for you to vanish into the fields alone?" he hissed.

"I was not alone," Elizabeth said at last, her voice stubborn, defensive.

Darcy's hands curled into fists. "Jane Bennet is not a bodyguard."

"And you are not my gaoler."

A sharp breath left him, but he refused to rise to the bait.

No. He was not her gaoler.

But hang it all, he was *responsible* for her. He had been charged with her safety, her life, and he had spent half the morning convinced she had been stolen from beneath his nose.

Elizabeth sighed, shaking her head. "We are here. We are well. Surely that is what matters?"

Darcy's throat burned. He forced his jaw to unclench, his hands to relax at his sides. "We must return," he said stiffly. "Now."

Elizabeth studied his face, as if weighing whether to argue further.

But then Jane Bennet turned back, calling for them to hurry along, and Elizabeth sighed, sending him one last pointed look before falling into step beside him.

Darcy said nothing else.

His hands were still shaking.

CHAPTER SEVENTEEN

NETHERFIELD'S DRIVE STRETCHED BEFORE him, dappled with late afternoon sunlight. He did not slow his pace. The needling sense of unease still gripped him, though he knew—*knew* this time—Elizabeth was perfectly safe at Longbourn. He had seen her safely inside and strictly charged Mr. Bennet to send him a message if she should do so much as sneeze without prior arrangement.

And yet...

Bingley's familiar drawl met him the moment he stepped through the doors. "Ah! I never know when to expect you these days, old man, so I simply keep a room waiting. Should I have the staff place a plaque outside? Mr. Darcy's Mysterious and Inconveniently Timed Retreats?"

Darcy exhaled, dragging off his gloves. "Amusing as ever, Bingley."

Bingley grinned, unperturbed. "You wound me. I am perfectly serious." He tilted his head, eyes bright with curiosity. "You are a creature of habit, Darcy, and yet lately, I have no notion of where you are or what you are doing. Do tell me, do you have a secret lover? A hidden smuggling operation? An undisclosed duchy you have yet to claim?"

Miss Bingley, reclining elegantly in a nearby chair, suddenly looked more interested in the conversation.

Darcy rolled his shoulders and gave Bingley a dry look. "No to all three."

"A pity." Bingley sighed theatrically. "I had my hopes on the duchy."

Miss Bingley's gaze sharpened. "You know, Mr. Darcy, you *are* quite an enigma. A gentleman of good family, certainly—nephew to an earl is something, you know—but one who does not speak of that family. One who disappears to London at the most unpredictable times." She offered a slow, assessing smile. "One who is, I suspect, far more than he appears."

Darcy's grip tightened slightly on his riding crop.

Bingley laughed. "Indeed! I have often wondered if my dear friend is secretly a covert agent for the Crown or some such intrigue." He turned to Darcy with a teasing grin. "Come now, old man, confess. Have you been leading a double life?"

Darcy forced a faint smirk. "Hardly."

Miss Bingley studied him, something speculative in her eyes. Then, she smiled with something approaching warmth. "I had not thought much of it before, but... Mr. Darcy, I should very much like to hear more of your work at the Home Office."

No.

No, no, *no*. He could not allow that.

Before she could say another word, Darcy cleared his throat. "Perhaps another time. If you will excuse me, I should like to change before dinner."

Bingley waved a hand. "Oh, of course. Your usual room, as always."

Miss Bingley's gaze lingered a moment longer before she, too, demurred, returning her attention to her embroidery.

Darcy wasted no time retreating up the stairs.

D INNER THAT EVENING WAS a more animated affair than usual. Colonel Forster, the officer in charge of the regiment stationed at Meryton, had been invited, and he had brought his new young bride along—Mrs. Harriet Forster, barely eighteen and delighting in every moment of her elevated position.

Bingley engaged the colonel in a spirited discussion about local society, while Mrs. Forster dribbled on and on about the upcoming planting festival to a tight-lipped Miss Bingley and Mrs. Hurst.

Darcy, meanwhile, listened.

Waited.

And then, quite casually, he asked, "I am curious, Colonel, how do you find Meryton? A quiet post, I imagine?"

The colonel wiped his mouth with his napkin before replying. "Oh, quite! A charming little town. No real disturbances to speak of. Such a peaceful winter we passed here—I quite fancy our little regiment has been forgot about, because we ought to have been sent to Brighton for training by now, but alas, here we remain."

Darcy nodded thoughtfully. "I should think your men must find it somewhat dull."

Colonel Forster chuckled. "Dull, perhaps, but the young ladies keep them entertained well enough."

Mrs. Forster giggled. "Indeed! My dear colonel can hardly keep them in line."

"I should hope you do not need to keep them in line," Bingley interjected with an easy smile.

The colonel shrugged. "A few minor disputes here and there. The usual foolishness."

Darcy tilted his head slightly. "Nothing more serious?"

The colonel hesitated briefly. "Well... I have had a few reports of strangers in town. Men who do not belong to the regiment, nor to the town itself."

Darcy's pulse quickened.

"Oh?" Bingley asked. "And what do they do?"

The colonel shook his head. "Nothing, so far. Just loitering. As if they are waiting for a carriage or some nonsense. It is probably nothing."

Darcy did not believe that for a moment.

He lifted his glass, masking his expression behind the rim. "Have these men been here long?"

The colonel frowned, thinking. "Not long. A few days, perhaps. They come and go. I cannot say whether it is truly something to concern oneself over."

Darcy could.

He placed his glass down with careful precision, his mind already turning. If these men had come in the past few days... it meant something.

And he did not like what it meant.

T HE RHYTHMIC CLACK OF billiard balls echoed through the dimly lit room. Darcy lined up his shot, focusing on the angle, the trajectory—only for the ball to glance off the side of the pocket, missing entirely.

Bingley, leaning easily on his cue stick, raised a brow. "You missed."

Darcy exhaled, stepping back from the table. "Astute as ever."

Bingley chalked his cue tip, his expression shifting from amusement to something closer to curiosity. "And unlike you."

Darcy said nothing.

Bingley studied him for a moment before turning his attention to his own shot. "Is something the matter?"

"No."

"You are certain?"

"Yes."

Bingley took his shot, sinking a ball with practiced ease. "You know," he said, in a tone that was almost too casual, "I have noticed a change in you of late."

Darcy's grip on his cue tightened. "Have you?"

"Indeed." Bingley straightened, glancing at him. "Since that business with the—what was it? The Holburn affair? Egad, you looked like a ghost when I saw you back in March. I think you went two months complete without eating or sleeping, and you have hardly got much better since."

Darcy inhaled slowly. He had not expected Bingley to mention that. "A great many things have occupied me."

"I imagine so." He hesitated, then added, "Have you had any progress in your petition regarding Pemberley?"

Darcy had been mid-motion, lining up another shot. The question made his muscles tense, his grip falter just enough that the ball veered wide.

Bingley sighed. "Ah. I take that for an answer."

Darcy straightened, setting down his cue. "It seems unlikely."

"A blasted shame," Bingley murmured, shaking his head.

Darcy strode to the sideboard, pouring himself a brandy. The amber liquid caught the low candlelight, reflecting in warm, shifting hues. He took a long drink, closing his eyes briefly against the heat of it.

For a moment, Bingley simply left him to think. To be silent. To drink to the memory of the home he had lost, the family legacy he could no longer claim.

"So... what is next for you?"

Darcy blinked. "I beg your pardon?"

Bingley gestured vaguely with his cue. "You have a life to get on with, my friend. You cannot put everything on hold and pretend the years are not passing. Pemberley is... well, nothing you can do about that. But *you* are not lost, are you?"

Darcy cleared his throat. This would not do. He thought quickly, hoping to shift the scrutiny away from himself. "I could ask the same of you."

Bingley let out a short laugh. "What do you mean?"

"You have done well, Bingley. I daresay you have done everything I ever advised you to do."

Bingley grinned. "Of course. I always heed your wisdom, dear sir."

Darcy nodded. "Save for one thing."

Bingley tilted his head. "And that would be?"

"Ought you not to be looking for a mistress for your new home?"

Bingley's laugh came, but this time it was slightly forced. "Ah. That." He cleared his throat, feigning interest in the billiard table. "I have been meaning to give it some thought. Perhaps I will go to London, attend some parties, mingle with society."

Darcy swallowed the rest of his brandy, setting the glass aside before returning to the table. "I am surprised none of the local Hertfordshire beauties have caught your eye."

Bingley twisted his hands on his cue stick, a flash of something painfully uncomfortable crossing his face. "There were one or two I considered," he admitted. "One, in particular... but I never felt a sense of actual inclination from any of them. It certainly was not for lack of interest on the part of their mothers, you understand."

Darcy smirked faintly. "Indeed."

"But none of the ladies I have met in Hertfordshire seemed..." Bingley hesitated, searching for the words. "Sweet. Personable. Interested in *me*."

Darcy coughed lightly, adjusting his stance. "I had thought there was one lady, at least. But perhaps I was mistaken."

Bingley frowned. "Who?"

Darcy took his time, lining up a shot, then said, as if it were of no great consequence, "Miss Jane Bennet."

Bingley blinked.

And then blinked again.

A pause.

Then—a laugh. "That is a preposterous idea."

Darcy lifted a brow. "Yes, perhaps it is."

Bingley shook his head. "No, truly. Miss Bennet? A charming girl, certainly—why, I daresay the prettiest girl I ever beheld, but I never had reason to believe she harbored any particular regard for me."

Darcy merely studied him.

Bingley hesitated, then ran a hand through his hair. "And besides, there is the trouble of her mother. And her younger sisters. Friendly enough, but hardly tolerable in company."

Darcy shrugged. "You are not wrong." He bent over the table and lined up his stick.

They played in silence for a while, each absorbed in thought.

Then, suddenly— "Are you quite sure?"

Darcy set down his cue stick, glancing at him. "I am nothing of the kind."

Bingley frowned in thought. "Well... Egad! You think there is any possibility?"

Ah, there it was... his opportunity. "That is not for me to determine," he said idly. "But we might call upon the family tomorrow so you might discover for yourself." He turned, casually selecting another cue. "A pleasant country walk, perhaps."

Bingley studied him, his expression uncertain.

Darcy arched a brow.

Bingley exhaled, shaking his head. "Oh, very well."

Darcy went back to the sideboard and hid his satisfied smirk behind another drink of brandy.

May 25, 1812

T HE BENNET HOUSEHOLD WAS rather quiet for this hour of the morning.

Darcy had expected as much. He and Bingley had carefully timed their visit—midmorning, when the younger sisters would most likely be out, flitting about Meryton with their usual unchecked enthusiasm. That, at least, was the hope. The fewer distractions, the better.

It was Bingley who knocked.

Darcy remained half a step behind, hands clasped neatly behind his back, affecting an air of casual disinterest as the door swung open to reveal the Bennet housekeeper. She blinked in slight surprise but curtsied quickly, ushering them into the small front hall before disappearing to inform the family of their arrival.

The moment she was gone, Bingley shot Darcy a glance. "Well, this is a fine surprise."

Darcy arched a brow. "Surprise?"

"I was half convinced you would find some reason to abandon me at the last moment."

"I might have done," Darcy admitted, smoothing a hand down the front of his coat. "But then I recalled how little entertainment there is at Netherfield before luncheon."

"And that Caroline has declared you to be 'fascinating.' She would have set upon you before your breakfast settled," Bingley chuckled, but the sound had barely faded before footsteps approached.

Mrs. Bennet arrived first, all flutters and exclamations. "Mr. Bingley! And Mr. Darcy! What a delightful surprise!" She turned over her shoulder. "Mr. Bennet, you did not tell me we were to have visitors!"

From somewhere in the depths of the house, Mr. Bennet's dry voice echoed faintly. "That is because I did not know, my dear."

"Oh, well! No matter, no matter." Mrs. Bennet beamed, clasping her hands before her. "Do come in! Girls!"

Elizabeth and Jane entered just as the matron's summons reached a piercing note.

Darcy's gaze flickered instinctively toward Elizabeth, finding her poised, composed, that ever-present curve lurking just beside her mouth.

Miss Bennet, however—her shoulders were drawn tight, her expression polite but unmistakably uneasy. Darcy did not immediately understand why. Then he followed the direction of her gaze.

She was not looking at Bingley, as he had expected.

She was looking at Elizabeth, almost as if seeking guidance.

Darcy glanced at Bingley, who was valiantly attempting to mask his curiosity, though his smile was just a fraction too bright, his stance just a touch too eager.

Interesting.

Mr. Bennet had ambled into the room by now, and he leaned against the doorframe. "To what do we owe the honor, gentlemen?"

Bingley straightened slightly. "I was of the hope that we might convince Miss Bennet and Miss Elizabeth to take a turn about the countryside this morning. The air is fine, and my horse is quite done in from a long ride yesterday, so—"

Mrs. Bennet clapped her hands together. "A walk! How charming!"

Mr. Bennet glanced between the ladies, his lips twitching faintly. "A most neighborly gesture, indeed. What say you, my dears?"

Darcy watched as Elizabeth's expression softened slightly before she turned back toward Bingley and, with a perfectly poised smile, said, "How very kind of you, Mr. Bingley. I believe a walk would be most agreeable. Do you not think, dearest Jane?"

Bingley's smile broadened.

Miss Bennet swallowed.

Mr. Bennet waved a hand toward the door. "Very well. Off with you, then. Do try not to lose them, Bingley."

Mrs. Bennet let out a delighted laugh. "Oh, Mr. Bennet, lose them? Heaven's sake, he cannot possibly lose them. Did you see how he was looking at dear Jane?"

Darcy barely resisted the urge to groan. Instead, he turned toward Elizabeth just as she met his gaze, her expression rather smug enough to suggest that *she* had arranged the outing rather than him. Then, with a delicate arch of her brow, she turned smoothly on her heel, linking arms with Jane Bennet and leading them toward the door.

Bingley followed immediately.

Darcy took his time. There was no hurry. He would have her attention soon enough, and it would be one of their less pleasant conversations.

E LIZABETH HAD NEVER KNOWN a man so easy to manipulate.

Well—perhaps *easy* was not the right word. Mr. Darcy was a suspicious, contrary, and dreadfully stubborn creature. But when he wanted something—when he was single-mindedly pursuing a goal—he became remarkably predictable.

Which was why, as they walked, she had little difficulty nudging Bingley ahead with Jane. A murmured comment here, an innocent question there, and before long, Bingley had taken Jane's arm and was leading her several paces ahead, entirely engaged in conversation about—oh, something or other. Elizabeth did not particularly care what.

She glanced up at Darcy, who was watching Bingley's retreating form with wary interest. He had not even noticed that she had maneuvered him. Or if he did, his purposes happened to align with hers.

Perfect, either way.

She clasped her hands behind her back, affecting an air of supreme innocence. "I do hope you have recovered from your heart seizure of yesterday."

Darcy's head snapped toward her. "I beg your pardon?"

She tilted her chin. "You know. The one that left you pale and trembling and in serious danger of expiring right there in the hedgerows."

His nostrils flared. "I was not—" He exhaled sharply. "I was concerned."

"Concerned. How very sweet."

Darcy's gaze darkened. "It was not a baseless concern."

She sighed. "Very well. I grant you that I was not where I said I would be."

He scoffed. "A gross understatement."

"And yet, here I am, perfectly well, having suffered no great misfortune beyond a rather wasteful afternoon spent in excellent company. Yet, your face still looks somewhat gray around the corners. I daresay, even if I had been shot by some ne'er do well, His Highness would only be slightly put out with you and would recover quickly enough. He can hardly afford to lose such a useful fellow."

Darcy said nothing to this. A few steps passed in silence as his face seemed to be tortured with a kaleidoscope of thoughts.

At last, he said, "There were men loitering about Meryton yesterday."

Elizabeth's brow furrowed. "I am sure there usually are."

Darcy's voice was even—too even. "Men I had not seen before. Strangers. They were not shopping, nor were they conversing with the townsfolk. They were simply... watching."

Her amusement faded entirely.

"That could mean nothing," she said carefully.

"It could," he admitted. "Or it could mean everything."

Elizabeth pressed her lips together. She was no fool.

The idea that she was being hunted, that someone still sought to silence her, was not a new fear. It had lurked in the corners of her mind since the day she arrived at Longbourn.

But hearing it put to words, seeing the quiet intensity in Darcy's gaze as he relayed the information...

It unsettled her.

"You could speak to Colonel Forster," she suggested.

Darcy nodded. "I did. He came to dine at Netherfield last night. He has noticed the same. And he has made inquiries."

A cool breeze stirred the air, ruffling the edges of Elizabeth's bonnet.

She swallowed. "And... Alice? Is anyone inquiring about her?" She hated how uncertain her voice sounded.

Darcy nodded. "Yes."

She gulped, hating to voice the quite reasonable fear that refused to be silenced. "Do you... do you believe she is alive?"

His jaw flexed. "That is what I hope to determine."

Elizabeth looked away, staring out over the rolling fields.

Who in her household could possibly be closer to her than her own maid? Alice had been the only person who had seen the tremble in her hands when she dressed for that radically impromptu audience with royalty... the one that she never returned from. It was only logical someone might think her maid could know something, have heard something. If someone had decided that Alice was another loose end to be... tied off—

Oh, dear... what had she done?

Darcy's voice was quieter when he spoke again. "If their intent is to secure *your* silence, I cannot think anyone would kill your maid. If anything, they might hold her until... Well. I am sure she is alive. We need only to find her."

She nodded jerkily. "How?"

"I have a man I trust assisting me in London. And he has men at his disposal, as well."

She glanced up at him. "Your cousin."

Darcy's gaze flickered to her. "Yes."

She exhaled slowly.

So.

This was the truth of it. She was *not* safe. She could not even clasp at the illusion of safety.

Darcy had not been panicking yesterday out of mere propriety or a sense of wounded pride. He had believed—truly *believed*—that she was gone. That realization made her blood turn to ice.

She pressed her lips together. "And you?"

He frowned. "What of me?"

She studied his face, her pulse thrumming a little faster than she liked. "What is your plan?"

Darcy hesitated.

And Elizabeth—quick, perceptive, always watching—caught it. And changed tactic. "No, nevermind that for now. Why are you doing this?" she asked suddenly.

Darcy exhaled sharply, his shoulders rolling back. "Doing what?"

She shot him a look. "Mr. Bingley did not think of coming today all by himself. You came to lecture me—I see it in your eye. You still look half panicked over something that, by your own admission, is already resolved."

His jaw tightened. "I have no intention of arguing with you further."

"That is not an answer."

He kept his gaze fixed ahead. "It is the only answer you will receive."

Elizabeth huffed a quiet laugh, shaking her head. "You are not my father, Mr. Darcy. And you are certainly not a philanthropist who looks after another's interests merely out of the good of your heart. And do not tell me 'The Prince Said So.' There must be a *reason*. So what is it?"

"I have a duty to my country, madam."

"No, no," she said, waving him off, "I expect better. A man of 'duty' alone would have long ago left me to rot. I have told you everything I remember. Go find your gunman and let me to my own fate. But you refuse to do that. Why?"

His lips parted slightly, but then he shut them again.

Elizabeth studied his face, searching for the telltale flicker of discomfort, the tightness around his mouth, the minuscule hesitation that *always* betrayed him. "Why do I get the distinct feeling that you are avoiding the truth?"

Darcy's steps did not falter, but there it was—something pinched, reluctant in the set of his jaw. A hesitation so minute that another person might have missed it. But she did not.

She had him now.

"You see," she continued breezily, "it leads me to a rather obvious conclusion, does it not? That you, too, have a *personal* stake in all of this."

His stride slowed just slightly. A guilty pause.

So. She had guessed correctly.

"Am I right, Mr. Darcy?"

"I am—" He stopped himself. The first word had barely left his mouth before he seemed to think better of it. He turned his head slightly, fixing his gaze on the distant horizon, the taut set of his shoulders screaming discomfort.

"Now, that is interesting. What could possibly be of such personal importance to you? I wonder... revenge, perhaps?"

Darcy's mouth opened, as if ready to refute her outright. But then—he hesitated again. His brows drew together slightly, his jaw locked. Something in his expression—something self-conscious—flashed too quickly to disguise.

Elizabeth's stomach curled with intrigue. *What* was he hiding?

"You are not merely some errand boy for the Home Office, nor are you a common investigator. You are not a soldier or a constable. The Prince has men for that. And yet... he chose you. Because *this*... something about all this... *is* personal for you."

Darcy's jaw twitched. "I fail to see—"

"Yes or no?" she cut in.

A muscle ticked in his cheek. He said nothing.

Oh.

He *did* have something.

She arched a brow, feigning a thoughtful look. "I shall take that as a confession." A score of possibilities ran through her mind at once, each more outlandish than the last. She discarded the ridiculous immediately.

The Prince had chosen *him* as her personal knight errant. That, in itself, was strange. Darcy might have come from better circles, but he himself was not a man of rank or influence. He was no statesman, no minister. His work at the Home Office was surely competent, but nothing suggested he was indispensable. Perhaps it was precisely because he was the opposite.

But why *him?*

Why this case?

Why her?

Was it... political? No. If it were merely about the case itself, he would not look so very much like a trapped animal.

Was it... financial? She pursed her lips, considering it. If he had something to gain, that would explain why a gentleman with no particular interest in her family should be so closely entangled in this affair.

But that explanation did not quite fit, either. Mostly because Darcy did not seem like the man to lose track of even a stray penny, let alone something large enough to engulf him in *this*. Not out of greed, but rather precision. He simply could not allow mistakes.

She studied his rigid profile, his obvious reluctance.

"Perhaps..." She exhaled, pacing herself. "Perhaps you have some personal connection to one of the men involved. The Prince, perhaps. Or the prime minister?" She paused. "The assassin?"

Darcy shot her a look so incredulous that she nearly laughed.

"Not that, then." She hummed in thought. "Perhaps your interest is in one of the suspected conspirators."

Nothing.

"Or perhaps—" she turned her gaze to him, scrutinizing, "—perhaps you are invested in the fate of another of the prime minister's enemies."

Darcy's jaw flexed, but he did not take the bait.

She sighed dramatically. "Nothing? No sharp inhalation? No guilty flicker of the eye? You are making this terribly difficult."

Still, he was silent as a stone.

Elizabeth huffed in frustration, thinking. If it was not politics, if it was not money, if it was not—

Oh.

Oh.

Her eyes widened in realization. *Of course.*

A slow, delighted grin spread across her face. "This was about *me*."

Darcy stiffened.

Elizabeth's chest warmed with self-satisfaction. She had unraveled him.

Darcy exhaled slowly, his gaze flicking toward Bingley and Jane, still ahead of them, before returning to the path. "That is hardly—"

"Oh, come now," she interrupted. "It is a simple question."

Darcy's teeth were grinding so hard she could actually hear them. And still, he did not answer.

That silence. That pause. That *guilt*. A thrill of realization swept down her spine.

He had *known her*. Or at least, known *of* her. Before London. Before the House of Commons. Before the assassination.

Which meant...

Her brows knit together as she turned the thought over, the implications unfolding like a map in her mind. *Why?*

Why had he never spoken to her? Why had he never made himself known? Darcy was a man of connections. His circles were not so far removed from hers that an acquaintance would be unheard of—indeed, had she not been introduced to his young sister? He ought to be *expected* to have made her acquaintance somewhere.

She took a slow step closer, watching him carefully. "I wonder..." she murmured, drawing out the words, "how long you have been avoiding me, Mr. Darcy?"

Darcy's gaze snapped to hers.

"You did! You knew me before this," she declared triumphantly, and then—even better— "And yet you never called. Never introduced yourself. Never sought an acquaintance."

His scowl deepened.

She bit her lip, shaking her head in exaggerated disappointment. "What a scandalous oversight."

Darcy exhaled harshly. "It was not an oversight."

Her brows lifted. "Oh? And what would you call it?"

Darcy's gaze cut sideways to her, something wary flickering behind his eyes as he muttered something low under his breath.

Elizabeth leaned in, her brow lifting. "I am sorry, what was that?"

He halted, and something in his chest was fairly trembling with some sort of pent-up... *something*. "Do not let your vanity fool you," he gritted between his teeth. "It is no work of intrigue or fascination to suggest I was familiar with your name before having you thrust upon me."

She drew back slightly. "I only meant—"

"Well, then, *have* your satisfaction!" he shot back. "Of *course* I knew who you were! Anyone who has eyes and ears within fifty miles of London knows who the Marquess of Ashwick's daughter is!"

Elizabeth blinked. "It is not by any design or quality of *mine*, sir. My father's name alone—"

"You think that, do you? Have you any idea what is said of you in the gentleman's clubs? How many wagers have been placed on your marital prospects, the exact size of your dowry, your measurements at the modiste's, and even on your virtue?"

Her face heated. "How should I know any of that?"

"Well, *I* have heard it all and then more—things you could never imagine. Things that would give you nightmares when you close those pretty long lashes of yours. So yes, *Lady Elizabeth Montclair*, I knew your name before we met. But I guarantee you had never heard mine before."

He began to stalk off, but Elizabeth followed, catching him by the elbow and forcing him to stop. "Just what is that supposed to mean? I said I knew your sister, did I not? I am not so unfamiliar with the name Darcy."

That drew a look from him that was altogether... she had no word for it other than to describe his expression as terrified. How odd, indeed!

"Meeting my sister once does not mean you are acquainted with my family," he managed at last.

"Now, that is a very strange thing to say. Are you trying to call me a snob, Mr. Darcy? I said I fancied her. Occasionally, I even have a generous feeling toward *you*, but you are acting rather like a petulant child just now."

"I—" His body surged forward as if he were about to unleash a tirade of justice upon her, but then he clenched his teeth and drew back. "I am *not* calling you a snob," he insisted.

"Yet you seemed so slighted when you said I must not know your name. How *should* I have known it, I ask you?"

His throat bobbed, and he looked away. "It is of no consequence."

"Yes." She fisted a hand on her hip. "You have the very look of a man to whom this conversation is 'of no consequence.'"

Darcy exhaled slowly, glancing on ahead at Bingley and Jane. They were nearly out of sight by now. "We should continue."

Elizabeth hesitated. Never in her life had she heard a man with "no secrets" defend them so vehemently. But there was no getting more from him—not when his teeth locked together like that and his eyes glittered with suspended wrath.

Just then, Jane's voice called out from ahead. "Lizzy, are you coming?"

Elizabeth drank in a sigh. "You are quite right. Let us catch them up and save this conversation for another day."

"I would rather not continue it at all, if it is all the same to you."

She squinted up at him. "It is not, but far be it from me to make the one man whose job it is to protect me despise my very face."

He had been in the very act of turning away again when she said that, and he stopped, regarding her with the oddest look. Frustration, perhaps, but there was a good deal of... was that tenderness mixed in? Surely not.

He blinked, and his chest rose and fell once. Twice. Finally, his lips parted and his voice, when he spoke, was rather husky.

"That is something you need not fear, madam."

"Good." She dared to step a little closer. "Then, if you please, sir, we ought to look like a gentleman and a lady out for a pleasant stroll. Do you mind?"

He narrowed his eyes and watched her in clear amazement as she reached boldly for his arm. She had to do it all herself—crooking his elbow so his fist fell just so in front of his chest, tucking her hand between his ribs and his sleeve, and angling her steps to match his. All the while, he looked as if he had forgot how to breathe.

"There," she declared in satisfaction once they started again. "My good sir knight, now I have no fear of rut or puddle or stone in my path. We shall make much better progress."

His mouth, which had been slightly open, clamped shut just in time to form a faint smile. "I think our 'progress' was not hindered by your lack of an arm to lean on, but rather by sharp tongues all around."

"And now, I am determined to be nothing but merry, sir. If you will be a good fellow and keep attempting to smile, we may almost have a pleasant morning."

At that, Fitzwilliam Darcy, the most vexing man alive... well, he laughed. Not loudly or vainly, but once the darkness cleared from his eyes, he produced a sound that pleased her very much. With a deep rumble in his chest, a tickle against her gloved hand and a thrill that laced from her ears all the way down her spine, he laughed.

And suddenly, she was feeling *entirely* too aware of him.

Of all people, it had to be Fitzwilliam Darcy who made her blood race like that.

CHAPTER EIGHTEEN

LONGBOURN CAME INTO VIEW, a welcome sight after the tumult of the afternoon. Darcy had half a mind to mount his horse at once, return to Netherfield, and spend the remainder of the day attempting to forget the utterly infuriating conversation he had just endured.

He had almost admitted too much.

Too much truth. Too much of himself.

Elizabeth had tricked him into it, of course. She had pressed and prodded, and before he knew it, she had nearly unearthed secrets he had no intention of revealing.

And worse still, she had made him laugh afterward. As if he could forget—as if all could be wiped away and the impossible might be made possible.

Well. It did not matter now.

He was here. He had ensured her safety. His duty was fulfilled for the day. He would leave—

But something caught his eye. A rider.

Coming from the direction of Meryton at a determined pace.

Darcy's gaze sharpened. He slowed his steps, the hairs on his neck prickling.

A messenger.

Bingley, beside him, glanced up in mild curiosity but said nothing. Elizabeth and Jane Bennet had slowed, murmuring something to each other as they approached the house. They had not yet noticed the rider.

Darcy had.

He stepped forward, his pulse beginning to thrum.

The messenger reached the drive at the same moment they did. He drew his horse to a halt before them, dismounting swiftly. He was a young man, dressed plainly but tidily, the unmistakable leather satchel of a courier slung across his chest.

"Begging your pardon," the man said, nodding first to the ladies, then to the gentlemen. "I was sent to deliver this for Miss Bennet."

Jane Bennet stepped forward instinctively, but the man glanced at his letter once more. "Are you Miss Elizabeth Bennet?"

Darcy went utterly still.

Elizabeth blinked. "For me?"

The man nodded, extending the letter.

Jane, clearly unaware of anything amiss, smiled. "Why, Lizzy, you seem so shocked! Indeed, I am surprised you have not had more letters before now."

Bingley chuckled. "Yes, surely your family must be anxious for news of you."

Darcy barely heard them. His focus was on the sealed note in the courier's hand.

The letter was creased. Slightly smudged.

The courier held it out, his expression one of complete disinterest. Just another errand to be completed.

Elizabeth reached for it, her fingers brushing the edge of the page before Darcy's hand moved faster, intercepting it before she could take hold.

She startled, looking up at him with wide, questioning eyes. "Mr. Darcy—"

He barely heard her. His focus was locked on the creases and folds, his pulse slowing, thudding in his ribs. The paper was slightly roughened from handling, the edges damaged, the wax seal broken with no attempt to mend it. Someone had read this. And then, there was the handwriting.

Not some unknown correspondent's. Not the rounded, simple scrawl of a country girl writing home to family. This was an elegant, disciplined hand, one instructed by a master—every stroke deliberate, every curve precise. A handwriting he had seen before—on official documents, invitations, correspondence between the highest of society.

Lady Elizabeth Montclair's handwriting.

A muscle tightened in his jaw, his grip unconsciously stiffening around the letter. He turned sharply to the courier. "Where did you get this?"

The man straightened slightly, boots scuffing the gravel as he answered. "Left at the Meryton post, sir. No sender. I was just told to bring it to Longbourn."

No sender.

Darcy exhaled slowly, the weight of those two words pressing heavily against his ribs. It should not be here. No one in Hertfordshire was supposed to have any connection to Lady Elizabeth Montclair, and no one outside Hertfordshire knew anything about "Elizabeth Bennet."

And yet, here the letter was.

Elizabeth took a step forward, frowning. "It is just a letter."

Before Darcy could reply, Jane Bennet's voice broke in, gentle but curious. "Is something the matter?"

Darcy turned sharply, schooling his expression into something impassive. "No, Miss Bennet." His voice was steady, clipped. "Only a minor confusion."

The lady still looked uncertain, but Bingley merely smiled. "Come, Miss Bennet," he said lightly, offering his arm. "I believe I promised your father a rematch at chess before we depart. We ought not keep him waiting."

She hesitated for only a moment before allowing herself to be led inside, her soft murmur of agreement fading as they stepped through the doorway.

Darcy turned back to Elizabeth the moment they were alone, his tone flat and precise. "No, *Lady Elizabeth*, it is not 'just a letter.'"

She hesitated, her brow knitting together in confusion, but Darcy barely noticed. The slow churn of anger in his chest burned too hot, too immediate.

His fingers curled tightly around the letter, the paper crinkling under the force of his grip. "Apparently," he said, his voice low and biting, "you wrote to someone, for the handwriting is yours."

Elizabeth went very still.

He did not stop. Could not.

"Tell me," he demanded, his tone cold and cutting. "Was I unclear when I told you that you could not—*must* not—draw attention to yourself?"

Her eyes flashed, her spine stiffening. "I hardly think a letter—"

"You hardly think at all!" The words snapped out before he could stop them, his fury overriding any sense of caution.

Elizabeth's nostrils flared, her chin lifting in immediate defiance, but Darcy refused to back down. His grip tightened around the letter before he thrust it toward her, forcing her to take it.

"Who was it?" he ground out. "To *whom* did you write?"

Her lips parted, as if weighing whether to tell him at all, but his dark stare pinned her in place. Finally, she exhaled sharply, barely above a whisper. "Charlotte."

Darcy nearly cursed aloud.

Of course. Lady Charlotte Wrexham. One of Elizabeth's closest companions—and the fact that he knew this smote all that was left of his pride. Blast him that he even knew Lady Elizabeth's inner circles, but the fact that she had written to *that particular* friend—a woman well-connected enough that letters to and from her would surely be noted!

He raked a hand through his hair, his pulse pounding in his temple. "And you thought that wise?"

Elizabeth squared her shoulders, her chin tilting just so—a telltale sign that she was about to say something insufferably flippant. "I... I was so homesick! And I did not write to my father or my mother—you told me I should not, so I did not. I thought it safe enough to write to Charlotte, especially if I sent it by way of a different—"

"Safe?" His voice dropped, rough with frustration. "This was intercepted, opened, and returned to you. How does that strike you as safe?"

The color drained slightly from her face.

At last.

He watched as her gaze lowered to the page in her hands, scanning the seal, the rough folds, the telltale creases of a message that had been tampered with. The moment she understood it, a sharp breath escaped her lips. Her hands trembled—only slightly, but enough.

Darcy did not move.

He knew that look. He had seen it before in men who realized—too late—that their position on the battlefield was compromised. That the safe ground they had relied on was an illusion. Whoever had intercepted her letter had done so deliberately. And now, they had sent it back.

Not as a mistake.

As a warning. Someone wanted her shaken... wanted her to run.

His anger did not dissipate. It only coiled tighter, heavier. "You should get inside," he said stiffly.

Elizabeth swallowed, then nodded once.

Darcy turned toward the house, his posture rigid, his thoughts already racing ahead.

Someone had her in their sights. Someone who had taken the time to intercept her correspondence, to ensure she understood she was not hidden. Not forgotten.

They knew exactly where she was.

T HE DOOR TO MR. Bennet's library closed with a gentle click, but the sound echoed in Elizabeth's chest like a thunderclap.

She had always liked this room. It had reminded her of a more homey version of her father's study—quiet, comfortably cluttered, filled with shelves that smelled of leather and paper and thought. But now, it felt entirely foreign. Mr. Bennet stood behind his desk, the letter she wrote to Charlotte held loosely in his hand. Darcy hovered nearby, arms folded, gaze simmering with wrath.

Elizabeth had never felt so small.

"I believe," Mr. Bennet said slowly, "that I have just learned more about my summer guest in five minutes than in the entire length of her stay."

His voice was deceptively mild, but the look in his eyes was not.

Elizabeth forced herself to meet it. "I am sorry."

"Indeed?" he said, raising a brow. "And which part, precisely, are you sorry for? Writing a letter that placed us all at risk? Or failing to mention that you were present for the murder of the Prime Minister?"

She flinched.

Darcy remained silent. He had not said a word since they entered the room. But Elizabeth could feel his disapproval, sharp and hot like the tip of a sword against the back of her neck.

Mr. Bennet gave a short sigh, rubbing the bridge of his nose with one hand. "Let me see if I have this correct. You were present in the House of Commons the day of the assassination, you fled the city under royal protection—in the form of Mr. Darcy here, which I have yet to understand—your maid was likely abducted or worse, and someone has now intercepted your letter and sent it back to you as a warning."

Elizabeth lowered her gaze. "Yes."

"Splendid." He gave a dry chuckle, devoid of humor. "And here I thought the greatest danger to Longbourn this summer would be Lydia's penchant for impetuous officers."

"I never meant—"

"I do not care what you meant." The words landed like a blow. Mr. Bennet's voice remained quiet, but each syllable was edged with something Elizabeth had not expected:

real anger. "What matters is what you have done. Your own house was burned. Is mine next?"

She sniffed once, staring at the floor. There was nothing else to say.

"I let you into this house because I trusted my friend." He looked toward Darcy. "And I trusted that you would not bring ruin to my daughters' doorstep."

Elizabeth's throat burned. She had never felt shame like this before. Not even when her father scolded her. Not even when the Queen's men first whisked her away under armed escort. This was different.

This mattered.

"I am sorry," she said again, the words low and unsteady. "Truly."

Mr. Bennet stared at her for a long moment, then turned to Darcy. "What now? Do you intend to take her elsewhere?"

Darcy opened his mouth—but before he could speak, Mr. Bennet waved a hand.

"No, no. I will not have it." He turned back to Elizabeth. "You will stay here."

Elizabeth blinked. "What?"

Darcy's brows drew together in clear confusion. "Surely, sir—"

"Where else, precisely, can you take her? Hmm? Short of hiding her away in a cabin in the woods or trundling her off to Scotland…"

Darcy coughed. "As a matter of fact, I—"

Bennet raised his hand again. "She certainly cannot take up residence at Netherfield, even with your sterling reputation, Mr. Darcy. And despite her… questionable choices, she has proved herself remarkably adept at beating me in chess, which makes her the most tolerable companion I have had in years."

Elizabeth stared. "You cannot be serious."

Mr. Bennet's smile was tight. "I rarely am. But in this, I am entirely earnest. If whoever sought to harm you could have got to you here, they would already have done so. However, so far, it appears that you suffer from a bewildering combination of good luck and bad timing. Like enough, sharing a room with another girl was enough to give them pause, and anyone would have to be the veriest fool to try to attack you when Lydia is around. She would set up the hue and cry louder than one of His Majesty's guards. I should think the very best thing you could do would be to remain at Longbourn."

"But sir," she protested, "they did not shrink from attacking my bedroom in London or abducting my maid. What do you think will keep your family safe if I am already discovered?"

Bennet frowned, then nodded at Darcy. "That chap there, I suppose. One day I will have the truth of it—what *do* you do, sir?"

Elizabeth shifted her gaze to the rather bothersome tyrant who had posted himself between her and disaster... time and again. He had been staring at the floor, but he lifted his eyes just once, flicking them between her and Mr. Bennet... and then his jaw clenched and he looked away.

"You may stay," Mr. Bennet said, returning to his chair and reaching for a book, as though that settled the matter. "But from now on, I expect full honesty. No more surprises, Miss Montclair. You are not the only one with something to lose."

She felt a strange heat prick at her eyes—exhaustion, perhaps. Or something else. Gratitude. Grief. Elizabeth nodded, swallowing hard.

"No more surprises," she whispered.

D ARCY HAD MADE MANY difficult decisions in his life.

He had stood before generals and lords, had been entrusted with tasks that would see lesser men ruined. He had faced down enemies in dark alleyways and sat across from politicians with blood on their hands.

But this—this wretched woman—had managed to put him in the most impossible position of all.

And the worst part?

She did not even seem to realize it. Probably not, at least. Perhaps it was better to say that the odds were not in his favor.

Darcy stood rigidly by the fireplace, the flickering light casting sharp shadows across his face. Mr. Bennet had just declared that Elizabeth would remain at Longbourn, a decision that, while practical toward the lady's interests, did little keep others safe, or to quell the storm brewing within Darcy.

Elizabeth sat across from her host, her posture uncharacteristically subdued, eyes fixed on her hands clasped tightly in her lap. The usual spark in her gaze was dimmed, replaced by a sheen of remorse that Darcy had seldom witnessed. It almost looked genuine.

Mr. Bennet cleared his throat, breaking the heavy silence. "Well, it seems we have settled that matter." His attempt at levity fell flat, the gravity of the situation rendering his usual wit ineffective. He rose from his chair, casting a lingering glance at Elizabeth before nodding curtly to Darcy. "I trust you both will exercise more caution henceforth."

With that, he exited the room, leaving Darcy and Elizabeth alone amidst the oppressive quiet. How the devil Bennet meant to explain leaving him alone in his study with an unmarried female to his wife and daughters, Darcy had no idea. He would probably find himself "betrothed" to the woman before the day was out, but what did that matter? "Elizabeth Bennet" did not exist, anyway.

But Lady Elizabeth Montclair... he had a word or two to say to *her*. Once he trusted himself to speak at all.

The flickering candlelight caught the edges of her dark curls, framing a face full of defiance and wariness. "You have not said anything," she observed.

Darcy exhaled slowly. "You wish for me to speak?" His words were clipped, cutting. "Very well. You have jeopardized everything. Everything."

Her chin lifted slightly. "I did not mean—"

"Oh, let me guess." His tone was venomous. "You did not *mean* for your letter to be intercepted. You did not *mean* to reveal your location. You did not *mean* to compromise your safety and put every soul in this house at risk."

Her lips parted, then pressed together in frustration.

He continued, relentless. "Tell me, 'Miss Bennet,' when you wrote this letter, did you consider—for even a moment—that the men who killed the Prime Minister might still be watching your friends? That they might not have fallen for the same 'holiday with the Queen' ruse that fooled your father? That there are people who do not wish for you to speak?"

She hesitated. It was brief. Almost imperceptible.

But he saw it. And he felt sick.

Because she had not thought of it then.

She had not thought of it at all.

She swallowed, her eyes flashing up to him. "And what would you have had me do? Pretend my friends do not exist? Let them worry for me? Assume I have vanished off the face of the earth?"

"Yes," he said flatly.

Her nostrils flared. "That is—"

"Necessary."

She let out a sharp breath, lurching back in her chair as if he had struck her.

Darcy turned away, pacing a few steps. He could not bear to look at her just now, not when anger still clawed at his chest like an unrelenting beast.

Not when fear still gripped him, despite his best efforts to force it down.

"I thought it would help."

Darcy whirled. "What?"

Elizabeth closed her eyes, and a single tear leaked down her cheek. Genuine or not, at this point, he did not care. Or, at least, he *should* not care.

"I thought if Charlotte had word from me, she would not worry. That she would corroborate the story put out by Her Majesty, and no one would be the wiser."

Darcy's shoulders sagged. "Truly? Or are you inventing this tale now, after you have been found out, to make yourself look less culpable?"

She raised her gaze to him. "You hold such a dim view of a lady's intellect that you truly believe such a creature would *not* be suspicious if her friend disappeared? You think a woman like Lady Charlotte Wrexham, or her mother, the Duchess—who *both* knew what I saw that day in the House of Commons—would not find it slightly alarming that I was suddenly 'spirited away with the Queen's ladies'?."

Darcy swallowed. "I am certain Her Majesty—"

"Knows nothing of me!" she finished for him. "Do you suppose Her Majesty knows how I part my hair? Whether I prefer cream or lemon in my tea? That I have my own funny way of crossing my writing in correspondence, that I misspell the word 'harbor' every third time I write it?"

He stared at her. Of course not. He had not thought—had not cared—about cream or lemon. About the quirks of handwriting or the pattern of errors in a word. He cared only for her safety. For silence. For simplicity.

Elizabeth pushed on, her voice trembling but firm. "Do you imagine her secretaries can forge a friendship? The kind that knows when you are frightened from the way you sign your name?"

Darcy opened his mouth, but there was nothing to say.

He turned from her, jaw tight, the letter still crumpled slightly in his fingers. The blasted thing had compromised everything—and yet she sat there, explaining how she had meant well, as if that erased the danger.

"It was not your place," he muttered, barely trusting himself to speak at all.

"And yet *I* was the one who was taken," she said. "Not you. Not Her Majesty. *Me*."

Darcy's spine stiffened. She was right.

It did not make her actions less reckless. It did not absolve the risk. But it reminded him that all his caution, all his careful guarding, had come after the fact. She was the one who had witnessed a horror, and had her life upended because of it.

"I *was* trying to help," she added softly, the light catching the shards of amber in her eyes as she turned her face toward the window. "To keep someone from worrying unnecessarily and stirring up the sort of gossip we wished to avoid."

Darcy stared at her profile—so calm, so stubborn. She had disobeyed his orders—orders meant to keep her alive. She had endangered herself, as well as the entire Bennet family. But in her mind, she had done it to protect the thin lie that was currently keeping her hidden.

And somehow, infuriatingly, he could not condemn that.

"Whatever your intentions *were*, you are now compromised," he said at last, his voice low.

Elizabeth swallowed so hard he could hear her throat working across the room. "I know."

"And do you understand what that means?"

She held his gaze. "That they know where I am. And who is sheltering me. And if they have half a wit, they have probably put together the name of the man protecting me."

Darcy unleashed a sigh. So, she *had* spared the matter some thought. Some remorse. "Yes."

She exhaled slowly, nodding, her face carefully blank. But there was something in her eyes—a flicker of something she had probably never let herself feel before.

Fear.

Not the petty fear of inconvenience or discomfort.

Real, honest terror.

She understood now.

Darcy's jaw clenched. "I must stay."

She blinked. "What?"

"I was meant to return to London. But I cannot leave now. Not when we know someone is watching you."

She stared at him, incredulous. "You would abandon your work?"

His fingers twitched at his sides. "If my work follows you here, then my duty is here."

Elizabeth swallowed. Her throat moved slowly, deliberately. "What do we do?"

Darcy straightened. "We must be vigilant. Trust no one outside this household—save, perhaps, Bingley at point of need. Any further correspondence must be scrutinized."

She nodded jerkily. "I understand."

Darcy's mind moved faster now, pulling threads and sorting them into patterns. He paced once more, two strides to the hearth and back again, the beginnings of a plan taking form even as his pulse still thrummed with unease.

Elizabeth was being watched. That much was now certain. And they apparently *wanted* her scattered, terrified, thinking about running again...

Then... why not use it?

He turned to her abruptly. "If they are watching your movements—if they intercepted your letter—then they are intercepting from somewhere close."

She frowned, following his logic, but wary. "You wish to draw them out."

"I want to know where your letter was taken. Who had the opportunity. Which hand betrayed you."

"And you think you can track that?"

He nodded once, sharp and certain. "It will take planning. I shall have to coordinate with Fitzwilliam, and perhaps involve a man or two from the Post. Quietly."

Elizabeth tilted her head, her expression guarded. "You want me to write another?"

"Yes. Nothing too pointed. Another note to Lady Charlotte—or even another friend. One who would expect to hear from you. Something innocuous. And this time, I will control its path. I will mark it, perhaps plant false information in it—details only a spy or traitor would note. And then I shall see where it ends."

A silence fell between them, full of possibility and risk.

"You're using me as bait," she said at last.

His jaw tightened. "I am using you to find the men who want you silenced."

Her eyes did not flinch from his. "And if they bite?"

"Then I shall be ready. This time, I will not be two steps behind. This time, I will meet them face to face."

Elizabeth was silent for a long moment. Then, at last, she said quietly, "Very well. But if I am to play the mouse, Mr. Darcy... *you* had best be the hawk, rather than some other."

His mouth twitched grimly. "I intend to be."

CHAPTER NINETEEN

MR. COLLINS ARRIVED BACK at Longbourn in high spirits—and with a loud voice in the hall to prove it. Laughter followed him—Kitty's shrill giggle and Lydia's breathless commentary on something they had seen in town.

The noise carried into the drawing room, where Elizabeth sat with her pitiful first attempt at embroidery, watching Jane blushing at Mr. Bingley. Mrs. Bennet perked up immediately at the sound of voices returning to the hall.

A moment later, Mr. Collins stepped into the room, still rubbing his hands because his gloves had proved a bit too tight. Kitty and Lydia tumbled in behind him, chatting animatedly.

"Oh, Mr. Collins!" Mrs. Bennet called brightly. "We did not expect you back so soon!"

"Indeed, indeed, madam, I found my errands in Meryton quickly concluded." He turned around and swept the room with a pleased swagger of a greeting, then stopped cold as his eyes fell on the doorway.

Mr. Darcy stood just outside the sitting room, having only just emerged from a quiet conference with Mr. Bennet. At the sight of him, Collins blanched, and Darcy... Darcy went entirely red in the face and looked as if he had seen a demon.

Collins' back straightened with almost comic rigidity. "Mr. Darcy," he stammered, "I was unaware of your presence here."

Darcy inclined his head slightly, his expression impassive as he entered the room enough to permit a greeting. "I think you will find the feeling mutual, Mr. Collins."

Mrs. Bennet, oblivious to the sudden drop in temperature, fluttered her hand. "Yes, how delightful you have already been acquainted! Mr. Collins, Mr. Darcy is a guest of Mr. Bingley's once again. Such a pleasure. Could not keep away from our lovely ladies in Hertfordshire, I daresay," she added with a giggle.

Collins gave a jerky nod, his eyes still fixed on Darcy, the color in his cheeks becoming splotchy. "I confess myself quite shocked," he said, his voice choking on the word "myself." "To find Mr. Darcy of all people here—in a respectable household!"

The air in the room froze.

Mrs. Bennet blinked. "What a very odd thing to say, Mr. Collins. Mr. Darcy is Mr. Bingley's friend. Why should he not be here?"

Collins looked flustered, then pounced on the opening with the eagerness of a man who had waited too long to deliver his piece. "Ah, but madam, surely you have heard—his family name, once so celebrated, has fallen into disgrace."

Elizabeth turned sharply toward him. "Disgrace?"

Collins lifted his chin, hands clasped before him in mock solemnity. "Lady Catherine de Bourgh herself, my most esteemed patroness, has spoken of it. The Darcys of Pemberley—what is left of them—are no longer received in certain circles."

The silence that followed was almost surreal, for the Bennets were a family that were not known for quiet reflection. But now, the clock was the loudest noise in the room.

Jane's gaze flickered uncertainly between Collins and Darcy. Mr. Bingley's brow furrowed and his eyes narrowed dangerously—if, indeed, so affable a man could look dangerous. Even Mrs. Bennet, normally eager for gossip, looked somewhat unsure.

Darcy stood perfectly still. His face betrayed nothing, but Elizabeth could see it—the stiff set of his shoulders, the iron thread of tension running through his jaw. He was enduring this. Silently. Proudly. And not, she suspected, for the first time.

Collins continued, emboldened by Darcy's silence. "It was all very tragic. The estate, you see, was lost to the family. Ruined. A dreadful scandal, everyone says as much. Though Lady Catherine did not speak of particulars, only that her nephew was no longer... suitable company. A *libertine*, she has pronounced him, and for good and proper reasons, I am certain."

A quiet gasp escaped Kitty. Lydia, for once, said nothing at all. Bingley managed a weak, "Now, see here..."

But it was Elizabeth who rose slowly from her chair, the embroidery hoop falling unnoticed to the floor. "Mr. Collins," she said, "I do not think this is the sort of thing one says in another man's drawing room."

Collins turned toward her, blinked, and then said with obsequious confidence, "I only meant to spare the family any embarrassment. One would not wish to form close associations with a gentleman whose circumstances are so very... tainted."

Elizabeth opened her mouth to speak again, but another voice beat her to it.

"I believe," said Mr. Bennet, emerging from the hallway, "that if anyone in this room is causing embarrassment to my family, it is not Mr. Darcy."

A hush settled over the room again.

Mr. Collins sputtered. "But... but I said! The man *is* a libertine! I—I merely repeated what I was told by a most reputable—"

"Yes," Mr. Bennet said dryly, "and with such excellent timing, too."

Elizabeth glanced sideways at Darcy.

He had not moved. Not so much as blinked.

But his gaze was fixed, unwavering, on the fire. And in his stillness, she saw the tight control of a man who had borne humiliation before. Alone. And who expected to bear it again, the same way.

Something ached deep in her chest.

Not pity.

Something more complicated than that.

And far more dangerous.

T HE CARRIAGE RIDE BACK to Netherfield was conducted in near-total silence—at least, for the first ten minutes. Darcy sat rigid, jaw clenched, eyes fixed out the window, hardly breathing. The fields of Hertfordshire blurred past unnoticed.

At last, Bingley shifted beside him. "Well," he said, with painful cheer, "that was... enlightening."

Darcy did not answer.

"Come now," Bingley added. "At least it was a man nobody knows or cares about, and not a parliamentary inquiry."

Darcy closed his eyes briefly. "He is hardly someone 'no one knows or cares about.' Do you not know who he is?"

Bingley blinked innocently. "Should I? I suppose I found it odd that he was talking about your aunt. How does he know Lady Catherine?"

"He is her bloody parson! I met him when I went with Richard to Rosings last summer—fool, I, I thought perhaps she would speak to me after ten years, but I could not have been more wrong."

Bingley frowned and shifted in his seat. "Still bearing that grudge because you were 'unfit' to marry her daughter, eh? Look, Darcy, I would not worry about it. Who cares if Collins decides to run his mouth a bit? You saw how Bennet silenced him. I doubt anyone in town listens to a word he says."

"No, no, you do not understand. If Lady Catherine learns I was not only present in the Bennet household but consorting with—"

"'Consorting,' good Lord," Bingley said under his breath. "You sound like Collins."

Darcy turned a slow glare on his friend. "If I'd had any idea *Collins* was Bennet's heir... He will not let this rest quietly, and therein lies the trouble."

Bingley laughed. "Likely not. He is probably composing a letter to your aunt as we speak. Written on the very finest vellum, in the most atrocious hand, with half a dozen flourishes to call you a libertine without using the word, because I doubt he could spell it properly."

Darcy said nothing. He felt... hollow.

No, worse. *Exposed.*

He had spent the better part of the last ten years trying to reclaim his name with caution and calculation—and now, with one blowhard parson and a single vulnerability—thanks to the Prince's idea of a joke or a test, or whatever this was—it was all unraveling.

And Elizabeth had heard it all.

Bingley studied him more carefully now, all traces of his hopeful sort of humor fading. "I am sorry, Darcy. I know what this means to you."

"No... I cannot think you possibly could," Darcy replied quietly.

Bingley sucked in a breath and sat back, chastened. They said nothing else for the remainder of the ride.

When they arrived at Netherfield, Darcy did not even wait for the footman to lower the steps. He jumped down and strode toward the house, ignoring the startled greeting from the butler, his coat whipping behind him in the breeze his strides created. Bingley followed at a more sedate pace, catching up only when Darcy had already pushed open the door to the study.

Darcy crossed to the hearth, standing with his back to the room as Bingley closed the door.

"Brandy?" Bingley offered.

Darcy did not answer.

Bingley poured two glasses anyway, setting one on the desk and holding the other loosely in his hand as he perched on the arm of a chair. "Do you want to talk about it?"

"No."

Bingley nodded. "Excellent. Let us sit in silence, then, while your blood pressure quietly murders you."

Darcy turned at last, his expression carved from stone. "He *will* write to her."

"Then let him," Bingley said. "She will huff and bluster and complain to her dogs, and the sun will still rise tomorrow."

Darcy stared at him. "You have no idea what she is capable of."

Bingley blinked. "Perhaps not. But I do know you. And I have never seen you this rattled." He stood fully now, his tone turning careful. "This is not just about your name."

Darcy's jaw tensed.

Bingley narrowed his eyes. "What *is* going on?"

Silence. A long one.

Darcy's hand twitched near the untouched glass on the desk. "There are things I cannot tell you."

"You mean you *will* not tell me."

"I mean," Darcy said evenly, "that the fewer people who know, the safer it is for everyone involved."

Bingley stepped back, folding his arms. "So that is what this is. A matter of safety."

Darcy said nothing.

Bingley exhaled. "Well. That is more of an answer than I expected." He reached for his own glass and took a drink. "Is it *her?*"

Darcy looked at him sharply. "I do not know what you mean."

"I mean your mysterious 'Miss Elizabeth Bennet.'"

Darcy stiffened. "*My* Miss Elizabeth? Bingley, you are imagining an attachment where none exists."

"Am I? You are always watching her. Protecting her."

Darcy scoffed. "Nothing of the kind. I like Mr. Bennet. His eldest daughter is tolerable enough, and as I said, she seems to have a *tendre* for you. I endure the rest of the family for—"

"Poppycock. She is no 'long-lost cousin.' She 'arrived' at Longbourn with absolutely no warning whatsoever—"

"Mr. Bennet is oddly capricious in the disclosing of planned guests. Only look at Mr. Collins' similarly unannounced arrival if you need evidence of that."

"—The very same day you returned from London, after a summons so 'urgent' that you left off a planed leave that you had so desperately earned?" Bingley clicked his tongue. "Come, Darcy, I may not know the exact nature of your business at the Home Office, but I am not incapable of drawing a straight line between two points. She is no more a Bennet than I am."

Darcy lowered his eyes. "She is... important," he confessed. "And for now, Bennet is the safest name for her to use."

Bingley finished the bite he had just taken and swallowed. "I suspect that is the best reply you mean to give me. If I can help, you need only ask."

Darcy's voice was quiet. "I know."

Another beat of silence passed.

Then Bingley muttered, "Still, I rather wish I had struck the man. Just once. For sport."

That earned the faintest twitch of a smile from Darcy. "You are not alone in that."

"Drink your brandy," Bingley added, "before it evaporates just to spite you."

Darcy lifted the glass. It did not steady his pulse. But it helped. Slightly.

May 26, 1812

THE MORNING SUN CAST long shadows across the manicured lawns of Netherfield as Darcy stood near the window, a letter trembling slightly in his grasp. The elegant script on the envelope was unfamiliar, but the contents within were unmistakably urgent.

"Mr. Darcy," it began, *"I trust this letter finds you well. I have come across information regarding the payments to Bellingham that you inquired about. It is imperative that we discuss this matter in person. Please meet me at the Red Lion Inn in Meryton at your earliest convenience. Discretion is advised."*

The letter was signed simply, *"A Concerned Friend."*

Bold. Terribly bold. Or desperate.

Darcy's brow furrowed. He had spent years delving into the murky depths of corruption, but this was the first time someone had reached out to him so directly—and so mysteriously. The timing was suspect, especially given recent events.

He folded the letter meticulously and slipped it into his coat pocket. Turning from the window, he found Bingley observing him with a mix of curiosity and concern.

"Another anonymous missive?" Bingley inquired, his tone laced with forced levity. He was seated at the small breakfast table, a half-eaten piece of toast forgotten on his plate, his eyes flicking between Darcy and the sealed letter in his hand.

"Something of the sort." He did not bother to sit, merely stood at the window, scanning the words again with narrowed eyes. "A potential lead on the Bellingham matter."

Bingley's fork paused halfway to his mouth. Slowly, he set it down, his expression hardening. "The Bellingham matter," he echoed. "Do you mean the fellow who shot Perceval? Darcy, is that what you've been chasing all this time?"

"Among other things. I shall be going for a ride later, alone."

Bingley exhaled sharply. "Well, that explains a good deal." He leaned back in his chair, frowning. "You are not working on a typical tea smuggling inquiry, are you? This is not merely corruption or bookkeeping trickery."

Darcy turned to face him fully. "It was never about smuggling. Not truly."

Bingley stood. "Then what, Darcy? Political assassination? Treason?"

Darcy gave him a long look.

Bingley ran a hand through his hair. "And you're going to meet this anonymous source alone?"

"I must," Darcy said. "If there's a trail, it's gone cold in London. But this—" he tapped his coat pocket lightly, "—this may be something."

Bingley looked stricken. "You cannot go unarmed into this. If they knew where..." He stopped and cleared his throat. "A certain... person... was—"

"I am not bringing her into it," Darcy snapped, then instantly regretted the sharpness.

Bingley blinked, startled not by the words, but by the tone.

"Apologies," Darcy muttered. "This must be handled delicately. Quietly. Any attention could ruin the lead."

Bingley gave a low whistle. "Darcy, if you are right... you are hunting something far more dangerous than stolen banknotes."

Darcy nodded once, grimly. "Which is why I cannot afford to miss this meeting."

"And which is why you bloody well should not go alone," Bingley said. "At least take a weapon. Or someone you trust. Do not be a martyr."

"I trust you," Darcy said after a pause. "But I need you here. And if anything happens to me, you must protect... *her*. Trust only Fitzwilliam."

Bingley's face sobered at that. He nodded once. "Then promise me you'll return."

Darcy hesitated at the door, just briefly, then gave a single nod.

"I always do."

LATER THAT AFTERNOON, UNDER a sky thick with the promise of a late spring thunderstorm, Darcy made his way toward the Red Lion Inn—a modest, half-timbered establishment nestled at the edge of Meryton. The sign swung slightly in the wind, its creaking hinges drowned out by the chatter from within.

Inside, the inn was dim and smoky, crowded with the usual mix of laborers, tradesmen, and travelers. The scent of some sort of hot pottage clung to the air, mingled with the bitterness of spilled ale and sweating men. Darcy paused in the entryway, letting his eyes adjust to the low light as he scanned the crowded room.

His gaze landed first on a man seated by the hearth, nursing a tankard and saying nothing. Broad-shouldered, with a deep scar trailing one side of his neck. His coat was travel-stained, but of good cut. He was out of place—too alert, too still. Darcy's attention lingered for a breath too long.

Then the man beside him laughed, and the stranger turned to clap him on the shoulder. "Same fool stories, Tom? Thought you'd have grown out of 'em by now."

The local—Tom, apparently—grinned and swore that his tale about a haunted mill was entirely factual. The tension in Darcy's spine eased. A local, then. Or pretending very well.

His gaze shifted again, this time to a corner table near the hearth, where another man sat alone, fidgeting with a weathered hat in his lap. He was thinner, more anxious, and dressed with care that did not suit the surroundings. His eyes darted toward the door the moment Darcy entered, and for a fleeting second, their gazes met.

Darcy approached with deliberate calm, loosening the top button of his coat. "Is the sun shining in London?" he asked quietly, resting one gloved hand on the back of the chair opposite.

The man flinched slightly. "Not since nightfall."

Darcy nodded. "Darcy, at your service."

"Eddleton, at yours," the fellow replied. "You're late."

"I am early," Darcy corrected, "by four minutes. If you are who you claim to be, then we cannot afford to waste time." He did not sit.

Eddleton hesitated, then reached into the inside of his coat and produced a small brass token—barely larger than a coin—stamped with a unique cipher known only to the Home Office.

Darcy's eyes narrowed. He withdrew his own from his pocket and laid it flat on the table beside Eddleton's. They matched. That was the final proof he needed.

Satisfied, he took the seat opposite, angling his body to keep the wall at his back and his view of the inn unbroken.

Eddleton leaned forward, lowering his voice to a near whisper. "I was told to come to you if I found anything more. Fellow in a red coat—said you'd know 'im—said to use no names. So I didn't. But I have something now. Something... real."

Darcy's eyes sharpened. "Speak."

Eddleton produced a folded packet wrapped in oilskin, tattered and smudged at the corners. "I found references to Bellingham—indirect, buried in old ledgers from the Treasury Office's auxiliary funds. Names I've seen before, from a previous inquiry. One I was warned to drop."

Darcy took the packet and did not open it. Not here.

"These names—" Eddleton wet his lips. "They're tied to shell accounts. Untraceable without deep authorization. But there are enough patterns, enough trails... They were paying him. Regular sums. Spread over months."

"Are the accounts still active?" Darcy asked.

"I do not know," Eddleton admitted. "But someone does. And they're making it very clear that this trail is not meant to be followed. Threats, blackmail."

Darcy's expression hardened. "Have *you* been threatened?"

"No," Eddleton said quickly. "But I was followed. My flat was broken into last week—nothing taken. Just... touched. I found my desk drawer open, and my ink bottle spilled."

A warning, then. Whoever this was had enough on Bellingham to force him—or trick him—into a fool's errand that could only end with a bullet or a noose. Surely, they were leaving nothing else to chance.

Darcy pocketed the oilskin. "Your identity will be protected."

Eddleton offered a dry, humorless laugh. "It's too late for that, I think."

He hesitated, then added, even lower: "There's talk. Quiet, but spreading. Someone saw something that day at the Commons. A witness." His eyes flicked to Darcy. "They think he was behind a pillar. A junior clerk, perhaps. But there's noise about... silencing him."

Darcy did not speak. His jaw locked tight.

If Eddleton had heard even scraps of rumor, then the secret was unravelling far too fast. And he was out of time.

They rose together, the scrape of their chairs drowned by a burst of laughter from the nearby table. Darcy nodded once and stepped away—but paused at the threshold.

"You will go to ground," he said without turning. "Do not return to your flat. Do not speak of this again. You will be contacted, if needed."

Eddleton gave a faint nod, and Darcy slipped out under a gathering summer storm.

He had barely gone ten steps before he felt it again—that prickling sensation at the base of his neck. A subtle shift in the air.

He glanced back once.

The man by the hearth was gone.

And so was the laughter.

CHAPTER TWENTY

THE AFTERNOON WANED, THROWING long shadows across the drawing room floor. Elizabeth sat with her badly botched embroidery balanced on her knee, though her needle had stilled some time ago. She barely noticed the thread looped loosely between her fingers. Her thoughts were far from domestic concerns, tugged instead toward darker corners—unfinished sketches, whispered suspicions, and the gnawing certainty that something more was coming.

She was just contemplating whether to rise and take some air when Mr. Bennet appeared in the doorway. His expression was, as ever, difficult to read, though his eyes held a gleam of something—amusement, perhaps, or perhaps a warning.

"My dear Elizabeth," he said with a hint of gallantry, "I have received a rather charming note from my cousin Daniel. I suspect you might find it diverting. You will find it on the desk in the study."

Elizabeth blinked, startled. His cousin Daniel...? *Oh!* Right. She rose quickly. "Of course."

He stepped aside, gesturing with a slight incline of his head. "I shall leave you to it."

She crossed the hall, the quiet clack of her slippers against the wood barely audible. As she entered the study, the familiar scent of pipe smoke and leather-bound books greeted her—along with something else.

Darcy was already inside.

He stood near the window, having apparently just climbed through it, one hand still brushing dust from his coat. He turned at once, eyes locking with hers, his expression dark.

And she was very suddenly, very completely, alone with him.

"Miss Ben—oh, bother with the disguise. I rather despise it, anyway."

She puckered her mouth. "Is that what you crawled through a window to tell me?"

Darcy's expression was taut, his jaw clenched in a way that betrayed more than mere unease. He paced a step away from the window, then stopped himself.

"I apologize for the ruse," he said stiffly. "Recent developments have necessitated caution, and I would not that Mrs. Bennet... or anyone else... knew I was here."

Elizabeth stepped forward, hands folding reflexively in front of her. "I understand," she said quietly. Then, after a beat, added, "If this is about what happened yesterday—Mr. Collins—"

He looked up sharply, surprised. "Collins? No."

She tilted her head. "Because I thought perhaps you had come to... I do not know. Clear the air? That man has no sense of tact. And you did not deserve—"

"This is not about Collins," he interrupted, not unkindly. His voice was quieter now, hoarser. "Though if I began addressing every insult he offered, I should never finish."

She gave a wry smile, but it faded as she took in the rest of his expression. Tension hummed off him like a wound wire, and beneath it—something darker. "Then what is this about?"

There was a pause. Darcy's hand drifted toward the inside pocket of his coat, but he did not reach for anything. Instead, he fixed her with a look that made her breath catch.

"The sketch," he said at last. "The man you drew."

Her brows furrowed. "What about him?"

"I believe," he said carefully, "we may now know who sent him."

"Oh?" She drew closer. "Then why did you come to me?"

Darcy reached into his coat and pulled out a folded paper. "I may have a name for the man providing the money, but I am still at a loss for the identity of the man who pulled the trigger. I..." He heaved an exasperated sigh. "Egad, I do not know why I am showing this to you. You have given me what you could, but we are running short on time. I suppose I hoped you might recall something more. Anything..."

Elizabeth accepted it, unfolding the paper to reveal the sketch she had drawn days earlier. The sight of it sent a shiver through her; though it was her own handiwork, the man's visage now felt eerily unfamiliar. As though the work belonged to someone else. She stared down at the stark lines, the shadowed angles of the man's face, the narrowed eyes.

"It still troubles me," Darcy said, watching her closely. "The detail in this is exceptional. Clearly, you *saw* this man. Anyone who knew him could point the finger at him. I just have no idea who it is. He does not resemble anyone I can implicate."

Her eyes traced the lines, absorbing each detail anew. A nagging sensation stirred within her, as if a crucial element hovered just beyond her recollection.

"I wish I had introduced myself, then," she said tartly, and trying to hand the paper back. "How terribly negligent of me."

But Darcy refused to take the drawing. "Elizabeth," he said, his voice edged with urgency, "I must ask—did you... imagine... or embellish... *any* details of this image? Is it *truly* an accurate representation?"

Elizabeth's head snapped up, eyes flashing with indignation. "I assure you, Mr. Darcy, I did not invent this man. Every line, every shadow—I captured them as faithfully as memory allows."

"'As faithfully as memory allows...'" he repeated. "Surely there is *something* you may have missed. Overlooked. The turn of his nose, the set of his mouth... Are you sure that was what his hat looked like?"

"No, no, those are quite..." She tilted her head. "But perhaps..."

He exhaled sharply, running a hand through his hair. "Then what is it? What detail eludes you?"

She returned her gaze to the sketch, frustration knitting her brow. The man's face, his posture, the surrounding elements—all seemed in place. She had even captured the pillars behind where he stood when she saw him. Yet, an intangible void persisted.

Suddenly, her breath caught. Her eyes locked onto the man's hand, the one holding the pistol, and clarity struck like a bolt of lightning.

"The ring," she murmured, almost to herself.

Darcy's posture stiffened. "What did you say?"

She looked up, eyes wide with realization. "I remember seeing a flash of gold when he was putting his pistol back in his coat. It caught my eye, but then I was looking more at the pistol."

"Do you recall anything about it?"

She squinted, as if trying to pull the wisps of memory into something tangible. "Thick, with an image in the center. I think it might have been signet ring. There was a figure in the center, set in ebony."

He blinked. "You are sure? You are not simply 'recalling' this to appease me? Your memory is accurate in this case?"

She narrowed her eyes and shook her head. "No, I can see it—I could not have invented that memory."

Darcy stepped closer. "Describe it to me."

Elizabeth closed her eyes briefly, summoning the image from the depths of her memory. "Gold, with black details. Not large or ostentatious. I know this sounds strange, but I could swear it bore the design of a jagged 'J' shape. Or perhaps a hippocampus—a sea horse."

Darcy's expression darkened, his jaw tightening as if restraining a surge of emotion. "You are *certain?*" he pressed, his voice a shade deeper.

She nodded slowly. "As certain as one can be from recollection. Why? What does it signify? Perhaps it was not a hippocampus, but that is the shape my mind sees—"

Darcy turned away, pacing a few steps before facing her again. "I doubt you invented something so odd and yet so coincidentally significant. The hippocampus is the emblem of the King's Fellowship for Civil Order—a society with noble beginnings but... rather questionable endings."

Elizabeth's mind raced, attempting to connect the dots. "And the man who wore this ring?"

Darcy's gaze met hers, a storm of contemplation and concern swirling within. "If he possessed such a ring, it suggests he was a member—or perhaps an associate—of the Fellowship. This ties him to influential figures, potentially even... egad, I dare not name him yet, but there is... an individual... one I already had reasons to suspect, who has known affiliations with the group."

Elizabeth's skin prickled.

She had drawn a face from memory. She had added detail. Shadow. Line. Structure. But until this moment, she had not known that a ring—something she had not even consciously registered in the moment—would be the key to unmasking an entire network of corruption. Of danger. And possibly, of murder.

"You said 'questionable endings.' Is this... Fellowship... defunct?" she asked carefully, watching the muscle twitch in his jaw.

Darcy gave a short, humorless laugh. "It should be. It was meant to be dissolved a decade ago. But some men do not relinquish power so easily."

"And you know people connected to it?"

"I cannot say. Not with certainty. But a man from the disbanded regiment that bore this crest—one of its fiercest loyalists—disappeared about three years ago. He was presumed dead. I investigated his 'murder' myself." Darcy's voice dropped. "But I suspect now that he is very much alive. And if he was at Westminster..." He trailed off.

Elizabeth felt the breath tighten in her chest. "Then he could be the one who pulled the trigger."

Darcy said nothing. His silence was confirmation enough.

She folded her arms. "Why would he wear the ring? Why leave such a mark?"

"Men like that... they do not fear being seen. They leave symbols behind the way a cat leaves feathers—trophies. Warnings. And sometimes... declarations."

She swallowed. "Declarations of what?"

"Allegiance. Or ownership."

Elizabeth blinked. "By whom?"

Darcy raised a brow. "I think, Lady Elizabeth, it might be safer for you if I said nothing more until I can be sure."

She sighed in disappointment. They stood in silence, the crackle of the hearth filling the space between them. Darcy had been watching her, then it was as if his eyes stung and he had to look away.

It was Elizabeth who spoke first. "I wish you would let me say how sorry I am," she said softly. "For what happened yesterday."

Darcy's brows drew together. "You need not—"

"But I do," she said firmly. "You were humiliated, and I..." She hesitated, glancing away. "I should not have appeared to find any of it amusing."

That earned her a look—half disbelief, half something else. "I did not accuse you of that."

"No?" she asked, the corner of her mouth twitching. "You think I did not notice how your jaw clenched every time he mispronounced 'libertine'? You think I did not smirk at the way his face was turning purple with ugly yellow splotches?"

A faint flush crept along the edge of his collar. His hand flexed at his side. "I... noticed. You, that is. Not him."

She tilted her head. "You take every insult like a blow. A man like you can hardly afford—"

"Afford what?"

She sighed. "I have few useful skills—you have said as much yourself. But this, I know, for my father told me often enough. Feelings are costly, Mr. Darcy. Dignity... it is dear. Most cannot afford to defend it, but *you*— Well, you looked as if you would have broken Mr. Collins in half if it were not another man's drawing room he stood in. And *I* thought *I* was the reckless one."

He looked up sharply. But not in protest. "I do not think you are reckless."

"You most certainly do! How many times have you had to thunder after me when I was up to some foolhardy mischief?"

Darcy's throat worked. "I have… tried to understand your perspective. And I think you are brave. Clever. And utterly impossible." He hesitated. "And I think if I were a better man, I would have stayed away from you."

She mouthed the words in repetition. *Stayed away…*

"But I am not," he said simply. "And I did not."

She blinked. "Why would you think you had to stay away from me? Am I so terrible?"

Darcy exhaled, his jaw tightening. "No… *I* am. If I were stronger, more prudent, I would have found a way. But I am not. And—"

"The prince did not give you a choice," she finished.

"No," he said. "But even if he had…" His voice faltered.

"Mr. Darcy, you make no sense. First, you act as if I am some leper forced upon you, and now you say it was because of some misplaced sense of fault of your own. I insist—"

"I *will* tell you everything," he said quietly. "Just not now."

That sounded rather final. And for once, Elizabeth said nothing at all. What could she say to the man who had risked everything to come back here? To protect her. To see her. Even if he never said it aloud.

Especially because he never said it aloud.

Her voice was very soft. "I suppose we are both guarding some secret."

A faint twitch pulled at the corner of his mouth. "A matched set… Elizabeth."

Her lips parted—to say what, she did not know. Correct him on his omission of her proper title? Dig a bit more into the morass of his private thoughts? But before the moment could fracture, before she could say something ruinous, Darcy turned back toward the window.

"I must go. There are people I need to speak with. Someone is trying to erase their trail, and they have killed to do it. But now… we have something to start with."

"The ring," she said.

"And the lady who noticed it," he added.

She smiled faintly. "That makes me dangerous, I suppose."

"Yes. It does. I will return tomorrow and we will work up that letter I spoke to you of yesterday."

And then he was gone, slipping through the window the same way he came—like a ghost. Like a shadow.

Leaving Elizabeth alone with her sketch, her thoughts, and a heart that beat a little too fast for comfort.

May 27, 1812

T HE PROBLEM WITH BAIT was that it tended to attract more than one kind of predator.

Darcy stood beside the writing desk in the Mr. Bennets' study, watching Elizabeth pace. Her arms were folded tight, her brow drawn in contemplation—or resistance. Possibly both.

"I am not fond of the idea," she said finally.

He had not expected her to be. "Nor am I."

Her pacing stopped. "Then why suggest it? What if it brings harm to the Bennets?"

"Because whoever returned your letter intended a threat, not silence," he said. "They already know you understood it as such. What they do not know is how much we learned from it—or what we intend to do next."

Elizabeth gave him a long look. "So this is not to fool them."

"Partly," Darcy said. "But mostly, it is to provoke them into tipping their hand."

Her mouth pressed into a thin line. "And if it works?"

"Then they will act—and we will be watching when they do."

She set her fist on her hip.

The stance was pure defiance—shoulders squared, chin lifted, the curve of her waist drawn in silhouette by the afternoon light. There was a flicker in her eyes, something bright and amused and entirely too knowing, as if she was daring him to object. Darcy exhaled slowly and looked away.

He was beginning to suspect she knew exactly what she was doing.

Then, to his surprise, she sat beside the desk, reached for the paper, and dipped her pen. "Very well. Let us set a trap."

She wrote quickly, fluidly—nothing obvious, nothing alarming. A charming note to Lady Charlotte Wrexham, full of droll observations about village trivialities and the burdens of rustic leisure. Elizabeth made light mention of her "holiday," carefully threading in a detail Darcy had offered—that Her Majesty had indeed retired to Frogmore, just outside Windsor, for the season. It would lend her lie a veneer of credibility for anyone curious enough to test it.

"Is it truly Frogmore?" she asked without looking up.

He leaned forward slightly, reading over her shoulder. "It is. I heard it confirmed while in London last week. Her Majesty prefers the gardens in early summer."

"How quaint. Perhaps I shall mention the lilies." Her tone was dry, but her eyes sparkled. "Would Her Majesty prefer white or yellow, do you think?"

"She prefers peace," Darcy said, watching the fine movement of her hand as she wrote. "And does not care what color it comes in."

Elizabeth hummed under her breath. "Pity. I should have liked to embroider some symbolism."

"You are *embroidering* quite enough."

"Cad that you are! You must have been hearing rumors from Jane, because I could not embroider a convincing flower if my life depended upon it. Though it is not for lack of diligence on her part to teach me."

"I can hardly believe you let anyone teach you anything at all."

"Now, see here, sir, I—" She turned slightly at that—just enough for him to realize how near they had become, her shoulder brushing his sleeve, her scent—clean linen and some pale trace of lavender—*disruptively* close.

Darcy straightened too sharply and folded his arms behind his back. "The 'cousin,'" he said, changing the subject. "Have you named him?"

"Mr. Redfield," she replied at once, eyes still on the page. "From Hampshire. Very fond of trout fishing and political radicalism."

Darcy arched a brow. "Inventive."

"I thought so." She dipped her pen again and read aloud as she wrote. "He has invited me to St. Albans next week. I think I shall decline. There is something suspect about his waistcoat. Then again, his breeches are rather fetching, so perhaps it might be worth a foray. What say you, dear Charlotte?"

"*Breeches?*" Darcy scoffed. "Lord have mercy."

"You think ladies do not notice how a man looks in his breeches? I assure you, we do. For instance…" She tossed a saucy glance over her shoulder, letting her eyes trail suggestively toward his waist and downward.

Darcy moved to stand behind her more completely—out of her field of view. "Finish writing, if you please. We shall be at this all day."

"You are terribly dull sometimes. Very well." She blew out a huff that feathered the hair falling over her face, and dipped her quill again.

Darcy watched her lace in the misleading cues they had agreed upon: a reference to "poppies in bloom"—a red herring suggesting surveillance nearby; the invented cousin, "Mr. Redfield"—a trigger word Fitzwilliam's men would now be able to track in any intercepted intelligence; and the mention of a planned excursion to St. Albans, which they had no intention of making.

The message, though addressed to Lady Charlotte, was written for someone else entirely.

He watched her dot the final sentence and set down her quill with a small sigh of satisfaction. "There. I believe I have lied thoroughly enough for one day."

"You did not lie," he said. "You rearranged the truth into something more useful."

Elizabeth glanced sideways, smiling faintly. "That sounds suspiciously like what the Home Office does."

"It is."

Something passed between them then—dry amusement, shared complicity, and something quieter beneath. It left the air thinner than before. Darcy turned away first.

"I am going to London to make my report to Prince George tomorrow. I shall send this from the posting inn at St. Albans," he said. "With luck, they will believe the bait. Or chase a ghost to St. Albans. Either way, Richard's men will start following it—see whose hands it passes through."

Elizabeth stood and stretched slightly, arms over her head. "Poor Mr. Redfield," she said. "Always embroiled in the wrong sort of company."

"You are fortunate he is not real," Darcy replied, reaching for the letter.

She arched a brow. "Why?"

"Because," he said, "he would be entirely unsuited to you."

And before she could reply—before she could smile that knowing smile that made his thoughts scatter—he turned and started for the window so he might climb back out onto the lawn, with no one—least of all, Collins—the wiser.

"Do tell your cousin to keep his wits about him," she said, stopping him. "If anyone is going to be captured following a decoy, I should prefer it not be someone I do not dislike."

Darcy inclined his head. "He will be thrilled to know you care."

"I do not. But you will be insufferable if anything happens to him, and I dislike you less when you smile on occasion."

She was already halfway to the door leading out into the hall when she tossed it over her shoulder, casual as anything.

Darcy watched her go, heart clenching in that maddening, inevitable way it always did now.

Chapter Twenty-One

May 28, 1812

THE CANDLE ON HIS desk had long since guttered to a stub. A second one burned low beside it, throwing distorted shadows against the far wall of the study at Netherfield. Darcy sat with his back to the fire, boots polished, coat ready, and his plans drawn out with a precision bordering on desperation.

At first light, he would ride for London.

He did not like it. He had left her once before, and in the space of a single morning she had found her life threatened and her trust shaken. But this could not wait—not with the Prince expecting an account, and not with the ghost of a man he once chased beginning to take shape again.

Three years ago, a man named Hugh Maddox had vanished amid whispers of a disgrace too sensitive for the courts. Darcy had been dispatched—quietly, without written orders—by the King himself to investigate the death no one dared confirm.

Maddox had once been a silent hand of the Crown, a fixer who operated in shadow and left no trace. The King never admitted it, not openly, but Darcy had pieced together enough to see the truth—and His Majesty, in a rare flicker of lucidity, had let slip a phrase that confirmed what Darcy already knew.

"Officially," Maddox was dead. Disavowed. Buried. But off the books... well, there was no proof of anything.

The only likeness Darcy ever saw had been a miniature, painted when Maddox was scarcely out of boyhood—useless now, against the man in Elizabeth's sketch. But the ring on that man's hand—the hippocampus seal of a now-disbanded regiment—Maddox would have worn one. And years before, he had shared political sympathies with Sir William Cunningham, back when opposing Perceval's reforms was fashionable treason.

If Maddox still lived, and if he was working for Cunningham now, then the rot stretched deeper than anyone feared. And Darcy could not unmask a ghost from Meryton.

He closed the leather folio with a snap and turned as Bingley stepped in, hair still rumpled from sleep.

"Good heavens, Porter was right. You're up and dressed at this ungodly hour," Bingley said, rubbing the back of his neck. "Which is either a good sign or a terrible one. Judging by your expression, I will assume terrible."

"I ride to London at dawn."

That woke him fully. "Alone?"

"Yes. I will hire as many horses as I need, ride quickly and stop only when necessary. I can be there and back in a day."

Bingley folded his arms and leaned against the doorframe. "And what am I meant to do while you are galloping off toward glory?"

Darcy exhaled. "Stay at Longbourn."

Bingley blinked. "You cannot be serious. How long?"

He looked up. "All day. From the moment Mr. Bennet lumbers down the stairs to sneak into his study until the moment the housekeeper shoos you out the door because she has run out of her day's allotment of candles for the drawing room. I do not care if you are seated beside Lydia Bennet while she recounts the entire lineage of the dragoons. I need a familiar presence in the house."

"Darcy—"

"She is not safe." The words came sharper than intended.

He stood, crossing to where Bingley waited. "We are being watched. I need to leave—briefly—but I will not do so unless I know someone is in that house who will notice if she vanishes."

Bingley made a wry face. "From what you say of lady, she vanishes rather easily."

"All the more reason for you to stay close. And if it can be said so lightly, there is more at stake here, even than her life. Or mine."

At that, Bingley's expression sobered. "Does she know?"

Darcy hesitated. "Not all of it. Not yet."

Bingley considered him. "Is it truly *her* safety you are guarding, or your own sanity?"

Darcy did not answer.

Bingley pushed off the doorframe and clapped him lightly on the shoulder. "Very well. I shall smile at Miss Bennet until my face aches. I shall attempt to match wits with Mr. Bennet in chess—"

"No chess."

Bingley's brow furrowed, still somewhat cloudy from sleep. "Eh?"

"Bennet is too much of a distraction. You may smile at his eldest daughter all you like, because *she* will not let Elizabeth out of her sight, and *you* will not lose Miss Bennet. But do not, for the sake of all that is decent, let Mr. Bennet suck you into his study for a round of chess."

Bingley sighed and nodded wearily. "Very well. Your Elizabeth will be guarded. And with any luck, your future mother-in-law will attempt to fatten me until I cannot fit into my carriage for the journey home."

"You mean *your* future mother-in-law. Bingley, you had better get some more sleep."

Bingley rubbed his face. "My what? Something the matter with Mrs. Bennet?"

Darcy gave a huff of breath that was not quite a laugh. "I suppose that depends. The lady *is* a gracious hostess, if something of a mercenary one. You will not eat half the ham she offers."

"I shall eat all of it," Bingley declared, tossing a jaunty salute. "For queen and country."

Darcy chuckled. "Good. Mr. Bennet is aware of certain... matters. A quiet word with him, and he will make excuses for your presence all day if needed."

"Excellent. Then I shall install myself in their drawing room with every intention of overstaying my welcome." Bingley paused, his tone softening. "Ride fast. Return faster."

Darcy nodded once and turned back to the desk. He had letters to burn, notes to hide, and a pistol to clean.

He would be gone no more than a day.

He only prayed it was not too long.

T HE MORNING HAD BEGUN innocently enough.

The family was just sitting down to breakfast—a modest affair, despite Mrs. Bennet's regular attempts to bully the cook into producing something grander—when Hill entered, cheeks flushed and voice breathless.

"Mr. Bingley, ma'am," she said, bobbing a curtsy. "He is on the front steps."

A spoon clattered. Lydia gasped. Kitty squealed.

Mrs. Bennet leaped to her feet so fast her chair tipped backward and nearly toppled Mary. "Mr. Bingley? At this hour?" Her voice rang with triumph and something very near hysteria. "Well! I told you all! Did I not say he would come to his senses? Oh, Jane, this must be in your honor!"

"*Mama!*" Jane hissed, mortified.

But Mrs. Bennet was undeterred. "He has repented, I am sure of it! Blind he may have been these six months, but no man could stay blind forever when confronted with such beauty. Oh, I *knew* you could not be so lovely for nothing!" She gave Jane a look so pointed it might have left a bruise.

Jane's blush bloomed instantly. Elizabeth, watching from across the table, wanted to bury her face in her hands in secondary embarrassment.

Mr. Collins cleared his throat loudly, his expression twitching between confusion and indignation. "Mr. Bingley?" he repeated. "At Longbourn? Without invitation? At breakfast?"

Mrs. Bennet fluffed her skirts, pinched her cheeks, and fluttered toward the hall. "Well, he shall have it now, sir! We are not so high in the instep as to turn away a man of such fortune. I say, he may have all the eggs and ham from the larder if it keeps him here long enough to effect his purpose!"

A moment later, Mr. Bingley was ushered into the dining room looking exactly as he always did—sunny, affable, entirely unbothered by the rules of decorum he had just trampled.

"Good morning, ladies!" he said cheerfully. "I hope I am not too early? The air was so fine, I thought I should take advantage of it—and then my horse rather insisted we head this direction."

Elizabeth stared at him. His coat was unwrinkled. His cravat was neatly tied. Not a man out for an idle ride—but one with an agenda. And she was no simple country girl, easily led by such tales—she knew a determined gentleman caller when she saw one.

He greeted them all in turn, his gaze lingering on Jane just long enough to make Mrs. Bennet beam and Jane squirm.

Then he settled in beside Mr. Bennet, who looked up from his eggs only long enough to say, "I see you have been conscripted, Mr. Bingley."

Elizabeth's eyes narrowed.

"I—pardon?" Bingley replied, almost too innocently.

Mr. Bennet only gave a small smile and returned to his toast.

Elizabeth did not miss the way Bingley shot a nervous glance at her—then quickly buried himself in conversation with Jane about the garden, the weather, and anything else unlikely to reveal classified intelligence.

Conscripted, indeed. So, this was how Darcy planned to report to the Prince and still keep a close eye on her.

B REAKFAST ENDED IN DUE course, and the entire family gathered in the drawing room, with Mr. Bingley and Mr. Collins each making a dash for the seat nearest Jane—a contest that was only ended when Elizabeth declared that to be *her* favorite seat. Mr. Bingley surrendered cheerfully, Mrs. Bennet frowned, Mr. Bennet chuckled and disappeared into his study for the morning, and that was the end of it.

But then, no one quite knew what to do with themselves. Sunlight spilled through the lace curtains, setting every dust mote aglow and making the faded upholstery look warmer than it deserved. Elizabeth had taken her embroidery in hand—not because she had either the intention or the ability to stitch a single useful thing, but because it offered an excuse to observe Bingley.

He had been perfectly cheerful, of course. Too cheerful. *Suspiciously* cheerful, as though he were not just tolerating the Bennets' company, but was determined to relish it or perish in the attempt. He need say nothing to confirm it for her—Darcy had clearly sent him.

The Bennet household had risen to the occasion. That occasion being Mr. Bingley must not be allowed to leave. Mrs. Bennet simply would not have it, no matter how awkward the conversation or how many hints Collins dropped about wishing to walk into Meryton. Rather, she plied her guest with tittle-tattle and tea and more than one pointed insinuation that Bingley might enjoy the prospect of the room better from the very seat he had surrendered to Elizabeth.

The plan was sound. Elizabeth simply had not anticipated how long a day could be when everyone was playing a role and no one admitted why.

By ten o'clock, Lydia had already suggested two games, demanded one walk, and asked Kitty six times whether officers might call. Kitty had no answers, but this did not stop her from whispering possibilities like a schoolgirl reading tea leaves.

By eleven, Mrs. Bennet had produced a pudding.

"Breakfast is over," Jane had whispered.

"Then it is a midmorning refreshment," Mrs. Bennet had declared, plopping the dish down on a little table beside Bingley with such force the table rattled.

Mr. Bingley, undeterred, beamed at her. "How very delightful, ma'am."

He was going to die here, Elizabeth thought, *and he would be smiling as he did it*.

By noon, even Mary—usually immune to social tension—had looked up from her sermon notes and remarked to Kitty, "This is quite a lot of effort for one man."

Mr. Collins had taken grave offense at that. "It is a great deal of effort for the *wrong* man," he had muttered.

Elizabeth had not missed it. Nor, apparently, had anyone else, but Mr. Bingley kept smiling, anyway.

Now, seated in a half-circle around the drawing room, with a blazing fire they did not need and conversation they did not enjoy, they all suffered together. Jane poured tea. Lydia whispered. Mr. Collins, seated beside the fire like an unmovable statue of pomposity, cleared his throat with theatrical weight.

"I must observe," he began, in the tone of a man who had been waiting far too long to speak, "that it is unusual for a gentleman of no landed estate to remain so long in company without a stated purpose."

Bingley, to his credit, blinked only once. "As to that, I *do* have an estate, sir, even if it was not a hereditary one. More to the point, I had understood my company was welcome, sir."

Mr. Collins sniffed. "It is not my place to determine who is welcome in my esteemed cousins' home. But I must be vigilant, as I am sure Lady Catherine would expect, when a man of no known connections to the family lingers among its unmarried daughters."

Elizabeth set her teacup down with a distinct clink.

"I believe," she said sweetly, "that Mr. Bingley is a favorite neighbor who has often dined under this roof. He is also an old friend of Mr. Darcy, who is a guest of Mr. Bingley's at Netherfield. And as Mr. Darcy has been a frequent and welcome visitor to Longbourn, and both gentlemen share a particular friendship with my uncle Mr. Bennet, I daresay the matter of connection is quite settled."

"I question the wisdom of calling Mr. Darcy welcome," Collins said with a tight little smile. "He may be my honorable patroness's nephew, but he has long disdained to acknowledge it. And now he lurks in Hertfordshire with no stated business and an attitude of entitlement that I, for one, find most unchristian."

Elizabeth's vision sharpened to a dangerous clarity.

"You are free to find fault in whomever you like," she said, "but I must correct the record. Mr. Darcy is in Hertfordshire on his own terms, which need not concern you, and he has behaved with nothing but civility toward this family. As for you, Mr. Collins, it would be well if you remembered that hospitality once extended obligates a guest to discretion."

Mr. Collins flushed. "You presume to rebuke me, Miss Elizabeth?"

"Oh, I should hope not," she said brightly. "I was aiming to insult you outright."

There was a long, pinched silence.

Then Mr. Collins, straightening, turned to Jane. "I do beg your forgiveness, cousin. I had not intended to create unpleasantness. I had merely hoped—" he coughed— "that the affections we once shared might yet endure."

Jane, who had shared precisely nothing but a strained smile, looked confused.

Mrs. Bennet, now glowing with the kind of horror only unprofitable suitors could bring, fluttered a handkerchief. "Oh! Mr. Collins, I am sure Jane is not inclined—"

But Mr. Collins had moved on.

"And speaking of cousins... and attachments... I must confess," he said, "that I had begun to entertain suspicions regarding Miss Elizabeth."

The room fell silent.

"I confess it strange to me. Now, it is true that my father had little contact with the Bennet branch of our family, but he did show me the family lineage on more than one occasion, by way of advising me of my..."

At this juncture, Collins placed a hand over his heart and bowed his head toward a gasping Mrs. Bennet. "That is to say, how the *misfortunes* of one branch of the family created something of a blessing for me. I must say, there was no record of my cousin Daniel Bennet ever having a daughter. And while the resemblance to your family is... plausible, it is hardly conclusive. Moreover, Miss Elizabeth, your manner is, I daresay, nearly as refined as the delightful Miss Anne de Bourgh's. I must question whether such elevated training could have been afforded by so modest a family as my cousin's must be."

Elizabeth could not speak.

"I have made inquiries," Collins went on. "And I have written to my esteemed patroness, Lady Catherine de Bourgh, to ask her advice, both on this matter and that of her profligate nephew ingratiating himself among unsuspecting families. She is most shrewd in such matters. I expect her express reply within the next day or two."

Elizabeth opened her mouth.

And found she had nothing to say.

Nothing that would satisfy Jane's soft, uncertain eyes watching her across the room. Nothing that would explain the burn rising in her cheeks or the sudden ache in her chest.

"I am certain," she said finally, "that any doubts you may hold will be answered in time."

Her voice was too quiet. Her lie was too thin.

Jane knew.

Of course she did. And Elizabeth, who could deflect nearly anything with charm or laughter, felt herself shrink under the weight of that silent, gentle gaze.

Bingley, who had been staring at the hearth as though trying to crawl into it, suddenly turned. "You wrote to Lady Catherine?"

His voice was not cheerful now. Not surprised or angry, just... cool. Stripped of its usual warmth. And harder than Elizabeth had ever heard it.

Collins nodded. "Naturally. She will know what is best. And she will likely write to her nephew, if she believes he is acting imprudently."

Elizabeth's head snapped toward Bingley.

The blood had drained from his face.

"You had no right," he said quietly. "None at all."

"I wrote only what I observed," Collins huffed.

"You wrote to a woman who believes herself superior to every soul in England and thinks nothing of making lives miserable when her pride is bruised." Bingley stood. "And you may have placed others in danger for no reason beyond your own wounded vanity."

"My—! Danger? Sir, I—!"

"I think," Bingley said, voice shaking with fury, "that we have had enough entertainment for one day."

He strode to the door to the hallway and yanked it open. Cool air flooded the room.

Elizabeth rose too. She had to leave. Had to think. Besides, Darcy had sent Bingley to watch *her*. If he left—

But Jane caught her wrist gently. "Lizzy," she whispered. "Please."

Elizabeth looked down. Jane's fingers were slender, steady. There was no anger in her expression—only hurt. And perhaps a trace of betrayal.

"Jane," she said quickly, "will you walk with me?"

Jane blinked. "Now?"

"Yes. Please. Just for a moment." Her voice was quiet, urgent. "I will explain."

Jane hesitated only a second before nodding. She rose and joined her without a word.

Elizabeth cast one last look behind her. Collins was sputtering, Lydia had begun whispering furiously to Kitty, and Mrs. Bennet looked torn between rage and triumph. Mr. Bennet, wisely, had disappeared.

Elizabeth turned and followed Bingley out into the sunlight, Jane at her side, and let the door close on whatever fresh outrage Mr. Collins was now shouting behind them.

Chapter Twenty-Two

D ARCY WAS USHERED THROUGH the wrought-iron gates of Carlton House, the Prince Regent's London residence, its neoclassical façade exuding opulence and authority.

Inside, the entrance hall unfolded in a spectacle of extravagance. Walls adorned with intricate gilded moldings rose to meet a ceiling frescoed with scenes of classical mythology. Rich crimson draperies framed towering windows, their heavy tassels swaying gently in the draft. Marble statues stood sentinel in alcoves, their cold gazes indifferent to the human dramas playing out before them.

A liveried footman led Darcy through a series of lavishly appointed rooms, each more ostentatious than the last. They passed through the Gothic Dining Room, its dark wood paneling and vaulted ceilings evoking the solemnity of a cathedral. Sunlight filtered through stained glass, casting kaleidoscopic patterns upon the gleaming floor.

Finally, they arrived at the Blue Drawing Room, a space where the Prince often held informal audiences. The footman announced Darcy's presence with a crisp bow before retreating silently, leaving him to face the Regent alone.

The Prince lounged upon an ornate chaise longue, swathed in a silk dressing gown of deep sapphire, embroidered with golden fleurs-de-lis. His ample form was partially concealed beneath the folds of the luxurious fabric, but there was no mistaking the corpulence that had become his hallmark. In one hand, he cradled a delicate porcelain cup of steaming coffee; in the other, a snuffbox encrusted with jewels that caught the light with every lazy movement.

His gaze lifted as Darcy entered, a slow smile spreading across his florid face. "Ah, Mr. Darcy," he drawled, his voice a rich blend of amusement and condescension. "Come to regale me with tales of your derring-do, have you? Pray, do sit. I find the sight of a man standing so tediously formal."

Darcy inclined his head, suppressing the irritation that threatened to surface. He took the proffered seat, the upholstery yielding beneath him with a sigh.

The Prince regarded him over the rim of his cup, eyes gleaming with something between mischief and malice. "So, tell me, what progress have you made in this sordid affair of Perceval's demise? I do hope you have brought me something more than excuses."

Darcy met the regal gaze evenly. "Your Royal Highness, my investigation has uncovered several leads of significance. The matter is intricate, with threads that extend further than initially anticipated. I respectfully request additional time... and monies... to pursue these avenues thoroughly."

The Prince's smile faded, replaced by a theatrical sigh of boredom. He set down his porcelain cup with a careless clatter and leaned forward, his gown parting to reveal a waistcoat groaning in desperate protest against its fastenings. "Time, Mr. Darcy? Time is what you request? It has been a fortnight since I entrusted you with this task. A Prime Minister is dead, and I have no names, no confessions, no justice to soothe my poor mother's cares about the safety of her family. What, pray, have you been doing with yourself in the countryside? Gardening?"

Darcy's jaw tensed. "Your Highness, I have reason to believe Sir William Cunningham is involved."

That gave the Prince pause. His expression tightened, just slightly, before he masked it with a scoff. "Cunningham? A boor, certainly, but a traitor?"

"And I believe he may be employing a man long presumed dead. Hugh Maddox."

Now the Prince blinked. "Maddox?"

Darcy reached into his coat and produced Elizabeth's drawing. "This likeness was sketched by Lady Elizabeth Montclair."

The Prince's brow creased, and he frowned. "Who?"

Darcy sighed. His Highness could *not* be so inebriated that he had already forgot about Elizabeth.

"The witness, Highness. The Marquess of Ashwick's daughter."

"Oh..." The Prince's features cleared. "Yes, the lady. Cheeky thing. Might make a fetching diversion for... well, never mind. Egad, Darcy, you needn't look so scandalized. I suppose she is still alive?"

"Quite. As I was saying—"

"You seem very assured of that, yet I do not see her with you. You must have seen her recently, then, my good fellow?"

Darcy fought to smother a sigh. "Rather, Your Highness. Yes, she sketched this from her memory of the second gunman. I say it is striking enough in detail to lend it credibility. Does the face look familiar to you?"

The Prince took it with two fingers, as if the paper might soil him. He studied it for a long moment, then frowned. "Never seen the blighter."

Darcy did not move. "Your father gave me a quiet order to investigate Maddox's death three years ago."

The Prince handed the paper back without meeting his gaze. "My father gave orders to a great many people. Usually after supper, and rarely in his right mind."

"His mind was clear that day. Maddox was once a Crown agent, was he not?"

The Prince flapped a hand at the air. "If he was, he is not now. You know how these things go. Men become inconvenient, or inconvenient truths become men." He picked up his snuffbox and tapped it idly against his palm. "And if Maddox is alive, as you claim, why has he not been seen?"

"Because he knows how to vanish when it pleases him. And because those in power are protecting him. Or using him."

"You mean Cunningham, I suppose."

Darcy nodded once. "He and Maddox have history. And political motive. Perceval was tightening control over funding. He may have been getting too close. As for how they got Bellingham to stand in front of Perceval and fire the first shot—well, Your Highness, Bellingham did have his own motives, some of which came out during his trial. But I suspect we might find that Bellingham was threatened, as well. Perhaps his family."

The Prince stood abruptly, robes billowing like a stage curtain. He crossed to the window and stared out, the light outlining the paunch of his figure and the restless tapping of his fingers against the sill. "I brought you into this because you were discreet, Darcy. Useful. Cold-blooded when necessary. Not to serve me riddles wrapped in shadows."

"Then let me finish the work."

The Prince turned, the light now showing a dangerous glint in his eye. "Finish what? It seems you have scarcely made a beginning. Perhaps I should give the task to someone else. Someone more decisive. More... obedient."

Darcy took a single step forward. "And if that someone causes the truth to leak? If it becomes public that Bellingham was coerced? That another man, still free, orchestrated the death of a Prime Minister? What then? How secure is your position, Highness, if foreign papers begin to whisper that the Crown hanged a mere scapegoat?"

The Prince's jaw ticked. He did not like that word—*scapegoat*. Nor the suggestion that his already fragile image could be further smeared.

"You brought me in because I do not blunder. I do not speak. And I do not fail. But I must be allowed to do the job."

A long silence fell. The Prince returned to his seat with exaggerated languor, as if to show he had never truly been rattled. He plucked at a cushion, rearranged his robe, and finally gave a careless wave. "Very well. Another week. But if you do not bring me something—something with teeth, Darcy—I shall install someone else. And you may explain to your pretty witness why the fox is now guarding the henhouse."

Darcy inclined his head, though every muscle in his body itched to bolt from the room. "Thank you, Your Highness."

But as he turned to go, the Prince's voice, suddenly sweet, halted him once more. "Oh, and about your little petition—your charming bid to reclaim that dusty estate of yours..."

Darcy turned back, wary. "Yes, Your Highness?"

The Prince smiled. "I gave it due consideration, of course. Quite touched by your devotion to ancestral rafters and carpets and all that. But alas, my hands are tied. My father's order was very firm, as it always was in such... cases. I might have doubted the credibility of the charges if you yourself could prove unimpeachable, but given how little you have managed to achieve thus far..."

A cold flush washed over Darcy, but he schooled his features into an impassive mask. "Your Highness, the accusations against my father were disproven. Every witness recanted. Every document verified. I have provided ample evidence to that effect."

The Prince chuckled, a low, mirthless sound. "Yes, well, evidence can be so dreadfully dull, don't you think? It is *action* this world wants. Now, do be a splendid fellow and catch this murderer, won't you?"

Darcy's fists clenched at his sides, hidden by the folds of his coat. He bowed stiffly. "As you wish, Your Highness."

T HEY WALKED IN SILENCE for some time, following the worn path behind Long-bourn that led toward the brook. The breeze was mild, and the tall grasses whispered with every step. Elizabeth kept her arms folded, eyes on the ribbon of water ahead, aware of Bingley to her left, Jane quietly between them.

She owed them an explanation.

Bingley had barely spoken since they left the house, though his strides had been purposeful, his jaw tight with residual fury. He had not looked at Elizabeth—not directly—but he had hovered just enough to make clear that he meant to stay between her and any danger, seen or unseen.

Finally, Elizabeth slowed. "This is far enough."

Jane turned to her, brow creased. "Lizzy—what Collins said—he is not a clever man, nor indeed a very agreeable one. You need not explain—"

"No," Elizabeth said, then shook her head. "No, I think I must."

She drew a breath and looked between them. "First, I must thank you. Both of you. For what just happened in that room. I have almost never in my life seen anyone stand up against a slanderer for someone who is not even present as you did for your friend, Mr. Bingley. I daresay it was one of the most... *honest* things I have ever seen."

He shifted on his feet, visibly uncomfortable. "Well. I did not do it for thanks. I did it because Mr. Collins is an insufferable fool."

Jane cast him a look that would have silenced any other man, but Bingley gave her a sheepish smile.

"Truly," Elizabeth said, "I have no doubt that he will make trouble. And I fear it will be directed at your household, Jane."

Jane reached for her hand. "What can he possibly do? I am not worried about that."

"But you should be." Elizabeth hesitated. "Because none of this is simple, and I have not been honest. I was placed with your family under false pretenses. You have shown me nothing but kindness, and in return I have lied."

Jane flinched, but she did not let go.

Bingley stepped forward at last. "Miss Elizabeth, before you say more, may I... explain one thing? Just so we are all clear."

Elizabeth nodded.

"I do not know everything," he admitted, "but I do know that my friend—Darcy—was tasked somehow with ensuring your protection. I know that he did not want to involve the Bennet family, but it became the best of a poor set of choices."

"You... know that much?"

"I was told just enough to be useful," Bingley said, lips quirking upward. "And given to understand that if I failed to remain at Longbourn for the entire day, Mr. Darcy would be forced to find a new friend."

Elizabeth gave a small, surprised laugh.

Jane's eyes were wide. "Then you... you are not here to..." She cleared her throat. "Well, to court me?"

"What?" Bingley blinked. "Oh. Well—" He flushed. "I would be most honored to—well, that is—I had hoped to—but not today! I mean, not as a ruse. Never as a ruse."

Elizabeth covered her mouth to keep from laughing.

Jane gave him a look of such confused warmth that Bingley visibly forgot what he had been saying.

Elizabeth cleared her throat. "Well, I shall let you two sort that out later. As to Mr. Collins' insinuations... yes. He is right. I am not Daniel Bennet's daughter. I never heard of the man before I came here."

Jane flinched again and glanced at Bingley, as if seeking some support. "Oh."

"My true name is Lady Elizabeth Montclair. My father is the Marquess of Ashwick. You may have heard of him. Most people have."

Bingley's brows rose, and a soft, "Ah," escaped him, but he said nothing else.

"I was in London on May eleventh. The day of Prime Minister Perceval's murder—I had left my friends, sneaked into the House of Commons to catch a glimpse of... well, *that* hardly bears repeating. I saw Perceval shot—I saw Bellingham... and I saw someone else."

By this time, Bingley was clamping his teeth into his upper lip as if biting back words, and Jane's face had gone rather pale. "Someone... else?" she asked.

"Bellingham's pistol misfired, or... or something. He was right there—so close, and Perceval jerked when the gunshot rang out. But the shot failed... I do not know exactly how. The second man's, however, did not."

"Second man!" Bingley exclaimed.

Elizabeth paused to close her eyes. "He was behind a pillar, waiting—I think he meant to shoot Bellingham if he failed to carry the deed out, but it was Perceval he shot in the end. The shots were less than a heartbeat apart, so tight it might have sounded like a ricochet or an echo of the first blast to others. But the man saw me, gaping at him as he was putting his gun away. He stared straight back at me... saw my face, as surely as I saw his."

"Good Lord," Bingley breathed. "That... explains a great deal."

Elizabeth swallowed and lifted one shoulder. "Anyway, because of that—because I have a fearful habit of wandering from where I ought to be and seeing and doing what I should not—I have been hunted. They set fire to my chambers in my father's house, captured my maid... I am only 'lucky' because I was no longer there when they struck."

Jane's hand flew to her mouth.

"It was not my choice to be placed with your family. I had no say in the matter. Mr. Darcy was charged with keeping me safe, and when he had no other options, he brought me here and bade me to behave myself... for once in my life. I... I never meant to lie to you." Tears filled her eyes. "And I never meant to put your family in danger. I am sorry."

Jane reached for her and pulled her into an embrace, holding her tightly. "You silly, brave, impossible creature," she whispered. "Of course I knew you were lying."

Elizabeth froze. "You did?"

Jane laughed softly. "Not about everything. But enough. I know very well Uncle Daniel never had children. His wife was so often ill, poor creature. But Papa vouched for you, so I never pressed. And Lizzy, you said once that you did not like tea, but I have seen you drink three cups in a row just to avoid conversation. And I am rather certain you were inebriated the day you first came to Longbourn, yet I have not seen you touch a drop since. That is not the behavior of a normal girl."

Elizabeth let out a watery laugh. "And I thought *I* was the sly one, but all along, you were a step ahead of me."

"You were never our cousin," Jane said, cupping her cheek fondly. "But you were always our Lizzy. And I loved you like a sister from the first day."

Bingley cleared his throat awkwardly. "If I may... this is all quite touching, but if matters are as you say, Miss... egad, I am not even sure what to call you."

Elizabeth tried to laugh again, but it came out as a near-sob. "Mr. Darcy calls me 'that impossible woman,' I am quite sure. You may as well do the same."

Bingley gave a vague smile and a shake of his head. "I think you might be surprised... but no matter. Perhaps we should return to the house before Mrs. Bennet sends out a search party. Or Heaven forbid, sends Mr. Collins."

Elizabeth nodded, glancing over her shoulder. "You are right. Mr. Darcy warned me against exposing myself where I could be harmed, and we are rather far from the house."

"Do you think he will truly write to Lady Catherine?" Jane asked.

"I am certain of it," Bingley said grimly. "And if she takes it upon herself to interfere..." He trailed off, his face darkening.

Elizabeth frowned. "Why would she? Surely she has no influence over what Mr. Darcy does."

"Oh, she believes she does," Bingley said. "And that belief, unfortunately, is a danger in itself."

Elizabeth tilted her head. "I know she is Mr. Darcy's aunt, but she lives in Kent and he is a grown man. Why would her 'disapproval' matter in the least? And... and why would Collins call him... *indecent?* From what I have seen, he is the farthest thing from it."

At that, Bingley shifted uncomfortably, pulled off his hat and ran a hand through his hair. "That tale is mostly Darcy's to tell," he said. "And he would likely disown me for even speaking this much. But since we are already so far down the road of shocking revelations..."

He sighed. "His family once held a title—his father was the Eighth Earl of Pemberley. Wealth. And land. A great deal of both, in fact. Pemberley is... good heavens, I saw it once, and I still think it the fairest estate in all of England. But it belongs to another now—not even a proper relation, but a family endowed by chance or favor. All of it stripped away and given to a miscreant by royal order."

Jane gasped softly. "Stripped? By the Crown?"

"That... that is not done lightly," Elizabeth murmured.

"Indeed, but it was done to the Darcys," Bingley said. "Unjustly, I assure you. The charges were... well, grievous, to be sure, but entirely false. Still, it was a fearful scandal—one I am not at liberty to explain. Darcy was away at Eton when it all began. He had no hand in it. But people like Lady Catherine"—he scowled— "never forget such things. Or forgive them. Particularly not when she imagines herself the sole guardian of propriety in England."

"And Collins?" Elizabeth wondered.

"Oh, Collins parrots whatever she says. If Lady Catherine declared Mr. Darcy a pirate, Collins would be drawing maps by morning."

"But why now?" Elizabeth asked. "What could she think to do to him now, of all times?"

"Embarrass him, I should think. Make him enough of a spectacle that anyone will think twice before being seen with him. She has done it before. Darcy and I were on holiday in Bath two years ago and when she heard of it, she sent a single letter to some friend of hers and by the next day, neither of us were admitted to the Pump Room. It is all because she once thought Darcy would eventually marry her daughter, you see, and when the family was disgraced, I suppose she could not peddle her daughter's virtue elsewhere, so they remain at Rosings as two bitter creatures, each so weary of the other's face that they must seek their entertainment by the post."

"So... she would see all Meryton turn against him," Jane murmured. "That is a pity. Most people in town were just learning to like him. It must be hard for the poor man to make friends."

"I am afraid it is worse than that." Bingley glanced at Elizabeth and his fists flexed as he swallowed. "Darcy cannot afford any sort of particular attention. Not now. Not when he is already working under royal sanction, and certainly not while trying to keep you alive. He needs to blend in, like any other man. To be unobtrusive."

He met her eyes. "Darcy knows your location is no longer a secret, but so far, he believes *his* connection to you has remained secure, which buys him time and a bit of leverage. But Lady Catherine's idea of 'loyalty and duty' is to shout his name from the rooftops while denouncing his every move. If she arrives in Meryton waving a letter from Collins... well. The quiet is over."

Elizabeth stared at him. "Then the hunt begins."

"Yes," Bingley said softly. "And we will all be caught in it."

D ARCY FOUND COLONEL FITZWILLIAM in his flat, coatless, cravat hanging loose, and sleeves rolled to the elbow as he bent over a sprawl of papers that would have given most clerks vertigo.

"You look entirely too cheerful for a man elbow-deep in Home Office filth," Darcy said, closing the door behind him.

Fitzwilliam looked up and grinned. "Do not let the candlelight fool you. I am wallowing in moral decay."

Darcy sank into the armchair opposite. "Any news of Alice?"

The grin slipped. Fitzwilliam set down his pen and folded his arms. "Some. Not enough. I have intelligence that she is alive—or was, as of three days past."

"Three days ago? What does that mean?"

"There is rumor she escaped. Slipped her guards near Brighton. Possibly headed north, though it is difficult to track a girl with no friends, no money, and a name she probably dares not give."

Darcy pressed his lips together. "So she is alone."

"If she is the one these reports refer to," Fitzwilliam said carefully. "There were no clear identifiers, but it matches what we know."

"No ransom demand. No threats. No message of any kind," Darcy said. "They did not want her alive, did they?"

Fitzwilliam gave a tight nod. "She was not the target. And either she knew nothing of value, or she already told them what she could. I expect they were taking her somewhere to make her disappear."

Darcy exhaled slowly. "Let us hope she proves as elusive as her mistress."

Fitzwilliam cracked his knuckles and leaned forward. "Now. Cunningham. Anything new there?"

"Perhaps." Darcy pulled a folded paper from his inner coat and handed it across the desk. "That sketch again. Take another look."

Fitzwilliam gave it a glance, then paused. "Am I supposed to recognize this devil? I already told you—"

"Do you recall that business with Hugh Maddox? Disappeared three years ago. Any chance this could be him?'

Richard turned the drawing in the light. Squinted. "Devil take it... that *might* be him."

"You think so?"

"The jawline is right. Hairline, too. I never met Maddox, but I once saw him riding out with Lord Beresford's company near Portsmouth—couple of years before he disappeared."

Darcy's brow rose. "Do you recall the miniature?"

Fitzwilliam snorted. "Painted by some society wife's cousin, if memory serves. She also painted pigs with cherubic faces. Not exactly known for anatomical fidelity."

"That explains a great deal."

Fitzwilliam studied the drawing once more. "If Maddox lives—and if he is with Cunningham—then we are not just dealing with a scandal. We are dealing with state treason at a level I have never seen before."

Darcy nodded once. "And I have spoken with Eddleton."

"The clerk who left breadcrumbs in the Treasury?"

"Shell accounts. Regular payments. From a fund tied to the Auxiliary Services, funneled through charities and printing houses—every one of them linked to Cunningham's known associates."

Fitzwilliam exhaled slowly, brows drawn together. "He gave you this himself?"

Darcy nodded. "Two days ago. We met at an inn—privately. He was nervous. Said someone had broken into his flat. Drawers opened. Ink spilled. Nothing taken. A warning."

"And?"

Darcy's jaw tensed. "He handed me the ledgers and left through the back. I told him not to return home. To go to ground."

Fitzwilliam glanced away. "Then you should know—yesterday morning, a body was pulled from the Thames. No identification. The coroner marked it vagrant, possibly suicide. But—" He hesitated. "One of your sources, Tibbs, was at the docks. Said the man wore a Treasury seal under his coat. Described him as thin, anxious. Brown coat. Frayed cuffs."

Darcy was silent.

"I cannot confirm it was Eddleton," Fitzwilliam said, more gently. "But I am fairly certain it was."

Darcy pressed a hand to his temple. "He was only trying to help."

"They always are," Fitzwilliam murmured.

A brittle silence fell between them.

Then Fitzwilliam asked, "Do you think the Prince will investigate it?"

Darcy's mouth twisted. "His Highness suggested I was... failing him. Then laughed off the entire affair over a plate of candied almonds."

Fitzwilliam gave a short, mirthless laugh.

Darcy looked up. "And then he threatened to pull me off the case. Replace me with someone quicker. More obedient."

Fitzwilliam's expression darkened. "He would not."

"He would," Darcy said flatly. "And he might. If only to be rid of the discomfort. But that would leave her exposed."

Fitzwilliam swore again. "Well, what came of it?"

Darcy stood and crossed to the window. "I convinced him to give me more time. Barely."

"You should stay in London," Fitzwilliam said. "You can push this through from the inside. Leverage my contacts. Use your resources at the Home Office. Turn up enough proof to make a scandal irrelevant."

"I cannot."

Fitzwilliam turned in his chair. "Why not?"

Darcy's gaze did not leave the window. "Her location has been compromised. I left Bingley in my place for the day, but I must return."

"Bingley," Fitzwilliam repeated. "You left Bingley in charge of an assassination witness. I would not trust him with a plate of jellied scones."

"Better him than a regiment," Darcy muttered. "He smiles too much to be suspicious."

Fitzwilliam raised both brows. "Well, that answers part of what you never told me. So, she is in Meryton, eh?"

"I have set a trap," Darcy said. "If someone moves to silence her, I intend to be there to catch them."

Fitzwilliam nodded slowly. "So the lady is no longer just a witness."

Darcy turned. "What is that supposed to mean?"

Fitzwilliam's expression was maddeningly neutral. "It means that you have never gone to such lengths for any other informant."

"She is *not* an informant," Darcy snapped. "She is an innocent woman—"

Fitzwilliam grinned. "And we are back to the part where you're pretending not to be smitten."

Darcy stiffened. "I am not—"

"You are," Fitzwilliam said, leaning back. "You would not be this defensive if you were not."

"I am not some besotted idiot drooling over the first fine pair of eyes to look my way. She is reckless. Infuriating. Entirely unsuited to the role she has been forced to play. I am simply doing my duty to protect—"

Fitzwilliam waved a hand. "Yes, yes. Your sacred duty. Just admit she has you twisted round her little finger and save us both the agony."

Darcy's glare was eloquent.

"Very well," Fitzwilliam said, unrepentant. "Deny it. But you are riding into the lion's den with barely a sword, and you are doing it for *her*, not some vain hope—misguided, I am sorry to say—of restoring Pemberley."

"I am doing it for England," Darcy said coldly.

Fitzwilliam chuckled. "Of course. God save the King and all that. Do try not to get yourself shot."

Darcy picked up his gloves. "That would be terribly inconvenient."

He was nearly at the door when Fitzwilliam said quietly, "I will make inquiries in the regiments. If Maddox is out there, someone has seen his shadow."

Darcy paused. "Thank you."

"Send word the moment you reach Meryton," Fitzwilliam said. "I will do the same the moment Alice surfaces. Or Cunningham slips."

Darcy nodded and was gone.

CHAPTER TWENTY-THREE

D ARCY ARRIVED AT NETHERFIELD long past twilight, his hired horse blown and
his coat dusty from the road. He had traveled hard and fast, and every bone in his
body felt it. The sun had already vanished beyond the trees as he dismounted, muscles
aching with the stiffness of a long day's ride. He passed his reins to a sleepy stableboy and
strode into the house, bracing himself for the laconic cheer of a country drawing room.

Instead, he was greeted by the butler with a blink and a bow—and unexpected news.

"Mr. Darcy. We did not expect you until tomorrow. I am afraid Bingley has not yet
returned, sir."

Darcy paused on the threshold, one brow raised. "Not at all?"

"No, sir. He departed for Longbourn before breakfast and has not been seen since."

Darcy exhaled slowly, lips pressed together in something dangerously close to a smile.
"Very good," he said. "I shall wait for him in the study."

He did not even bother removing his coat. He poured himself a glass of something
brandied and stood before the hearth with it untouched in his hand, waiting. When
Bingley finally did return, the clock in the hall had struck half-past ten.

His friend entered with the flush of wind and candlelight, his coat flung back, his hair
askew from a ride taken at more than gentlemanly speed.

"You look half-murdered," Bingley said cheerfully. "Have you eaten?"

"No," Darcy said. "Nor, I presume, have you."

Bingley grinned. "Not in any way Mrs. Bennet would consider adequate, no."

"I take it our Miss Elizabeth did not attempt to give you the slip today?"

Bingley shook his head. "No, no, quite sedate and well-behaved, in that regard. I expect
she is even now retiring to bed, so no gallivanting the countryside for your wayward miss."

Darcy's posture relaxed slightly, and he set down his untouched drink. "And? Did he
do it?"

"Eh?"

"The parson. I assume he wrote to my aunt and is rather proud of himself for it."

"Collins?" Bingley sighed, tossing his gloves onto a side table. "Yes. He admitted it this afternoon, and I do not think he regrets it."

Darcy's jaw tensed. "I expected as much," he said. "Did he... say anything else? To *them*, I mean."

Bingley hesitated. "I am not sure that he even knows the full truth, but he certainly hinted. Nothing explicit. Nothing that would make too many ripples in polite society, but enough that Miss Bennet looked ready to bite through her teacup, and Miss Elizabeth was set to lob hers at his head."

Darcy frowned. "I expected he would scold or insult—he is always insufferable—but nothing more."

Bingley hesitated. "There *was* more."

Darcy's head turned sharply. "More?"

"Not about you, this time, but about Miss Elizabeth. He was rather put out that she defended your honor in public, so he decided to attack *her* credibility."

Darcy stiffened. Elizabeth had... defended him? That almost pained him more than if she had denounced him outright. "What did Collins say?"

"He said," Bingley began, choosing his words carefully, "that he never believed she was a Bennet cousin. Claimed Daniel Bennet never wrote of children, and that Miss Elizabeth's manner did not match her supposed upbringing."

Darcy stared at him. "He said that in front of the family?"

Bingley nodded grimly. "In front of everyone. Loudly enough that Mrs. Bennet nearly choked on her tea."

Darcy's gaze darkened. "And how did that fall upon Mrs. Bennet's ears?"

"She was ready to throw him out of the house," Bingley said with a small, dry smile. "Well, that was how we found matters when we came back. I am afraid I quite lost my temper as well, and the ladies and I... we took some air for a bit."

Darcy swallowed the rest of his drink without tasting it, without even seeing the glass. "Well? Where stand matters?'

"Oh, Mr. Bennet smoothed it over. Something about Elizabeth being sent to live with some wealthy aunt as a child because her mother's health could not manage the raising of a small babe, and that she had only lately returned. It was nonsense, but plausible nonsense. Enough for Mrs. Bennet, for she was instantly distracted by the notion of a 'wealthy aunt' she never heard of before and forgot entirely about the lady's parentage. I doubt Collins will actually accept that, though."

Darcy turned away, pacing a step. He had counted on Collins's ignorance. That veil was now torn. "What of the sisters? Will any of them talk?"

Bingley's smile gentled. "The younger sisters? They believed what their father told them. But Miss Bennet already knew."

Darcy whirled. "How?"

"She is more perceptive than either of us gave her credit for, I suppose. She said she always knew something was off. But today, when we were out walking, Miss Elizabeth told her everything."

Darcy's brows lifted. "Everything? As in... *everything?*"

"Everything pertinent, I suppose."

Darcy heaved a sigh. "So. You know the truth, too."

Bingley chewed his lip and sucked in a breath. "Yes."

Darcy nodded and paced away.

"You need not have hidden so much," Bingley said softly. "I would have helped you more, had I known."

"I know."

"But I understand why you did. The more people who know..."

Darcy nodded once. "Indeed."

Then Bingley chuckled. "Well, I suppose one good thing came of today... I have changed my mind."

Darcy blinked and turned around. "About what?"

"About the lady."

Darcy's shoulders straightened. "Which lady? Miss Elizabeth?"

Bingley smiled like a man with a secret too fine to keep. "No! Miss Jane Bennet."

Darcy's stomach uncurled, and his mouth twitched. "Ah."

"I have secured her blessing to court her. And her father's, and, naturally, her mother's. I will be calling often—*very* often, I hope."

Darcy tried for a smile, but he had burned through every ounce of warmth in London. What emerged was a faint, tired curve of the mouth. "I told you that you misread her."

"You did," Bingley agreed. "And I am very glad I listened."

Darcy reached for the brandy again, this time with purpose. "I am pleased for you, Charles."

Bingley clapped him on the shoulder. "Go to bed. You look like death. I will see you in the morning."

T HE HOUSE HAD FINALLY settled.

Dishes had been cleared, chairs straightened, and Mr. Collins—thankfully—had taken himself off to bed after yet another long-winded grace. Now only the low creak of floorboards overhead and the distant ticking of the hall clock gave any sign of life beyond the drawing room, where Elizabeth sat with Jane in comfortable quiet.

A pile of half-folded linen rested between them. Jane was methodical—neat corners, soft hands. Elizabeth's pile had already toppled twice, and the sheet in her lap had somehow acquired a corner torn along the seam. She blamed Collins. No one could fold after a dinner like that.

But the quiet was welcome. Needed, even.

"I used to dream of a house like this," Elizabeth murmured. "Warm. Noisy. A little unkempt."

Jane smiled faintly. "Unkempt is kind. You have seen Mama's ribbon drawer."

"I have seen her kitchen." Elizabeth smirked. "I am fairly certain your cook keeps a poultry ledger more meticulous than the Home Office."

Jane laughed—a soft, surprised thing—and folded another pillowcase. "Hill is efficient, but I think it is rather *in spite* of Mama than *because* of her."

Elizabeth snorted a silent chuckle, then went still, her eyes glazing a little as she watched Jane's hands. "My father's house is beautiful," she mused. "Marble floors. Carved panels. A garden so vast we once lost a French tutor in the yew maze for half a day."

Jane looked up, one brow raised in curiosity. "It sounds lovely."

"But cold," Elizabeth added. "And too quiet."

Jane chuckled and tossed her folded linens aside. "I did not know such a thing could exist."

Elizabeth shook her head. "My mother could not bear it. She left for Devonshire when I was nine. She said she would rather listen to seagulls than my father's opinions. I visited her, of course. Back and forth, for a time. And she comes to London on occasion—she was there when I was presented at Court. But neither of them... truly wanted company. Certainly not mine."

Jane's face softened with sympathy.

"I was not neglected," Elizabeth said quickly. "Not really. I had governesses and chaperones. I had all the tutors I could ask for, a private education worthy of a son rather than a daughter. I was introduced. Danced. Made friends." She paused. "But friends cannot replace family. Not forever."

"Surely your parents care for you," Jane supplied hopefully. "Not all are capable of expressing their feelings, but I cannot think they were entirely ambivalent toward you."

Elizabeth lifted one shoulder. "No, I was useful. Sometimes. Mother would send me lists of things to look for when I went shopping, Father would use my friendships to strengthen his alliances..."

"Surely there was more than that!"

Elizabeth looked down, fingering a loose thread on the coverlet. "I doubt my mother even knows I am not in London. As for my father, he has supposedly received letters purporting to be from me as I am out 'on holiday,' and I doubt he has bothered to notice the handwriting is not mine."

Jane fell silent.

Elizabeth glanced toward the fire, where the last coals glowed faint and red. "I must confess, Jane, I thought it would be fearfully dull and provincial when Mr. Darcy insisted I was to come here. I thought I would be bored into a stupor. Instead I found noise. Laughter. Kitty and Lydia arguing over jam. Your mother shouting across the garden for Mary to put down that dreadful book before she trips over the cat."

Jane ducked her head, trying not to smile. "Mama is... dramatic sometimes."

"Your mother may be dramatic, Jane, but she cares about you. Desperately."

The smile faded into something gentler. "She does."

"I envy you that," Elizabeth whispered.

They fell to staring at the fire in silence.

A few minutes later, as Elizabeth stood to take the bundle to the hallway, Mr. Bennet stepped in through the side door—book in one hand, slippers scuffing quietly on the rug.

"Ladies," he said with a mild nod.

"Papa." Jane rose, brushing a thread from her sleeve.

"Mr. Bennet." Elizabeth bobbed a slight curtsy, linen still in her arms.

He eyed the pile with a touch of mock suspicion. "You have not taken to housemaid duties, I hope. I shall be forced to speak to Hill about exploitation."

Elizabeth offered a crooked smile. "I suspect Hill would say it is I who require the supervision."

"She would not be wrong." He approached the hearth and tapped a finger against the mantel, as if checking for dust. Then his eyes flicked back to Elizabeth. "You are well?" he asked quietly.

"I am," she said, surprised by how much she meant it.

He nodded once. "Good. Then I shall not worry until I must." A glance at Jane. "Which I am sure will be sometime tomorrow."

"Papa."

He patted Jane's hand, turned back toward the door, and ambled out without another word.

Elizabeth stood still for a moment, listening to the familiar sound of his uneven gait retreating down the hall.

The home was not hers. The name was not hers. Nothing about this life was meant to last.

And yet—when the door closed behind him—she felt, for the first time in her life, as though she belonged.

May 29, 1812

D ARCY HAD BUILT THE network years ago, brick by brick, favor by favor, until it stretched like a silent lattice beneath the polished surface of respectable England. It had begun during a quiet inquiry into the forgery ring that nearly unseated a viscount—and grown in complexity with every mission the Crown had entrusted to him since. He had learned early that success in this work depended not only on discretion in action, but in the company one chose to trust.

So, he had trusted almost no one.

His informants were as disparate as they were discreet—post riders, ostlers, taproom boys, stable hands, innkeepers who kept two ledgers, and messengers who asked no questions. None of them knew more than a sliver. None knew they were part of a whole. Each had been paid in coin, favor, or silence, and each was instructed to pass their information only to a courier bearing a false name, at a false hour, their faces concealed.

This was not a web—it was a maze. And only Darcy knew the shape of it.

By Friday morning, the pieces began to arrive.

One report from a stable east of St. Albans: a red coach, lacquered but not new, had changed horses under cover of rain. The ostler noted its trim—black piping, nothing else—and said the driver had looked wrong for a gentleman's servant. Shifty. Too thin. A southern accent.

More curious still, the driver had asked for directions to the road west—not toward London, but Oxfordshire.

Two towns over, one of Fitzwilliam's men, posing as a common traveler with a toothache and an urgent parcel, had seen the same coach again before dusk. Still no passengers. Still silent.

The bait had worked.

They were chasing a ghost, and now, Fitzwilliam had tails on them.

Darcy spread the notes across the writing desk in his room at Netherfield, eyes flicking from one detail to the next. The paper was cheap, the ink smudged, but the pattern was unmistakable. Someone had taken the hint embedded in Elizabeth's letter—had seen the name "St. Albans" and moved in haste.

He could not know for certain if it was Maddox. But it could not be coincidence. No one else would have the means or the motive to react so quickly. Perhaps a proxy. Perhaps Maddox himself. Either way, it meant the game had changed.

He reached for a fresh sheet and composed his reply to Fitzwilliam in a hand so tight and controlled it barely resembled his own.

> New directives: any further sightings of the red coach were to be recorded, not intercepted. Let them run. Let them believe they were gaining ground. Let them think the quarry just ahead.

Darcy sealed the letter with wax, pressed no signet, and handed it off to the groom with careful instructions.

Only then did he let himself sit back in the chair and close his eyes, just for a moment. They were chasing a ghost. But it was better than being hunted by one.

HE DID NOT LEAVE Netherfield that day. The storm clouds that threatened the horizon had not yet broken, but he could feel them gathering at his back, every hour wasted a provocation to fate. Still, he stayed.

He wrote letters and burned half of them.

Missives to his associates at the Home Office—he had his regular duties to pay heed to as well—inquiries to lesser informants...

...A half-started note to Elizabeth he should never have considered writing... He crumpled that one and then, not satisfied, threw it in the fire and waited until it was ash.

At one point, he found himself composing a dry, formal warning to the innkeeper in St. Albans who had reported the red coach—only to ball it up, too, and hurl it into the grate before it reached its third line. There was no reason to warn the man. No one knew the trail had been laid but those he trusted. And yet he could not shake the feeling that they were all standing atop a cracked floor, waiting for it to give.

He stood long at the window, watching the road to Longbourn, arms folded tight across his chest.

Caroline Bingley discovered him there just after noon, sweeping into the study without so much as a knock. She wore a muslin dress that fluttered as she walked—carefully chosen, no doubt, to draw the eye—and carried a deck of cards in one hand.

"I declare, Mr. Darcy, if you remain posted at that window much longer, you shall be mistaken for a governess waiting on the post," she said with a lyrical laugh. "Come, do let me distract you. I am positively dying of tedium, and Charles has been no help at all—off chasing pheasants with the steward or some such thing."

"I am occupied," Darcy said without turning.

"Then let me be occupied with you. Whist? A stroll in the orangery? I have heard the roses are nearly in bloom." She came to his side and peered out the window. "You know, I have often thought roses are quite vulgar when left to their own devices. Rather like some people, do you not agree?"

"Caroline," came Bingley's voice from the hall, all affable warning and just enough steel. "There you are."

"Oh, dear," she sighed. "I thought you were out, Charles."

"Not all day. You are needed in the drawing room. Louisa is searching for you to advise on the new pianoforte arrangement."

Caroline blinked. "The pianoforte—? But she—"

"Now, if you please." His tone did not shift, but it was final.

She hesitated, casting a glance between them—then turned on her heel and swept out, muttering something about the tyranny of being useful.

Bingley stepped in behind her, his expression apologetic and faintly amused. He gave Darcy a conspiratorial smile and crossed to the door, speaking low to a waiting footman.

"See that Mr. Darcy is not disturbed again," he said. "By anyone."

The footman bowed, and Bingley clapped his friend once on the shoulder before departing, whistling.

Darcy exhaled heavily and returned to the window.

Longbourn remained out of sight, hidden behind the sweep of trees and the rolling hedge. But he could see the path that led there. See the cart that trundled by at midday. The dust kicked by an afternoon rider. The slow progress of a shepherd's flock across the distant pasture.

He asked himself, more than once, what the devil he thought he was doing.

This was not Pemberley. These were not his affairs. Elizabeth Bennet—no, *Lady Elizabeth Montclair*—was not *truly* his to guard... certainly not indefinitely. She was the daughter of a marquess, destined for some viscount or duke or, God help her, a political attaché with a gift for boredom. What right had he to pace like a sentry, to chase rumors and rearrange the chessboard of his life for the sake of a woman whose trust he had not even earned?

But he stayed.

And when the sun dipped low, he made ready to ride. Not for reconnaissance. Not for strategy.

He needed to see for himself that she was safe.

B Y NIGHTFALL, THE AIR had turned cool and damp. Clouds veiled the stars and turned the sky to ink. The wind moved low through the fields, brushing over the grass with a hush, as if the earth itself were holding its breath.

He rode out alone.

No servant. No house crest on his saddle. Just an ordinary brown gelding and a dark riding cloak. He did not take the main road. He had no wish to be seen. Instead, he followed the edge of a copse to the west, where the trees pressed close and the fence line curved along the rise of a shallow hill.

From there, he could see the house.

Longbourn stood quiet in the distance, its sharp roofline softened by the dark. Two windows glowed gently above the parlor—golden and warm in the night. Jane Bennet's, he guessed. And Elizabeth's, since Collins' arrival necessitated that they share.

She would be preparing for bed.

Perhaps she was brushing out her hair, grumbling about "those dratted curls" again—the ones that gave her a crown of so many intricate luxuries that he had yet to glance at them without losing his breath.

Perhaps she was reading by firelight, her brow drawn, her lips twitching faintly at the margin of some inner thought. Perhaps she was already asleep, her hands tucked under her cheek the way he had seen her once before, after that first mad dash out of London. He had not meant to watch her then, either.

But he watched now.

There were no figures in the windows. No movement. No sign of unrest. Just the quiet of a house at peace.

He stayed in the shadows a long time.

It was absurd, and he knew it. For tonight, at least, she was safer than she had been in weeks. The trap had worked—the letter had drawn attention. Fitzwilliam's men and his own informants were reporting in regular intervals. Longbourn had not been breached. No stranger had been seen on the road.

And yet, he could not leave.

He had hardly slept the night before. His limbs ached from a full day in the saddle, followed by a day of idleness at his desk. His shoulders ached worse. His eyes stung, and he still carried the scent of coal smoke from the Prince's insufferable study in his clothes.

But this—this silent vigil under a moonless sky—felt more vital than anything else he had done. More necessary than any report, any strategy, any gallows-bound theory.

She was in there—and now, at least, she trusted him.

He thought of what Bingley had told him—about Collins, about the things that had been said in that drawing room. Elizabeth was not stupid. She would begin to think things... ponder things... Egad, how had she not already put it all together?

Still, she had stayed, heeded his words, because he had asked her to.

He had no claim to her. Not as a protector, not as a suitor. Not even as a friend. He was only the man who was supposed to keep her head on top of her shoulders until another could claim her hand.

He shifted slightly in the saddle, his hands tight on the reins. The gelding snorted and shook his head.

He had no right to want her.

But want her, he did. Every time she turned her head toward him with fire in her eyes, every time she caught him staring and said nothing, every time she had stood unflinching while the world shifted beneath her feet—he had felt it pulling him closer, past reason, past restraint.

He would not act on it. Not ever. She deserved better than a man in exile from his own name, with no title, no standing, no future to offer but disgrace. She was the daughter of a marquess. He was nothing now, but a tarnished tool the Crown found convenient.

And yet—God help him—he could not rule his heart.

He watched those two golden windows from the safety of the trees, unmoving, unblinking, as if something in the candlelight might speak to him.

He knew what was coming.

The letter trap had bought them a little time, but not enough. Once Lady Catherine's reply arrived, the story Collins had started would blaze through Meryton. Elizabeth's false identity would not hold. His own would be dragged into the light beside it.

They would have to run. And soon.

But not tonight.

Tonight, he only watched. And for a moment—just a moment—he let himself imagine that he belonged there, too.

CHAPTER TWENTY-FOUR

May 30, 1812

LONGBOURN WAS IN CHAOS.

Ribbons trailed over chairs, bonnets dangled from banisters, and the scent of lavender starch clung to every hem as the Bennet household prepared to descend upon Meryton's annual Planting Festival—a yearly affair where country manners collided with town gossip and no one's waistcoat escaped unwrinkled.

"I need my green gloves!" Lydia cried from somewhere upstairs. "Not the yellow—Kitty, did you take them?"

Kitty's voice echoed back. "Why would I want your ridiculous gloves? You sit in the grass and then cry when they stain!"

Mrs. Bennet was in rare form, fluttering between rooms and demanding that someone pin her brooch straighter. "The festival will be half-wasted if we do not arrive before the Netherfield party," she declared. "And I want us seen. All of us! Even you, Mary, though heaven knows you will scowl your way through the flower carts. Lizzy, *do* try to smile—oh, I shall have to introduce you to Mrs. Long and Mrs. Purvis..."

Elizabeth stood in the corner of her room, twisting the tie of her bonnet with a reluctant hand.

"It will not kill you to smile," Jane said, adjusting a pearl-tipped pin above her ear. "The festival is harmless, and Mama has been planning our arrival for more than a week."

Elizabeth gave her a dry look. "So has Napoleon. That does not make me eager to march into battle."

Jane suppressed a smile. "Hardly a battle. It is only a village fête."

"A fête where half the guests think I am someone I am not, and the other half wonder why no one has asked. Forgive me if I do not thrill to the prospect of parsnip displays and curious glances."

"No one doubts you, Lizzy, and before you protest, let me remind you that nobody listens to Collins. You are being dramatic."

Elizabeth turned from the mirror. "I am being strategic. I spent the first week in this village blundering around in borrowed shoes. I would rather not compound that by letting the vicar's wife ask if I am fond of root vegetables while she tries to place my face. What if someone recognizes me?"

Jane leaned over to adjust the ribbon on Elizabeth's bonnet. "You have been to Meryton half a dozen times before and no one knew you as anyone but our cousin. Why should today be any different?"

"Because we…" Elizabeth stopped and lowered her voice to a whisper. "Because Mr. Darcy sent a letter that made it seem like I had gone elsewhere. What good will that do if I am seen in town today?"

Jane frowned speculatively. "Well, I know nothing about that. But I do know that Mr. Bingley spoke to him at length about plans for the day, and Mr. Darcy voiced no specific concerns."

"You mean beyond his usual glowering and grumbling?"

Jane squeezed her hand. "Nothing will go wrong. Mr. Bingley will be beside us at all times, and Mr. Darcy close by. You will not be alone, Lizzy."

"The prime minister was not alone when they shot him, now, was he?"

Jane's face paled, as if it was the first time she had thought of it. "Well… But surely, if Mr. Darcy did not think it too dangerous…"

Elizabeth sighed. "Very well. But I draw the line at admiring anyone's marrow crop."

Downstairs, a loud crash signaled the fall of someone's bonnet box. Elizabeth sighed and tied her bonnet with an air of martyrdom.

They descended together into the fray, stepping over a fallen shoe and dodging Mary's attempt to read aloud from a volume of devotional poetry.

In the foyer, Mr. Bennet leaned against the newel post, watching the scene like a man observing a distant battlefield.

"Well, this is festive," he said. "All this for the chance to stand about a muddy field admiring turnips and pretending to care what the vicar's wife planted last year."

"I was just saying the same," Elizabeth murmured, drawing alongside him.

Mr. Bennet cast her a sidelong glance. "Ah, but your reasons are likely nobler than mine. I simply hate crowds. You, I suspect, are concerned about being noticed."

"Should I not be? I still cannot believe my 'guardian' thought this at all a reasonable idea. Should I not be hiding here at Longbourn while we wait to see if that decoy letter has fooled anyone about my whereabouts?"

"Unfortunately, my dear 'niece,' I am afraid that would only cause more talk, for Mr. Collins would find it irregular enough to make a comment or three, do you not agree?"

She grimaced and nodded. Not only Mr. Collins, but Mrs. Bennet and Lydia would express their disappointment over her absence rather vocally as well.

"And it would be inadvisable for you to be here alone, so naturally you must have a capable 'bodyguard.' If it were observed—as it would be, of course—that Mr. Darcy is similarly absent from the festivities, we would have a different sort of scandal on our hands. So, you see, there is some safety in numbers."

"There is 'safety' in company that does not gossip," she muttered.

He patted her hand. "I used to entertain that fantasy myself, until I learned its futility. It will pass, my dear. Just keep walking and do not answer any questions you do not like. It is what I have done these past twenty years."

A footman opened the front door, and the breeze caught Mrs. Bennet's voice mid-command. "Girls! Into the carriages now—unless you mean to miss every eligible gentleman within thirty miles!"

Mr. Collins, meanwhile, stood stiffly by the door with his hat clutched to his chest and a grim sort of anticipation gleaming in his eyes.

"Mr. Bennet," he announced, "as your guest and as a devoted servant of Lady Catherine de Bourgh, I believe it is most proper that I should escort your eldest daughter in the first carriage. Miss Bennet, if you please—"

But before Jane could formulate a reply—whether courteous or otherwise—the clatter of hooves on gravel interrupted them.

A chestnut gelding crested the drive. Mr. Bingley, beaming and windblown, doffed his hat.

"Good morning, Longbourn!" he called. "Have I missed the parade?"

Mrs. Bennet clutched her shawl in delight. "Mr. Bingley! Oh, what a joy—you must ride beside us to the green! Such a gallant escort! Jane, Lizzy, and... oh, I suppose Mary, you shall ride in this carriage so that Mr. Bingley may ride beside us."

Mr. Bennet gave a soft grunt of amusement. "Timely, that one," he murmured to Elizabeth.

Mr. Collins blinked rapidly and took a step back, clearly flustered. "Well... I... I suppose—though—I had intended—that is, it would have been—"

Mr. Bennet, without blinking, said, "I suppose that leaves us in the second carriage, Mr. Collins. Kitty, Lydia, you as well."

Mr. Collins opened and closed his mouth like a startled fish.

Bingley dismounted to aid in assisting the ladies into the carriage. "My sisters are still dressing, and Mr. Hurst volunteered to accompany them. I thought I might ride ahead and offer my services as."

"Consider yourself most welcome, sir," gushed Mrs. Bennet as she patted his shoulder when he helped her inside. And Elizabeth had to suppress a giggle when she turned to Jane and, in a rather loud-ish "whisper," bubbled something about feeling no padding under the gentleman's coat.

Mr. Bingley only blushed at her remarks and leaned a little closer to Elizabeth as he offered to hand her in. "Darcy will be arriving separately, but rest assured, he intends to remain... vigilant."

Elizabeth blinked, then nodded once. "Of course. I would have expected nothing less."

Bingley smiled. "Shall we, then?"

And with that, the door of the carriage closed, and the slow descent into the lion's den began.

D ARCY STOOD JUST BEYOND the main green, half-shielded by the edge of a vendor's canopy, trying to look disinterested. A boy darted past him with a fistful of barley-sugar sticks, nearly colliding with his boots, and Darcy took a slow breath.

There she was.

Elizabeth moved through the crowd like she had always belonged to it—ducking between flower stalls and ducking again as Kitty tossed a loose shuttlecock that nearly hit her bonnet. She laughed, quick and bright, and reached to return it, her grip steady, her back straight. Darcy watched the motion—a flick of her wrist, a shift in her weight as she sent the bird whirling upward again. It arced too wide for Lydia to catch.

The Bennet girls shouted at their friends—the Lucas girl and someone named Mary King. Scattered, regrouped, and set for play again.

That was when Elizabeth's gaze cut toward the crowd, scanning.

And then—she stopped.

When she saw him.

Her eyes caught his, just for a heartbeat, and something in her expression softened. Her lips parted, curved. She turned back to the game too quickly, as if nothing had happened.

He exhaled. Too sharply. Almost angrily.

God help him, he had waited for that smile.

"Rustic," came Caroline Bingley's voice, somewhere off to the right.

Darcy blinked, turning just enough to see her gliding toward the circle of girls with her most brittle smile in place, a fan dangling from one gloved hand.

"You exhibit such... charm in this quaint pastime," she said, aiming her words like darts. "Perhaps the game of graces would offer a more elegant display."

Elizabeth turned, and whatever she had been about to say died on her lips. Darcy saw the spark in her eyes. She was not flustered. She was planning something.

"I adore the game of graces," Elizabeth said. "Shall we?"

Caroline smiled and granted a dip of her head. Darcy crossed his arms and prepared to be amused. Caroline had no idea who she was trying to best...

The footman fetched the rods and the hoop. The Bennet girls drew back, making space.

Darcy watched, arms crossed, mouth set.

The first pass was Caroline's—slow, stiff, overly rehearsed. The ribbon fluttered. Elizabeth caught it easily and launched it back in a clean arc, the motion so fluid it barely looked intentional.

They continued, and Caroline's timing frayed with every exchange. Elizabeth never looked triumphant. Just amused. Calm. Bright-eyed and maddening, like she always was.

Darcy wanted to laugh and strangle something at once.

Then Elizabeth sent the hoop high and spinning, and Caroline lunged too late. It fell at her feet.

There was a pause. Then polite clapping. Lydia giggled.

Elizabeth stepped forward and bent—graceful, always graceful—and handed the hoop back with a bow of her head.

"A delightful diversion," she said sweetly. "Thank you."

Caroline took it without reply, her knuckles white against the ribbon.

Darcy turned away before anyone could see the expression on his face. He needed air. And distance. And a stronger will than he possessed.

For the next quarter hour, Darcy stayed where he was, at the edge of the festivities, half in shadow and half in torment. Elizabeth had moved on from the game of graces and now stood beside Jane Bennet near the booths lined with preserves and hand-painted ceramics. An older matron was gesturing grandly with a pot of quince jam, but Elizabeth's attention kept drifting. Every few minutes, she would glance sideways, scanning the green, eyes moving past the horses, the fiddlers, the girls with sugar sticks, until—

There.

Her eyes met his again. No flourish. No surprise. Just a spark of greeting, or perhaps relief, and then—deliberately—she looked away.

Darcy felt the moment like a blow to the chest. She was content to know he was there, watching, but she did not need him for her pleasure. Never would.

Nor should she.

He turned aside, pretending to study the angle of the sun through the trees, as if that might explain why his breath had caught or why his stomach twisted whenever she looked at him like that. She was not flirting. She never flirted. That was part of what made her so damnably dangerous. She just *saw* him.

And it undid him.

A bobbing horse head cut through the crowd, threading in the opposite direction of most of the activity.

Darcy straightened instantly, instincts overriding emotion. This rider had all the look of a courier, carrying a message.

Not one of his.

No, an express rider. Horse lathered. The man rode with an object, weaving between festival carts and startled children. His coat was unmarked, but his satchel bore the crest of a noble household—which one, Darcy could not see from that distance. Dust caked his boots to the knee. He dismounted near the market stalls, his eyes scanning faces. Then he began moving from group to group, asking questions.

Darcy could not hear the words, but the gestures were clear. The rider lifted a folded express—thick, with a large seal set in wax—and pointed vaguely across the green.

Darcy moved without thinking, weaving through a knot of teenagers near a cider stand. The rider was asking again—this time a butcher's wife—and she pointed, almost too casually, toward the far end of the field.

Where Collins stood.

Darcy's blood ran cold.

The vicar was at his most insufferable, posturing beside a rather uninspired squash display. His hands moved as if delivering a sermon on the moral superiority of root vegetables. The express rider cut across the field.

Darcy stopped walking.

The rider reached Collins and handed him the envelope with a crisp bow. Collins's face lit up like a boy being given a puppy. He broke the seal immediately, eyes devouring the page.

Darcy did not need to read the words to know.

Lady Catherine.

A flush of self-importance colored Collins' cheeks as he cleared his throat and, without hesitation, began reading aloud to those nearest him. Heads turned, conversations hushed, and a ripple of whispers spread outward like wildfire.

Darcy's pulse thundered in his ears as he slipped through the crowd, trying to remain unseen without being unseen—a trick he had mastered in drawing rooms, but never before in a public square ripe for spectacle.

Collins was still crowing over the letter, now fluttering it in the air for the benefit of a clutch of middle-aged matrons who leaned closer with a kind of delighted horror. Darcy could not make out the words, but he could see the effect. The women gasped and tittered, glancing toward the cider stalls—and then directly at him.

One put a hand to her mouth.

Another whispered something to her companion, and they both turned away, but not before he caught the faintest sneer.

And that was only the beginning.

Caroline Bingley stood several yards away, dressed too finely for an open-air gathering and watching the scene with a tightening frown. She had not heard Collins' letter—of that, he was certain—but she was hearing enough now to know something was amiss. A gentleman near her made a remark Darcy could not catch, but he gestured toward Darcy, then toward Bingley. Caroline's head jerked, her fan stilled mid-sweep, and her mouth fell slightly open.

She turned in a slow, horrified circle, scanning faces. Looking for her brother.

He moved again, quickly now, toward the cider cart where a knot of laborers and farmers had formed an unhurried ring around a barrel-top table. Tankards in hand, boots scuffed from the field, they leaned on elbows and spoke in half-lowered tones, the kind reserved for matters both scandalous and satisfying.

Darcy slowed his steps, pausing just beyond the edge, half-shielded by a faded canvas tent. A potboy from the inn dashed past with a pitcher. No one noticed him listening.

"...never liked the look of him," one man was saying. "Too stiff. Walks like he is afraid to catch a crease."

"Thinks he's better than the rest of us, that's plain," said another. "Did you hear what was in that letter?"

A scoff. "Letter, nothing. Old Carrick knew something weeks ago. Said the fellow tipped obscenely high and asked too many questions."

"That's the one—Darcy, is it? The guest at Netherfield? Wonder if Mr. Bingley ever heard of this. Shoddy affair, it is."

A collective murmur of agreement passed through the group.

"Strange business, him coming down here at all. Nothing to interest a London man in a place like Meryton. Not unless he was hiding from something."

"Or someone."

Darcy's pulse flickered. He shifted slightly, just enough to catch a different angle of the crowd. Beyond the green, Elizabeth moved with her sisters among the booths—trailing just behind Kitty and Maria Lucas, who were laughing over a painted fan and mostly ignoring the murmurs.

But they had caught Elizabeth's ear... he could tell that by the flicker of her jaw muscles. She turned her head, searching.

Found him.

And something in her face softened.

Pity.

He looked away first. Pity was the one thing he could never bear... most particularly not from her. He swallowed once. Hard.

"Strange lot, the whole company," a voice was saying now. "Darcy, and that red-haired one—Bingley."

"He is polite enough," another offered, "but I would wager he knows something. Always flitting after the Bennet girl, that quiet one."

"Miss Jane?"

"No, no, the other. The one who showed up out of nowhere."

There it was.

Darcy did not move.

"...and she said she was a cousin, right? Only did you hear what that fellow Collins said yesterday? No one remembers Daniel Bennet ever having a daughter. Odd, that."

A grunt. A shrug. Then— "Odd, nothing. Remember that afternoon—first day she was in town? Walked out of the inn half-blind and barely standing?"

"Aye, dunk as a lord, she was," came the answer. "And it was him—Darcy—who paid her reckoning and bundled her off into a carriage. Told Carrick to keep it quiet. And gave him a purse fat enough to buy his silence."

A pause.

Then a sharp intake of breath. "You are sure it was the same man?"

"Aye, the tall one. Darcy."

The name passed between them like the first spark from a flint.

Darcy closed his eyes.

He could still see the flash of her pale face that first night, the way she clung to the doorframe, blinking into the lamplight, and how she looked at him with something like loathing.

Not *at* him, precisely—but at the rescue. At needing it. At what it said about her. And he—fool that he was—had thought that if he paid enough, concealed enough, covered his tracks well enough, kept quiet long enough, it would never follow her.

It had followed.

He opened his eyes.

A pair of young ladies hurried past behind him, hands clutched together, faces turned toward the green.

"...not even a cousin, they say. Invented the whole connection. Imagine the audacity—"

"Mrs. Blount told Mama it was some scandal in Town. That she fled from it."

Darcy's eyes snapped to their retreating backs.

Someone else whispered, "She's ruined, surely. And him with her. What will come of Mr. Bingley, I wonder?"

Heads turned.

First toward Darcy.

Then toward Elizabeth.

A single ripple had become a flood.

T HE BENNET DRAWING ROOM was too full—of voices, of panic, of the smoke-sweet breath of lamp oil thickening the air. Elizabeth stood in the center of it all, hands clasped tight before her, feeling the walls press inward like jaws.

Mrs. Bennet was crying into a handkerchief that had not been clean since breakfast, her voice rising with each fresh wave of despair. "Ruined! Absolutely ruined! I told you that cousinship was nonsense from the start! A scandal, in our very household, and with the worst man in England, no less!"

Jane had a gentle arm wrapped around her mother, but her eyes were fixed on Elizabeth. Wide, stricken. Uncomprehending.

Kitty and Lydia huddled near the hearth, their skirts bunched in their fists, whispering. Mary stood a little apart, her brow drawn in fierce lines of confusion, clinging to a prayer book like a shield.

Collins, puffed with indignation, stood in the center of the room like a self-inflated toad, his eyes darting between Darcy and the Bennet family with theatrical horror. "It is appalling, utterly appalling," he declared, his voice climbing in righteous volume. "Had I known she was no relation—had you all not insisted on lying about it—I should never have permitted such familiarity beneath this roof. I acted only in good faith, under the impression she was family. Instead, I find myself entertaining the company of a woman of mystery and a *man*"—he turned and jabbed a finger toward Darcy— "whose disgrace has been well-documented by better sources than mine!"

Darcy's eyes glittered with rage, but he did not move.

Collins wheeled on Bingley next, his voice reaching a new pitch of self-satisfaction. "And you, sir, playing host to such a man! You cannot plead ignorance, not when Lady Catherine de Bourgh herself has spoken. She wrote me in the strongest terms. She is aggrieved, naturally, but not without compassion. In her beneficence, she has taken care to warn the good Mr. Wickham—yes, he is in London for the Season, as you may know—that her nephew is once again stirring trouble, this time from such a close vicinity as Hertfordshire!"

Darcy's spine snapped rigid. Elizabeth could almost hear the bones and sinews cracking as his frame flexed from sheer wrath, viciously checked.

Bingley took a step forward. "She did what?"

Collins blinked, as if surprised anyone would interrupt such a noble pronouncement. "She felt it her duty to protect decent society. Naturally, she wrote to me at once—and to Mr. Wickham, who will, I daresay, not be slow to act if his generous nature is once again tested by Mr. Darcy's... presence."

"You fool," Bingley breathed. "You absolute cretin."

Mr. Bennet stepped forward then, his tone unflinching, each syllable cold and clean as a blade.

"Collins."

The parson turned, puffing up again. "Sir?"

"Get out of my house."

"But I—I am the heir!"

"And I am still very much alive. Collect your things while I still grant you time to do so. You may *walk* back to Meryton to catch a post-chaise or hire a hack, I care not what."

"But... but I have a trunk! My prayer journals, my clothing!"

"And whatever you cannot take with you now, I shall burn tomorrow. Out, sir."

Collins gaped at him, jaw slack, as though he had been struck. Then, flustered and muttering about duty and the burdens of moral guardianship, he turned and made for the hall door—only to trip over the hem of the rug in his haste. He stumbled into the entryway with all the grace of an overturned teapot, clattered up the stairs to his room, and the door slammed behind him with a clap that echoed like a final verdict.

Elizabeth's voice, when she finally found it, was soft. Broken, even. "I... I never meant for it to fall on all of you."

Jane caught her hand. "You have not done this. *They* have."

Mr. Bennet, grim-faced, turned to Darcy and Bingley. "My study. Now."

Elizabeth met Darcy's eyes as he passed her. He did not speak. He only looked. And she knew well enough what that look meant.

She turned to Jane. "Come help me, Jane. I need to pack."

Jane's brows flew upward. "Lizzy—no. What are you talking about?"

Elizabeth's voice cracked like glass. "I cannot stay."

Jane stared at her, lips parted in shock, but she said nothing. She only turned, lifting her skirts, and followed Elizabeth up the narrow stairs without another word.

Their small shared room was warm and dim, the scent of rosewater lingering in the folds of the curtains. Elizabeth did not hesitate. She crossed to the wardrobe, yanked open the doors, and reached for the old linen wrap she had folded there days ago. Not the trunk

Darcy had procured for her—there was no time for that, no strength to carry it, and no sense in taking more than she could run with. Just a satchel, a warm cloak. Just enough.

She gathered only the essentials—a change of gown, a ruby ring she had worn to Buckingham House that first night tucked in a kerchief, a clutch of undergarments procured for her by a bachelor, and the most unremarkable bonnet she could find.

"Lizzy," Jane said behind her, helpless, clutching a pair of gloves in both trembling hands. "Where will you go?"

"I do not know. But I cannot stay here. I have made your home unsafe. For you. For your father. For everyone."

"You cannot just vanish into the night!" Jane whispered.

"I can," Elizabeth replied, wrapping her things tighter. "And I must."

Jane stepped closer, resting a hand on Elizabeth's shoulder. "But what will you do? Who will be with you?"

Elizabeth paused. Her hands stilled around the knot in the fabric. "He will help me. He is already thinking of a plan, I am sure of it."

Jane blinked. "Mr. Darcy?"

Elizabeth nodded once.

Jane's eyes went wide, her lips parting in horror. "But... he is not your husband! If you go with him now—Lizzy, you would be—"

"Ruined?" Elizabeth let out a breathless, broken laugh. "It will certainly not be the first time I vanished into the night with him. Remember?"

Jane flinched as if struck. "That was under the Prince's orders. This... this is Collins' stupidity and that pompous patroness of his. It is not fair, Lizzy."

Elizabeth turned to face her, bundle in her arms. "None of this is fair. But if I stay, I will die. Maybe not tomorrow, but soon, and probably others with me. I would rather be ruined and breathing than dignified in a box."

Jane's eyes filled again. "You cannot know that would happen."

"I do. And he knows it too. He has had some trouble keeping me alive this long, and now it is worse. They know the name I have lived under. They know this house. And worse, thanks to all the gossip in town, they know now that Mr. Darcy was the one helping me to remain hidden. They will try to kill him now, too, Jane. We cannot wait for them to come knocking."

"But... *where* will you go?" Jane demanded once more, as if she still could not believe Elizabeth truly meant what she said. "Where can a bachelor and an unmarried woman run off to together? And this late in the day!"

"I do not know," Elizabeth said again, this time softer. "Wherever he thinks safest."

Jane's face crumpled. She crossed the room in two steps and flung her arms around Elizabeth, clutching her with a desperation that shook them both.

Elizabeth closed her eyes. "You are the closest thing to a sister I have ever had."

"Oh, Lizzy!" They held each other like girls again, like they had never pretended to be ladies, and time had not passed so cruelly.

"You must write to me," Jane said fiercely, pulling back just enough to look at her.

"I will. When it is safe. Not before." Elizabeth gave a damp, tired smile. She reached out and brushed a tear from Jane's cheek with her thumb. "In the meantime, you must promise to think of me every time you smile at Mr. Bingley."

Jane laughed and mopped her sodden cheek with the back of her hand. "Why should that be my particular memento?"

Elizabeth sniffed and grinned. "Because I know it will be often."

Jane laughed again, burying her face in her sleeve until she sobbed. Then they both stood in silence for a moment, until Elizabeth pressed a kiss to Jane's forehead and stepped back, her small bundle clasped tight in her hands. "Goodbye, sweet Jane."

No trunk. No plan. Just a promise.

And a man waiting below.

CHAPTER TWENTY-FIVE

A LOW MIST COILED through the hedgerows behind Longbourn as Darcy waited beneath the cover of an ancient yew, listening for hoofbeats that were not his own.

His gelding stood quietly beside him, his reins looped loosely in his gloved hand. The second mount—a smaller, fleeter mare he had borrowed from Bingley's stable—pawed once, twice, before falling still. She had carried couriers before. She would carry a secret tonight.

Darcy glanced toward the narrow track behind the house, half-concealed by the thicket. They would not use the main road. He had planned for that. Every choice from this moment forward had to be quiet, quick, and unpredictable. Somewhere out beyond the trees, Selwyn would already be lighting the lantern. The safe house near Cambridge—little more than a country waystation in his father's time—had stood empty for nearly a decade. No servants. No family. No reason for anyone to watch it. Until now.

A flicker of movement caught his eye.

Two figures emerged from the shadowed side door of Longbourn—Mr. Bennet first, his coat unbuttoned, shoulders unusually stiff. Behind him, Bingley. Both approached without haste, but with purpose.

Darcy stepped forward.

Bingley offered no jest tonight. He clasped Darcy's arm in silence and held it a beat longer than usual. "Take care of her," he said. "And of yourself."

Darcy inclined his head. "Thank you, Charles. I trust you will look after the Bennets. I fear they may be a target now as well."

Bingley gave a crooked smile. "Jane says to write. Mrs. Bennet did not say anything at all. Which I take as a form of gratitude."

Darcy might have laughed if his chest did not feel so tight.

Mr. Bennet extended a small packet, sealed with wax. "For her," he said. "If she should need reminding that not everyone prefers her absent."

Darcy accepted it with a quiet nod. "I will do what I can."

Bennet's eyes were sharp behind his spectacles. "Do not do what you *can*. Do what she *needs*. There is a difference, and you strike me as a man who often forgets it."

Darcy smiled tightly. "Sir, if I may, I heartily suggest that your family be seen at church tomorrow *without* Elizabeth. Put it out loudly and to anyone who will hear it that she returned to... wherever it is you all claimed she was from. Protect your family by making it known that your house is no longer her shelter."

Bennet nodded. "Let us concern ourselves with that, sir."

"I mean to sit up with him all night 'drinking,'" Bingley supplied. "And keeping our powder dry. We will be careful, Darcy. I pray you will be as well."

"I do not need to be more 'careful.'" Darcy sighed. "What I need is a bit of luck to turn our way for once."

Before Bingley could respond, the door creaked again, and Elizabeth stepped into the clearing.

No laughing smile. No fanfare. Just a cloak drawn close, and a satchel slung over one shoulder. Her eyes found his instantly, as if she had always known exactly where he stood.

She crossed the lawn with no hesitation and stopped just short of him. "I am ready."

Darcy gave a small nod, then helped her mount the mare. She did not flinch when he touched her elbow. She did not smile, either.

He kept them to the side lanes, avoiding the turnpike and every coaching inn marked on the general maps. Even before he left Meryton that afternoon, he had put the first signal into motion. Selwyn would receive it through an intermediary—no names, no seals, just a symbol etched in charcoal on the corner of a supply chit. That had always been the agreement.

Selwyn did not know who he was. Darcy had been adamant about that when the arrangement was first made, years ago during a particularly volatile inquiry into naval procurement fraud. Selwyn thought he worked for a minor functionary in the War Office. He had no reason to suspect otherwise.

The safe house itself was no great comfort. A squat brick structure at the edge of an old Cambridge holding, it had been purchased under an alias and stocked only for emergencies. There were shutters that locked from the inside, a cold cellar, false flooring, and a rear exit that led directly to an overgrown game path. It had once been used to move wounded couriers during a failed Irish rebellion. Darcy had sworn then he would never need it himself.

And certainly not for this.

There would be no servant waiting, no one to light the hearth or tend a meal, and certainly no chaperon. The very idea of bringing a lady here alone would have scandalized the man he once was. And yet here they were—riding through a nearly moonless night to a place built for silence, not comfort.

He glanced once at Elizabeth as they turned northward past a low stone boundary. Her cloak fluttered slightly in the breeze, but her seat was solid. Daughter of Lord Ashwick, she had probably grown up chasing the hounds. How strange that now they were chasing her.

Still no questions.

Still no fear.

Only trust.

It humbled him more than he could bear.

I T WAS PAST TEN when they cleared the last hedgerows of Longbourn. The stars had just begun to push through the thinning clouds, and the road beneath them stretched like a ribbon of ink through open fields.

Elizabeth rode side-saddle, one hand wrapped tightly around the reins, the other gripping the pommel so hard her knuckles had gone numb inside her gloves. The horse beneath her was solid and sure-footed—Darcy had chosen well—but after the first hour, every jolt of its gait sent a fresh ache up her spine.

She had not spoken since they left the tree line.

Darcy had not offered conversation. He rode just ahead, his cloak whipping behind him in the wind, his silhouette stark against the dim sky as his head swiveled constantly about them. He had said nothing when she mounted. Nothing when they turned east. Nothing as Meryton fell behind them and the last pinpricks of candlelight vanished into the dark.

But he checked the road with every rise.

Twice, he paused to listen. Once, he dismounted and led her horse through a narrow copse, their path swallowed by brambles. She said nothing—would not give him the satisfaction or bother of fielding a complaint—but by the third hour her thighs trembled with effort and her hands could no longer feel the reins.

He knew. Of course, he knew.

Darcy slowed once they reached the river valley, allowing her a chance to flex her legs. "Another hour," he said, his voice low in the close dark. "There will be a place to rest then."

Elizabeth nodded. Practical, efficient, no sentiment. But the meaning was clear enough.

She had always thought herself capable. Her father had seen to it—long days in the saddle, summers in Devon with more mud than manners, winters where she rose with the sun and did her own grooming. She had never wanted to be one of those society girls who needed a footman just to mount, and more than once, her skills had proved the envy of her friends.

But this ride—this constant vigilance, this lurching, winding, aching ride—was something else entirely. Her stomach twisted with exhaustion.

And still he said nothing.

At the top of a narrow ridge, they paused. The moon had risen now, low and pale, casting silver across the fields. Elizabeth tugged her gloves tighter and looked out across the countryside. There was no road in sight by this time. No travelers. No sound but the wind in the hedges.

Darcy turned in his saddle, his profile etched in moonlight. "You are keeping up."

It was not quite praise.

"I am not made of lace, Mr. Darcy," she said, her voice hoarse.

A flicker of something passed through his eyes—amusement, maybe—but he gave no reply. He merely inclined his head and turned back toward the east, spurring his mount into a steady trot.

She wanted to hate him for it.

Wanted to scream at him, rail against him, throw her aching body to the ground and demand that he see her—see her for who she was, not a burden, not a charge, not a problem to be managed. But she knew what this was. This was purpose. This was the man he became when everything else fell away.

He would carry her to the ends of the kingdom before he let her fall. But he would not touch her hand unless duty demanded it.

The thought sent a throb of something sharp and burning straight to her chest.

They crested another hill just as the first grey hint of morning filtered over the horizon, pale and cold.

Elizabeth's entire body throbbed. Her eyes burned from lack of sleep, and her fingers—now locked in a permanent curl from gripping the reins all night—had gone stiff and useless. She had lost all sense of time hours ago, the road behind them melting into an endless stretch of wind and hoofbeats.

Then, at last, Darcy raised a hand. "There."

Below them, half-shrouded in mist and crouched in a grove of trees, stood a cottage. Low and narrow, built of old stone. The chimney bore no smoke, and its dark shutters gave no sign of life. But as they approached, Darcy gave a sharp whistle—and after a beat, the door opened.

A man stepped out.

No lantern. No greeting. Just a brief nod. And safety at last.

Darcy helped her down. His hands were warm, steady beneath her arms. She tried not to lean into him, but the moment her feet hit the ground, her knees buckled. His grip tightened. Their eyes met in the dark.

"You are shaking," he said, and his voice was the only warm thing she had felt on her skin for hours.

"I am tired."

He did not answer. Just steadied her under his arm, holding her close to his side as he handed the horses to the man and guided her toward the door.

Inside, the cottage was cold, but clean. A single room, with a hearth long gone cold, a cot at the back, and a table with a pitcher of water beside a long wooden bench.

Darcy lit a lamp. The yellow glow washed over him—and for the first time, she saw how worn he looked. Dust in his hair. Creases around his eyes. His jaw set too tightly.

This was not a man playing the hero.

This was a man trying very hard not to fail.

She sank onto the bench, every inch of her body humming with pain. He poured water into a cup and handed it to her.

She drank in silence. Then, quietly, she said, "You signaled him before we left."

He looked up.

"That man outside," she added. "The one who met us. You arranged it before we even left Meryton for Longbourn yesterday afternoon. You had to have."

"Yes."

"He does not know who you are."

"No."

She nodded once. "You have had this place ready all along?"

His expression did not change. "I hoped I would never need it."

Her throat tightened. "Especially not with a woman."

A long silence. "No," he said at last. "Most especially not with a woman."

She looked down at her hands. At the trembling she could not hide. And then, slowly, her gaze lifted back to his.

"Who... who *are* you, Mr. Darcy?"

He did not answer. Instead, he moved past her to the hearth where Selwyn had left a parcel wrapped in oilcloth. Darcy unwrapped it and passed her a small loaf of bread and a wedge of hard cheese. It was cold, rough food, but Elizabeth took it gratefully and ate in silence, her hands clumsy with fatigue.

When she had finished, he nodded toward a narrow cot in the far corner. "There. Try to sleep."

She wanted to protest. To ask what came next. How he meant to keep half the world from discovering them this time.

But her legs moved without waiting for her mind, and she sank down on the thin mattress. Her eyes swam with exhaustion. The air had grown paler now—the fragile grey before dawn—and her stomach twisted with nausea.

She lay back, arm curled beneath her head.

As her eyes slipped closed, she mumbled, "Where do *you* sleep?"

Darcy's voice came from somewhere near the door. "I do not."

And that was her last thought before she drifted into oblivion—the assurance that he would keep her safe.

May 31, 1812

DARCY HAD NOT SLEPT.

Not truly.

A handful of times, he had closed his eyes—leaned his head back against the cool stone wall, just long enough to lose track of thought. But sleep never came. Not while *she* lay a few paces away. Not while he still had breath to guard her with.

Selwyn was gone. The last signal exchanged, and the man vanished into the woods as quickly as he had appeared, leaving behind only the ghost of reassurance and two worn blankets.

Darcy had already tended the horses twice. He had checked the perimeter three times. He had washed his face in the shallow stream behind the house until his skin stung.

Anything to stay awake.

Anything to keep his eyes open—and off of her.

She lay still in the far corner, curled beneath a blanket. Her bundle of outer clothes lay at the foot of the cot, her boots neatly placed beneath. One hand rested over her midsection, the other under her cheek, her dark hair worked loose from its pins and tangled against the pillow.

She did not stir. Not even when the blanket she had tossed over herself so haphazardly slipped down from her shoulder.

Darcy moved before he thought.

He crossed the room in silence, crouched beside her, and gently, carefully, tucked the blanket back into place. His fingers brushed the curve of her shoulder, and he felt the warmth of her through the fabric. He could not help it—he studied her face in the pale light that filtered through the shuttered windows.

Even now, in sleep, in exhaustion, there it was.

A hint of it.

That familiar smirk—curved like a secret. She was tired, worn, and hunted... and yet she looked like she might open her eyes at any moment and laugh. At him. At the world.

He swallowed hard.

Perhaps that was what had drawn him to her from the very first time he saw her. The way she laughed, as though nothing could touch her. As though life—real, flawed, dangerous life—was a joke she had already heard the punchline to.

He stood quickly and walked away.

It was early afternoon when the spell broke.

He had been sitting by the window, staring through the warped glass into the trees beyond, when something touched his shoulder.

A hand. Warm. Gentle.

He did not startle at first. His mind was too slow, his body too numb. It took a breath. Then another. And then he turned.

Elizabeth stood beside him.

She was barefoot. The linen of her borrowed gown sagged at one shoulder, and her hair was a riot of waves down her back. In her hand, she held a glass bottle—half-full, dark amber, unlabeled.

"I found this beside the cot," she said softly. "I thought it might fortify you."

He stared at the bottle. Then at her. And he shook his head.

"It would only make me sleep."

She tilted her head. "Yes. That is rather the point."

"I cannot," he murmured, dragging a hand through his hair. "Not yet."

"You can," she said, firmer this time. "And you must."

He blinked at her.

She crossed her arms. "Do you think I am entirely useless? I can keep watch."

"You should rest—"

"I *have* rested. You have not. I will not let you fall asleep just as someone comes to kill us both."

He opened his mouth, then closed it again.

She set the bottle on the windowsill, folded her arms tighter, and gave him a look that brooked no compromise. "I will wake you if there is so much as a squirrel."

He gave a dry huff of laughter and rubbed his eyes. "Half an hour."

"*One* hour."

He sighed, dragging himself to his feet.

"If I wake up and you are playing cards with an assassin, I shall be very cross."

Elizabeth smiled faintly as he passed her, every step heavier than the last. He stumbled once against the edge of the hearth but caught himself.

He made it to the cot.

He could feel her watching him as he lowered himself with the stiff awkwardness of a man twice his age. One arm flung over his eyes. His chest rising and falling in the first uneven rhythms of surrender.

He was asleep within minutes.

T HE COTTAGE WAS QUIET.

Elizabeth sat on the low stool by the hearth, knees drawn up, blanket draped around her shoulders. The late spring wind outside had slowed to a whisper, and the birdsong—so bright just an hour ago—had faded into the hush of a lazy afternoon.

She had not been raised for this.

Rough stone floors. Musty blankets. Half a heel of bread and a slice of dried meat to call dinner. Every muscle ached from yesterday's long ride, and she could still feel her thighs twitch faintly each time she stood. Her arms trembled when she tightened the blanket. The exhaustion would catch her again soon—but not yet. She had promised—her breath snagged on an unbidden yawn—*promised* to stay awake. To keep watch.

So she decided to fill her mind with distraction. Where did she leave off with life before this? Oh! Yes, the festival. Yesterday.

Was it *truly* only yesterday?

But it must have been. She wrinkled her forehead and tried to remember all. Caroline Bingley, prim and sparkling in her expensive lace, trying to outshine her at the game of Graces—and losing, all while pretending not to care. Of Kitty and Lydia teasing one another near the cider booth, their laughter high and thoughtless as they tried and failed to make Captain Denney look their way. Of Jane, glowing, absolutely glowing, as Mr. Bingley hovered near her elbow with the sort of shy, persistent attentiveness that made younger sisters giggle behind their gloves.

And her. Paraded about the green by Mrs. Bennet, proudly brought to the notice of every acquaintance and stranger in equal measure, as if she had always belonged... until everyone discovered that she did not.

The ache behind her eyes sharpened. Why the devil had silly Mrs. Bennet's preening and plucking made her belly feel so warm and pleasant? It was... well, it was silly. It should have been annoying, but it...

She should have thought of Devonshire.

It struck her now, with quiet absurdity, that she never had. Not even once, in all the time since she had been dragged unceremoniously from her meeting with the Prince at Buckingham House. She never thought of Ashwick.

That had been her first home—the estate that would eventually pass to her upon her father's death, unless by some miracle he sired a son and proper heir before then. The place where she had learned to walk, learned to ride, learned to be everything she was.

Her mother was there still—indulgent, talkative, extravagantly affectionate when it suited her. Had Elizabeth shown up on the doorstep in flight from danger, there would have been no questions. No rebuke. Likely a party by the end of the week.

And yet, not once had she longed for it.

Not even when the shadows closed in.

Even now, with the weight of exhaustion in her limbs and the stale, unwelcoming air of the cottage pressing close, she did not crave the velvet cushions and sweetmeats of her mother's world. That life was safe. At least in theory. But it had never felt like hers.

And it could not have actually been *safe*, anyway. Anyone chasing her would have looked there first. They did not hesitate to set fire to her room in London, so why would a lofty old mansion in Devonshire slow them down?

Still, it startled her—that the thought of Devonshire came not as a regret, but as an afterthought.

Should that not have been instinct?

Home, after all, was meant to be where you ran, or at least *wanted* to run, when the wolves were close. But her heart had never turned in that direction.

It turned here.

She let out a soft breath and rested her chin on her knees.

Her thoughts wandered, drifting past Devonshire and its honeyed edges, past the mother who had given her life but never direction. And without quite meaning to, her mind settled back on the place she had just left behind.

Longbourn.

A creaky old house, cluttered and chaotic, full of mismatched furniture and louder voices than she had ever been raised to bear. And yet—

There had been laughter. Music. Banter over breakfast and squabbles over gloves. Hands reaching for hers without calculation. Faces lighting when she entered the room.

And one man seated behind a newspaper who never asked questions he already knew the answers to.

A father...

Not the Marquess. Not the title.

The other man. The one who gave her sanctuary. Who made her laugh when she thought she had forgot how. Who looked at her with knowing eyes and said nothing at all when everything hurt.

Mr. Bennet.

Her hand reached instinctively for the small bundle she had found earlier—tucked into her satchel with neat care and quiet foresight. A parcel. His writing on the paper, just a few words.

A few things in case you need reminding that someone expects you to come home.

Home! Such a fond word for a place she had known so little. She did not open it. Not yet. But she held it tight against her chest.

A fortnight.

That was all it took for one man—and one messy, imperfect, beloved family—to make her feel more like a daughter than her own ever had in twenty years. She blinked back the ache behind her eyes.

And then—there was Darcy.

She turned slightly, glancing across the room.

He had not shifted in sleep—too tired for that, probably. One arm flung across his eyes. The rest of him too long for the narrow cot, his boots still on. She had watched his chest rise and fall for nearly ten minutes before he made a sound.

Then came the snore.

Soft, a bit uneven. The sort that caught in the throat and hiccupped out again.

She smiled. It should have been irritating. But somehow, it was not. Somehow, it was... right.

He had brought her here. He had guarded her steps, watched her sleep, refused food and drink so she could have more. He had held her world together with nothing but sheer force of will.

And when this ended—*if* it ended—what then? Logically, something must change, for they could hardly hide here forever. Long enough for the scent of their trail to fade. The heat of immediate exposure to cool, and her stubborn knight errant to recover the strength to stagger back to his horse, back to the hunt.

Surely the assassins would be caught. Maddox exposed. Cunningham dragged from whatever darkened parlor he was hiding in. The Crown would thank its faithful servants. The scandal would fade. Eventually.

Even if it did not, how long would they really keep hunting her? Surely, at some point, they would either succeed in silencing her or just... give up. If no one caught the wrongdoers, if they had seemed to get away with it, why would they keep up the risk of exposing themselves trying to kill the daughter of a nobleman? Would there not come a time when her father's name protected her more surely than Darcy's arm?

Someday, somehow, this would end—it had to. And then what?

Would she go back to London? Back to her father's house, where the chandeliers gleamed and silence passed for affection? Where her absence had been tolerated with equanimity—perhaps even preferred?

The thought felt like putting on a gown that no longer fit.

She shifted, curling her feet more tightly under herself, still staring at the far corner where Darcy slept. He stirred a little now—the snoring stopped when he rolled into a deeper slumber, one arm flung carelessly off the cot so his hand scraped the floorboards. The cloak she had balled up under his head for a pillow had been pushed off the mattress, but she resisted the impulse to rise and fix it. Let him rest. Let him have this moment of peace. Heaven knew he deserved it after all he had endured for her sake.

That was when a cold stab crept down her spine—a thought she had never encountered before. Would she ever see him again? What would happen to him after this ended—after they survived it?

If they survived it.

She tried to picture him in the drawing room of her father's London townhouse, sipping brandy with bored peers and refusing to dance. It was a laughable image. He did not belong there any more than she did.

And yet...

He had become such a fixture in her life in two short weeks that she hardly knew how to breathe without him. Her gaze lingered on the hair tumbling over his brow. The loosened cravat. The shadow of stubble on his jaw. The deep steadiness of his breath.

She closed her eyes and rested her cheek on her knees.

No, she was not at all sure she could ever go back to "not knowing" Fitzwilliam Darcy.

And then—*crack*.

A sound from outside. Clean. Sudden. Like a foot snapping a twig beneath weight.

Her head jerked up. Heart pounding. Breath caught. Ears straining against silence.

She did not move. Neither did the trees.

But something had. She was certain of it.

CHAPTER TWENTY-SIX

H E STOOD NEAR THE edge of the ballroom, where the candlelight struck the gilded walls in golden waves and the string quartet played something lilting and strange. The air smelled of roses and jasmine. Somewhere behind him, a footman murmured something about refreshments, but Darcy hardly heard.

She was there.

Not across the room. Not tucked behind some gaggle of giggling girls. No—she stood alone, one gloved hand resting on the curve of a chair, the other playing idly with the flowing satin at her waist. Her gown was a molten gold that gave warmth to her cheeks and shimmered like a treasure chest beneath the chandeliers, and her smile—he swore it could cut through the fog of London itself.

Then she looked up, and the smile tilted.

Teasing. Knowing.

Darcy's throat went dry.

He meant to say something. He stepped toward her—just one step—and her laughter came like a bell, light and clear, and—

"Mr. Darcy," she whispered. "Sir—I need you."

He stepped closer—her eyes bright, her fingers poised as if to catch his sleeve. "Lady Elizabeth," he murmured. "Rather forward, do you not think?"

"Mr. Darcy," she breathed. "I must tell you something."

He stilled. Her voice wrapped around his name like a ribbon. "You may tell me anything."

But she shook her head. "Darcy! Blast you, wake *up*."

His brow furrowed. The music dimmed. Her face flickered. "I beg your pardon?"

"Darcy! Please!"

The room around him tilted. The candlelight shuddered. He blinked—

And flinched.

Breath caught in his throat as the dream broke apart, fragments dissolving before he could hold them still. A dull ache bloomed at the base of his skull, and for a moment, he did not know where he was.

Not the ballroom.

Not London.

Just the cottage. Cold air. Damp stone. The scent of must and soot and something vaguely like sheep. Rough wool beneath his cheek. The thin, uneven padding of a cot beneath his back.

"Darcy, I swear if you do not wake up, I will steal your pistols and fire a warning shot myself!"

Well, *that* was certainly no dream.

He opened his eyes—and she was leaning over him, her face drawn tight with worry.

"E... Elizabeth?"

Her fingers gripped his arm, her voice barely above breath. "I heard something."

He blinked. "What—?"

"Outside." She looked over her shoulder. "It was sharp. Like a snap. A branch, I think. Someone is out there."

Now fully awake, Darcy shoved upright. His limbs screamed in protest, stiff from too little rest and too much tension. But the fog was gone. The sharp chill of the stone walls. The scent of damp earth. The tremor in Elizabeth's voice. All of it sharpened his focus.

His eyes swept the room, quick and precise. "Where were you when you heard it?" he whispered, already reaching for his coat and the pistol buried inside.

"By the hearth. I was watching." Her eyes shone with fear, but her voice was not panicked. She was perfectly rational. "It was nothing at first. Just rustling. But then—it was sharp. Close. I had to crawl halfway across the room to wake you without making noise."

He was already moving. He grabbed his second pistol from the saddlebag and checked the load. Then he turned to her, his voice low and urgent. "Those two floor boards there are loose. Pull them up and climb under them. Get out of sight and stay there until I come back."

She bristled. "I am *not* hiding. What's the point if they kill you first? They will just come for me, anyway."

He stared at her.

"I can be useful!" she hissed fiercely.

A muscle in his jaw jumped—but he did not argue. He simply glanced around the room, spotted the iron poker by the hearth, and nodded toward it.

She followed his gaze, caught the meaning, and retrieved the poker silently. It looked absurd in her hand, but her grip was solid.

Darcy gave her one last look—steady, silent, full of the words he did not have time to say—and slipped out the door.

The air was still. The woods thick with early summer green.

He moved in a crouch, eyes scanning the thicket. Each breath was tightly wrapped in control. Every sound sharpened. No wind. No movement. He rounded the edge of the cottage, pistol raised—

—and stopped.

A shape shifted beside the woodpile.

For one breathless moment, he thought it a man. Large, slow-moving, head bowed.

Then it turned, slowly, and stared at him.

It was a sheep.

A bedraggled, matted old ram, wool overgrown and wild as moss. The creature stared back at him with blank, mildly curious eyes, then nosed the ground and returned to its grazing.

Darcy stared. Then let out a breath that nearly unbuckled his knees.

He watched the animal wander off into the trees, shaking its overgrown fleece with a stupid sort of majesty. Then he turned back toward the cottage.

Elizabeth met him at the door, poker still raised.

He holstered the pistol with a sigh. "A sheep," he said flatly. "Possibly the dumbest one in England."

She blinked. "A sheep?"

"Enormous. Filthy. Utterly disinterested in us."

Elizabeth's shoulders relaxed—but only slightly.

Darcy rubbed a hand over his face. "I should have expected it. Selwyn said the fences here were barely standing."

She looked out into the trees. "Still... better to check."

"Yes," he said. "Better to check. And a bloody good thing it was just a sheep, because between you trying to rouse me and the squeaking of that door hinge, it is a wonder all of Cambridge did not hear us."

He gestured for her to go inside first. And once the door shut behind them, neither of them reached for sleep again.

E LIZABETH SLICED THROUGH THE dried sausage with a dull penknife, the motion jerky from fatigue. A heel of black bread followed, divided as evenly as she could manage on a flat tin plate. She crossed the room in her stocking feet and set the meal in front of Darcy, who was crouched near the door, oiling the hinges with something he had pulled from a battered kit under the cot.

"Eat," she said simply, nudging the plate toward him.

He glanced up, surprised. Then nodded once and pulled the food toward him without a word.

She did not sit. Instead, she crossed her arms and leaned against the wall. "So. What now? Where to?"

Darcy chewed slowly, then wiped his mouth with the back of his hand—a necessity she was certain must have pained his sense of propriety. "*You* are not going anywhere."

"I know that," she said. "I meant you."

"I can hardly leave you here alone, can I?"

"So we are simply to sit here until we run out of food?"

He gave a long, tired exhale. "If I am to find Maddox... if we mean to catch any of them... yes. I will have to do... something else."

"But you might not," she said quickly.

Darcy looked up, brow furrowed. "What?"

"We might already be setting a trap." She tilted her head toward the cottage window. "We *might* have been followed."

He froze for just a beat. Then he set the bread down. "If we have been followed, it means I failed to cover our trail."

"Not necessarily," she said. "You are not the only one trying to outwit the enemy, remember. Someone may have been watching Longbourn for days."

He rubbed his eyes. "I had hoped the decoy letter would suffice to scatter them. But after that scene in Meryton yesterday... Well. At least it gave us enough time to get out.

If they were that close, they would have had any number of chances to shoot us before now."

Elizabeth swallowed. "I *knew* going to that festival was a bad idea."

"*Not* going to it would have been a bad idea as well," Darcy sighed tiredly. "I should have dragged you to Scotland and hidden you under a frost heave. Perhaps nobody would have found you then."

A smile threatened to tug on her mouth. "I also know you well enough to expect you have formed a backup plan by now."

He arched his brows tiredly as he chewed. "I asked Bingley to send a message to Richard. A coded express, last night. If all went as planned, Richard should already know where we are. Ten pounds says he is on his way already."

She smiled weakly. "You do not have ten pounds."

He lifted one shoulder. "Then it is a good thing I feel confident in the wager."

Elizabeth dropped onto a footstool beside him with a long exhale, her limbs still aching from the night's ride. She reached for the tin plate without thinking, tore a corner from the heel of bread, and took a bite—only to find Darcy watching her, one brow raised and the barest hint of a crooked grin at the corner of his mouth.

"Oh... oh, that was yours." She swallowed. "Surely, I... there is a bit more. Let me—"

He nudged the plate toward her without comment.

She narrowed her eyes at him but accepted the offering, chewing the rest in silence before pushing the final bite back his way.

"For all this," she muttered, brushing crumbs from her fingers, "I hope someone, somewhere, is pleased with the results. The whole of England is rumbling, and what do we have to show for it? Stale bread, dried-up sausages, and an assassin's bounty on my head."

Darcy said nothing, but his jaw twitched. He turned to the door hinge again and gave it another careful turn of the cloth.

Elizabeth stretched out on her stool. "We ought to go to America," she said brightly. "Disappear entirely. I have heard they outlawed nobility, rejected kings, and run about happily without a single overfed marquess or bobbing old earl to tell them what to do."

That earned her a glance—faint amusement flickering in his eyes. "Is that so?"

"It is," she declared. "No dukes. No viscounts or knights of the realm. No scheming courtiers or secret fixers with hippocampus rings. Just endless wilderness and bears and...

and maize. I am sure Mr. Bennet told me his cousin boasted about this vegetable they call maize. I hear it is terribly wonderful."

Darcy huffed a quiet laugh. "*I* have heard they scorch their tea and cannot tie a proper cravat to save their lives."

"Savages!" she cried, grinning. "That settles it—we cannot possibly flee to there."

He shook his head, turning back to the hinge, but not before she saw the smile still playing at the corner of his mouth.

She leaned in conspiratorially. "I suppose I might bear the cravat-less men, but I draw the line at over-steeped tea. What would we even drink? Coffee?"

Darcy affected a shudder. "I would rather face Maddox with both hands tied."

Elizabeth gasped. "And here I thought you were brave."

"I have my limits."

"Then it is settled," she said solemnly. "We shall remain in hiding in this noble and drafty cottage until the end of time. You may pass the days oiling hinges, and I shall perfect the art of moping. There. I think have affected a passable frown, what do you say?" She pulled a pout and rested her chin on her hand, wigging her eyebrows at him.

He laughed then—unexpected and full, the sound startling even himself.

"A laugh!" she crowed. "I knew you could still do it."

His smile softened as he looked at her. "You make it difficult not to."

"I do try, you know. I absolutely cannot abide the idea of frowning all the time, and you are just starting to make a passable companion. If we go elsewhere, I shall have to start all over on another project gentleman."

He laughed again—freely, this time. But it faded too quickly. His smile dimmed as some shadow crossed behind his eyes. His fingers stilled on the hinge, and his eyes fell.

"What, what is this?" she asked.

His chest rose on an indrawn breath, and his mouth shaped to frame words. "I..." But then he stopped and rose from his crouch abruptly to begin working on the upper hinge of the door.

Elizabeth's eyes rose with him, and dash it all if it was not uncomfortable to be squatting at his feet on a stool, so she sighed and clambered back to her feet on weary legs.

Darcy acted like he was ignoring her, jaw tight as he worked the pin through the joint to oil it. The movement was calculated, methodical—too methodical for a man who had just been laughing. Elizabeth watched his hands move, then his shoulders shift as he leaned into the task.

She cleared her throat softly. "Mr. Darcy?"

He did not answer right away.

She picked the empty plate up off the floor to set it on a nearby table, and returned to stop a few feet behind him. "Sir, I think it is time you told me whatever it is you are keeping from me."

That drew his attention. He turned, slowly, his brow lifting with practiced neutrality. "What do you think I am keeping from you?"

"Oh, come," she said, folding her arms. "What about the scandal that drove us out of Meryton yesterday? You might at least admit what it was."

His gaze fell away. "Surely you heard everything."

"Actually, I did not," she said with a huff of a laugh. "I was not near Mr. Collins when he received that letter. I saw the effect—but not the cause. Once I saw the faces in the crowd, I knew we would have to leave at once, so I moved quickly to the carriage. Mr. Bennet, Mary, and Jane joined me—and none of them seemed inclined to speak so much as a single syllable. So... I truly have no notion what it was yesterday that turned you into a pariah in a town that once thought well of you."

He looked back at her sharply.

"I did know there was a scandal," she said, softer now. "That something terrible happened to your father when you were a young man. Mr. Bingley told me only that much. He did not feel at liberty to say more."

Darcy's mouth pressed until his lips were almost invisible. He returned his focus to the hinge, testing the door at last. It swung silently.

Then he stepped back and turned, wiping his hands on a cloth from the floor. His eyes scanned the room as though hoping for a distraction—any distraction—but found none.

At last, he exhaled.

"You may as well hear it, then. There is no escaping it now."

He paced once, stopped, then paced again before dragging a hand through his hair. "I confess... I half-believed you already knew. That someone would have told you, in London, before you ever met me. I thought surely the gossip had reached even your circles. Your father had to have known, of a certainty, and you are clever enough... I kept waiting for you to say something, but you never did. I never dared to hope you were truly ignorant of everything."

She shook her head slowly, watching him.

Darcy moved away from the door at last and crossed to the hearth, but he did not sit. His hands braced on the back of the nearest chair, head bowed. The stillness of him was disquieting.

"When I was fifteen," he began, his voice trembling faintly—the first time she had ever heard that— "my father was still the Eighth Earl of Pemberley. A title centuries old. Revered, in some corners. Envied, in others. Pemberley itself—our estate in Derbyshire—was the jewel of our line. My father took pride in that. In our tenants, our land, our name."

He paused, lips parting as if to continue—but the words stalled. When he spoke again, it was even more shaken.

"We had a steward, Mr. Wickham. A man of uncommon acumen. He kept our accounts in perfect order. Saw to the farms. Negotiated leases. Even kept a weather eye on the law when local disputes arose. I remember my father praising him often. Saying we were fortunate to have him."

Darcy straightened but did not look at her.

"He was ambitious. Loyal, outwardly. But beneath that..." He exhaled. "Jealous. His own son—George—was clever, if spoiled. He had everything I did—ponies when we were boys. The best tutors. A gentleman's education. But no matter how bright he was, how much he was given, he would never inherit Pemberley. He would never be *me*, is the sum of it. And his father—his father could not abide it."

He paced a few steps, not looking at her. "I was at Eton when it began. Home only during holidays. I did not see it unravel, not with my own eyes. But I remember the tone of my father's letters changing. His weariness. There were whispers. Rumors about strange absences—unsubstantiated, but that did not matter. He wrote once that the local magistrate had begun inquiring after impropriety—without naming the charge. He told me at the time he did not know the source of the rumors."

Darcy turned and looked at her now, the pupils of his eyes now grown dark.

"And then, one day, it was made plain. Accusations. Two sworn statements. A coachman. A scullery boy. Claims of... conduct unbecoming. Involving my father."

Elizabeth's mouth parted. "I... I do not..."

"They called him... a sodomite. Said he kept unnatural company, hosted deviant gatherings. Mr. Wickham went on record at last, saying he had once caught my father in the act."

"*Oh,*" she breathed. Her ears burned to scalding. So *that* was why he had been so uncomfortable speaking of it.

"He denied everything. Of course he did, because there was not even a grain of truth in it. Innocent moments twisted to look nefarious. The kindness of a true gentleman in the intimacy of his own home, but never *that*. But by the time the King's couriers arrived—by the time the accusation reached the Crown—the scandal had grown. Whether anyone truly believed it scarcely mattered. A nobleman accused of such things... it was easier to silence the embarrassment than question its origin."

His hands flexed once, then closed into fists—slowly, deliberately, as if to keep something darker from escaping.

"The title was revoked. The estate was meant to be absorbed by the Crown. But in a turn so inexplicable that it could only have been the deliberate work of a criminal upon a mad king, His Majesty granted our land, our holdings... to the steward. To Wickham."

Her eyes widened, not in horror, but in disbelief—like someone told the sky had fallen and expected to see it lying neatly in pieces on the floor. "To... the man who accused him? But... *how?*"

Darcy gave a bitter laugh. "He said it was to 'preserve the local order.' That the steward had managed the land for years, and would see it done properly. I was seventeen. I returned from school to find the gates of my childhood home locked against me."

"And your friend the heir in your place," she murmured.

"He was never my friend. George made my life a living hell whenever he could. Taunting me, living in dissolution and making me pick up the pieces to keep from shaming our fathers... If only I had known how little his own father cared about shame!" He swallowed. "My father died three years later. Alone. With nothing."

Elizabeth stepped toward him, her fingers daring to stretch for his coat sleeve, but stopping short. "I do not know what to say."

"There is nothing to say," Darcy replied, voice ragged. "Only that I have been paying for it ever since."

She did it this time—she reached for him, slowly.

He did not flinch. But his expression turned inward, as if refusing to accept comfort from her.

"Perhaps it is human nature to try to claim one knows where it all went wrong. To place blame on the victim, saying if they had only seen... been more aware..." He shook his head. "I have spent the last ten years trying to be nothing like him, and yet everything like him. Trying to atone for a crime he did not commit, but there is no wiping that stain from my family's name."

She blinked, recalling something. "Your sister... what of her?"

He gulped a long breath of air and walked away from her, leaving her hand dangling after him. "She manages. She ought to be one of the diamonds of the *ton*—like you—but not now. I think she rather likes being invisible. My aunt and uncle took my sister in to be one of their own daughters, though I am distressed to hear of my cousin's... behavior towards her."

"It was not all that terrible," Elizabeth inserted. "She did not mock her or make her sweep the floors or anything so insulting. She just treated her as a bit of a... a novelty, I suppose. And truly, if I had a cousin living with me who could play as well as your sister does, I think I would want others to hear her as well."

"You needn't make excuses for my cousin Julia. I know very well who and what she is. Still..." He lifted one shoulder. "I hardly have any right to complain after everything else. The earl and countess have been kind—were it not for them, and for Richard, I would not even have been allowed to finish school. My uncle advised me to take up at the Home Office, vouched for me to secure the place, and I was able to work my way up from there. I only wish... well, I suppose there is nothing to be done now."

"Oh, now, you cannot stop there. What do you wish?"

He glanced up once, then turned away, as if it all had become too heavy to face her. He swallowed, and was a moment in replying.

"I thought... if I could serve the Crown, if I could carry out work that mattered—quietly, effectively—then perhaps I might restore some portion of what was lost. Not the land. Not the title. Those are gone. But perhaps the honor."

"But that..." She sucked in a breath. "Oh! I *knew* you had something personal—some secret that made you particularly beholden to the Prince. You—you have been trying to clear your father's name, have you not? It makes sense now."

He gave a bitter half-smile, facing the hearth now, not her. "I have worked rather diligently to make myself 'useful.' And my plan seemed to be working, too. My petition was noticed, my character and work esteemed just enough to make me a curiosity. The Prince promised me an audience shortly after he was made Regent. Suggested he might be willing to review the ruling—quietly, of course. 'Informally.' It was the first hope I had been given in years."

Elizabeth wetted her lips, leaning forward and holding her breath. "And did he?"

"You saw the man. He laughs at everything. Including that promise. He dangled it in front of me like a reward, and yanked it back the moment I asked him to make good his word. Not for the first time, either."

Her hands gripped the edge of the table, knuckles white.

"So yes," he said, turning slowly. "That is what they meant. That is the scandal. The disgrace. That is what Lady Catherine used to cast me out of Meryton. What Mr. Collins will whisper to every parlor and pew. That my father was a sodomite, and I—the shameful heir—am likely no better."

Elizabeth stepped toward him. "There is nothing 'shameful' about you, and the truth is what matters."

He shook his head, dark eyes flickering with something like pain. "You do not understand. It does not matter what I am. Only what they believe. That scandal lives beneath every interaction, every invitation withheld. Every door quietly closed."

She took another step. "But it is not true."

"No," he said simply. "But truth was never the point."

"Well... what *is*? Surely, His Highness knows the truth. Why would he keep... *teasing* you like this? For his own amusement?"

Darcy lifted a shoulder. "Very likely."

She shook her head, snorting in disgust. "I do not understand. How are you supposed to appease him enough to make him keep his word? Are you supposed to... to dance a jig? Come bathe his feet for him, feed him grapes while someone strums the harp, *what*? What the devil does he expect you to do?"

He closed his eyes, biting his top lip between his teeth. "Ruin you."

CHAPTER TWENTY-SEVEN

"*R*UIN ME? AS IN... *ruin?* The... you know. The—" Her hands shaped in the air and gesticulated somewhat crudely. "*Everything?*"

Darcy swallowed. He turned from the fire and pressed both hands to the back of the chair between them. "That is what he would prefer."

Realization dawned slowly. "You mean—this *entire time*—he meant for you to...?"

"Yes."

Elizabeth's breath left her in a slow, stunned hiss. "No, no. I was there! I heard his command. He said he wanted me *protected*."

"He did. But not only that."

She moved toward him—one step, maybe two—but her eyes never left his. "You mean to say I was bait. For... an entirely different sort of trap."

Darcy only nodded.

Elizabeth's expression contorted—outrage warring with humiliation. "He wanted you to prove yourself a man? *That* was the test?"

A faint, bitter smile ghosted across Darcy's mouth. "He believes in appetites. Wine, women, sensation. Scandal entertains him. Virtue bores him. And my life has never entertained him."

Her hands clenched into fists at her sides. "He was willing to destroy *me* for that? Just to watch you slip because he thought it would be *amusing?*"

His gaze flicked up, meeting hers. "Yes. And do not think your father's standing mattered one whit to him. That probably only made it all the more entertaining as far as he was concerned."

Elizabeth stared at him. Her mouth opened, then closed. "You knew. From the first night, you knew."

He nodded. "I did."

She let out a soft, incredulous breath and turned away, pacing to the far end of the hearth. "So... this was never about the assassination. Not really. It was all about you and trying to get Pemberley back and a spoiled, selfish Prince who thought this was all a good joke."

"No," he said quietly. "It was and is about the murder. Maddox still lives. Cunningham still hides. The Prime Minister was gunned down in daylight, and a scapegoat was hanged for it—there is real justice at stake, and there really are men who would very much like it if *you* never spoke another word again. But the Prince... he saw an opportunity to accomplish many things at once. Temptation of every sort to dangle before *me*, and *you* entirely without choice in the matter."

Elizabeth spun back to face him, fury flickering in her voice. "You should have told me! Before it was too late, before I was dragged away from—"

"How?" he scoffed. "Announce it right there when we were standing outside the gates to Buckingham House? You would have stormed the palace and thrown your gloves in his face, and then we would have been hanging *two* people at Old Bailey."

"I still might!" she snapped.

His mouth twitched despite himself. But there was no laughter in it. "It was cruel. I know it."

Her chest rose and fell. "And yet you played along."

"No!" he said sharply. "No—I refused to."

Something in her expression shifted. Doubt. Wonder.

"I have obeyed his command," Darcy continued, "and I have protected you—with my own life, I have protected you. Nothing more. Nothing less. Not one step beyond what duty required. I have *not* touched you, and I *will* not."

Elizabeth stared at him. Then—softly— "Why not?"

His mouth dropped open. "I... *what?*"

Her voice broke. "It would have been so easy for you, you know. Seduce me. Trade my honor for yours. One night. One misstep—a bottle of ale, a few promises you have no intention of keeping. That is all it would take, is it not?"

The look she gave him stopped him mid-breath. His chest shot through with quiet, blazing pain. A question and an answer and a wound, all at once. "I am not such a fool that I ever accounted that... or *anything* about you... easy."

She took a step forward.

Then another.

He did not move.

She crossed the room with no hesitation now, only the quiet certainty of a woman who had made up her mind. He told himself to stop her. He told himself to turn away.

He did neither.

She came to stand before him, close enough that he could feel the warmth of her skin, the faint rise and fall of her breath. Her hands reached up—tentative at first—then firmer, fingers slipping behind his neck. She had to stretch on her toes to reach him, and still he did not move.

So she pulled.

And he let her.

Their lips met—soft, testing, unbearably tender. His breath caught. For one suspended second, he kissed her back—and then he tore away.

"This..." he said, voice raw, "this was not what I wanted."

She looked up at him. "Are you sure?"

"No. That is..." His hands fisted at his sides, nails digging into his palms—anything to keep from reaching for her. "I never asked for this."

Her head tilted just slightly. "Then do not lean down. I cannot reach you if you do not lean down."

She kissed him again... because she could.

This time, he tried.

He truly did.

His hands came up—caught her by the shoulders—not roughly, not firmly, only enough to slow her. His lips parted, his breath ragged, but he could not seem to make the words come. Her mouth was already pressing to his again, soft and sure, and the moment he tasted her, all his strength faltered.

She was warm beneath his hands. Warm and willing and alive in a way that made his heart seem to burst. Her kiss deepened—more bold now, more certain—and he groaned as her fingers slid over his chest, over his shoulders, tugging him closer.

He wrenched back with effort. "Elizabeth," he managed, hoarse. "This is... a bad idea. We should not—"

"Then tell me to stop," she whispered.

Her eyes met his, wide and sure and gleaming in the low light.

He opened his mouth, but nothing came.

So she reached for him again.

When he kissed her back—truly, fully—it was like drowning. His hands tangled in her hair, and her arms wrapped around his neck. There was nothing gentle in it now. Her lips parted beneath his with a sigh that was half a moan, and he drank it in like salvation. Her body pressed to his, mouth opening for him again and again, and he was lost. Devouring her. Consuming her. Every sound she made shot through him like fire. When he kissed down her neck, she arched, gasping encouragement.

He was already gone.

He could not think. Could not reason. He knew only her fingers twisting in his hair, her mouth trailing heat along his jaw, the intoxicating press of her curves beneath his hands. She clung to him, pliant and eager, and he burned for her.

She whispered his name—his given name—and it wrecked him.

He picked her up—one seamless, breathless movement—and she laughed against his throat, the sound barely audible, more sigh than laughter, but it curled around his spine like a brand. Her arms wound tighter around his neck, and her lips found the line of his jaw again just before she pulled back to look at him.

His eyes met hers. He should have set her down. He should have said her name—gently, warningly, with all the strength of a man still in control.

Instead, he carried her to the cot.

The room seemed smaller, dimmer, pulsing with the sound of his own heartbeat. He knelt over her, his hands braced on either side, trying—truly trying—to draw one last breath of sense before he lost it entirely. But she was already pulling him down with her, fingers in his hair, cradling his head to her chest like she meant to keep him there forever.

And he went. Helpless. Wanting.

Her breath hitched as his lips found her throat, lingering there. Kissing lightly, then deeper, letting his mouth speak the things he could not yet say aloud. Her scent, her skin, the shiver she gave when he moved—he had never known desire like this. It consumed. It commanded.

He could make this right. Even now... even if...

She would be ruined, yes—her reputation shattered beyond repair—but not by force, not by deceit. By choice. By her own will. Her own fire. *She* had come to *him*, arms open, eyes clear, asking nothing but the truth of his heart.

And he would give her everything in return—everything that was his to give, at least.

Her father would surely protest, but he would prevail. He would tell all, if necessary, to prove that he was the only man she could possibly have. He would bind himself to her in every way a man could. She would never lack for protection, never fear disgrace. The world might talk—God knew it would—but he could shield her from the worst of it. With his name. His vows.

She would not fall alone.

The Prince would see it. That lecherous puppet master would count this as a victory. His little game played out. The noble, icy Fitzwilliam Darcy, finally tumbled by a woman. It would be proof enough, perhaps—proof that Darcy was, in the eyes of the court, a man like any other. Tempted. Mortal. Flesh and blood.

And no longer a worthy source of entertainment for a royal hedonist. The Prince might finally keep his promise... the scandal would fade. His name might be restored.

And he—he could go home. To Pemberley. To his birthright.

But not alone. Not this time.

He could bring her with him. Hand in hand. Queen of the place he had once been forced to leave in disgrace. The final piece of his shattered world made whole—his ruin and his redemption, wrapped in the same arms.

Her hands threaded into his hair and pulled him closer.

"I love you," she whispered, voice soft as prayer, fierce as battle. "I love you, Fitzwilliam Darcy."

The words struck him like a musket ball.

Clean through. No warning. No armor. No breath.

His hands froze where they rested—gripping her waist, her ribs, her heartbeat.

His lungs refused to work. His vision tunneled.

He lifted his head slowly, as if surfacing from a dream he had no wish to wake from.

And then—he pulled away.

Not gently.

He staggered upright, every motion abrupt, disjointed. His limbs no longer obeyed the rhythm of desire, only the jolt of panic pounding in his chest.

And he walked.

Blindly. As far as the room would allow.

The moment her voice broke the silence, soft and uncertain, he flinched.

"What did I do?"

He did not look back.

She was still seated, he could tell by the sound of her voice—muffled slightly by the press of the cot, by the distance between them—but her hurt rang through the question as clear as any bell. A tremor of disbelief, of aching confusion.

"Nothing," he said at last, his voice unsteady. "Lord help me, you did... everything right. That is the problem."

Behind him, he heard the creak of the cot as she shifted. Then her feet on the floor. Then a single step toward him.

He held out a hand, sharply, as if warding off a blow.

"Please!" he choked. "Do not come closer."

She halted. He could feel her stillness behind him like heat. Silence stretched between them until she spoke again—quieter, gentler.

"Is it... because I said I loved you?"

His eyes closed. His throat worked once before he found the words.

"It is because I cannot hurt you." He gripped the edge of the shuttered window in both hands, his knuckles white. "No matter what you believe now, what you might convince yourself you understand... if I take what you offer—if I give in, indulge my own pleasures—you will be the one to suffer."

"I told you, I understand the consequences—"

"No," he cut in, voice ragged. "You trust me. That is not the same thing."

She blinked, and her mouth dropped open for a half a heartbeat.

"I *do* trust you. And I know you are not a cad, but perhaps just this once, you should try acting like one. If you took me to your bed now, it would not be out of vanity or cruelty. I know that. I know *you*. And if you are right—if it meant your name restored, your family redeemed, your home returned—then perhaps I should let you. Perhaps the exchange would be worth it."

A bitter sound escaped his throat—half laugh, half groan.

"You think I have not thought of that?" he muttered. "That I have not imagined exactly how the Prince would react—how loudly he would laugh first, and then quickly he would declare his 'suspicions' laid to rest? How easily the path would clear if I gave him his entertainment?"

"But we could marry! No scandal, no... consequences to regret."

Darcy's heart lurched. She would have him? In *that* way, as well as *this*? Oh, how he had longed for... for even a kind word from her, but she was offering her entire self, all her future, for *him?* He closed his eyes and balled his fist, clenching it against his teeth to prevent himself from blurting out a *"God, yes!"*

Instead, he hung his head, shaking it. "Your father would send you to Scotland first. You would bear my bastard in disgrace and he would hide the child and cover it all, or sell you to the nearest lord in need of an heir before he would consider... It is impossible, Elizabeth."

"I... I can choose whom I please when I come of age..."

Darcy chuckled bitterly. "Next March? I am afraid that would be too late."

He turned toward her, but not fully. "It is no good, Elizabeth. I promised myself, from the first moment the Prince assigned me this task, I would not use you. I would not... trade you. I cannot buy back what was lost by harming what is most precious to me."

Silence.

Not confusion, this time.

Suspicion.

He heard her drawing closer, could almost feel the air stir as she sucked in a gasp. "What do you mean by that?"

Darcy turned slowly. The sight of her—eyes wide with hurt, lips parted in confusion—struck him with a force that nearly stole his breath. He clenched his jaw, swallowing the emotion that threatened to overtake him.

"What I mean," he began, staring at the floor so he would not look at her face, "is that you were right."

"Right? About what?"

He let the air out of his lungs slowly, his eyes searching hers. "That day outside Longbourn, when I confronted you about wandering from the safety of the house... you guessed not only that this was personal for me, but that I knew of you long before we met. That is... not the full truth."

He paused, a bitter smile touching his lips. "At the time, I retorted that everyone knew you—the daughter of a marquess with a dowry substantial enough to feed all of London for a year. Everyone was competing for your hand, yet you had satisfied none of them. You were the constant subject of society pages, with endless speculation about who you would choose."

Elizabeth's brow furrowed. "Yes, I remember. But that was not all?"

Darcy shook his head, his expression pained. "No. I first saw you at a ball. I declined an introduction. Refused a chance to dance with you."

She blinked, a little surprise flickering across her face before she smiled. "That does not astound me. I have always thought you the sort who would despise dancing."

He managed a faint grunt. "It is true, I have never been fond of it. But that was not the reason."

He turned away, running a hand through his hair. "My aunt, Lady Matlock, advised me to marry an heiress. She believed that was the surest way to restore some of our family's dignity. I loathed the idea of trying to rebuild my family on the back of another like that... but I had Georgiana to consider. I could not easily dismiss my aunt's counsel, so, I accepted her invitation to a ball. It was last year, early spring—one of the first balls of the Season."

Elizabeth squinted, and then a wrinkle appeared at the edge of her mouth. "Lady Matlock? I remember that ball. I wore a gold gown the Duchess of Wrexham helped to design—gold silk with a ridiculous number of rosettes. My hair would not stay pinned, and Lady Henshawe made me redo it twice before we even left."

He nodded, a distant look in his eyes. "It shimmered like liquid gold in the candle light. I remember, it was shortly after you made your curtsey to the Queen."

She let out a soft, incredulous laugh. "The first ball I attended after that, yes. You do have an excellent memory. I went with Charlotte and her mother, and we were nearly turned away at the door because someone forgot the invitation. I danced with Lord Densmore—who stepped on my foot—and then with Captain Harcourt, who would not stop talking about the weather." She tilted her head. "But I have no memory of Fitzwilliam Darcy."

Darcy swallowed. "No... you would not have. My aunt introduced me to numerous young ladies that evening—all respectable, many beautiful and well-dowered. I even considered asking one or two to dance. Your name was on everyone's lips before you even arrived—so much speculation about you and maybe one or two others who were expected to make an appearance that evening."

She blushed and looked down. "I never liked that bit. Of course, yes, it is flattering, but I believe it frightened away just as many people as were drawn to me."

He offered a dry huff. "Well, believe me, I thought it all rot at first. But then I saw you enter the room, and I had eyes for no one else. Nor did any other gentleman."

Elizabeth's eyes widened. "But I never saw you. Not even a glimpse. I feel sure I would have remembered."

He smiled ruefully. "No. Because I knew you were as far beyond my reach as the stars. Yet I could not look away."

She sniffed and swallowed, glancing at the window—the floor—his shoes. "I never meant to..."

"Yes you did." His voice softened. "You walked in like the room belonged to you, and perhaps it did. Not because of your father's name, or the whispers of your dowry. It was the way you moved, as if joy followed in your wake. The way you looked at each person who spoke to you—as though their words truly mattered."

He risked one step closer to her—just enough to reach for the worried knot of her fingers to try to soothe them. "I watched you laugh with a girl whose name I never caught. You tucked a flower back into her hair when it slipped from her ribbon and whispered something to her that made her glow. I watched you rescue a plate from a nervous footman and hand it off before the hostess saw. And I watched you take a seat beside an elderly lady who seemed utterly forgotten, and make her feel the center of the room."

His voice wavered. "You made the tedious seem delightful. The pomp and vanity of that hall dimmed in your presence. You... outshone everything."

She was still staring at their hands, letting him do as he pleased with her fingers. But at his last words, she locked her hand to capture his, not permitting him to withdraw it.

He hesitated, then continued, his voice thick with emotion. "There was a moment when you reached for a biscuit and found the plate empty. You blinked, made a face, and then laughed—laughed like it was the best joke you had heard all evening. And in that ridiculous moment, I knew."

"...Knew? What?"

She was gazing up at him now, eyes wide and glittering with a sheen of tears.

He worked one hand loose from hers and let his fingers trace her cheek, shaking his head. "I realized then that I had seen the woman to whom I would compare all others for the rest of my life. A woman I could never hope to even speak to."

She narrowed her eyes faintly and tried to open her mouth, but her voice cracked before she could release even a single word.

He exhaled a shaky breath. "I left the ball shortly after, apologizing to Lady Matlock for not dancing with any of her guests. She did not forgive me for months. And I did not forget."

Elizabeth finally cleared her throat. "You... you really thought all that, did you?" she whispered.

He smiled faintly. "When I saw you that night at Buckingham House," he murmured, "brought into the Prince's chambers, shaking and frightened... and then entrusted to *my* care..." He closed his eyes. "Great heavens, I felt unworthy. Incapable. My failures nearly cost you your life."

Elizabeth's eyes filled with tears again, but her features hardened. "No! The mistakes were mine, not yours."

He shook his head. "I cannot accept that. I could never live with myself if any harm came to you. Because the woman I once placed on a pedestal, whom I watched from afar, whose name I sought in every broadsheet, every carriage in Mayfair..."

He cupped her face gently. "You are no longer a distant dream to me, Elizabeth. You are a part of my heart. And I would sooner tear it from my chest than do anything to hurt you."

He leaned in, pressing a tender kiss to her cheek. As he pulled back, she caught his face in her hands, attempting to bring his lips to hers. But he resisted, stepping away.

Clearing his throat, he mumbled, "I should check the perimeter."

CHAPTER TWENTY-EIGHT

H E HAD FLED THE room.

Not in haste. Not in disgrace. But in that deliberate, careful manner he used whenever he was afraid he might do something reckless.

She had not moved from the chair by the window since.

The fire was low. The shutters still drawn, though she peeked through them every few minutes. And somewhere beyond the walls of this stone-wrapped sanctuary, Darcy was pacing the cold earth, trying to forget how it felt to touch her.

She curled her knees beneath her, pulling the blanket tighter around her shoulders, though she was not cold.

Half in love with her before they had even spoken.

Darcy's confession echoed again and again in her mind, recalling every stolen glance, every silent hesitation, every moment of misjudged reserve he had offered her since they met.

He had known her name long before she learned his. Had watched her dance, smile, tease some simpering peer in a golden ballroom, and had thought her beyond reach. And then, somehow, she had landed—quite literally—in his care. Bruised and hunted and more herself than she had ever been in satin and jewels.

She closed her eyes and sighed.

She should have been furious. He had let her believe he found her bothersome, a burden he would rather do without. Had spoken to her with ice in his tone and steel in his posture. But now, looking back, she could see the cracks in that armor, for they had been there from the start. Every flinch. Every hard-won word.

He had wanted her. Even then. Perhaps most especially then.

And now... now he was out there breathing cold air because he did not trust himself to breathe near her.

She rose slowly, smoothing the blanket and folding it with meticulous care, though her hands trembled just a little. She found the bucket and rinsed off the tin plates they had used earlier. Put the room to rights and then, when that was done, she went about tidying even what had not been disturbed.

And still he did not return.

When the door finally creaked open, she turned without haste.

Darcy stood in the frame, a satchel over his shoulder, a pail of water clutched in one hand. He did not speak. Merely entered, eyes down, jaw set. She watched him set things down with the same exaggerated calm he always used when he was trying not to feel.

"You were gone a long while. I was starting to worry you had been discovered."

"I apologize." He set the satchel down first, then the pail, careful not to spill. "The well is farther than I recalled. Selwyn left a note tucked in the door. There was another parcel out back—more provisions."

He did not look at her as he said it, only crouched by the hearth and began building the fire from the embers he had banked before. His hands were practiced and efficient, striking flint, nursing the flame, shielding it from the draught.

Elizabeth crouched beside the satchel and began pulling out what he had brought: more smoked sausage, dried apples, a larger round of hard cheese, a cloth-wrapped loaf of oat bread. Far more than she expected.

"I suppose we can breathe easier. At least we will not starve."

"No," he said, glancing at her. "Selwyn is cautious. He always prepares for three times what is needed."

She retrieved the little pen knife and began to slice the bread. Not because she was hungry, but because her hands needed something to do. It felt strangely like being in a play—her cutting food, him coaxing flame to life like a couple acting out a well-rehearsed routine. A play about a couple who knew each other inside and out, who did not require words to understand their parts.

The thought made her throat close. Because if there was one man she could ever imagine herself living the simple life with... building a home with, rather than just commanding the one given to her...

It was this man.

As the water warmed, he fetched two cracked mugs and poured what little tea they had left into one. He passed it to her without comment, and she accepted it without thanks, both of them too aware, now, of all that remained unsaid.

When the fire had caught, and the water simmered, he straightened.

"I will go back out. Surely you would like a chance to refresh yourself now that the water is hot." And then he left, closing the door behind him.

T HE NIGHT WAS THICK with silence—the kind that hummed in the ears and made even the settling of timbers sound like thunder. Elizabeth lay stiff on the narrow cot, her arms folded across her stomach, staring up at the uneven ceiling.

Her mind refused to still. Darcy's voice still echoed in her memory, low and rough with all he had tried to bury. She could not stop thinking of the way he had looked at her... the way he had held her, kissed her as if she were his only link to life... and then left the room in a rush because staying another moment might break him.

He now sat near the window, angled just enough away that she could not read his face. His outline was sharp against the soft gray spill of moonlight—broad shoulders drawn tight beneath his coat, one hand resting lightly on the table beside him. The other was close to the pistol he had placed within easy reach.

He had not spoken since his last return. Not a word. Not a glance. Perhaps because he would have had to see her hair drying or see her soiled dress laid out to be scrubbed.

Elizabeth turned her head slightly, watching him through the flickering light of the embers. He looked composed. Almost peaceful. But she saw the way his jaw flexed now and then. The way one boot tapped softly against the floor. He was trying to be still. Trying to seem distant. But she knew better.

That was no peace at all.

Elizabeth curled onto her side, the threadbare blanket drawn up to her chin, listening to the slow crackle of the fire dying in the grate. Its flickering warmth did little to chase the cold that had seeped into her bones—not from the night air, but from everything that had passed between them. The silence between her and Darcy was not hostile. It was reverent. Fragile. Weighted with too much.

She blinked slowly, trying to will her body into rest.

And then—

A crack like cannon fire tore through the room.

The window shattered in a volcano of breaking glass. Splinters and shards sprayed across the floor like a hail of razors. She gasped, too stunned to scream, as a second blast followed, closer this time—louder. Her heart stopped.

Darcy grunted—no, choked—and jerked violently in his chair.

His body collapsed sideways, slamming to the floorboards with a sickening thud. For one frozen second, he lay still.

And then the blood came.

It spread quickly across the white of his sleeve, soaking the fabric in a deep, vicious red.

"Fitzw—!" The rest of his name caught in her throat, lost to the terror clawing its way up her chest.

She flung the blanket aside and bolted from the cot. Her bare feet hit the floor hard—then hissed in pain as they struck something sharp. Shattered glass. She stumbled, barely catching herself as she skidded through the debris, the skin of her soles slicing open, warm blood meeting cold splinters.

She did not feel it.

Not truly. Not yet.

Her only thought was *him*.

She dropped to her knees beside him, heedless of the glass cutting into her skin, of the warm stickiness already streaking her legs. Her palms flew to his chest—searching, frantic—then to his throat, trembling fingers pressing into skin she could barely feel over the roar in her ears.

He was so still.

His eyes—closed. His jaw slack.

"Fitz—Fitzwilliam—please—"

Blood soaked through her fingers, seeping from the torn white of his sleeve. It felt endless. Hot. Terrifying.

She let out a strangled sob and bent low over him, her forehead brushing his cheek.

"Please," she whispered again. "Please do not leave me!"

Another shot rang out, and a splinter of wood burst from the wall above them.

She ducked instinctively, heart hammering against her ribs. There was no time. No time to think. Only survive.

"Darcy!" Her voice was a desperate whisper, her hands trembling as they hovered over his inert form. Another shot rang out, cracking the doorframe inches from her head. Panic surged, but she forced it down. *Think, Elizabeth. Think.*

Her gaze darted around the room, wild and searching. The shattered window gaped open, and more shots echoed—sharp cracks that sent fresh glass raining down from the frame. She flinched instinctively as a bullet tore through the edge of the cot behind her.

The floorboards.

She remembered—there, to the left of the hearth, the two boards Darcy had told her were loose. An empty space below to hide. Shallow, but maybe enough for both of them—if she could get to it.

Another shot slammed into the wall, and she dropped low, throwing herself across Darcy's body. Could she move him? His weight was ungainly, and dead weight at that—though she refused to think of it as such.

Not dead. He is not dead.

"Please—please forgive me," she whispered, her voice cracking as she hooked her arms under his and began to drag. How many glass shards was she raking across his flesh? Her back burned. Her palms slipped against his blood-slick shirt. Her wounded feet left streaks behind her on the floor. But she moved him—inch by agonizing inch—toward the place where the boards were.

A bullet tore through the windowframe. Another buried itself in the mattress.

She gritted her teeth and reached for the floorboards. The gap was just wide enough for her fingertips. She clawed at them, shoved, wedged the toe of her foot beneath one and wrenched it up. The wood came loose with a groan. She caught it before it could fall with a clatter, her breath ragged. One board free. Then another. She laid them carefully beside her, ready to replace.

The crawlspace gaped below—narrow, shallow, nothing more than packed dirt and cobwebs—but it would have to do.

There was no time to think.

She rolled Darcy onto his side, gritting out a sob as his head lolled against her shoulder. "I am so sorry," she whispered, bracing herself. Her only idea—the only way to get them both inside without further hurting him—was terrible.

And it was all she had.

She laid her body atop his, curling herself around him, her arms cradling his head as best she could. Then, with one desperate motion, she rolled them both sideways—over the edge, down into the dark.

They landed hard. Great mercy, but he was heavy!

The air rushed out of her lungs. His weight pressed her flat into the cold earth, the jolt making her cry out softly. But he was in. They were in.

Her arm trembled as she reached up, feeling blindly for the planks she had left within reach. She groped until her fingers found the edge and pulled, dragging one board across. Then the next. Another gunshot cracked above, and a splinter tore from the hearth overhead. Dust and fragments fell onto her hair as she eased the final board into place.

Darkness sealed them in.

Total. Breathless. Terrifying.

Elizabeth lay there, arms wrapped around him, the side of her face pressed to his chest. She waited.

Waited.

And then—yes. *There.* A faint thump beneath her ear. A heartbeat.

Still alive. Still hers.

Or was that only the thunderclap of her own pulse drumming in her ears?

Elizabeth froze beneath the floorboards, her body pressed against the cold, damp earth, cradling Darcy's inert form. The confined space was suffocating, the air thick with the scent of soil and her own fear. Above them, the cabin bore the brutal assault of their assailants.

The relentless barrage of gunfire continued, each lead ball tearing through the cabin's thin wooden walls with a sickening thud. Splinters rained down, and the stone hearth above them shuddered under the onslaught. Elizabeth flinched at every impact, her heart pounding so fiercely she feared it would betray their hiding place. She tightened her hold on Darcy, feeling the faint rise and fall of his chest against her own. The warmth of his blood seeped through her clothing.

Then, abruptly, the gunfire ceased.

The silence struck like a hammer. Not peace—no, never that—but something worse. Expectation. Elizabeth froze, blood galloping in her ears, listening to the world hold its breath.

They had stopped shooting. Not because they had fled or were satisfied. Because they were coming.

The thought slithered in before she could shove it away. Of course they would come now. To look. To finish. Her fingers dug into Darcy's coat, sticky with blood, and her mind scrambled for a new plan—*any* plan—but there was nowhere else to run.

And then she realized... The trail. The blood. Her own frantic crawl across the floor, slicing her feet to ribbons on the glass and dragging Darcy's bloodied body across it.

It was all there, pointing like an arrow. She had bought them minutes. Not safety. Minutes.

A shiver coursed through her as she heard the unmistakable sound of footsteps approaching the cabin. The door was kicked open with a force that rattled the walls, and heavy boots stomped inside. Through the narrow gaps between the floorboards, faint beams of lantern light pierced the darkness, casting eerie patterns on the ground beside her. She held her breath, every muscle taut with dread.

Voices, rough and laden with anger, exchanged terse words. "Where are they? They couldn't have gone far."

"The back window's shattered. Maybe they escaped that way."

A pause. Then another voice, sharper, more observant. "Wait. Look here—blood. Fresh. Leads this way."

Elizabeth's stomach clenched. They had found the trail. She felt nauseated with terror as she pressed closer to Darcy, her body the only shield she could offer for his. She willed herself to disappear, to become one with the earth. Tears pricked at her eyes, but she blinked them away, focusing solely on the faint rhythm of Darcy's heartbeat beneath her.

The intruders moved methodically, their boots thudding ominously above. Furniture was overturned, belongings rifled through. Each sound was a dagger to her fraying nerves. Then, the dreaded moment arrived.

The footsteps halted directly above them.

A guttural curse.

The floorboards above her shifted.

Light flooded in as the boards were yanked away, blinding her momentarily. Elizabeth instinctively positioned herself over Darcy, her eyes squinting against the harsh glow. As her vision adjusted, she found herself staring up into the cold, merciless eyes of a man whose face was twisted into a morbid grin. He leveled a pistol at her—Darcy's pistol, the one that he had meant for her protection. Now it would be her death.

"Well, well," he drawled, his voice dripping with cruel amusement. "The little lady has some fight in her."

Panic screamed in her ears, drowning out rational thought. The man loomed above her, his sneer a grotesque mask in the dim light. She could think of nothing else—it was sheer instinct when she surged upward, seizing the barrel of his pistol with both hands.

The metal was cold and unyielding beneath her fingers. With a desperate wrench, she shoved it aside just as it discharged, the deafening blast ringing in her ears. The acrid scent of gunpowder filled the air as the shot embedded harmlessly into the wall.

Capitalizing on his momentary surprise, Elizabeth lashed out, her fingernails raking across his unshaven cheek. He bellowed in pain, recoiling as blood welled from the fresh wounds. The feral satisfaction was short-lived; another assailant lunged at her from the shadows. She twisted away, narrowly avoiding his grasp, and kicked out, her foot connecting with his shin. He grunted, stumbling back.

The confined space erupted into chaos. They had no more loaded pistols, but they had their fists and their strength. Elizabeth fought with the desperation of the damned, her movements wild and unrefined. She clawed, kicked, and bit, her survival instincts overriding any semblance of decorum.

But the men were hardened and far stronger. One managed to snare her wrist, twisting it cruelly behind her back. She cried out as pain lanced up her arm. Another grabbed a fistful of her hair, yanking her head back to expose her throat.

"Feisty little wench," the first man growled, his breath hot and rancid against her ear. "You'll pay for that."

Elizabeth struggled, but their combined strength was overwhelming. The man she had scratched pressed a calloused hand against his bleeding cheek, his eyes narrowing with fury. He reached into his coat and produced a gleaming knife, the blade catching the dim light. Her heart seized as she recognized him—Maddox. The man who had stared up at her from her own sketch and haunted her nightmares.

"Remember me, My Lady?" He advanced toward her. "Yes, I can see that you do, and that is rather a problem. Time to finish what we started."

Terror coiled in her stomach, but she lifted her chin, refusing to let him see her fear. "Go hang yourself," she spat.

Maddox's eyes darkened. He raised the knife, the blade poised to strike. Elizabeth braced herself, every muscle tensed for the inevitable.

That was when the door exploded inward.

Not with ceremony or clarity—but with the raw, splintering force of men who had run too far, too fast, too long to wait another second. Boots thundered across the threshold, voices barked orders she could not understand, and light from a dozen lanterns struck her eyes like musket fire.

For a moment, Elizabeth could not breathe.

Colonel Fitzwilliam stood in the center of it all—weapon raised, eyes like stone.

"Stand down!" he growled, the sound so low and lethal that the world seemed to halt.

Maddox turned just slightly. That was all. But it was enough. A rifle cracked. One of Fitzwilliam's men charged. The chaos moved away from her.

And Elizabeth ran.

She did not remember standing. She did not remember crossing the room. But suddenly she was at Colonel Fitzwilliam's side, her fingers twisted in his sleeve.

"Darcy," she rasped. "They shot him. Please—he is under the floor—"

He caught her by the shoulders, steadying her. "Darcy is where? What the devil?"

His gaze dropped, following the blood trail she had feared, and a flicker of rage passed across his face. "Secure the room," he barked to his men. Then to her, more gently, he urged, "Show me."

She tugged him toward the gaping hole in the floor. Her throat would not work.

Two soldiers moved to the loose more boards, prying them back with haste to make a larger hole. Fitzwilliam knelt beside the opening before they had even cleared the way, his pistol discarded, his hands already reaching.

Elizabeth hovered, her whole body vibrating with held breath. And when Fitzwilliam reached inside—when he grunted under Darcy's weight and pulled him up like a broken doll from the earth—it was too much. She sank to the floor where she stood, knees hitting hard, hands trembling in her lap.

"Is he—?" Her voice cracked. "Please. Tell me he's—"

Fitzwilliam pressed two fingers to Darcy's throat. His jaw clenched. Then—after one long, unbearable moment—he nodded.

"He's alive."

She sagged, caught up from the floor only because a quick-thinking soldier was standing near at hand.

Darcy was alive.

And still—nothing in her body would stop shaking.

CHAPTER TWENTY-NINE

June 1, 1812

"THIS WAS A DEVILISH fine trap," Colonel Fitzwilliam muttered, tugging on his gloves as he surveyed the wreckage of the ruined cottage. "You drew Maddox out so we could kill him. We questioned the survivor—before he died, that is—and have the names of the ones funding them that happened to line up with our suspicions. All in one night."

Elizabeth turned toward him, her body aching, her mind still reeling from the terror of the night. Her feet were bandaged, her legs raw from cuts, and her hands... Good heavens, did she have any body parts that were not bleeding?

"A *trap?*" she repeated, her voice sharp with disbelief. "We did not *plan* this. We were running! Hiding—trying to keep innocent people from being shot with us! We had no idea anyone followed us. Mr. Darcy was so cautious!"

Fitzwilliam glanced sideways at her. "Darcy may have let you believe that, but he was no fool. He knew that letter to St. Albans did no more than buy you a day or two to take the fight elsewhere."

Elizabeth sniffed and crossed her bloodied forearms, blinking against the sting of tears. "You are not saying he... he *meant* to fight them? That he drew them here on purpose?"

The colonel drew a long sigh, making an almost painful effort at schooling his features to explain the matter patiently. "How long could you have kept running and hiding, Lady Elizabeth? Like enough, the only thing that protected you so long in Hertfordshire was the fact that you were constantly surrounded by a group of other females. Three or four gently bred ladies gunned down in broad daylight does cause talk. From what I gather, the house was too set in the open, so they probably could not get close enough to set fire to your bedroom again. But make no mistake, they would have found their moment soon enough. And this—" he gestured about the shattered cabin— "it worked. Maddox thought he had you cornered but he had no idea we were just behind him. Bloody good show of it, if you ask me."

Elizabeth looked away, throat tightening. That was not victory. Not to her. Good heavens, what of the Bennets? Maddox had to have had some way of following them from Longbourn. Was there any chance the Bennets had been attacked as well? Tortured to make them reveal her whereabouts? Her breath came in sharp stabs of panic, and her knees began shaking again, so hard that she had to sag against the door—the one where she had first kissed Darcy.

Fitzwilliam crouched beside the body of the man they had taken alive—apparently he was no longer so—and murmured instructions to one of his soldiers. His jaw was set, eyes hard. Whatever confession they had extracted, it was enough to move him.

"Cunningham's in Northumberland," he told her, standing again. "If I do not get to him before word of this spreads, we risk losing him."

"What of *him?*" she demanded, gesturing to Darcy lying half-conscious on the cot—head bleeding and chest bare while one of the colonel's men bandaged his many wounds. "You mean to just leave us here alone?"

The colonel dragged in a heavy sigh as he watched his cousin flinching and groaning, even in his delirium, as the officer probed the paths of the bullets—two, at least, perhaps more. "No, Lady Elizabeth. Quite the opposite, in fact. You must get him to Carlton House at once."

Elizabeth's eyes rounded. "*How?* He should not even be moved! You cannot put him on a horse all the way to London!"

"I had a thought to that. We have a carriage waiting, though I had not expected to have to put Darcy in it. I'm afraid it is the only way. It is no good me running to Northumberland to take a peer of the realm into custody without His Highness's knowledge and consent. That is for Darcy to secure, and with all haste."

"But..." Elizabeth swallowed. "Are you sure he can even make the journey? What am I to do if the bleeding does not stop?"

Colonel Fitzwilliam frowned and stepped to the cot to look over his bloodied cousin. He spoke a few low words to the soldier dressing his wounds, then returned to Elizabeth.

"He will not mistake this for a pleasure tour, but yes, he will survive. Keep him still. That wound at the base of his neck was almost through the artery—Heaven only knows how he kept from bleeding out at once. The shoulder wound will be the one that causes him the most pain, though. The ball tore clean through a deal of muscle, and I fear a fever. Keep pressure on the wounds. Change the bandages if they soak through. We shall send a poultice and whiskey in the satchel. If he stirs, talk to him—I daresay your voice will keep him in this sphere rather than the next."

She nodded quickly. "What about the wound on his head?"

"Looks far worse than it is. That one is probably why he was knocked out, but we got the bleeding stopped. He'll have the very devil of a headache when he wakes, but that one is the least of his worries."

Their carriage was waiting a few yards down the track—plain, dark, and unmarked. A traveling chariot, small and swift, with shuttered windows and a single driver handpicked by the colonel. It took some trouble and three men to move Darcy's body, but by the time another quarter hour had passed, the men were back on their horses, and a mostly unconscious Darcy was lodged inside.

Elizabeth had no choice but to climb in after him, but she leaned out before the door was closed behind her. "Where do you expect us to go once we reach London? Surely we will have to wait for an audience. Should I go to my father's house? Will Mr. Darcy go to Matlock House?"

"No!" Fitzwilliam said sharply. "You must go nowhere. Stop for nothing—not for fresh clothing, not to rest, not even to wash your wounds. I mean it. Drive straight to Carlton House. No detours. No delays. Do you understand?"

She blanched. "But we are covered in blood—we look like highwaymen! I am in no state to be seen by royalty."

"His Highness started this business," Fitzwilliam growled. "You are not there to impress him. You are there to end this. The driver has orders not to stop for anyone, but if something forces it..." The colonel extended a pistol. Darcy's pistol. "Do you know how to shoot, my lady?"

Elizabeth took the cold weight into her hand with a shuddering sigh. "My father treated me more like a son than a daughter."

The colonel grunted. "Well, that will have to do."

"Anything else?"

He gave her a grim smile and tipped his hat. "No. Godspeed. Tell Darcy I will see him in London."

And then he was gone, galloping into the woods with four men at his heels.

She sat with her skirts rumpled and drying blood caked on her knees, Darcy slumped beside her with his weight tilted heavily against her left side. His head lolled to the shoulder that had not been bandaged, and his breath came in soft, uneven hitches.

Once, as the sun began to rise in a haze of gold behind them, he stirred more deliberately, his lashes fluttering. Her heart leaped into her throat. Was he waking?

"Elizabeth?" he rasped.

She clutched his hand, pressing it between her own. "I am here."

"Did they..." His voice broke off.

"No. They are gone. You are safe."

"You... what about you?"

"I am well. Perfectly well."

He sank back into her side and did not speak again. And Elizabeth could do nothing but stroke his cheek and count his breaths. So long as his head rose and fell against her shoulder with each shudder of his chest, he lived.

They rode in silence, save for the endless drum of hooves and the rattling of the wheels. Outside, England sped past—green fields and hedgerows and towns that knew nothing of the war being waged in their capital. She wrapped her arms more tightly around him and closed her eyes.

She awoke some hours later to a burning in her stomach from hunger. Her eyes opened blearily, and she swallowed against a dry throat as she blinked out at the passing trees. They must be near Buntingford—at least, she thought that was what the sign read before it passed out of her view. Her stomach squeezed and gurgled, and she glanced round the carriage.

There was the satchel of provisions, but it was on the opposite seat. Just beside Darcy's pistol, which Colonel Fitzwilliam had loaded for her. And so, she sat there, gazing at the answer to the answer to the painful rumbling in her belly, but too unwilling to slip out from under Darcy's weight to retrieve it. Instead, she let her head slip back again—her temple supporting Darcy's cheek, the tickle of his hair ruffling the mess of her curls, and his hand fallen heavily, unconsciously, over her lap.

What would the Prince say to their audacity for stumbling upon his gates in such a state? The colonel had seemed so confident in their reception, as if this affair were the supreme anxiety resting upon the royal head just now. Or perhaps Darcy himself commanded some respect with the Regent. If that were so... well, perhaps not all was lost.

The carriage hit a rut, lurching her head rather sharply against his. Darcy stirred and grunted in pain—a grunt that dissolved into a faint moan.

"Fitzwilliam," she whispered, brushing a lock of hair from his brow.

No answer. But he shifted faintly, his brow twitching. His hand moved—just once—toward the wound on his chest.

Elizabeth sprang into action. She slipped from under his shoulder and fumbled for the satchel the colonel had given her, tugged it open with fingers that still stung from tiny shards of glass. Inside, she found not only a parcel of bread and cheese for her, but linen, a tin of salve, and a flask she dared not open yet. She found a clean cloth and peeled back the blood-soaked one that had been tied around Darcy's shoulder. He flinched, even unconscious.

"Oh—oh, I am sorry," she whispered, lifting the cloth gently.

The sight of the wound stole her breath. Angry red flesh, blackened at the edges with dried blood. The bullet had passed clean through, Fitzwilliam had said, but the exit wound was wider, raw, weeping.

She worked slowly, for it was all she could do to heave his body about and reach under his ruined shirt to nurse his bare flesh. Tucked clean cloth beneath him. Packed the salve against the wound. Rebound it with trembling hands, remembering the way Fitzwilliam had demonstrated it. The knot must be firm. The pressure even. She braced his weight against her body and tied the bandage tightly, whispering soothing nonsense all the while.

Darcy murmured something—her name, she thought. Or part of it. A fragment.

"It is all right," she breathed as she wedged herself once more under his ribs, propping him up. "You are safe."

The carriage jostled again, and he sagged harder against her, his bloodied temple brushing her jaw. She adjusted her posture to cradle him better, mindful of his wounds. Her legs ached, her hands throbbed, and her back screamed in protest, but none of that mattered. Not while he breathed.

Not while she had him.

His face was too pale. His lips, dry. She pressed the flask to his mouth, coaxed a sip between them. When he swallowed, she nearly wept with relief. A few more hours, that was all. A slow, excruciatingly slow rumble into London, and he would be able to rest.

And she would lose him to others.

As the afternoon light shifted, casting the carriage interior in muted shadows and stifling warmth, Darcy stirred more lucidly. His eyes fluttered open, meeting Elizabeth's with a clarity that had been absent since the attack. He attempted to shift, a grimace betraying the pain the movement caused.

She cupped her hand against his cheek and pressed a kiss to his forehead—soft, reverent, meant for comfort rather than passion.

But then, unable to help herself, she brushed another kiss—slow, aching—against the corner of his mouth.

His eyes fluttered open, hazy at first, but searching. And when they focused on her—truly saw her—his fingers twitched against hers and caught. "Elizabeth?"

"Fitzwilliam." Her lips parted, heart surging at the look in his eyes. She bent closer, meaning to kiss him fully... and he did not stop her.

Not this time.

Her lips met his—tentative at first, then deeper, fuller as the seconds slipped past and the carriage rocked gently beneath them. His hand, still tangled with hers, tightened. His other came up slowly, with effort, brushing the line of her jaw as though he meant to memorize it.

She sighed into the kiss, felt the warmth of him answering back, the faintest hum in his throat—one that was all relief, all yearning, all yes.

For one brief moment, nothing existed but the press of her mouth against his. The world narrowed to the shallow breath between them. And it was good. It was perfect.

And then his hand shifted, pressing lightly against her shoulder. Not urgent, not unkind. Just firm.

"Elizabeth," he croaked, voice hoarse and ragged. "No. Do not." He pulled away, breath ragged, and let his head fall back against the cushion.

"Do not what?" She picked up his hand and pressed it to her lips.

"Elizabeth," he murmured, eyes half-lidded with regret. "You know very well what I mean."

"Yes, and you know very well how impossible I am, so I have no intention of abiding by your wishes."

"Listen to me," he began, curling his fingers against her mouth and trying—unsuccessfully—to retract his hand. "When we reach Carlton House... you must be cautious in your speech."

She frowned. "Fitzwilliam, you are injured. I almost lost you! Carlton House is the farthest thing from my mind just now. We can discuss—"

"No! You must promise me. Do not... compromise yourself before the Prince. No matter the provocation."

Her stomach twisted. She knew what he meant. The lie unspoken between them, the role she could play if she wanted to seal his redemption. Her eyes searched his pale face, his bloodied coat.

"I cannot stand by while you suffer unjustly," she protested.

His grip tightened, a surprising show of strength. "You must. If you speak out, try to say anything to tickle His Highness's fancy, I will deny it. The consequences will fall solely upon you."

Still? Even now, he still thought this way? Tears welled in her eyes, blurring her vision. The protective barrier he sought to erect around her was both infuriating and endearing. "You will not. I know you better than that. You would not let me face that alone."

His cheek ticked. "Promise me, Elizabeth. I'll not see you ruin yourself."

She looked at him, really looked at him—so strong, so foolish, so utterly hers—and nodded, her heart breaking. "I promise."

Only then did his body ease. His hand slackened and his eyes closed again. She pressed another kiss to his brow, this one lingering, as the carriage wheels clattered on through the dawn toward their fate.

THE GATES OF CARLTON House rose like a judgment.

Darcy sat ramrod straight, despite the agony blooming beneath his bandages. He had barely spoken since the first London cobblestones clattered under the carriage wheels. The wound in his shoulder throbbed in time with his heartbeat, a dull, insistent warning. But pain was nothing. Pain could be borne. What waited for them inside—what he had known would come—was another matter.

The prince wanted blood.

Elizabeth had moved to sit across from him now, her posture rigid with tension. Even in her borrowed garments, with her sleeves pulled down to hide the bandages on her forearms and her hair bound in a hasty, unruly twist, she looked like nobility. Or perhaps something even rarer—like defiance shaped into elegance.

He watched her without letting his eyes linger. He could not afford indulgence. Not now.

They had not spoken again of their pact. There had been no need. But the silence wedged between them like a splitting maul.

The footman opened the carriage door.

Darcy descended first, careful not to show how the movement jarred him. He turned to offer his uninjured arm to Elizabeth, and she accepted it wordlessly. She would have need of it, for she was too proud to limp, too injured not to, and too stubborn to ask for help.

Inside, the great hall of Carlton House gleamed with marble and menace. Footmen moved like wraiths. The walls whispered power.

They were announced. Her name first, then his. He felt her fingers twitch at the sound of her title, as if it was now foreign to her. There would be no ceremony for her return to the life she had left dangling. There could be no celebration for her survival. Only this audience, and then she would be deposited back in the home whence she had come, just as if time had never stopped.

The Prince Regent received them in a tall chamber, its tall windows draped with heavy brocade that filtered the blaze of sunset into subdued amber tones. He lounged in a high-backed chair of crimson velvet, positioned beside a mahogany writing desk cluttered with sealed dispatches, half-eaten candied fruits, and an ornate snuffbox left ajar. A gleaming watch chain coiled like a golden serpent at his waist, catching the light with each of his languid movements.

He did not rise.

"Well," the Prince drawled, swirling a glass of ratafia in one hand. "Look at you both."

Elizabeth curtsied, and Darcy bowed deeply, trying not to wince. "Your Royal High ness."

The prince's gaze meandered over them, pausing to take in Darcy's disheveled appearance. "You look like a sailor dragged off to the docks," he remarked, his lips curling in a semblance of amusement. His eyes then flicked to Elizabeth, and he tsked softly, shaking his head. "And as for the lady... What have we here, Miss Montclair? Dressed like the undermaid of a provincial apothecary. And are those bandages? Good heavens, what an awful to-do."

Elizabeth's lips parted. Darcy saw the fire in her eyes before the words formed, and he stepped forward—not between them, but enough to remind her.

She caught herself. Barely. Her chin lifted.

The prince's smile widened, as if privately entertained by the lady's spark of defiance and Darcy's obvious diversion. "You have come to report, I trust?" he said, reaching for a sugared grape and popping it into his mouth with deliberate leisure.

"I have. Colonel Fitzwilliam is en route to Northumberland to apprehend Cunningham on charges of conspiracy to commit murder. One of the assailants who attacked us survived long enough to provide a confession. He identified Bellingham and two others as accomplices, and we recovered the insignia of the Fellowship from Maddox's body."

The prince exhaled slowly, setting his glass down with a soft clink. "So," he murmured, almost to himself, "the traitor was real. A good bit of luck there, Darcy."

A brief silence settled over the room, punctuated only by the distant chiming of a clock and the popping sound of another grape in the Prince's mouth.

"This presents a delicate situation," the prince sighed, his fingers drumming idly on the armrest. "The public must remain ignorant of such... unsavory affairs. The monarchy's image is, after all, a tapestry woven with threads of perception."

Darcy inclined his head. "Discretion is paramount, Your Highness."

"Indeed. Measures will be taken to ensure this remains within the confines of those who need to know." He leaned forward slightly, the movement causing the golden chain at his waist to glint. "You understand, Mr. Darcy, that such loyalty and service do not go unnoticed."

Darcy bowed. "I serve at the pleasure of Your Highness and the realm."

"Quite." The prince tilted his glass toward Elizabeth. "And the lady?"

Darcy's jaw clenched. "Survived, thanks to her own bravery and quick thinking."

"I dare say. A good bit of luck, indeed." The prince turned to Elizabeth. "And how did you find your guardian, Lady Elizabeth? A steady hand in troubled waters? I trust he did nothing... *untoward,* while he had you in his sole keeping."

Darcy held his breath.

Elizabeth flicked a glance to him...

Do not... he prayed silently. *Do not say it!*

But what if she did? What then? Was there any realm of fantasy in which he could make her his? Over her father's certain objection, over the derision of the *ton*...

Half of him longed for her to blurt the words in defiance... the whiff of salaciousness, the accusations of impropriety... She was just recalcitrant enough to do it.

Elizabeth swallowed and turned to meet the prince's gaze evenly. "Mr. Darcy," she said, "was ever the perfect gentleman. He protected me at great personal cost, and never once compromised either his honor or mine."

There was a long silence.

The prince blinked. Once. Then leaned back in his chair, the glass forgotten in his hand.

"Well," he murmured, "is that not a pity."

Darcy felt the air shift. He looked to Elizabeth, who had gone pale beneath her cuts and bruises. Her mouth was set in a thin, defiant line.

He said nothing. There was nothing to say.

"Well, I suppose there ends it. Back to Ashwick House, eh?" The prince rang a bell, and a steward entered.

"See to the lady," the prince said with a dismissive wave. "She is to be dressed, supped, and returned to her father. Use the Windsor silks—nothing too fine, but I will not have her arriving like a washerwoman."

Elizabeth looked back at Darcy—this time, with a hint of panic in her eyes.

He could not speak. He inclined his head instead, as formal as any stranger.

The steward guided her from the room... and the door closed off his view.

The moment she was gone, the prince turned back to him.

"You will go to the Home Office," he said crisply. "There is still paperwork to be concluded. Bring me everything that links Cunningham to the Fellowship. If I am to see the man dispatched or transported, I must think of a way to do it quietly. We have already hanged a man for dear Perceval's murder, God rest his wretched soul. I shan't have anyone else thinking it worthwhile to attempt likewise."

"Yes, Your Highness."

The prince looked down at his desk. "And Darcy."

Darcy paused. "Your Highness?"

"You may go."

No word of Pemberley. No gesture toward restoration. No mention of justice.

Darcy bowed once more. The ache in his shoulder flared.

He turned and walked away, leaving the prince in his sunlight, and Elizabeth behind him.

Perhaps for the last time.

CHAPTER THIRTY

The chamber they brought her to was larger than any she had entered in weeks, perhaps months—an opulent drawing room converted to a lady's dressing suite, with high ceilings, gilt-trimmed paneling, and a row of mirrors framed in gold.

Two women in aprons stood waiting. One of them, older and silver-haired, curtsied. "Your ladyship," she said, as though Elizabeth had not come in filthy boots and a bloody riding dress.

Elizabeth blinked. "You must be mistaken—"

"No mistake, Lady Elizabeth," the younger maid said gently. "We were told you had been through an ordeal. We are here to assist."

She wanted to protest—say something tart and proud—but her body sagged too heavily against the doorframe for pride. Her arms ached. Her ribs still felt every jolt of that cursed carriage. And she could hardly walk another step. She nodded once.

They stripped her carefully, murmuring apologies when they revealed the bruises on her legs and the cuts on her palms, shins, and feet. The elder woman gasped when she saw the angry gouge across Elizabeth's back. "Musket ball," she muttered. "Near miss."

"Oh!" the younger one cried. "It must have pained you terribly!"

"Not until about six hours ago," Elizabeth said with a shudder. "I did not even notice it at first."

The maids surveyed her with round eyes, but made no further comments about her injuries. They brought a shallow copper tub and filled it with heated water. Steam rose like a balm, and Elizabeth sank into it with a soft groan, arms floating at her sides, eyes closed. It made her wounds sting and scream in agony, but it was a good sort of pain.

At some point, one of the women found a purpling bruise beneath her cheekbone. "Ah," the younger one said, clucking softly. "I'll fetch the powder. No one need know."

Elizabeth opened one eye. "You are very good at this."

"I had four sisters and one brother who boxed for coin," the girl replied wryly. "I became a genius with rouge."

Her hair was next—a solid half hour of dunking, scrubbing, yanking tangles—amidst muttered apologies—and more dunking and scrubbing. For the first time in her life, Elizabeth ignored it. Or she did not care enough to *need* to ignore it. Whatever pain inflicted upon her scalp, it was nothing to the empty place in her heart.

While her skin dried and her wounds were re-bandaged with ointment and silk, Elizabeth's mind drifted—slipping past the quiet murmurs of the maids, past the perfume of lavender water, and back to the wet-black woods and gunpowder smoke of the cabin. The floorboards had been slick with blood. Her flesh still remembered the sting of glass, the slippery weight of Darcy's body, the hollow terror of thinking he might be gone.

How Darcy had slumped against her in the carriage, half-lost to pain and exhaustion, murmuring incoherently. Names. Places. Once, a prayer. But then—softly, brokenly—her name.

Always, he came back to her name.

And when his head had dropped to her shoulder, heavy and unguarded, she had not shifted a muscle. She had held still for miles, letting him lean into her. Letting herself believe, just for that magic time, that she was allowed to be the one he leaned on.

That weight had felt like both an anchor and a promise.

She reached for that memory now. Clutched it. Buried it under her ribs and held fast. Because she did not know what would come next. And she needed something to believe in.

A gown was produced—seafoam silk, finely embroidered—and she stepped into it, letting them button her up like a paper doll.

The mirror showed her a stranger.

There was no dirt, no blood, no signs of the shattered cottage. Her face was pale but composed, hair pinned back into elegant submission, her figure smoothed and shaped into a version of herself that fit Carlton House's expectations.

Except her hands. Those, only dark-colored long gloves would be able to disguise entirely, and if she moved her hands just so, even now, a little blood would stain them. How Alice would fret at her!

She closed her eyes and gulped. *Alice.*

She could not ask the maids. They bustled efficiently, their attentions fixed on ointments, ribbons, and hairpins. What would they know of a missing lady's maid vanished weeks ago into the belly of a conspiracy? They were servants of the royal household, not spies.

But she had asked the colonel. In the cabin, when the colonel's men were securing the surroundings and Darcy was half-drugged with spirits at her side, she had begged an answer to the question she had been holding on her tongue since the rescue.

"Alice. My maid. Has there been any word?"

His answer had been spare. "It appears she may have escaped. But as of now, no fresh intelligence."

Elizabeth had nodded, but the uncertainty had sunk its teeth into her and refused to let go. Escaped... to what? And was she truly alone? Or recaptured? Dead?

But then, even her fears for Alice had paled compared to her worry for Darcy.

Seated across from her in that same carriage, he had looked like something carved from cold stone—bloodied, silent, too pale. She had watched the pulse in his neck to be sure it still beat. She had whispered to him in the dark when he flinched in his sleep, and when he had murmured her name.

She had not told the Prince about the kiss. The near-seduction. It was the truth, after all, and it might have been enough.

She could have. She had been tempted.

One word, one cleverly dropped suggestion, and the scandal would have been theirs. Her ruination. His obligation. It would not have mattered what her father thought of him, not when honor demanded redress. Darcy would be hers, and if the Prince thought the whole thing satisfying enough, Pemberley would be his.

But she had said nothing. Because Darcy had looked at her with that gaze she knew too well by now—serious and shuttered and painfully noble—and warned her not to do it. He had promised he would deny it. That if she threw herself on the sword of scandal, he would not catch her, though she knew in the pit of her soul that bit was a lie on his part.

And so she had let the opportunity pass.

What now?

What would her father say, if he saw the truth of what had unfolded? Would he believe her untouched, when the whole of the Prince's household had seen her arrive bloodied and disheveled beside a man who was not her husband?

Could she ever see Darcy again without the shadow of what might have been?

She did not know. But the ache in her chest said she would never stop wishing it.

D ARCY FOUND HIMSELF STANDING on the grand steps, trying to force his posture erect. The oil lantern on the corner was blinding, and the early evening bustle of London streets seemed distant, muffled by the pounding in his head. His shoulder throbbed where the bullet had torn through, the graze at his neck burned, and the bruise on his temple sent waves of nausea with every heartbeat.

A carriage pulled up outside Carlton House, its lacquered panels gleaming with the Prince Regent's insignia—a symbol of power, opulence, and distance. But it was not for him. It waited for her.

Darcy paused at the edge of the square, one hand braced against the lamppost as though the iron might steady the unraveling ache in his chest. He was already meant to be gone—already late to collect his final documents—but the sight of the carriage held him rooted. A footman adjusted the harness; another swung the step into place. Above, behind one of the tall windows on the upper floor, a curtain shifted. A maid, perhaps. Or someone closing off the view. He would never know. But he felt it, that invisible pull in his chest, the absurd hope that it was her—watching, wondering, waiting.

His hand tightened on the post. And then the door opened.

He could not see her face. Only the flash of pale silk, a gloved hand. A woman's figure descending with care and a barely concealed limp—the same posture he had seen her adopt while carrying his pistol in her sleeve and blood on her knuckles. The royal livery moved to surround her, to escort her to the carriage with the same polished elegance used for foreign princesses and Her Majesty's own daughters.

She did not look back.

And then the door closed. The driver snapped the reins. The wheels turned, and the carriage—her carriage—vanished into the turning curve of Pall Mall.

He let go of the post. And forced himself to walk away.

Summoning what little strength remained, he signaled for a hackney cab. The driver eyed him warily, noting his disheveled appearance and the pallor of his skin. Darcy managed to instruct, "Whitehall. The Home Office." The driver hesitated, but, seeing the coin glinting in Darcy's palm, nodded and set the horses in motion.

The carriage wheels clattered over cobbles slick with rain, but Darcy barely registered the sound. His vision blurred; every jolt of the vehicle sent knives of pain lancing through his shoulder, his spine, his skull. He kept upright only by force of will, one hand braced against the wall of the compartment, the other pressed to his side. Sweat clung cold beneath his cravat. His coat, still stained dark with blood beneath the shoulder seam, stuck to him like a second skin.

London unspooled around him, grey and indistinct. Streets he knew by heart—Brook Street, Piccadilly, the turn toward Whitehall—blurred past without meaning. The chill in the air pressed in through the cracks in the frame. But he was beyond cold. Beyond exhaustion. All that remained was the mission.

The Home Office loomed ahead like a sentry in stone—cold, massive, watching. He nearly stumbled on the step down, catching himself with a grunt of pain that tore across his bruised ribs. The footman offered a hand; Darcy ignored it. He had to walk in under his own power.

He passed through the entrance and into the interior hush of bureaucracy. The familiar scent of ink and old paper replaced the smoke and ash that had clung to him since last night. His boots echoed down the corridor—too slow, too uneven—and heads turned. A junior clerk dropped his quill. A secretary stilled mid-conversation. They knew who he was, of course. Knew enough to whisper.

But no one dared stop him, or ask why his shirt bore crusted red stains.

His hand trembled as he reached for the key to his office. The brass stuck in the lock before clicking open, and the door swung inward to reveal the small, orderly room where he had spent countless hours unravelling treason.

He crossed to the writing desk, swaying slightly. With stiff fingers, he unlocked the drawer beneath. Inside, wrapped in linen and bound with twine, lay the last of the evidence. Folded ledgers. Crumbling correspondence. A banker's receipt in coded script, signed by a false name—one they now knew to be Cunningham's. Letters that would unwind him. Ruin him.

Darcy laid each piece on the blotter with reverence, as though touching something holy. Or dangerous.

Darcy left the Home Office with the documents tucked close to his chest, wrapped in oilskin and tied with twine. The corridors had quieted as he passed, but whispers rose in his wake. He did not look at them. Did not slow. Let them gawk. He was beyond the reach of their curiosity.

Outside, the cold bit through the linen at his collar. The weak moon had begun its ascent, and the damp air clouded in like a second weight on his shoulders. He turned west, toward his flat.

The walk should have taken fifteen minutes.

It took nearly forty.

By the time he reached his door, his right arm hung limp at his side, and his vision danced with light. He fumbled with the key three times before the lock finally yielded. The door opened inward to silence and dust. No fire laid. No supper waiting.

He made straight for the desk.

There, beneath a pile of military reports provided by his cousin and a discarded great-coat, lay the rest of it. More evidence. Copies of letters he had once shown to Richard—ci-phered notes, household accounts from the Bellingham estate, a sworn statement from a disgraced footman who once served in Cunningham's town house. He gathered them all, hands shaking, and then sat down to pen a cover letter for His Highness that he hoped would connect all the ruinous dots.

Then, and only then, did he pull the bell rope.

His manservant had been on leave for weeks—probably forgot the name of his em-ployer by now. But Darcy had made arrangements months ago for such a moment as this. A trusted courier, paid well for discretion, appeared within a quarter hour. He was a broad-shouldered man with pale brows and a weathered coat, and he said nothing about the state of the flat—or of Darcy himself.

"You are to take these to Carlton House," Darcy said, forcing the words out though his vision spotted. "Directly to His Highness. No detours. No intermediaries. Do you understand me?"

The courier nodded once, solemnly. "Yes, sir."

"Good. Go."

The moment the door shut behind him, Darcy staggered back to the sitting room. He leaned against the wall, willing the world to hold still—but it swayed beneath him. His knees buckled.

He made it to the bedroom. Just.

His coat dropped somewhere between the door and the edge of the mattress. His boots he did not bother with. He collapsed half onto the bed, one arm flung across his eyes, breath ragged and shallow.

The fever came for him like a rising tide.

Heat, cold, light—all blurred together. He drifted between lucidity and memory, but always, always came back to her.

The kiss.

Her hand at his cheek, her body pressed against his chest, the taste of breath and tears and something wild. Her lips. The impossible softness. The way she had said his name like it mattered.

Fitzwilliam.

He clung to it, even as darkness pulled him under.

AS HER CARRIAGE APPROACHED Ashwick House, Elizabeth's gaze lifted to the familiar façade. The stately townhouse stood in its customary grandeur, but her eyes were drawn upward—to the charred remains of her bedchamber's windows. The blackened edges stood in stark contrast to the pristine stonework, a silent testament to the recent fire. A lump formed in her throat as memories threatened to surface, but she swallowed them down, straightened her shoulders, and descended from the carriage.

Inside, the air hung thick with the rich scent of roasted duck and saffron rice, underscored by the faintest trace of clove-studded wine. Elizabeth paused just inside the threshold, her gloves still on her hands, bonnet slightly askew from setting down out of the carriage. A footman appeared instantly, offering to take them, but her gaze remained fixed ahead.

The dining room had changed not at all since her childhood: deepest mahogany gleaming under the gas sconces, a single taper lit at the center of the table. Her father dined alone at the head, shoulders faintly hunched, a glass of something dark and potent resting near his left hand.

Elizabeth mustered all her fortitude and stepped forward without much of a limp, forcing her shoulders to square, her lips curving into what she hoped passed for a pleasant smile.

Her father glanced up from his plate, brows lifting in surprise that seemed—momentarily—genuine. "Well! If it is not my wandering Petal returned to the fold. Come back so soon, eh?"

She flinched. Just a flicker, barely more than the tightening of her mouth, but it lanced through her all the same. Still, she crossed to the table and made herself answer lightly, "I thought you might have grown used to the peace."

He chuckled, gesturing toward the empty seat across from him. "Peace is a dull business. Sit, sit. You must tell me everything. I had understood the Queen would keep you tucked away at Frogmore for at least a month. What happened? Did she tire of you already?"

Elizabeth eased into the chair, smoothing her skirts as she gathered her composure. "She had... other matters to attend."

"Mm. And yet she sent you home without a proper escort or fanfare. Not quite the dazzling exit I might have expected."

She tried for another smile. "I had a royal carriage, Father. Guards and coachmen, all of it."

"Of course you did," he said airily, returning to his wine. "But surely your time was not wasted. You must have drawn attention—your mother would be apoplectic with envy. Was Lord Pembroke there? I hear he is back in circulation. Or that dashing young Viscount Stanhope—clever fellow, though rather too fond of racing debts. And what of the Marquis of Belgrave? He was positively sniffing after you last season."

Elizabeth's stomach twisted. She reached for her napkin and folded it with great care. "I saw none of them."

Across the table, her father smiled shrewdly. "Ah, then it was Prince Nikolaos. I have been hearing rumors about him. Come now, Petal, I—"

She swallowed, and the napkin fell to the table.

Her father's smile faltered. "What?"

"Please," she said quietly. "Do not call me that."

He blinked, caught off guard. "I beg your pardon?"

She lifted her gaze, and this time it did not waver. "That... name you always use. I am no longer a child to be petted."

For a beat, he said nothing. Then, with a mild shrug and a crooked smile, "Very well, my pet—ah—my dear."

The Marquess of Ashwick picked up his fork again, slicing into a cutlet with surgical precision. "Well, what of Her Majesty?" he asked between bites. "Did you make yourself agreeable?"

Elizabeth folded her napkin again, refolding it once more before answering. "As much as could be expected."

He snorted. "Which means you said something saucy and offended someone in lace." He waved his knife vaguely. "Really, Petal—my dear—you must learn to temper your wit in royal company."

She looked down at the tablecloth. "There was no incident. Her Majesty was perfectly satisfied."

"I daresay she was," he mused. "Though you being sent home so quickly... one does wonder."

Elizabeth lifted her gaze again, steady this time. "It was not a punishment. Merely a change in schedule."

"Hm." His eyes drifted to her gloved hands. "Is it unusually cold at Frogmore this spring, or have you taken to fashioning yourself a nun?"

She blinked once, then slipped her hands beneath the edge of the table. "It was drafty, yes."

He arched a brow at her evasion but did not press. Not yet. He merely sipped his wine and leaned back in his chair, his smile returning. "Well, even if the Queen did grow tired of your company, you cannot possibly have returned without some tale to tell. You may as well admit it—there was someone. Some romance. Your face gives you away."

She did not reply.

He set down his utensils with exaggerated care. "Come now. I may be your father, but I was once a young man myself. There is a look about you—you've either had your heart bruised or your pride wounded."

Elizabeth kept her gaze on the tablecloth. "The gentleman did not return my affections."

He scoffed immediately. "Then he's a damned fool."

Her eyes flicked to his, startled by the vehemence.

"I mean it," he said, waving his fork for emphasis. "Name the fellow. I shall see to it he understands what he has thrown away."

"I would rather not."

"Afraid I'll duel him?" he teased, clearly warming to his own narrative. "You must give me more credit. I have attorneys now. I let them handle my grudges."

Elizabeth forced a smile, then rose to her feet. "It truly is of no consequence. And I am... very tired. May I take my leave?"

He waved a hand, already reaching again for his wine. "Of course, of course. Ah—one thing. Your bedchamber will be uninhabitable for a time. A fire. Nothing serious, but the furnishings were ruined and the walls rather scorched. Select any of the guest rooms you like."

Her breath caught faintly. "I heard about it. And... Alice?"

He lowered his glass. "Alice?"

"My maid. I hope she was not..." Elizabeth swallowed. "That is, I hope no blame fell on her. She is not... dismissed, I hope?"

"Ah." He cut a bit of his meat and pierced it with his fork before replying. "I suppose she is around somewhere. I doubt she had anything to do with the fire. But if she's not to be found, someone else will see you settled. There is always someone."

Suppressing a sigh, Elizabeth rose and made her way up the staircase, her footsteps soundless against the plush runner. The house was quiet—too quiet. Every portrait along the corridor seemed to watch her pass, their painted eyes judging her as an interloper in her own home. When she reached the guest wing, she bypassed the grand chambers with terrace views and ornate balconies. No vistas. No trees. No French doors. She needed four walls and a single latch she could set herself.

The room she chose was modest, narrow, and square, with a single window that overlooked nothing but the inner courtyard and stable roofs. She closed the shutters before she crossed the threshold, twisting the latch firmly and testing it twice. The lamp on the bedside table cast a soft glow, flickering as though uncertain it had the strength to last the night.

She moved to the dressing table on legs that barely felt her own. The stool creaked faintly as she sat. The mirror offered her no comfort—only the dim outline of a woman she scarcely recognized.

She reached for the buttons at her wrists and slowly tugged at the gloves. The fabric caught where scabs had dried against the lining. When she finally pulled them free, she stared at the damage.

Her hands were a ruin—scraped raw across the knuckles, the pads of her fingers lined with angry red. Deeper gouges along her palms had reopened in places, the skin puffed and dark with bruising. There were cuts she did not remember getting. Scars that would stay.

She laid them palm up on her lap for a long moment. Then she turned back to the mirror and reached for the cloth and dampened it with the basin.

One pass took off the worst of the powder over her cheeks. Another revealed the truth. A dark bruise bloomed across her left cheekbone, half-hidden by clever cosmetics. A faint line at her hairline, where a shard of glass had nicked her. A smear of dried blood behind her ear.

She dabbed carefully at each spot, ignoring the sting. She did not stop until the cloth was stained, until every effort to look untouched had been undone.

Then she sat back.

And stared.

The girl in the mirror was not the one who had curtsied before royalty and danced under chandeliers. She was not the whispered-about heiress with the London suitors and the diamond pins. She was not the Marquess's daughter, or at least—she no longer knew what that meant.

She was a girl who had run through dark woods. Who had fought off trained killers with her bare hands. Who had hidden in floorboards with the man she loved, waiting to die.

Her throat clenched.

She had not cried at all. Not when she had held Darcy's unconscious body. Not when she had lied to the Prince's face. Not even when she had come home to find her bedchamber blackened and her maid vanished and her father only dismayed that she had returned so soon.

But now—

Now the silence gave her no more space to run.

Her shoulders trembled. Her breath caught. And the tears came—not sobs, not loud or messy—but quiet, steady rivers that would not stop. She buried her face in her hands and let them fall.

CHAPTER THIRTY-ONE

Darkness. And heat.

His throat was a ragged thing, scratched dry, his skin too tight across his bones. Something crusted at the corners of his eyes. He turned his head—no, tried to—and the world spun sideways.

The ceiling was there. That blasted cobweb in the corner he had always meant to clean. It stared back. Mocking him.

He was cold. Or hot. His hands trembled as he groped for something—cloth? The pitcher? Had he left it full?

Fingers found the tin cup, and he lifted it with a shaking arm, sloshed lukewarm water over his chin. Enough got in his mouth to swallow. He coughed, gagged, drank again. He would live another hour. Perhaps.

Blankets twisted around his legs like vines. He kicked. Or thought he did. Everything was so heavy.

Elizabeth.

The name pulled him under again.

They were running. Always running. Her hand in his. He could feel it—warm, firm, trembling. She was behind him, her skirts catching on branches, and he turned, lifted her over the fence, pressed a kiss to her temple before she could even speak.

Safe. Just keep going.

He mumbled her name. Again. Again.

Then cold. The floor. Hard beneath his cheek. Had he fallen? No—he was lying down. He must have made it to the couch. Or the bed. He tasted blood. No—iron. Water staled from the kettle, from the tin. It always tasted like that.

He curled tighter, groaning.

The corner of the room swam with shadows.

She was there. No, she—she had been. He had kissed her. Her lips were real.

And then he had walked away.

Fool. Heaven above, what a fool.

The room flickered. Light. Day. Then dark again.

Something in his stomach shifted. Hunger? He could not remember eating. He forced himself upright, staggered to a pantry. A door. There—hardtack, dry and stale—some haversack left by Richard. He chewed. Gagged. Swallowed. The corner of the counter bit into his hip.

Back to bed. Cold floor again.

He closed his eyes, and she was there. Always. Gold gown. Laughter. Blood on her hands. His hands. Crawling under the floor, the weight of her body shielding his. Her voice at his ear, whispering his name—"Fitzwilliam."

Was she real?

He did not know.

Time lost all shape.

Sometimes the door rattled in his dreams. Sometimes the wind screamed her name.

And still, he burned. Was that his heart, or just his shoulder?

Water. He needed—

No. Already drank it. Or spilled it. Or both. Was there more? He could not remember.

The tin cup was on the floor again. Or still. It clanged once, softly. That had happened before.

He groaned—soft, ragged—and rolled, or tried to. The blanket tangled again around his knees. No. Not a blanket. His coat. He had been wearing it and now he was not and now it was a pillow and none of it made any sense.

It was so cold. Except when it was hot. Everything was burning.

Elizabeth.

His mouth formed the shape of her name, but no sound came out. He thought he had spoken it aloud. Maybe he had. Maybe that was what brought her. She always came when he called. Or maybe he dreamed her—he did not know the difference anymore.

Sometimes she stood in the corner and watched him. Sometimes she came close. Whispered to him. Touched his hair.

He told her to leave. She never listened. He told her he was dangerous. She laughed. He told her he would die soon, and she pressed her lips to his and told him not yet.

Other times it was not her. Other times it was fire and pain and the sharp snap of gunfire in the dark. Sometimes he was crawling, sometimes he was running. Once he reached for her hand and found blood instead. His or hers—he could not say.

He remembered trees. Wind. Her breath in his ear. He remembered hiding. Holding her. Fighting for her. He remembered dying.

Maybe he had.

And then—

A sound.

Not in his head. Not this time.

Footsteps. Real. Heavy. Sharp-heeled boots on floorboards. Not hers. Too loud. Too certain.

The door slammed open. He flinched—tried to sit up—and the world reeled sideways.

A voice, harsh and distant and terribly familiar. "Bloody hell."

Darcy blinked. The light behind the man was too bright. It cut around his silhouette like a halo. Or maybe a noose.

More footsteps. Another voice. "Get the surgeon. And water—clean towels. Christ, Darcy, what the devil—"

Fitzwilliam?

No.

Yes.

Could not be. Richard was away. Chasing traitors.

The floor tilted again. A hand grabbed his shoulder. He shouted—tried to shout—maybe it was just a moan. Too much pain. Too much.

"Easy, cousin," the voice said. "Easy now. You are safe."

Safe.

He almost laughed.

Then another voice. Lower. Older. "This wound is badly infected. We must clean it immediately—I cannot believe it is not yet gangrene. Another day, and we would have lost him."

Hands. Too many hands. Lifting him. Cutting something—his shirt, he thought. He did not care. His skin peeled like paper and someone poured acid into the wound and he screamed.

Someone held him down. "Drink this. Darcy. Drink, damn you!"

Bitter. Sharp. The taste hit the back of his throat and he gagged, but it kept coming. Warm liquid. Too warm. He coughed. Then again. Then he drank.

Cool cloth on his face.

Bandages.

A voice—Fitzwilliam's voice again, lower now, close to his ear.

"You stupid bastard," the colonel said. "Why did you not send word? Why the hell did you not let someone know?"

Darcy tried to reply. Could not.

Fingers gripped his wrist. "You are going to live. Do you hear me? You *will* live."

He wanted to say he was not sure he wanted to.

But the voice was stubborn. The pressure on his arm strong. And Elizabeth's face was still in his mind—soft, smiling, fierce—and when sleep took him again, she was all he saw.

And this time, she did not leave.

June 10, 1812

THE DRAWING ROOM AT Wrexham House was a perfect, curated display of taste—high ceilings trimmed with plasterwork, a great floral arrangement crowning the center table, and a distant fire murmuring softly beneath the clink of teaspoons and the rustle of skirts. Afternoon light spilled through the tall windows, filtered by lace curtains so fine they seemed woven from mist. A footman had just departed with the silver tea tray when Lady Charlotte Wrexham gave an elegant stretch across her chaise longue and smiled wickedly.

"You cannot simply sit there and tell us nothing, Elizabeth," she said, a sparkle in her eye. "Everyone says Her Majesty summoned you to Frogmore. What was it like? What did she wear? What did she say? And—most importantly—was it terrifying?"

Elizabeth, seated upright on a velvet-backed chair with a cup of lemon-scented tea cradled between her fingers, smiled faintly. The porcelain was warm. Her fingertips, cold. Even inside her long gloves. "It was... a great honor," she said, the words tasting foreign. "And yes. A little terrifying."

The Duchess of Wrexham, who sat like a throned oracle near the fire, lifted her chin at that. "You were summoned by the Queen herself, my dear. One does not receive such an invitation without reason."

Elizabeth's mouth was dry. She took a sip to mask the ache rising in her throat. "Her Majesty was very kind."

"Kind?" Charlotte tilted her head. "Gracious heavens. That makes her sound like a benevolent aunt in the country, not the sovereign matriarch of the realm. Was there no scandal? No secret assignation with a foreign prince in exile? I expected far more intrigue."

"I doubt her household would permit such license," Elizabeth said mildly, setting her cup down with care. "And if they did, I assure you I would be the last to hear of it."

"Do not be coy," the Duchess interjected, her tone smoother than Charlotte's, but far more dangerous. "We heard the Queen sent for you after the Perceval affair. Your account must have impressed her. Or terrified her. Either will do."

Elizabeth lifted her eyes, meeting the duchess's gaze. "I only told her what I saw. Nothing more."

"A great deal more, I think," the Duchess replied, watching her over the rim of her teacup. "There were many who witnessed Perceval's death. None of them were summoned."

Elizabeth resisted the urge to shift in her seat. "Perhaps it was a kindness, then. A balm for a distressed young lady."

Charlotte gave a theatrical sigh. "If only *all* our nervous turns could win us a few weeks in the Queen's favor. I shall develop a tremor and see where it gets me."

"You shall not," her mother said crisply.

"I shall not," Charlotte echoed, with a wry giggle. She turned back to Elizabeth, eyes narrowing with gleeful suspicion. "Now—what about gentlemen? I know you will claim your time was occupied with noble purpose, but I am not so easily misled. Was Lord Pembroke there? He is always lurking about in royal households. Did he spill wine on your hem and beg your forgiveness?"

Elizabeth pressed her lips together to suppress a smile. "Lord Pembroke was not in attendance."

Charlotte's pout was immediate and dramatic. "Pity. I was hoping he had finally grown bold enough to propose."

"I do not believe he ever showed particular interest," Elizabeth murmured.

"Not in *you*, perhaps. But your dowry inspires courage in the faintest of hearts," Charlotte replied with a wink. "Did Lord Westing reappear? I know he danced with you at Lady Ravenshaw's ball and was positively luminous with hope. Or perhaps that odd little Viscount Stanhope? He still wears his collar three inches too high, but Mama says his estate in Kent is quite tolerable."

Elizabeth summoned a practiced laugh. "I was not paying much attention."

Charlotte narrowed her eyes. "That is a suspicious answer. You only say that when something interesting happened."

"Charlotte," the duchess said mildly, though she did not sound disapproving. "Let the girl alone. She has just returned from royal service, not a Bath cotillion."

But Charlotte only grinned. "I shall extract the truth eventually. Mark me."

The Duchess gave a soft, audible breath through her nose—her version of indulgent disapproval. "My dear Charlotte, perhaps your friend is simply not inclined to broadcast her affections."

"Or," Charlotte said, leaning forward with a grin, "she is concealing the fact that she fell madly in love with a stable boy and eloped to Dorset in secret."

Elizabeth smiled again, but this time, it felt fragile. "I fear I have disappointed you. There were no elopements. No proposals. No stable boys."

"Nothing?" Charlotte groaned. "Then I shall simply have to live vicariously through someone else. Mr. Audley, perhaps. Have you heard him lately? They say he has been carrying on at White's about secret shooters and government cover-ups. He has the look of a man quite determined to write a gothic novel, only without the talent."

Elizabeth's spine tensed. Her fingers found the edge of her saucer and gripped it lightly.

"Ah! There, I *knew* that name would provoke some sort of reaction. I believe you found him rather more than agreeable once, did you not, Elizabeth?"

"To be quite frank, I have many other things in my mind that seem far more important than one Henry Audley," Elizabeth replied.

"Just as well," Charlotte continued, "for I think he has gone dotty in the head. I sat next to him at Lady Matlock's dinner party last week and he nearly overturned the soup insisting there was more to Perceval's death than met the eye. I said, 'Well of course there was, Audley. There were pistols and bullets and probably a very cross debtor involved. What more do you require? A ghost?'"

The Duchess snorted—very nearly a laugh. "The man is a gossip in trousers. He ought to take up a hobby."

Elizabeth summoned her voice. "Perhaps he merely wishes for answers."

Charlotte shrugged. "Perhaps. Or perhaps he wishes for an excuse to be quoted in the papers. In any case, it is nonsense. Everyone agrees there was no grand conspiracy. Just an angry man and a pistol."

"Two," the duchess corrected, "if one listens to our dear Elizabeth."

Elizabeth cleared her throat. "Oh, I think there was nothing in it, Your Grace. Her Majesty spoke to me more at Frogmore and now I understand it was merely a... a constable in plain clothes, who thought he could stop the shooter and was too late."

Charlotte sighed. "Such a shame, really. It makes for a dreadfully dull story."

Elizabeth's mouth tasted of ashes. "Indeed. Dreadfully dull."

The conversation spun on, touching on a new dressmaker in Grosvenor Street and Lady Celeste's engagement to a man old enough to be her grandfather, but Elizabeth drifted from it. She smiled when expected. She laughed once or twice. But her thoughts had already left the room.

And by the time the visit concluded, she had made up her mind to write to Jane. There were too many things she could not say to anyone else.

Montclair House
London
June 11, 1812

My Dearest Jane,

How strange it feels to write to you from the silence of my father's house rather than the warmth of yours. And how much stranger still to call it yours, when to me, it feels like mine. I hope you will forgive my clumsy pen—there is so much I wish to say, and not nearly enough elegance in my fingers to say it.

How are you, dearest? Truly? I think of you more often than I can say and send a little prayer each evening that you are safe, content, and well loved. Has Mr. Bingley continued to make his admiration plain? I shall be quite cross with him if he has not. And you must not be too discreet, either—do let him see your heart. He is not the only one whose affections ought to be assured.

Give my regards to your father, and tell him I am quite certain I should have beat him in chess by now, were I allowed to remain at Longbourn. I do hope he has found a worthy opponent—Mr. Bingley is too easily distracted by your beautiful eyes, I imagine, and not nearly ruthless enough to be entertaining.

Are Kitty and Lydia well? I imagine Lydia has already appropriated your best bonnet and Kitty has feigned ignorance. Please tell them I expect no fewer than three proper curtsies when next we meet. If they will not learn them for Society, then let them learn them for me.

Enclosed you will find the new sheet music I mentioned for Mary—I have marked the passages I think she will most enjoy. And a lace handkerchief for your mother, which I believe would suit her best with that lilac gown she wore the day I arrived.

As for me... London is as it has always been. Grand. Glittering. And yet entirely hollow. I walk through it as though through a dream, half-listening, half-seeing. The season is in full swing, but I confess, I feel no inclination to dance.

Jane... I have not heard from Mr. Darcy. Not since we were separated. He was terribly wounded when we parted, and I desperately hoped to find out if he is well. I do not even know where he resides, or whether he is in town. There is no address, no calling card, no plausible reason for me to inquire after him. But if you happen to see Mr. Bingley, perhaps you might mention his friend in passing. I would not ask you to be too forward. Only... if you should hear anything—anything at all—please write and tell me.

I miss him.

And I miss you. More than I have words for. I hope soon I might concoct some reason compelling enough to satisfy my father and return to Hertfordshire, if only for a visit.

Until then, write to me, Jane. Often. Tell me every dull, delightful, maddening detail of your days. I shall devour them like sugar.

With all my heart,
Elizabeth

June 21, 1812

DARCY ADJUSTED HIS CRAVAT with care, his fingers lingering on the folds longer than necessary. The familiar weight of the fabric against his throat was both a comfort and a reminder—he was returning to the world of the living, to duty, after weeks lost to fever and pain. His shoulder throbbed beneath the layers of his coat, a dull ache that still pulsed in time with his heartbeat.

As he stepped into the Home Office, the murmur of clerks and rustle of papers greeted him, a symphony of bureaucracy that had once been his daily score. He nodded to a passing colleague, the man's eyes widening momentarily before he offered a hasty greeting. Darcy was accustomed to such reactions; his unexpected return from the brink had evidently sparked whispers.

Darcy sank stiffly into the chair at his desk, the leather unforgiving against the bruised edge of his spine. His shoulder ached—throbbed, really—and every reach across the blotter sent sharp warnings down his back. But he ignored them. He had come here to work. To reacquaint himself with order, with focus, with purpose.

Maddox was dead. Cunningham "sailed to Antigua" under odd circumstances. And there was a new prime minister, Lord Liverpool, who was both loyal to the monarchy and fairly capable—after all, Darcy had served under him when he was the Home Secretary. The world was coming back to order.

And now, for his little corner of it, it was time to do his bit. He pulled the first folder from the stack, squinting at the dull gray print of a coded report. "Nothing but grain tariffs," he muttered, flipping the page. "Fascinating."

A second folder yielded a half-written memorandum on port authority corruption. Another listed suspected tea smugglers along the Channel. Darcy skimmed them all with increasing impatience, stacking the irrelevant reports to one side and muttering under his breath about the state of filing systems at the Home Office.

Then something slipped from the pile.

He reached absently to catch it, grimacing as the motion tugged too hard on his bandaged shoulder. A folded broadsheet fanned across his desk, one of a dozen he had agreed to receive while recovering—meant to keep him informed, he reminded himself, though he had barely glanced at a single one.

"Must have delivered these yesterday," he murmured, trying not to sound as disgruntled as he felt. He reached for it, intending to set it aside.

But a bold headline stopped his hand.

"The Marquess of Ashwick and his daughter, Lady Elizabeth Montclair, Attend the Theatre with Prince Nikolaos of Württemberg."

The room tipped sideways. The engraving beneath the headline depicted a familiar scene: Elizabeth, radiant in an elegant gown, seated beside her father in a private box. Opposite them, a distinguished gentleman—presumably Prince Nikolaos—leaned in, his posture attentive, his gaze fixed upon her.

Darcy's fingers tightened around the broadsheet, the sharp edges cutting into his skin. He scrutinized the illustration, searching for nuances, for truths hidden within the artist's strokes. Elizabeth's face was turned slightly away from the prince, her attention seemingly directed toward the stage. Was it mere coincidence, or had the artist captured a deliberate moment of detachment? The prince's demeanor, however, was unmistakable—his body angled toward her, his expression one of admiration and intent.

He told himself it was only a drawing, a subjective interpretation, perhaps even an exaggeration meant to tantalize society's gossipmongers. Yet, the knot in his stomach tightened.

He forced his gaze to the dateline: yesterday. The ink was barely dry on the news of her public appearance with another man. A prince, no less. The article elaborated on the prince's visit to London, noting his rumored search for a suitable English bride to strengthen ties between Württemberg and Britain.

The room seemed to constrict around him, the ambient sounds fading into a distant hum. He became acutely aware of the rhythmic throb in his shoulder, each pulse echoing the turmoil within. The logical part of his mind chastised his reaction—Elizabeth was free to attend the theatre with whomever she pleased. It was not as if *he* could escort her, and he would not deny her the pleasure of social engagements. Yet, the image of her in the company of another man—a prince, of all things—gnawed at him with relentless ferocity.

His vision blurred as he stared unseeingly at the broadsheet, the words and images dissolving into meaningless smudges. A tremor coursed through his hand, and the paper slipped from his grasp, fluttering to the floor. He pressed the heels of his palms against his eyes, as if to block out the tormenting thoughts that assailed him.

The walls of the office, once a sanctuary of order and purpose, now felt like the confines of a prison cell. The weight of solitude, of weeks spent in isolation with only the company of a doctor, his cousin, and his own despair, bore down upon him with crushing intensity. He had believed that immersing himself in work would provide an escape, a reprieve from the memories that haunted him. But reality had a cruel way of intruding upon such illusions.

A ragged breath escaped his lips, and before he could steel himself against it, a sob broke free—a raw, guttural sound that seemed to reverberate through the empty room. He doubled over, elbows braced against the desk, as the floodgates opened and the tears he had so steadfastly withheld streamed down his face.

The image of Elizabeth's smile, the lilt of her laughter, the warmth of her touch—all surged forth with vivid clarity, each recollection a dagger to his heart. He had convinced himself that distance and time would dull the ache, that he could will himself to forget. But the heart was not so easily swayed by reason.

Minutes passed, or perhaps it was hours; time had lost its meaning. What was he to do? What *could* he do? One day, she would marry. Some lucky bastard with more money and titles than comprehension that his real treasure was the woman taking his name. It would be in all the broadsheets, and there would be no avoiding it for him. The only way to escape it was not to know of it, and the only way to do that...

He straightened, wiping the dampness from his cheeks with a trembling hand. The broadsheet lay crumpled on the floor, and he left it there.

Drawing a shuddering breath, he reached for a fresh sheet of paper, the familiar act of writing offering a semblance of control. With deliberate strokes, he began to pen a letter, each word solidifying his resolve to seek solace in duty, if not in love.

> *To the Right Honourable Secretary of State for Foreign Affairs,*
>
> *I trust this letter finds you well. In light of recent developments and my unwavering commitment to serve His Majesty's government, I respectfully request consideration for an overseas assignment where my skills might be most effectively employed. Portugal, given its current strategic importance, appears a suitable station, though I remain amenable to deployment wherever the need is greatest.*
>
> *I await your esteemed consideration.*
>
> *Yours faithfully,*
> *Fitzwilliam Darcy*

He sanded the letter, watching as the ink set into the fibers. Folding it slowly, he pressed it with the seal of his office. Summoning a passing clerk, he extended the missive.

"Ensure this reaches the Foreign Secretary's office without delay."

CHAPTER THIRTY-TWO

June 30, 1812

T HE SILVER TEAPOT RATTLED faintly as Elizabeth lifted it to pour her father's tea. No one else had entered the breakfast room—not a footman, not a maid—and the only sound was the swish of liquid against porcelain. She replaced the pot and folded her hands in her lap, listening for his approach.

The door opened without ceremony.

"You refused him," the Marquess of Ashwick said by way of greeting, striding to his place at the head of the table. No kiss, no "Good morning, my petal," not even the customary inquiry after her health.

Elizabeth inclined her head. "I did."

He sat, the napkin flicking crisply over his lap. "Without so much as a word to me."

"I did not think your answer would differ from mine."

"In that, you are entirely incorrect, but that is not the point."

She said nothing, reaching for the toast rack.

He snorted, watching her with a gaze sharpened by disbelief. "Her Majesty's favor is not offered lightly, Elizabeth. And Prince Nikolaos is a suitor blessed with royal sanction. A German principality may not be a throne, but it is hardly something to dismiss over your morning tea."

Elizabeth looked up. "You promised, when I came out, that I would be allowed to choose my own husband and that I would be granted time to look round."

The marquess's lip curled. "Yes, within reason. I had rather thought that implied you *would* choose someone. Eventually." He picked up his spoon and stirred his coffee with more force than necessary. "But it has been over a year since your curtsey to the Queen, and your affections remain a mystery to everyone—including, it seems, yourself."

Elizabeth's eyes cooled. "Not a mystery. Simply a matter I keep private."

His brows lifted faintly. "So there *is* someone."

She reached for her own cup. "That is not what I said."

He leaned back, the chair creaking beneath him. "Then explain why you have refused a prince. And why you persist in asking to travel to Hertfordshire, of all places. What do you imagine I will believe, Elizabeth?"

"My imagination is as vivid as the scope of your beliefs, Father."

His fist fell on the table—for the first time in Elizabeth's memory, his temper flared, his face reddened, and he was glaring... at *her*. She startled and straightened in her chair.

"It would not have anything to do with that Member of Parliament from Hertfordshire, Henry Audley, would it?"

Her eyes flashed with indignation. "Mr. Audley and I have hardly spoken to one another more than twice. Besides, he has a weak chin."

"I'll have none of your impudence, Elizabeth!" The marquess snarled. "Society is watching. My line is at an end, but a daughter with royal connections? Now, that is something that might have ensured the Montclair legacy! Refusing a prince's proposal is not a matter taken lightly, especially when the Crown seemed to favor such a union."

Elizabeth's temper flared, her composure slipping. "I will not be bartered like a prized mare at auction, regardless of the Crown's inclinations."

The Marquess of Ashwick surged to his feet, the chair scraping against the floor with a discordant screech. His face flushed crimson, and his hands clenched into fists at his sides. "You are being obstinate and ungrateful," he thundered, his voice reverberating through the room.

Elizabeth rose as well, her eyes blazing as they locked onto her father's. "And you are forgetting your promise," she shot back, her voice trembling with emotion.

His eyes narrowed, and he took a step closer. "Enough," he commanded, his tone brooking no argument. "Sit down."

Elizabeth's heart thundered in her chest, but she stood her ground, her chin lifting defiantly. "No. I will wait. Come next March, I shall reach my majority, and then I will require no one's permission to marry whomever I choose."

The Marquess of Ashwick's voice hardened. "Elizabeth, you are my only child. The continuation of our family line rests upon your marriage and the heirs you will provide. Do you not understand the gravity of this responsibility?"

Elizabeth's eyes remained fixed on her father. "I am aware of my duty, Father. But I will not sacrifice my happiness for the sake of a dying lineage."

His hand struck the table again, the sound echoing through the room. "Your *happiness?* This is about more than your personal desires! Our family's standing, our alliances, they all hinge on your decisions!"

"And what of my life? Am I to be a pawn in your political games, married off to live in Germany simply because the Crown approves of it?"

The marquess's eyes narrowed. "You speak of autonomy, yet your actions suggest recklessness. Refusing a prince without counsel, showing no interest in suitable matches. Society is beginning to talk."

"Let them talk. I will not be pressured into a union I do not desire simply to appease society's gossip."

He took a step closer, his voice low. "Your mother has connections, friendships cultivated over decades. Do you wish to see them strained, our family isolated because of your obstinance?"

She met his gaze unflinchingly. "I cannot even recall the last time I spoke with my mother or received a letter from her that contained more than the most banal of trivialities. Why should I care for her inconvenience when she hardly seems to care for mine?"

The marquess exhaled sharply. "You are playing a dangerous game, Elizabeth. Time is not on your side. Eight months until your majority, and you believe you can withstand the pressures that will come?"

Elizabeth swallowed. "I do."

His eyes searched hers. "And if I were to arrange another match, one that would benefit our family immensely? There are agreeable gentlemen, daughter. I do not speak of wedding you to an ogre."

She shook her head. "It would be futile. My answer would remain the same."

The marquess's shoulders bunched as his fist closed around his teacup. "You are determined to defy me at every turn."

Elizabeth's voice softened, but her resolve remained. "I seek not to defy, but to choose a man I find worthy. Can you not understand that?"

He glared at the table. After a moment, he spoke, his tone weary. "Do what you will, Elizabeth. But know this: your choices carry weight, and the consequences will be yours to bear."

"Understood." Elizabeth rose from the table and left the room, not waiting to be dismissed. The door clicked softly shut.

Eight more months.

She could outlast him.

ELIZABETH RATTLED UP THE staircase, her steps coming in a disorganized flurry of anger. The morning's confrontation with her father left a residual heat in her chest that could only be satisfied by screaming into her pillow. But as she reached the landing, the murmur of voices and the shuffle of movement stopped her in her tracks.

Two maids bustled in and out of her former bedroom, arms laden with gowns and personal items. Their brisk efficiency suggested a task both urgent and familiar.

Elizabeth approached the doorway, her brow furrowing. "What is happening here?"

The younger maid, startled, nearly dropped the stack of hatboxes she carried. "Begging your pardon, my lady," she stammered. "The repairs are finished, and His Lordship ordered us to move your belongings back into this room."

Elizabeth's gaze swept the room. The walls, once a muted cream, now bore a fresh coat of soft blue. The heavy drapes had been replaced with lighter fabrics, allowing sunlight to spill generously into the space. The familiar scent of lavender sachets, placed in drawers and armoires, wafted through the air.

She stepped to the window, drawn by an inexplicable pull. The street below bustled with midday activity—carriages rattling over cobblestones, vendors calling their wares, pedestrians weaving through the throng. Her eyes scanned the crowd, landing on a figure standing motionless across the way. A man, his face obscured by the brim of his hat, seemed to be staring directly at her window.

A cold wave of fear crashed over her. The room, moments ago a sanctuary, now felt exposed, vulnerable. She recoiled from the window, her breath coming in shallow gasps.

"No," she said, her voice tight. "Move everything back. I will remain in the smaller room."

The older maid hesitated, a crease forming between her brows. "But, my lady, this is your rightful chamber. The other room is scarcely fit for—"

"I said no." Elizabeth's tone brooked no argument. "Please, do as I ask."

The maids exchanged uneasy glances, but nodded. "As you wish, my lady."

Turning on her heel, Elizabeth almost raced back toward the smaller room. Toward safety. As she rounded the corner, she collided with a figure emerging from the doorway. An armful of gowns tumbled to the floor between them.

Elizabeth recoiled a step as though she had seen a ghost, her pulse slamming against her ribs. And then she recognized the face.

"Alice?" she whispered.

The young maid froze, the bundle of gowns sagging slightly in her arms. Her eyes, wide and glistening, darted to the floor. "My lady—"

"Alice!" Elizabeth surged forward and grasped her by the forearms, the stiff silk of her own sleeves rustling with the suddenness of her movement. "Where have you been?"

Her voice cracked. She could not help it. Her hands clenched tighter around Alice's arms, not enough to hurt, but enough to make sure she would not vanish.

"I—I did not mean to go. I swear it, my lady. I did not—"

"I thought you were dead!" Elizabeth's breath shuddered out of her lungs as she crushed the poor girl, along with the bundle of gowns, in an awkward embrace. "We searched. That is... I know you were tracked—good, clever men searching for you! I asked everyone. I feared—" She stopped herself. "You were gone."

"I was taken." Alice's voice broke on the words. "I could not stop them."

Elizabeth stared at her—really stared. The hollows beneath her eyes, the faint scars along one cheekbone, the way her shoulders tensed under the weight of both memory and fabric.

She stepped aside and pushed open the door to the nearest room. "Come in here," she said, not waiting for Alice to agree before tugging her inside. "Tell me. Tell me everything."

Alice hesitated only a second before obeying. The gowns spilled onto the chaise as she lowered her arms, her posture awkward, wary.

"I was taken," she said again. "After the fire. I had stepped out to fetch more water. Someone grabbed me at the alley near the chemist."

Elizabeth sank onto the window seat, her legs suddenly weak. "You were alone?"

Alice nodded. "He said you would be joining me soon. That... that I would be a companion to you. But he lied."

"What happened?" Elizabeth's fingers dug into the window cushion, her knuckles white against the fabric. "How did you get away?"

Alice's eyes flicked to the floor. "They questioned me, my lady. About you. Where you had gone. Who you might tell. They thought I knew more than I did. I told them you were summoned to be with Her Majesty but they would not believe me."

Elizabeth's heart plummeted. "And made you suffer. Because of me."

Alice twisted the edge of her apron tighter between her fingers. "They kept me in a cellar. I do not know where. The windows were too high to see out. They brought me stale bread and water, and sometimes... sometimes nothing at all."

She drew in a trembling breath. "The man who came the most—he was always angry. Said he'd seen me walking with you. Said I had to know something. When I told him I didn't, he hit me. Backhand, mostly. Sometimes the belt."

Elizabeth's breath caught. "Good Lord..."

Alice went on, as though afraid to stop. "Then one night, the one who watched me drank too much. He slumped in the corner of the coach when they moved me. I waited, pretended to be asleep. When I was sure he was out cold, I opened the latch with my teeth and pushed the door open."

"Good heavens! You jumped from a moving carriage?"

Alice gave a small, humorless laugh. "They were going slow through a village. Not many lights. I leaped."

Elizabeth stared, horrified. "With your hands tied?"

"I hit the road hard," Alice said, pressing a hand to her ribs as if she still felt the bruise. "I could not breathe at first. My knees were skinned bloody. But I got up. And I ran. Through a hedge. Across a field. I tore my skirt climbing a gate, and I kept running until I could not feel my legs. I do not even know how far I made it. Just that when I collapsed, it was at the foot of a stranger's door."

Elizabeth rose to her feet, tears pricking at her eyes. "And he—this stranger—he helped you?"

Alice nodded, finally looking her in the eye. "Yes, my lady. He opened his door and found me bleeding and filthy and crying like a child. He said he had nothing to offer but porridge and clean sheets, but I thought it was heaven." Her voice faltered. "He never asked what I had done. Only what I needed."

"He took you in?"

Alice nodded. "He let me stay. Fed me. Nursed me. When I could walk again, I helped with the garden, the chickens. We... grew fond of one another."

A silence fell.

"And then?" Elizabeth asked gently.

Alice's eyes flicked upward. "We married. Quietly. My Bernard is kind, my lady. So kind. But he used everything he had to care for me. We live simple, but I wanted to work—to repay it. So I came back."

Elizabeth stared at her in stunned wonder. "You... came back *here?*"

Alice gave a small nod. "I thought it would be best—they knew me here. But the housekeeper said I was disgraced, and she did not mean to take me back, until Kenny from the stables spoke up for me. Said he had it on authority from some gentleman from the government that I'd been collected to attend you at some royal house. What was I to do but agree? It's only until I've saved enough. My Bernard is waiting. I just— I wanted to do right by him. By you."

Elizabeth stood without thinking, crossed the room, and drew Alice into a fierce embrace.

"You foolish, wonderful girl," she whispered. "You should have asked to speak with me the moment you returned. You need not stay a single hour longer."

Alice looked confused. "But—"

"Come with me." Elizabeth dragged Alice back to the room she had been sleeping in, a protective arm around the maid's shoulders as others passed through the door. Once they were alone, she broke away only long enough to pull open the drawer of her writing desk and drag out a heavy locked box.

She opened it and spilled the contents—coins and folded banknotes—into a cloth satchel she laid out on her mattress. Every bit of her own savings, collected from gifts and careful accounting over the past years. A few hundred pounds, probably, but she had never bothered counting it. She pulled the corners of the cloth together and tied them at the top.

"Take it," she said, pressing it into Alice's hands. "It is far less than you deserve, after all you endured for my sake. Go home. Go to your husband. And write to me. I want to know you are safe. Happy."

Tears spilled over Alice's cheeks. "My lady—Lady Elizabeth—I cannot—"

"You can," Elizabeth replied, folding her fingers around the satchel. "You will. Quickly, before someone else comes in and sees."

Alice clutched the purse to her chest, tears spilling over. "Thank you. Thank you, my lady."

"Do not." Elizabeth put out a hand. "Do not thank me. This is more than a debt and larger than what coins can repay, but I hope it will at least see you into a new life."

As Alice slipped out, still clutching the coin bag against her chest, Elizabeth stood motionless beside the door. Her hands, empty now, remained outstretched for a moment longer before she drew them back and clenched them at her sides.

The room was quiet. Too quiet. The kind that used to comfort her, and now only made her skin crawl.

She turned toward the narrow dressing table, ran her fingers over the edge. The wood was scarred and warped from age—never meant for someone of her station, yet lately, it was the only place in the house that felt hers.

She stared at her reflection in the mirror. A fine gown. A house full of staff. A title.

None of it mattered.

She reached for the ribbon at her throat and pulled it loose.

There had to be a way. If Alice could walk barefoot into the night, bleeding and half-dead, and still find her way into the arms of the love of her life—

Then Elizabeth would find hers.

"Mr. Darcy—this just arrived for you, sir."

He looked up slowly, the page's voice barely registering over the throbbing behind his right eye. He had been staring at the same report for nearly an hour and had absorbed none of it.

The letter was sealed with a plain red wafer. No crest. No ceremony. Just a name scrawled across the front in a hand he recognized as belonging to a junior secretary under Lord Sidmouth.

Darcy broke the seal with his thumb and scanned the page.

Your transfer request is granted.

Expect departure within the week. You are advised to prepare any immediate family or dependents for extended absence. Further instruction to follow.

His lips thinned. That was all. No formal approval yet, no post named, but it might as well have been done. It was coming. Portugal, almost certainly. Lisbon, if he was lucky. Somewhere more remote, if not. He folded the letter carefully, tucked it into his coat, and stood.

The ache in his shoulder was a warning, but he ignored it. He could take a carriage. It was a long walk to Mayfair, and his boots were not new.

But a carriage cost money—and he had spent enough of that during his convalescence to make even a gentleman feel unease. He preferred the control of his own two feet, and besides... walking cleared the mind.

Or at least, it used to.

He set out just before midday. The streets of Westminster were already warm with the breath of summer, and the air hung thick with dust. He kept his head down as he crossed into St. James's and then past Piccadilly, weaving his way toward the familiar grid of streets he once walked with such easy confidence.

Each block brought back the memory of another life. Turning the corner at Bond Street felt like stepping into a painting—one he could no longer touch.

He meant to go straight to Matlock house. To speak to Georgiana, to tell her what little he could about what came next. But then, as he passed into the heart of Mayfair, his eyes caught on something that stole his breath.

A placard. Tied with blue ribbon to the wrought-iron gate of a tall, stately home.

FOR SALE.
Inquire within.

Darcy stopped walking.

Because this was not just any house. This was *his* house.

Or rather, it had been.

The London townhouse of the Darcy family—Pemberley House, as it had once been styled, though there was no longer any Pemberley title to speak of—stood quiet behind its neat fence. The windows were shuttered. The knocker polished. The brick the same golden-red as he remembered.

Only the sign had changed.

He stood there so long that someone on horseback passed him twice.

Darcy's lips parted, but no sound escaped. The sensation was oddly physical—like finding a blade buried in his ribs after the duel was long over. He swallowed, a sour taste rising behind his teeth. How many times had he walked that threshold as a boy? How many hours had he spent pressed against the balustrade of that balcony, listening to summer thunder?

His feet carried him closer without conscious thought. His hand lifted toward the gate.

He wanted to leave. He *should* leave. Matlock's townhouse was only five doors down. Georgiana was waiting. But the ache in his shoulder suddenly pulsed with more than pain. It was something else. Something cold and bitter and ancient.

Anger. Not at fate. Not at the king. Not even at Wickham.

But at himself—for allowing it to feel like grief. For feeling anything at all.

The front door creaked open, and a young man in a cravat too bold for the neighborhood poked his head out.

"Looking to view the property, sir?" he chirped.

Darcy's eyes narrowed. "I have... 'viewed' it before."

The young man blinked. "Ah. Well—uh—it just came available, sir. We have a viewing scheduled in half an hour, but I can make allowances. Would you care to have another look inside, sir?"

Darcy hesitated, the question hanging in the air. His initial impulse was to decline, to walk away and leave the past undisturbed. Yet, an inexplicable urge rooted his feet to the spot. Before he fully comprehended his own decision, he found himself nodding.

"Very well," the agent replied, producing a set of keys from his pocket. He pushed the door back open, his demeanor professional yet eager, as if this was his very first showing. "This way, if you please."

Darcy followed, his steps faltering slightly as they approached the front entrance.

"After you, sir," the agent gestured.

As he crossed the threshold, Darcy was enveloped by a flood of memories. The scent of aged wood, worn leather, and faint traces of dust from his mother's favorite rugs lingered in the air. The unwaxed marble floor of the foyer gleamed softly in the muted light, each tile a silent witness to the passage of time.

The agent began his rehearsed spiel, his voice a distant murmur to Darcy's ears. "As you can see, the entrance hall is quite spacious, leading directly to the main reception rooms. The previous occupants maintained the original features, preserving the property's historical charm."

Darcy's gaze drifted upward to the grand staircase. He could almost see his younger self descending the steps, his father waiting at the bottom with a proud smile. The echoes of laughter and the rustle of elegant gowns during evening gatherings seemed to resonate within the walls.

They moved into the drawing room. The agent held up a hand in demonstration. "This room offers ample space for entertaining. The large windows allow for plenty of natural light, and the fireplace remains fully functional."

Darcy's fingers brushed against the mantelpiece as he recalled winter evenings spent before the fire, his mother reading aloud while he and Georgiana listened raptly. The warmth of those moments contrasted sharply with the cold emptiness he now felt.

The dining room was next. The long table had been removed, leaving the room feeling hollow. "Perfect for hosting dinner parties," the agent noted.

His mother always kept the table set with fine china and silver, her face brilliant even when the conversation swelled with politics and finance. His father's laughter used to rise above the clatter of cutlery, and Georgiana, as a child, would sneak candied almonds beneath the table until she was caught and scolded with a smile. It had been a place of comfort, of ceremony—of belonging.

He had once imagined continuing that tradition. Had pictured himself seated at the head of the same long table, perhaps grumbling inwardly over the number of guests, but secretly pleased by the sparkle in his wife's eyes as she orchestrated it all. A wife he would never deny. He had imagined enduring the fuss of floral arrangements and wine pairings and all the silly little details of society entertaining, just to see her pleased. Just to hear her laugh.

And of course, now, that wife had a face.

Sharp eyes and chocolate-dark hair that snarled into the most delicious knots at the barest breath. Wit that bit. Kindness that soothed. A voice that haunted his dreams.

Elizabeth.

He could see her standing at the end of the table, smoothing over a footman's error, or slipping her hand through his arm as she passed him a private smile. Filling the house with warmth. Filling it with life.

And now—he was only a visitor here. And she... might never know it had once been meant for her.

The staircase came next, its curve still elegant beneath the fading runner. Each step creaked under his boots with a familiar protest, like an old friend chiding him for being away too long. The agent continued his polite commentary, gesturing toward the upper floor with a rehearsed flourish. "And here we have the master suite. Generous space, as you see. A fine dressing room just beyond that door."

Darcy followed him in silence.

The room was unchanged. Tall windows let in the weak July sun, illuminating the carved moldings and the faint ghost of old wallpaper. He crossed to the window without thinking, hands clasped behind his back. Outside, the street stirred with late afternoon traffic—horses, wheels, a fruit seller shouting his wares. Nothing extraordinary.

Except that he had once stood here, in this exact spot, a boy barely old enough to tie his own cravat, dreaming of all the years to come. He had imagined standing here with a wife. With a son, perhaps. Or a daughter who would tug his sleeve and beg to be taken to the park.

He turned slightly, his gaze catching the half-open door across the chamber—the entrance to the mistress's rooms.

His face heated. The blush crept up his neck like a thief.

It had never been his habit to indulge in fantasies, but... he had once imagined *her* there. In the dressing room. Her voice calling lightly to him as she complained about the bothersome tangles in her hair that always dazzled his eyes. Elizabeth, wrapped in a silk robe, barefoot on the cool floors, laughing as he caught her hand and pulled her back toward the bed. Not out of hunger, but reverence. Worship. The thrill of knowing she was his, and he was hers.

He turned quickly back to the window, ashamed of the heat still prickling beneath his collar. It was foolishness. All of it.

And still, it would not leave him.

Finally, they went down the stairs and the agent made for the last door in the corridor—the one Darcy had both longed and dreaded to see. His father's study.

"This room has been repurposed into a gentleman's retreat," the agent said, his tone bright. "Ideal for a private office or a quiet library. Fine light from the south-facing windows, and the built-in shelves are—"

He pushed open the door and faltered mid-sentence.

"Oh. I... had thought you had already taken your leave, sir." His brows knit in confusion. "I beg your pardon."

Darcy stepped past him—and froze.

Behind the desk, slouched in the leather chair once reserved for the Earl of Pemberley, sat George Wickham. His boots were crossed lazily on the blotter, scuffed soles resting where the elder Mr. Darcy once signed official documents. A crystal glass—brandy, likely—glistened in his hand.

"Well, well. If it is not dear Fitzwilliam. Come to buy back the house, have you?"

The agent blinked between them. "Ah... it seems you are... acquainted. I shall give you both a moment."

He stepped back quickly, the door clicking shut behind him.

Darcy did not move. His hands were at his sides, clenched tight, but otherwise, he remained perfectly still. Wickham's presence—his very ease in the chair, the way he tilted his glass in mock salute—was a provocation. An insult. A desecration.

Darcy's gaze swept the room. His father's desk, once so meticulously kept, was scattered with playing cards and empty glasses. The shelves, where once had stood volumes on estate law and history, now held cheap knickknacks and half-filled decanters. A cravat had been discarded over the arm of a chair like a soiled napkin.

It was filth. Disrespect. A house turned inside out by a man who had never been invested in it. And yet here he sat.

Wickham raised the brandy to his lips and sipped leisurely. "You look well. A bit thinner than I remember. Heard you were sick. Something about a bullet? Two?"

Darcy said nothing.

"Oh, come now. We used to be such friends." He gestured to the chair opposite. "Sit down, do. Let us reminisce."

Darcy did not sit. He stepped forward once, eyes narrowing as he surveyed the wreckage of the study—the ruined papers, the smeared ink, the ring stains on the walnut surface. His father's nameplate was gone. The brass lamp that had stood in the corner for decades was missing. In its place was a gaudy crystal monstrosity.

Wickham watched him take it all in. He seemed to savor every flicker of disgust.

"I heard about your little petition," he said lightly. "Stirring up trouble again, are you? Still hoping for a royal pardon? Or just trying to get back what is no longer yours?"

Darcy's voice, when it came, was quiet. "You have no right to this house."

"Oh, but I do," Wickham said, lifting the brandy glass to his lips again. "Gifted by the Crown, no less. That must sting."

Darcy's jaw flexed.

Wickham leaned back further in the chair, arms wide. "You always had the land. The name. The fortune." He grinned. "Or so you thought."

Darcy's fists clenched until they trembled, but he locked them at his sides.

Wickham's smile widened. "Lady Catherine wrote to me, you know. Weeks ago. Thought I should be warned about you. Said you were making a mess of things up in Hertfordshire. Cavorting with gentlewomen well above your station. Trying to stir sympathy in the court."

Darcy's heart went still.

"Some girl, she said. Claimed a connection to one of the local families. Mysterious little thing, too well bred for country stock, but nobody could pin down exactly who she was."

He tilted his head, watching Darcy closely. "Funny, that. You, showing up in the country just as a pretty, unknown 'cousin' appears? Lady Catherine seemed convinced you were using her for something. Stirring up sympathy. Playing the country hero. Or was she just a bit of fun before you came crawling back to London?"

He gave a low, deliberate laugh. "Always had a knack for choosing your amusements carefully, did you not?"

Darcy's biceps were now quivering, his jaw ticking.

Wickham smiled wider. "What is this? Touch a nerve? She must have been some little piece of flesh."

Darcy moved before he even registered the decision. He crossed the room in three strides and struck Wickham across the jaw.

The brandy glass toppled to the floor and shattered. Wickham reeled, crashing against the desk before surging upright. For a moment, he looked stunned. Then his expression darkened. He swung wildly, catching Darcy with a blow to the shoulder.

Darcy gasped, his injured side collapsing inward with pain. He staggered, gritting his teeth, trying to right himself—but Wickham was already on him.

They went down hard, grappling, fists flying. Wickham was stronger, and Darcy—still weak, still recovering—could not keep pace. A punch landed to his ribs. Another to his already bruised temple. His vision went white.

And still Wickham snarled insults in his ear. "Always so bloody noble," he spat. "Still fighting battles no one asked you to."

Darcy clawed for purchase, found the edge of the desk, tried to haul himself up.

Wickham kicked him back down.

"Stay down, Darcy. It is where you belong."

Darcy coughed, blood in his mouth.

And Wickham, smirking now, stepped over him—then kicked his hat aside as he sauntered out the door.

CHAPTER THIRTY-THREE

July 2, 1812

L ADY ELIZABETH MONTCLAIR HAD always been strategic in her social engagements—raised to understand, as she was, the nuances of rank and influence. A simple morning call could topple an alliance or create a stir that would reverberate throughout London for weeks.

Thus, when she resolved to reconnect with Lady Julia Fitzwilliam, daughter of the Earl of Matlock, it was with deliberate intent, careful planning... and no little chagrin.

She had not called on Lady Julia in more than a year—not since that brief friendship during her first season. It had not ended in acrimony; rather, Elizabeth had simply found the girl uninteresting. Too dull. Too prim. And altogether too pleased with herself for keeping her cousin Georgiana perpetually underfoot. Still, Julia was well-connected, easy to impress, and—most importantly—the daughter of an earl... an earl who happened to be Darcy's uncle.

Elizabeth did not need to *like* her. She just needed to gain her trust.

The carriage rocked slightly as it came to a stop, the horses snorting. A footman opened the door, and Elizabeth stepped down without hesitation, skirts brushing the stone. She did not pause to adjust her gloves or glance up at the windows. She simply walked to the door and knocked.

The butler, upon recognizing her, executed a deep bow. "Lady Elizabeth Montclair, an unexpected pleasure. Her ladyship is in the music room. May I announce you?"

"Thank you," Elizabeth replied sweetly. "However, I had hoped to see Lady Julia. I hope my unanticipated visit does not inconvenience her."

"Not in the least, my lady. Lady Julia always welcomes your company. She is in the drawing room."

BETTER LUCK NEXT TIME

As she was guided through the familiar corridors, Elizabeth's eyes flitted over the portraits lining the walls—generations of Fitzwilliams, each rendered in oil and shadow. She searched their faces without meaning to. The arch of a brow, the curve of a mouth. Did that gentleman resemble Darcy about the eyes? Did that lady carry his sister's gentle expression? These were his people. His mother's blood. Elizabeth had passed through this house before without giving them a second glance. Now, they felt like echoes. A family she might have called her own.

The drawing-room doors were opened, revealing Lady Julia seated by the fireplace, an embroidery hoop in hand. At Elizabeth's entrance, she set aside her work, a genuine smile gracing her features.

"Lady Elizabeth!" she greeted, rising gracefully. "What a delightful surprise."

Elizabeth curtsied subtly. "Lady Julia, I hope I do not intrude upon your morning."

"Not at all. Please, sit."

As they settled, a maid appeared with tea, the delicate clinking of porcelain filling the brief silence.

"It has been some time since our last meeting," Elizabeth began, accepting a cup.

Lady Julia nodded, her eyes full of more curiosity than her words let on. "Indeed. I heard you were at the theatre recently. I saw an opera last week, so it seems the Season has kept us all engaged. How have you fared?"

"Well enough," Elizabeth replied, with that practiced smile her mother had taught her. Lady Julia was fishing for gossip about Prince Nikolaos, but Elizabeth had more interesting topics in mind. "However, I have decided I do not care for the theatre. It is not for lack of effort on my part, I assure you. I simply do not prefer it."

Lady Julia's lips drew together in a bow, and her brows climbed upward. "Indeed? Why, half of London saw that engraving of you and... oh, some gentleman or other, I can hardly keep them straight. It looked as though you were enjoying yourselves tremendously."

"Artistic license, I am afraid. No, I have recently taken an interest in the musical arts. I can play, to be sure, but I rather prefer to listen to others."

"Do you?" Lady Julia sipped her tea nonchalantly. "I am content with either. However, Viscount Bromley has asked me to play so often when we are in company that I think I might come to agree with you."

Elizabeth smiled at that thinly veiled bit of false modesty. "Oh, but you are not the only musician in the house, at least. I recall that your cousin—whatever was her name, dear? She was rather accomplished."

Lady Julia set down her cup with a flourish. "Georgiana, yes. She is a dear girl," she said. "Though I daresay Mother has kept her too often alone—at her brother's request, I am afraid. She has been permitted precious little society."

Elizabeth lowered her cup. Ah, they were getting to *him* already. This would be easier, even, than she had hoped. "I do not recall you mentioning that she had a brother."

"Oh, yes. He is great friends with *my* brother Richard, else I doubt we should ever see him. Fitzwilliam is... particular about Georgiana's company. As if the girl were made of glass!"

Elizabeth took a quiet sip of her tea. "Perhaps her brother believes she would be happier in smaller company," she said lightly. "A shy young lady, though very sweet. I hope she is well?"

"She is, though still not formally out." Lady Julia gave a slight roll of her eyes. "Everyone treats her like some cloistered nun rather than the niece of an earl. But I suppose that is a Darcy for you."

"Is she often in Town?" Elizabeth asked, keeping her voice mild.

Lady Julia's eyes lit up, sensing an opportunity. "She is staying here in London just now. I daresay she must be dreadfully bored. Prefers the country, that one."

Elizabeth allowed a small smile. "Then perhaps she might welcome a walk in the park some afternoon? I think I should like to know her better. Anyone who plays as beautifully as she does might enjoy a friend with a similar passion for music."

"I shall send for her at once," Lady Julia said, already reaching for the bellpull. "It would be the very thing. She has been sighing at pianoforte scores and writing letters to no one for days. And I cannot think of a better companion than Lady Elizabeth Montclair."

She turned toward the footman who presented himself by the door. "Have Miss Darcy brought to us at once."

The man bowed and vanished, and Elizabeth folded her hands in her lap to still their sudden restlessness. Her heart gave a quiet thud.

"She spends far too much time upstairs," Lady Julia added. "Sketching, mostly, or brooding. You would think her brother were the only man in England worth pining over."

Elizabeth did not reply. She could feel her pulse in her throat.

The door opened.

Georgiana Darcy entered with hesitant steps, her eyes flicking between her cousin and their guest. She had grown taller, perhaps a touch thinner than Elizabeth remembered.

But her face was the same—gentle, watchful, guarded. Her hands were clasped before her in a way that reminded Elizabeth uncomfortably of Darcy at his most reserved.

"You remember Lady Elizabeth Montclair, of course," Lady Julia said airily. "She was just saying how she hoped you might keep her company."

Georgiana curtseyed. "Yes, my lady. I remember."

Elizabeth stood. "Miss Darcy," she said warmly. "I hope I have not imposed."

Georgiana's gaze lifted to meet hers—shy, but not overly reticent. "Not at all. I am glad to see you again."

And there it was. Not only a memory, but a possibility. A door cracked open.

Elizabeth stepped closer. "Perhaps you will sit with me?" she asked. "Only if you were not otherwise engaged before we pulled you away."

Georgiana hesitated, then nodded at once, and Elizabeth could see it—the faintest flicker of relief in her eyes that she had not been summoned here to perform and impress. She sat beside her on the settee, and Lady Julia, sensing herself dismissed from her own drawing room, reached for her embroidery frame with a very self-satisfied smile.

Elizabeth settled deeper into the settee beside Georgiana, offering a warm, encouraging smile. The younger woman sat with her hands folded neatly in her lap, her gaze lowered, the very picture of modesty.

"Miss Darcy," Elizabeth began gently, "I recall from our previous meeting that you have a talent for the pianoforte. Do you still find joy in playing?"

Georgiana's cheeks tinged pink, and she nodded slightly. "Yes, my lady. I practice when I can."

"Music can be such a solace," Elizabeth said. "Especially amidst the bustle of London. Do you find the city agreeable?"

Georgiana hesitated, her fingers tightening together until the knuckles whitened. "I... I prefer the countryside," she admitted.

Elizabeth nodded. "The countryside does have its charms. But surely, London offers its own diversions? Have you attended many events this season?"

Georgiana's eyes flickered toward Lady Julia, who observed the exchange with a faint smile. "Not many," Georgiana replied. "My family is... particular about the company I keep."

Elizabeth sipped her tea thoughtfully before venturing, "Ah, yes. Lady Julia was just mentioning your brother's protective nature. It is commendable how he looks after you."

At the mention of her brother, Georgiana's composure faltered. Her eyes welled up, and she glanced down, dabbing at them with a handkerchief. There was a marked sniff.

Lady Julia sighed, setting her hoop down with more than a hint of exasperation. "Georgiana, must you always be so dramatic? It is not as if he is dead."

Elizabeth stiffened in alarm. Not dead, but... but what was the matter with Darcy? Lady Julia seemed to think whatever it was of little consequence, but Lady Julia had also been heard to laugh off the little matter of another war with America, so that was no sound indication.

Had something happened to him? Was he ill? That bullet wound in his shoulder... had it got infected, after all? Had he lost... Oh, good heavens, pray he did not lose his arm!

She leaned forward, a spiraling series of fresh nightmares tumbling through her mind. She held on to her teacup like a lifeline, lest she claw for Georgiana's hands instead. "Miss Darcy, I apologize if I have upset you. Is something the matter with your brother? Is he..."

Georgiana shook her head, her voice trembling. "It is just... my brother is leaving soon. He intends to take a post halfway around the world, and he is to sail tomorrow. I fear I shall never see him again."

Elizabeth sat frozen, her teacup suspended halfway to her lips. The china began to tremble faintly in her grasp.

Leaving?

Her thoughts raced, scrambled, failed to catch up. Mr. Darcy—Fitzwilliam—was leaving. Not for the country, not for some brief errand or posting in a neighboring county. Halfway across the world.

She blinked once, twice, her breath shallow as if someone had knocked it from her lungs. A strange, cold nausea stirred low in her belly.

And Georgiana... sweet, shy Georgiana, who clearly adored her brother with quiet reverence—Georgiana believed she would never see him again.

Elizabeth swallowed hard. Something cracked open inside her, sharp and breathless. There was no room now for pretense, no excuse to retreat into careful civility. She had not come merely for news.

She had come for him. And he was about to vanish.

D ARCY KNELT BEFORE THE half-packed trunk, sleeves rolled to the elbow, his shirt damp with the effort of sorting through the detritus of a life he had not intended to abandon so suddenly. A pair of boots thudded to the floor beside him. He straightened, reached for the stack of folded shirts on the nearby chair, and began placing them neatly inside.

His manservant, Mr. Simmons, had left the day before. His departure was hardly a surprise. Darcy had never been one to need constant assistance, and Simmons had been more a fixture than a servant, more accustomed to dusting the furniture than providing meaningful help. Now, Darcy was left to sort through the remnants of his life alone.

Tomorrow, he would board a ship to Portugal.

Every movement felt mechanical. Shirts. Books. A custom shaving kit he had barely touched. A second trunk waited open by the hearth, filled with things he had no intention of taking—items destined to be sold, given away, or forgotten.

He picked up a stack of papers from the desk, a few contracts, letters he had never bothered to read. They went into the trunk without much thought. There was little enough left for him to take—no more than could fit inside a few small trunks. He was leaving everything behind: the place, the life, the man he had been.

But there were a few things he could not part with—things he knew Georgiana would appreciate. Some of his mother's old jewelry, the last of his father's books, a few knick-knacks of sentimental value. He wrapped them carefully, placing them to one side.

His hand brushed against something unexpected. He had nearly forgot about it—tucked in the corner of an old drawer. It was a drawing, neatly folded and already yellowing from too much handling. The sketch was of Maddox. Elizabeth had drawn it in that hasty, almost unconscious way she had, capturing him with lines so precise they almost hummed with life.

Darcy stared at it for a long moment. Why the devil did he still have it? Maddox was dead. Nobody needed this anymore. Why had he not thrown it out, burned it? It was a reminder of a time he should have left behind.

He held it in his hand for a while longer, almost mesmerized by the simplicity of it. How easily she had drawn it. Had she thought of him while sketching it? He could almost hear her voice in his mind as she had talked to him back then, teasing him about the "scoundrels" they were surrounded by, drawing that inimitable smile from him, one of those rare smiles that no one ever saw except her.

Shaking his head, he tucked the drawing aside, but then his eyes fell on something else—a familiar pair of ladies' gloves. They had been carelessly folded and left in one of the pockets of his best coat.

The gloves Elizabeth had worn to Buckingham House—the ones he had made her remove so she could blend in, disappear in plain sight. As if *she* could ever disappear! He had not realized he had kept them, had not even remembered to return them.

For a moment, he simply stared at them. His pulse quickened, and before he could stop himself, he brought them to his nose. Her scent. That faint, unmistakable fragrance of rosewater. He closed his eyes as the memories washed over him.

Buckingham House. The mad dash into darkness. She had been frightened, furious, utterly disoriented—torn from everything familiar, from the illusion of safety she had always known. She had lashed out with words sharp enough to draw blood. And still...

Even then.

Even with her temper high and her pride higher, he had barely been able to take his eyes off her.

She had worn these gloves. Pale grey, soft as breath, with a bit of fraying along the edge where she worried the seam with her thumb. He had watched that thumb for an hour, sitting across the room while she slept—legs folded under her on a filthy cot, her face half-turned into her arm, that indomitable spine finally softened by sleep.

He had watched her and known, with the terrible clarity of a man doomed by his own conscience, that he could never have her. Not without cost. Not without destroying her.

And yet he had wanted. Desperately.

He lifted the gloves to his face and closed his eyes. If this was all he could keep... Well. Odd how something so small seemed to have the power to destroy *him*.

He opened his eyes again, startled by his own emotion, and gently placed the gloves in a pile of things for Georgiana. Best that he let go, while he still could.

He breathed in deeply, trying to clear his head. He had a choice to make, a future to build, even if it meant a life alone.

Darcy had just begun to fold his two spare cravats when the latch turned and the door to his flat pushed open with a clatter.

"Packing already?" Richard called out, striding in like he owned the place, though his smile came too quickly and sat too loosely on his face. "You could have told me. I would have brought a bottle of brandy and made a ceremony of it."

Darcy did not turn. He closed the trunk with care, then fastened one of the latches. "I have little enough to take. The rest is of no use to me now."

Richard looked around the modest apartment, taking in the spartan furnishings, the half-filled shelves, the solitary trunk resting at the center like a coffin. "Still feels a bit grim, does it not? You are quite sure about this?"

Darcy straightened slowly, lifting his eyes to meet his cousin's. "Yes. I am quite sure."

Richard rubbed the back of his neck, then wandered further in, tapping a knuckle absently against the mantle. "Portugal," he said at last. "Not exactly the tonic I would prescribe. But I suppose if the plan is to put the whole of England behind you, that is one way to do it. You do set off in a dashed hurry, though."

Darcy moved to the writing desk and began sorting a few items into a leather folio—letters, a few clippings, a folded map. "You would not understand."

Richard scoffed. "You are right. I cannot possibly comprehend the desire to flee to the farthest corner of Europe because you are too pigheaded to—"

He broke off, sighing. Then, as if deciding something in that instant, he reached into his coat and drew out a square of torn paper. He crossed the room and held it out.

Darcy frowned, glancing at it without taking it. "What is that?"

"Read it," Richard said, flatly. "You are the one always harping on about reading the evidence."

Darcy took it, unfolded the scrap. It was from the society pages, a narrow column trimmed unevenly from its neighbors. His eyes scanned the words, his stomach twisting as he read:

> *One of the ton's brightest gems seems to shine a little less brilliantly today, as whispers abound of a certain lady's recent refusal of a royal offer from none other than the Prince of Württemberg. Speculations run rampant about the reasons behind such a surprising demurral.*

Darcy said nothing. He folded the page again, carefully, too carefully. He held it out to Richard. "Why have you brought me this?"

Richard did not move to take it. "I thought you might like to know what the rest of London has been whispering about for the last few days. You remember London, do you not? The place you live in, where the woman you are running from still resides?"

"Her affairs are no concern of mine," Darcy replied, placing the scrap on the edge of the writing desk with a precision that betrayed him.

"You are insufferable."

"I am aware."

Richard paced away, stopped at the window, then turned back. "You love her."

Darcy's voice was low. "It makes no difference."

"Then why do you look like that?"

Darcy did not answer.

After a long moment, Richard reached for the torn page and stuffed into the pocket of Darcy's own coat, hanging on the hook. "I came to walk with you. You will want to bid Georgiana farewell, and I have a few matters to settle with Father."

Darcy nodded once, reached for his coat. Neither man said anything more as they stepped into the hall, the door closing behind them.

Richard hailed a carriage with a sharp whistle, stepping into the street with a confidence that brooked no argument. Darcy followed, his steps dragging somewhat.

"Come now, Darcy," Richard chided, clapping a hand on his shoulder. "Must you always pinch pennies? Allow me to indulge in this extravagance. My treat."

"Your generosity is noted, though unnecessary."

Richard only grunted in response, tossing a few coins to the driver as he ushered Darcy into the waiting carriage. His eyes flicked once—just once—toward the far end of the street, where the familiar corner of Grosvenor and Upper Brook loomed. "Humor me," he said, too casually, climbing in behind him. "Even you must admit that limping up Mayfair on foot with half your shoulder still stitched is not the ideal farewell."

Darcy did not reply. He folded his arms with stiff discomfort, the movement tugging at half-healed skin. He turned his head deliberately toward the carriage window and fixed his gaze on the drab brickwork of the shops and façades they passed.

It was cowardice. He knew it. But still he refused to look.

The carriage turned.

He felt it in the curve of the wheels before he saw it. His throat closed.

Pemberley House.

He kept his eyes on the far side of the street. A milliner's display flashed past—a garish explosion of ribbons and bonnets. Next, the butcher's, and then the tobacconist. His reflection stared back at him in every shop window. Tight jaw, hollow eyes. Unflinching.

He did not look. But he could see it, anyway.

The pale, elegant façade. The gate with its spear-point finials. The ivy that climbed along the western wall. The gleam of brass on black iron.

And the sign.

He did not need to read it again. "FOR SALE. Inquire within." A stranger's hand affixed it. Wickham's final insult.

The house his grandfather had bought. The one his father had loved. The one he had once imagined passing on to a son of his own. To Elizabeth's son.

Darcy swallowed hard and clenched his gloved hand into a fist. If Richard noticed, he said nothing. The carriage wheels rolled past, and Pemberley House vanished behind them.

Only then did Darcy exhale. The carriage's interior was stifling, or perhaps it was the maelstrom within his own mind that suffocated him. The broadsheet clipping Richard had shown him burned in his pocket, its words seared into his consciousness.

She refused a prince...

Yet, once, she had offered herself to a man stripped of title and fortune.

Would she still? What if he asked her... now—today, even?

The notion was absurd, reckless. To ask her to abandon her world, to accompany him to a foreign land where neither rank nor wealth could shield them. In Portugal, her titles would be whispers, her influence diminished.

But perhaps that might be what she desired—to escape the relentless scrutiny, the ceaseless gossip.

The thought was intoxicating, a vision of a shared exile where they could forge a new existence, unburdened by expectation.

Yet, she is not yet of age.

March 20th.

The date loomed in his mind, a barrier insurmountable. Without her father's consent, marriage was an impossibility. And even if they waited, even if he dared to hope—

Eight months was an eternity in this world of alliances and strategic matches. By then, she would have moved on. Forgot all about him in favor of someone better suited to her.

The carriage jolted, the sudden halt snapping him from the dizzying reel of thoughts that had looped without mercy. He blinked, disoriented, as if surfacing from underwater.

Matlock House rose before them, prim and dignified in its symmetry, just as it had always stood. The same brass knocker on the black-lacquered door. The same climbing roses curling around the window frames. But something inside him recoiled. It was not the house that had changed.

It was him.

Darcy reached for the latch and paused. His hand trembled once before he willed it still.

This was farewell. One last duty to perform. One more mask to wear.

He stepped down. The cobblestones were warm beneath his boots, the air thick with London heat, and every muscle in his body ached with the knowledge that this might be the last time he saw his sister's face in many years.

He drew a breath.

And walked to the door.

Chapter Thirty-Four

"Portugal—some business or other for the Foreign Office. He said he would be away for some years, perhaps. I am afraid it shall be forever," Georgiana whispered, her voice thin with grief.

Elizabeth blinked hard, trying to focus. The walls tilted, ever so slightly. Her teacup clinked sharply against the saucer as she set it down with trembling fingers.

"Elizabeth?" Lady Julia's voice held a note of alarm now. "You look quite pale. Shall I call for salts?"

"No," Elizabeth breathed. "No, I—" She pressed her fingers to her temple. "It is only... the heat."

It was not. It was the world collapsing inward. The air was thick and impossible. Her stays too tight. She had come here to find out if he was well, to discover where he had gone—and instead she had learned he was leaving the country. Leaving England. Leaving *her*.

"He cannot," she murmured.

"Elizabeth?" Lady Julia stepped closer. "Do you—"

From the corridor beyond the door came a familiar cadence: footsteps, booted and brisk, and low voices in conversation. Georgiana's head snapped up.

"That is Richard," she said, rising from the seat. "And—oh!"

Lady Julia turned sharply toward the door. "Is that Mr. Darcy with him?"

Elizabeth rose unsteadily. Her heart had already leaped a thousand times in an instant. She knew that voice. She had replayed it in her mind too many nights to mistake it now. *Fitzwilliam.*

The door had not yet opened, but she was already moving. Her blood simmered. Her limbs, moments ago heavy as stone, were carried now by something else entirely.

There were words just outside—the colonel's voice, chiding him over something. "—I told you it was idiotic, but do you listen? No, of course not. You are going to Portugal, and for what? To avoid—"

Darcy's voice cut him off. "I have come to see Miss Darcy," he said to the footman outside.

Elizabeth was already surging forward, already fixed on the door.

"Yes, sir. She is in the drawing room with Lady Julia. I am afraid they do have a caller—"

"Georgiana is entertaining callers?" the colonel's voice echoed outside. "Darcy, perhaps we should—"

"Forgive me, but I prefer not to tarry long enough to be detained by the earl. I will ask her to step out for a word."

The door opened. The footman stepped aside, halfway through a proper announcement. But Elizabeth was already there, already waiting to intercept him, chin high and back straight.

Darcy entered, and for a moment, a smile of greeting flashed on his face. Then he halted mid-stride. His eyes jumped past his sister and cousin—straight to her.

She did not wait for pleasantries. "*Portugal?* Why the devil are you running away to Portugal?"

Darcy's mouth opened, but no sound emerged. He appeared entirely at a loss, his usual stoicism faltering.

Richard stepped between them. "I told him it was idiotic," he said helpfully. "But he never listens." He turned to Elizabeth with a quick bow. "Lady Elizabeth, always a pleasure."

Lady Julia's mouth was hanging open, and she was gasping like a fish. "You... you are... *acquainted?*"

Elizabeth ignored her. "Well?" she pressed, taking a step closer to Darcy. "Have you nothing to say for yourself?"

Darcy's throat bobbed as he swallowed, his gaze dropping momentarily before meeting hers once more. "I... I did not think it would be of interest to you," he managed.

Elizabeth's eyes flashed with a mix of hurt and indignation. "'Not of interest?'" she echoed. "You believe I would not care to know that you intend to exile yourself to the far reaches of Europe?"

The colonel cleared his throat. "Yes, yes, Darcy is an idiot. On that, we can all agree. Perhaps we should all sit down," he suggested, though no one moved.

Lady Julia's brow furrowed deeper. "I must insist on an explanation," she declared. "How is it that you are all so familiar?"

Georgiana's gaze mirrored her cousin's bewilderment. "Brother?" she prompted, seeking clarification.

Darcy exhaled slowly, his gaze never leaving Elizabeth's. "Lady Elizabeth and I became... acquainted this spring," he said weakly.

Elizabeth's fists balled. "*Acquainted*," she repeated, the word tasting bitter on her tongue. "Is that all it was?"

Darcy's jaw tightened, a muscle feathering beneath the skin. "Elizabeth..."

The use of her given name sparked a handful of gasps from the others, and sent a shiver of warmth through her belly. Oh, how many times had she heard him saying her name in her dreams? But she was too angry with him to soften so easily.

She crossed her arms. "I demand an answer. More 'smuggling' to tamp down for the Crown? A life given over in service to a Prince who can hardly be bothered to remember your existence, save when you can be prodded into amusing him?"

His throat bobbed. "It was not like that. I—"

The colonel clapped his hands together. "Darcy, shut up. You will only make it worse for yourself."

"Richard," Darcy growled between his teeth, his eyes never leaving Elizabeth. "This is a private conversation."

"There you go again. I swear, man, it is like you have a death wish. Well, now," he said, forcing a chuckle. "Shall we at least attempt civility? Let us call for more tea. Julia, dear, ring for Mother. I've a feeling we could use a bit of leaven in the lump. For a certainty, we cannot leave them alone, or one of them may not survive."

Lady Julia's eyes narrowed. "Richard, what have you involved yourself in?"

He held up his hands in mock surrender. "I assure you, dear sister, I am merely an innocent bystander in this tale."

Georgiana stepped forward tentatively, her gaze pleading. "Lady Elizabeth, please... what is happening?"

Elizabeth tore her eyes from Darcy's, turning to the younger woman with a softening expression. "I am attempting to understand why your brother seeks to abandon his entire life for some foolhardy quest."

Her chest rose and fell in rapid, uneven breaths. She looked once more at Darcy, whose face had lost all color. His lips parted as if to speak, but still, nothing of any use came out.

Lady Julia made a sound—half outrage, half confusion—and turned on her heel. "This is intolerable. I *shall* fetch Mama. At once." She swept from the room, skirts swishing behind her, the door clicking shut with a finality that felt almost symbolic.

Richard exhaled and folded his arms, muttering, "Well, that ought to go well."

But Elizabeth ignored him. She took another step toward Darcy, her voice low and trembling. "If you think to disappear to Portugal without so much as a farewell, then you are a coward."

His eyes snapped to hers. "Do not call me that."

"What else would you call a man who flees the very thing he wants?" Her voice broke. "Have you even spoken to Mr. Bingley? I can see by your face you have not. You said nothing—*nothing*—to me or anyone else who cares for you. No word, nothing! I feared for a while that you might be dead and I knew not how to find out. After everything. After being shot, after—"

"You think I did not want to?" he interrupted, his voice hoarse. "You think it has been easy to stay away?"

"Then why did you?" she cried. "Why vanish? Why say nothing? Why Portugal?"

He ran a hand through his hair, exasperated. "Because I was trying to survive. Because I thought it would be easier, less painful, to vanish from your world than remain in it with no place and no claim—"

"You are a fool," she whispered.

He blinked. "I know. A fool, and... and yes, a coward."

"No," she said louder, eyes glistening. "The man I met—he was not a coward. He waited, he planned, he turned and fought. He went back for the people he loved, even if it meant a bullet or the noose."

Darcy flinched.

Elizabeth pressed on. "So do not tell me this is about survival. Do not insult me by pretending this is noble."

"I am not pretending!" he snapped. "Do you not understand? I have nothing left. No home. No family lands. No standing. Nothing I could offer you except the pleasure of having your name dragged through the muck alongside mine."

"You think I care about any of that?"

"I know you do not. But your father does. And your family. And every last smug bastard in the *ton* who would say I lured you into disgrace."

"You did not lure me," she hissed. "I *ran* to you."

Darcy looked away, gritting his teeth and closing his eyes as his fists worked.

Georgiana, still near the settee, emitted a tiny sound—half gasp, half squeak—and pressed a hand to her mouth.

Richard cleared his throat behind them. "I am still here, you know. And... uh... Georgiana is somewhat more innocent than the rest of you lot."

"Feel free to leave then, Colonel," she snapped without looking at him. Her gaze was fixed on the man whose body was listing toward her, even though his words and his manner were clearly screaming his desire to bolt.

The door opened again, unannounced this time, and the Countess of Matlock stepped inside with the slow, commanding grace of a woman who had never once been uncertain of her welcome in any room. Her eyes scanned the scene—and paused.

Elizabeth stood just left of center, her cheeks flushed, her posture rigid, her hands balled at her sides. Darcy was scarcely a foot away, equally still, his mouth parted, breath shallow, his eyes locked onto Elizabeth's as if unable to look anywhere else.

At the far end of the drawing room, Colonel Fitzwilliam was perched lazily on the edge of a low ottoman, teacup balanced precariously in one hand, looking as if he were watching a play.

A moment of silence passed like a thunderclap.

The Countess blinked once, then again. Her eyes narrowed just slightly. "I... assume we are interrupting something," she said, her tone laced with the exquisite poise of a woman who had stepped straight into scandal and found herself vaguely intrigued.

The Earl of Matlock stepped in behind her, halted dead in his tracks, and muttered, "Good God. It's Ashwick's daughter. What the devil—"

Richard gestured airily with his spoon. "Ah, good afternoon, Mother. Father. You are just in time for the climax."

Elizabeth turned toward them, not retreating. Not explaining. "Forgive me, my lord and lady," she said with a perfunctory curtsy. "But I mean to marry your nephew, whether he likes it or not."

The room froze.

Darcy's hand shot up, palm outward, a soundless plea for restraint. His eyes, wide with alarm, locked onto Elizabeth's, silently urging her to reconsider. But Elizabeth was already walking toward the Earl, her expression composed, her voice sweet.

"Lord Matlock, you are well acquainted with my father, the Marquess of Ashwick, are you not?"

The Earl, still clearly trying to make sense of the scene before him, nodded slowly. "Yes, indeed. Ashwick and I have shared many a table over the years."

"Excellent." Elizabeth's gaze shifted to the Countess. "And you, Lady Matlock, have a passing acquaintance with the Duchess of Wrexham, if I am not mistaken. I recall seeing you both in conversation at several balls."

The Countess inclined her head. "That is correct."

A serene smile curved Elizabeth's lips, though a storm brewed beneath her composed exterior. "Wonderful," she said softly. "Then, my lord, I trust that when you speak to my father this afternoon, you will be able to convey that the magnitude of the scandal shall be in direct proportion to the disagreeability of his reaction."

The Earl blinked in confusion. "'This afternoon?' Magnitude? I am sorry, Lady Elizabeth, but to which scandal are you referring?"

Elizabeth took a deliberate backward step toward Darcy, her eyes never leaving the Earl's. "This one."

And with that, she turned to Darcy, closing the distance between them. Rising onto her toes, she reached up, her hands gently cradling his face. For a heartbeat, time seemed to suspend as she looked into his eyes, searching, imploring.

"Elizabeth, no," he breathed.

She only smiled back at him. Then, with deliberate intent, she pulled him down and into a kiss that was anything but chaste.

The moment her lips touched his, the world reeled.

She felt it before she heard it—a collective intake of breath, like the room itself had gasped. Somewhere at the edge of her vision, Lord Matlock's form shifted violently, as though struggling with whether to exclaim or sit down. She did not look. She did not care.

The countess moved—Elizabeth caught the flick of a fan rising, rapid and practiced, and knew without turning that it was Lady Matlock. She imagined those shrewd eyes watching her behind a veil of painted ivory.

And Richard... there was a sound, like a muffled snort of laughter. A scrape of boot against marble. If she turned her head, she might see his grin. But she would not. Not now.

All she knew—truly knew—was Darcy's mouth against hers, the tentative tremble of him as his hands found her waist, and the way her whole body sang with the shock and sweetness of having him, just this once, not stepping away. Not retreating. Not telling her no.

She stepped back at last, breathless but triumphant, her gaze locked on Darcy's—daring him to contradict her. He did not. His mouth was still slightly parted. He looked stunned. She half expected him to scold her or flee the room.

He did neither.

"Elizabeth," he murmured, his voice a raw whisper, "what have you done?"

She smiled and caressed his cheek. "I have given us no choice but to face what we both know to be true."

The silence around them was staggering.

When she finally looked up, it was to find the Earl of Matlock frozen mid-step, his eyes wide, mouth agape in a way that would have been comical in any other setting. His cheeks were an alarming shade of crimson. He looked as if someone had struck him with a brick.

Georgiana had gone rigid, one hand clapped over her mouth, the other fisted in the folds of her gown. Her wide eyes darted from Elizabeth to her brother and back again, horrified and enthralled all at once.

Lady Julia stood behind the settee with a hand pressed to her bosom, her jaw visibly working as though she was struggling to articulate even a single syllable.

But it was the Countess who drew Elizabeth's attention.

Her fan was raised, fluttering gently. Her expression was cool—pleased, almost smug. As if she had seen something like this coming for some time and was only surprised that it had taken so long. There was the faintest upturn at the corners of her mouth, and when Elizabeth dared meet her eye, the Countess gave the smallest, most imperceptible nod. Approval, sharp and quiet and not at all unimpressive.

The Earl finally cleared his throat, though it came out more like a wheeze.

"Well," he said gruffly, "this is most... unconventional."

The Countess tilted her head slightly. "But perhaps not entirely unwelcome," she said, with lavish calm.

Richard gave a bark of laughter. "Darcy," he said, shaking his head. "It appears you have been outmaneuvered."

Darcy looked at her. A beat passed. Then another.

And he smiled.

A real one—slow, boyish, warm and astonished.

"It would seem so," he said.

The Earl drew himself up, squaring his shoulders like a man about to do something unpleasant but necessary. "I shall... repair to Ashwick House at once."

"Please do," Elizabeth replied serenely. "And I would advise haste, for Lady Julia over there is already trying to decide which friend to call on first to air the gossip."

That earned a sputter from Julia and a choked sound from Georgiana, who slapped her hands to her mouth again, as though trying to suppress a scream.

"Do not dawdle, Father," Richard added, clapping the older man on the shoulder as if the entire thing were a lark. "And I think I shall come along for... for a bit of fortification. Ashwick will not be in a cheerful mood when he hears of it."

The Earl blinked as though reeling from a blow he could neither name nor avoid, then turned stiffly and exited the room.

Chapter Thirty-Five

E LIZABETH SAT UPRIGHT, HANDS folded tightly in her lap, the rigid line of her spine betraying the chaos roiling beneath her calm exterior. To her right, Georgiana shifted closer, the younger girl's knee brushing against hers in a silent show of support.

To her left, Fitzwilliam Darcy remained stoic, his posture a perfect study in restrained composure—until his thumb moved, slow and deliberate, tracing a soft, unhurried arc along the inside of her palm.

Elizabeth's entire body flushed. The contact was fleeting, barely more than a whisper of touch, yet it sparked through her like flint to tinder. How could the mere brush of his thumb make it feel like he was caressing every inch of her?

She was probably blushing to the roots of her hair. She sniffed, shifted, had to clear her throat, and then clenched her hand down on his when he moved to withdraw it. And was that an almost silent growl of satisfaction rumbling in his throat?

Across from them, Lady Julia slouched into her chair with all the wounded pride of a girl excluded from the heart of the drama. Her expression—part scandalized, part sulking—shifted in quick glances from her mother to her cousin, clearly itching to leap up and whisper this tale to every dowager and debutante within her acquaintance. But she did not dare.

The Countess of Matlock had positioned herself like a sentry at her daughter's side, not merely presiding over the room but commanding it. Her hands rested lightly on her fan, which she had not opened since the kiss, and every flick of her gaze was sharp enough to silence gossip before it began.

Despite the warmth of Darcy's hand, Elizabeth's thoughts spiraled. She had done the unthinkable—no, the unforgivable, at least in her father's estimation. She had flung aside every expectation, every careful hope of alliance and influence he had ever curated for her, and she had done it publicly. Before the daughter of an earl. Before the earl himself. And if she knew anything about her father, it was that he would not forget who had witnessed it.

Her fingers tensed within Darcy's, but his touch remained steady, anchoring. She turned her face slightly to glance at him, but he was looking forward, serene—no, not serene. Resolute. Whatever the consequences, he would meet them beside her.

She tried to take comfort in that. But her stomach roiled. Her father would be livid, of course. But it was not the anger that unsettled her.

It was the grief. Her own. For she had begun to hope, quietly, stubbornly, that one day she might have a different kind of father. A gentler one. One who valued her for more than what she could secure for his name. She had caught glimpses of such affection in Mr. Bennet. The way he looked at Jane. The way he allowed his daughters to speak freely, even when he did not agree.

Ashwick would never become that father to her now.

She had shut the door on that hope herself. She had chosen a man without a title. Without fortune. A man who had risked everything for her but carried the disgrace of a lost estate and a family name maligned by gossip. A man who now sat beside her with fire in his eyes and her hand in his.

As if sensing the exact moment her spirit quaked, the Countess of Matlock turned her head and addressed her with perfect calm.

"Do not fret, my dear," she said, her tone lightly imperious but unexpectedly kind. "The Earl will do everything in his power to smooth matters with your father."

Elizabeth blinked, caught off guard. "You believe he can?"

The Countess's eyes gleamed just faintly above the rim of her fan. "He will. Because I shall tell him to."

And there was something about the certainty in her voice that made Elizabeth, for the first time since the kiss, draw a full breath.

The distant crack of the front door slamming open rang through the corridors like cannon fire. The staccato rhythm of angry boots followed, accompanied by a raised voice—her father's voice, unmistakable in its clipped, disdainful fury.

Elizabeth jolted upright on the settee, her spine locking as though bracing for impact. Her eyes darted toward the doorway just as the drawing room shuddered faintly beneath the approaching storm.

Darcy's hand on hers tightened. "Wait," he said lowly, not looking at her. Then, already rising, he added quietly, "Let me."

He was halfway to standing before she could argue, and then, with no hesitation, he turned and extended a hand to help her rise as well—just as the double doors swung open.

The Marquess of Ashwick stormed into the room like a thunderhead, his eyes wild and his gloves clenched in one white-knuckled fist. The Earl of Matlock followed more sedately, though his lips were pressed into a hard, inscrutable line.

Elizabeth had no chance to speak. Her father's gaze zeroed in on her—then on Darcy, whose position between them was deliberate, unmistakable.

"Lord Ashwick," Darcy said, his tone courteous but firm. "Before you speak, I ask that you allow me to explain."

Ashwick drew up short, his nostrils flaring. "Do you, indeed?" he sneered. "Explain what, sir? That you have defiled my daughter in the drawing room of an earl? That you have thrown the Montclair name into every salon in London? That you have undone her future for good and all with your desperation and—"

Darcy's voice remained even, though the strain behind it showed in the taut set of his jaw. "No. Only that I love her. And that whatever else you believe, I would never harm her. I have done what I must to protect her from the beginning, and I would do it again."

Ashwick turned a livid shade of red. "Protect her? From what? From a prince? From wealth? From the match of a lifetime? Tell me, Darcy—what exactly do you offer that outshines all that?"

Elizabeth moved to speak, but Darcy held out one steadying hand, not touching her, only halting her with a slight movement. His eyes did not leave her father's.

"Only myself," he said simply. "Whatever is left of me."

The words fell into the silence like a stone into still water.

It was then that Elizabeth noticed—Colonel Fitzwilliam was absent. Vanished. Perhaps wisely.

Ashwick barked a bitter laugh. "And you think that is enough?"

"No," Darcy said, and this time, he did not look away from Elizabeth as he spoke. "I think it is everything."

The Marquess looked as though he meant to throw something.

But Lord Matlock—still behind him—cleared his throat sharply. "Ashwick. Sit down. For God's sake, we are not at Parliament."

And the Countess, seated in quiet command, added dryly, "I am afraid if you raise your voice again, I shall be forced to remove Lady Julia from the room. She is impressionable."

Lady Julia, who had not moved once, glared hotly at everyone.

Elizabeth swallowed the tide of emotion swelling against her ribs and folded her hand back into Darcy's. For the first time since her father had stormed into the room, she saw the faintest flicker of confusion break through his rage.

Darcy's voice cut through again. "We can speak as men, Ashwick. Or we can shout. But I believe your daughter has chosen her course."

He did not say, *"And it is not one I asked for."* But Elizabeth heard it anyway.

Ashwick's chest rose once, sharply. Then again. But his eyes were not fixed on Darcy any longer. They flicked to his daughter—and held.

"Elizabeth," he said, his voice low and tight, "you will not do this. I am your father."

She met him head-on. "Yes. You are. And when I made my curtsey to the Queen, you promised me I might choose."

Ashwick bristled. "Among those I deemed suitable! How conveniently you forget that part. This—" He stabbed a hand in Darcy's direction. "This is not what I meant. This is *not* suitable!"

"Enough," Darcy said sharply, stepping forward.

Ashwick whirled. "I will not be silenced in my own daughter's—"

"She is not a child," Darcy said. His voice was low, even—but there was something steely in it now, something forged. "You may shout, my lord, if it pleases your pride. But do not presume she needs protecting from me. I am merely counseling you not to say something you cannot retract."

Ashwick drew several heaving breaths, struggling to steady himself.

"So, *Lady Elizabeth*," he growled, turning his fury back to her, "you will shame your mother's name for this? Your father's? For this man, who has nothing but a salary and a family name blackened by royal decree?"

Elizabeth stepped forward—past Darcy's shielding form, not flinching, not blinking.

"His name," she said, "is the one I will bear."

He stared at her, as if unable to comprehend it. "Good Lord. It is already too late, is it not? You are already defiled! By this—"

"I assure you, that is not the case," she interrupted. "He had every reason to take advantage of me once. He had the power, the opportunity. I was alone. Unchaperoned. I threw myself into his arms and begged him to give me any excuse—any hope. And he refused."

A silence fell, sharp and abrupt. Her father's mouth seemed to be trying to shape itself around the words she was saying, but he could not comprehend them enough to repeat them.

She went on, quieter now.

"He protected me, when no one else would. Not for his gain. Not to force an attachment. Simply because he could. And I would rather tie my life to a man who refuses to profit from another's pain than all the dukes in Christendom."

Ashwick swayed slightly. "*Unchaperoned*... how?" His voice rose. "*When?*"

Elizabeth merely raised a brow. "There were times you never heard me, Father, but others listened. *He* listened."

Ashwick blinked and put out a hand to steady himself on the back of a nearby sofa. "No fortune. No title. Not even a home," he murmured. "You would truly give all that up?"

She only lifted her chin.

Ashwick stared at her. Then looked at Darcy. "And you?"

Darcy's eyes never left Elizabeth's. "I would have walked into exile with her and counted myself rich."

There was a pause. Lord Matlock cleared his throat again. "Well. If no one else will say it," he muttered, "I suppose I shall. That sounds rather like a settled matter."

Ashwick looked as though he wanted to punch someone. But instead, after a long silence, he sank into the nearest chair, one hand covering his eyes. "God help me," he muttered. "You are your mother. This... I cannot mend this, Elizabeth! You have gone too far."

Lady Matlock, lips twitching, murmured, "And about time, too."

A sudden voice called out from the doorway, causing heads to turn. "What ho, is everyone in here?"

Colonel Fitzwilliam reentered at that moment, snatching a biscuit off the tea tray, and glanced around the room. "I trust no blood has been shed in my absence?"

Darcy, who had moved back to stand between her and her father like a living shield, exhaled slowly and did not move. His back was straight, his expression calm—but she could see the tendons in his neck, tight with effort.

Lord Ashwick growled, "If you left in order to let your cousin do something stupid and irrevocable, you timed your exit perfectly."

"And yet," Richard replied, strolling further in, "it seems we are all still breathing. I must say, I am impressed."

"You will not be if you hear what your cousin has done," Ashwick snapped.

"He has done nothing," Elizabeth said, stepping forward. "I am the one who—"

"Be silent," her father barked. "I will not have you humiliate yourself further."

"I am not humiliated," she said coldly. "And I have nothing to be ashamed of."

Darcy's hand closed gently around her wrist—support, not restraint.

"Where will you live?" the marquess demanded. "Do you have a residence suited to her rank?"

"I do not," Darcy said quietly. "And I probably never will have anything worthy of her."

"So, what is your plan, man?"

Darcy hesitated. "I have a... a connection in Hertfordshire that might serve our immediate wants. Or we may remain in town. Temporarily."

"With what income?" Ashwick barked. "What will you use to feed her? Clothe her? Good intentions?"

"I am... employed."

Ashwick scoffed. "At the Home Office? You can hardly afford to keep yourself. That is not enough!"

Darcy's jaw ticked. "Then I shall find something that is."

The marquess snorted, derision curling around every syllable. "You intend to keep her like a governess? Shall I expect to see her giving lessons to other people's children?"

Elizabeth flinched. Her father might be angry, but he was not cruel—at least, not usually. That he would stoop to mockery meant he was floundering. Losing ground.

The Countess's voice cut clean through the air. "You are being dramatic, Ashwick."

He turned to her in disbelief. "You cannot seriously be encouraging this!"

"I am not encouraging anything," she replied, eyes glinting. "But I am acknowledging what is already done. And you might consider that, in the right light, it may not be a disaster."

"Indeed," the Earl agreed, in a voice that sounded like a steaming kettle that had been close to boiling over before he gave it vent. "Darcy's character is unimpeachable. As for the title, it might be extinct, but the Darcy name is older even than the Montclair—"

"*Extinct?* How very tactful of you. No, it was *revoked*," the marquess growled. "Forfeit! 'Unnatural circumstances,' as I recall. The father was... unlawful! How should I think better of the son?"

Darcy opened his mouth—then closed it again.

"Well, if you had any questions about *that*," Colonel Fitzwilliam scoffed, waving the last bite of his biscuit, "I daresay you missed all evidence to the contrary. We'd a fair proof of that earlier, did we not? Lady Elizabeth, kiss him again and let us see his hair curl once more."

"Richard, please," Lady Matlock hissed.

"Sorry, Mother." Richard cleared his throat. "Shall I leave now? Because I should like to know whether to pour more tea or fetch a clergyman."

No one even blinked. The silence that followed Richard's flippant jest stretched on—long enough for the last of Elizabeth's heartbeat to slow from its thundering gallop. Her father had sunk into his high-backed chair as though the air had been knocked from his lungs. His face was flushed; the deep creases at his brow had not smoothed. But his voice, when it came again, was quieter. No less furious, but resigned in the way a man is when he knows he has already lost the argument.

"Do not imagine I will condone this," he said, not looking at her. His gaze was fixed somewhere beyond the mantel. "You will find no support from me. I will not host your wedding. I will not fund your trousseau. You have chosen to disgrace this family, and it will be borne alone."

Elizabeth's eyes blurred. She had hoped... well, that was a foolish idea, anyway. She had lost her father. Her throat tightened, and she sniffed. "I understand."

That was when Darcy's hand found hers.

Her father inhaled sharply, as if the sight pained him. "I had always assumed you would do your duty. Not with pleasure, perhaps—but with the sense of obligation you were raised to possess. I did not think I had raised a fool."

"You did not," she said softly.

Her father's lip curled. "You will live in squalor. You will starve in the hedgerows with such a husband."

"I would rather starve with him than dine alone in a palace."

Lord Matlock let out a sound that might have been approval. The Countess was watching with frank amusement now, as if the outcome had never been in doubt.

Ashwick's eyes flicked toward them, and he seemed to realize the game was lost. He looked around the room—at Georgiana's open admiration, at Richard's smug and knowing grin, at the Earl of Matlock whose family name would now be further tied to his.

And perhaps worst of all—at Elizabeth herself.

He exhaled slowly. When he spoke again, it was almost a murmur. "I will make you an offer, Darcy."

Elizabeth's pulse stuttered. What was this?

Ashwick stood slowly. Straightened his coat. "I will settle a sum upon you—a generous one. Enough for land, for comfort. For your sister's security. A tidy estate. Respectable tenants. The illusion of a life well-preserved."

He paused. "But only if you give her up."

Darcy's fingers tightened around hers, so briefly she might have imagined it. When he answered, his voice was calm.

"No."

"Do not be hasty," Ashwick urged him. "You could build something honorable. You would never want for anything."

Darcy said nothing.

The Marquess took a step forward. "You cannot build with a scandal. You will never outrun it. But wealth—wealth dulls disgrace. It buys silence."

Still, no answer. Just a tightening of his fingers around hers.

At last, Elizabeth turned to Darcy. His jaw was tight. His brow furrowed. But there was no hesitation in his eyes. He looked down at her. Only her.

And then he looked back at the Marquess of Ashwick. "Keep your fortune."

Ashwick let out a slow, bitter laugh. "You are as much a fool as my daughter."

And then he turned and walked out, the tails of his coat slicing through the air like a blade.

Elizabeth stared after him, her heart full and breaking all at once.

"Was that it?" Richard asked after a moment. "He did not even shout or call for his attorney. I am almost disappointed."

Lady Matlock rose gracefully to her feet. "Well," she said, smoothing the skirts of her gown, "now that the unpleasantness is behind us... perhaps someone will call for a fresh tea tray."

Elizabeth turned to Darcy. He was still watching the door where her father had gone.

But he was still holding her hand.

CHAPTER THIRTY-SIX

July 4, 1812

T HE TRUNK GROANED AS he knelt beside it, the hinges complaining under the pressure of his hand. Darcy paused, the folded shirts and carefully arranged parcels inside looking absurdly obedient for a life that had just unraveled and spun itself into something completely new.

He was not going to Portugal.

He was supposed to set sail yesterday. That ship, now halfway down the coast of France, had been meant to carry him from this country, from a scandal he could never live down, from the woman he loved and could never have.

Only now... he *did* have her. Or rather, she had him—because he could not claim to have won her so much as surrendered.

His mouth curved into a grin, unbidden, as he pulled a linen shirt from the top of the trunk and tossed it aside. He could still see her face in that moment—eyes blazing, voice determined, the press of her lips on his so fierce it had driven every rational thought from his head. She had chosen him in a display meant to shock half the British aristocracy, in a house not her own, with no hope of apology or retreat. His fiancée.

Fiancée.

The word still made his chest swell and his stomach swoop as if he were a schoolboy on his first errand of daring. Two days. They had been engaged for two days, and in that time, he had upended every plan, burned every bridge, and now stood on the precipice of a life he had never dared imagine.

He was, as of yesterday, unemployed. He had not officially resigned from the Home Office before—there had not been time—but now, he had sent word of his change in circumstances. He was supposed to be on his way to Portugal—his old position terminated, all his duties assigned to another.

Whether they would welcome him back now was another matter. A man whose personal life had become this public, this tumultuous, did not make for an ideal servant of the Crown. Still, he hoped.

He also hoped for a reply from Bingley. He had written the moment he realized he would not be leaving—sent off a rambling letter full of apology and explanation, though God only knew how Bingley would take it. Darcy had not told him everything about Elizabeth, not before. The truth had been too raw, too uncertain. Now it was unavoidable.

And if the Home Office did not take him back... then what? He could not very well install Elizabeth in his bachelor's rooms at Albany, even if he *could* afford to keep them. He had nothing to offer her but the remnants of a gentleman's salary and the scraps of pride that came with refusing charity.

Bingley would take them in, and he just might have to accept... at least, in the beginning. But he would not live off his friend's goodwill. He could not bear to see Elizabeth treated with condescension—or pity.

He leaned back on his heels, pressing a hand to his face and laughing quietly.

She had refused a prince. For *him*.

That was enough. That was the stone on which they would build.

The last of the linen shirts lay crumpled in his lap when the knock came—sharp, official, and utterly unwelcome.

Darcy groaned and ignored it. Perhaps it would go away—not likely, because scandal did not work that way, and Darcy was certainly at the heart of a scandal by now.

A second knock, brisker this time.

He stood slowly, tugging the front of his waistcoat, heart tightening as he crossed to the door and unlatched it. The man on the threshold wore livery Darcy recognized too well. Red and gold, crested with a crown. A royal messenger.

Darcy's shoulders tensed. "May I help you?"

The man bowed crisply. "You are requested immediately at Carlton House, sir. His Royal Highness says it is a matter of urgency."

Darcy blinked. "There must be some mistake. I am no longer employed in any official capacity. His Highness surely wants someone still in a position to be of use."

The messenger did not waver. "There is no mistake, Mr. Darcy. His Royal Highness specified you by name. A carriage is waiting."

Darcy exhaled. He glanced past the messenger to the window above the street. Sure enough, a black-lacquered coach stood at the curb, a footman poised at its door like a marble statue.

He did not need to ask what this was about.

Elizabeth.

He pinched the bridge of his nose. "Of course," he murmured. "He did not even wait until tomorrow for the banns to be announced. A prince's pride must be stroked."

The messenger, to his credit, neither blinked nor shifted.

Darcy stepped back into the room, reaching for his coat. "Tell him I shall attend him within the hour."

"No, sir." The messenger was suddenly firmer. "The prince said *immediately*."

Darcy's eyes narrowed. Of course he had.

THE OPULENT GRANDEUR OF Carlton House never failed to impress, though today, Darcy found it more oppressive than awe-inspiring. The gilded ceilings and lavish furnishings seemed to mock his current predicament. He was led through a series of ornate corridors before being ushered into the Prince Regent's private chamber.

The Prince lounged on his favorite chaise, swathed in a robe of deep crimson velvet embroidered with gold filigree, one slippered foot dangling off the side with studied indolence. A snifter of brandy twirled lazily between his fingers, and his powdered wig sat slightly askew, as though to remind the world that rules of appearance did not apply to him.

"Darcy," he declared, lips curling into a satisfied smile as though he had summoned the man by sheer will, "at last. Do sit. Or stand and glower, as is your habit—I leave it to you."

Darcy remained precisely where he was. "Your Highness," he said with a controlled bow. "You summoned me with some urgency."

The Prince made a show of sniffing the brandy, then looked over the rim of his glass with theatrical relish. "Urgency, yes, but not alarm. One should never be alarmed at good news, Darcy. I have reviewed your petition."

Darcy's expression did not shift. "I see. And what does Your Highness require of me this time?"

The Prince gave a bark of laughter, the sound echoing off the gilded walls. "So jaded! So delightfully suspicious. Tell me, do you treat all your benefactors with such grim reserve, or am I merely lucky?"

Darcy's brow twitched. "I have learned to temper my expectations, Your Highness."

"Quite right. Prudence is the balm of the disappointed." The Prince leaned forward suddenly, the silk of his robe swishing against the upholstery. "But not today, Darcy. Today, you are to be astonished. Flabbergasted. Aghast, even. I have made my decision."

Darcy's jaw clenched. "Regarding—?"

The Prince gestured grandly with his glass, nearly sloshing brandy onto his silk sleeve. "Your family's estate and title. The matter of Pemberley. I am overturning your father's disgrace. The revocation was—what was the phrase they used in chambers?—ah, yes. 'A poorly justified political expediency.'"

Darcy stared, as if the words had reached him from a great distance. "You... have decided to reverse the ruling?"

The Prince raised both brows. "Well, I do not simply *decide* things. I order them. But yes. Yes, I have." He grinned again, teeth flashing beneath his curled lip. "Try to look pleased, Darcy. This is the part where you fall to your knees and thank me, is it not?"

Darcy blinked once. "I confess I am... surprised."

"Oh, that is dull." The Prince drained the last of his brandy and reached to refill it from a crystal decanter beside him. "Say something interesting. Ask me why. Ask me what devilish scheme I am about. Or ask me what she wore when she kissed you in the Matlock drawing room—because I *do* know. I imagine half of London does."

Darcy's throat worked, but no sound emerged.

The Prince chortled into his sleeve. "Oh, you are priceless. And you owe me a new scandal soon, Darcy. The court has grown dreadfully dry."

Darcy's brow furrowed. "This is... because of Lady Elizabeth?" he asked slowly. "The scandal. You mean to say—"

The Prince's laughter erupted like a cork popping from a champagne bottle. "Oh, Darcy. You do make it sound so sordid. 'Because of the scandal,'" he repeated, as if savoring the phrase. "You wound me. Do you really think me so petty?"

Darcy said nothing—it seemed more tactful than the truth.

"Though," the Prince added, eyes gleaming, "if I were so inclined, it would be a delightful sort of pettiness, would it not? No, my dear man—it was not the scandal itself, but the way it unfolded. The theater of it. The sheer, glorious madness of it all."

He leaned forward, voice dropping conspiratorially. "I received an 'anonymous' letter the day before the news hit the salons. A warning, you might call it. Your cousin the colonel has rather distinct handwriting, by the way."

Darcy's mouth parted. "Fitzwilliam?"

"Oh yes. Full of righteous fury and familial concern. Quite touching, really." The Prince took another sip of his brandy. "He wrote that you had been wronged, that the girl was the same Lady Elizabeth Montclair whom everyone had believed vanished off to Devon or France or the moon, and that the scandal you were about to cause would likely make headlines unless someone, say, a certain royal personage, chose to get ahead of it."

Darcy stared, reeling. Of course. Richard's abrupt departure, the way he had vanished just after the kiss, only to reappear as if summoned by providence—it was all beginning to make sense.

"And then came the moment itself," the prince continued with a laugh. "A Montclair in the arms of a Darcy. In public. The Marquess of Ashwick frothing at the mouth while the Earl of Matlock looked on. Really, I could not have staged it better myself."

He set the brandy down, shaking his head with something that resembled fondness. "You, sir, are far more interesting than I gave you credit for. And as for Lady Elizabeth... well. One does not dim such a light. She would make a bishop recant."

Darcy exhaled, trying to tether his thoughts. "And... this decision—"

"Is final," the Prince interrupted, all lightness gone for a moment. "Your family was wronged. You have paid enough for your father's misstep—or whatever it was that led to all those accusations. It is time to restore what was lost. You may inform your bride that she shall not be marrying a disgraced pauper after all."

Darcy swallowed hard. "Your Highness... I am—"

"Yes, yes," the Prince waved a hand. "You are honored, humbled, grateful, all the usual nonsense. There will be formalities. A signing. An announcement. Some sighing from Cabinet and the old sticklers at the College of Arms. But you may consider the matter settled."

Darcy inclined his head. "Then I thank you. Sincerely."

The Prince had already returned to his brandy. "Yes, yes. Do tell your good cousin to write when the next scandal brews, won't you? I rather like his turn of phrase."

Darcy bowed, deeper this time. "Your Highness."

He turned on his heel and left the chamber, boots silent against the plush carpets. The corridors of Carlton House stretched before him, long and bright, but the world beyond the doors had narrowed to a single point of clarity.

He had *her*. And now... he could give her everything.

DARCY STOOD BEFORE THE imposing façade of Ashwick House, its stone edifice as unyielding as the man who ruled within. The grand entrance loomed ahead, flanked by towering columns that seemed to guard the secrets held within. Drawing a quaking breath, he ascended the steps and rapped the brass knocker against the heavy door.

The butler, a man of advanced years with a demeanor to match the house's austerity, opened the door. His eyes flicked over Darcy with a practiced neutrality.

"Mr. Darcy," the butler intoned, his voice devoid of warmth. "To what do we owe the pleasure?"

"I seek an audience with Lady Elizabeth. I have news of significance to share with her."

Before the butler could respond, a familiar figure emerged from the shadows of the hallway. The Marquess of Ashwick approached, his gait deliberate, eyes narrowing as they settled on Darcy.

"Mr. Darcy," the Marquess greeted, his voice carrying the bite of restrained civility. "Your presence is... unexpected."

Darcy inclined his head respectfully. "And unwelcome, I see, my lord. However, I have just come from Carlton House and wish to convey some good news to Lady Elizabeth."

Ashwick's gaze sharpened, his lips pressing into a scowl. "Good news, you say? Perhaps you might enlighten me first. It would be... prudent, would you not agree? Such transparency might persuade me to permit you into *my house* to see *my daughter*."

"With all due respect, my lord, my concern lies solely with Lady Elizabeth's opinion. It is her I wish to inform."

Ashwick's eyes bored into Darcy's, searching for any sign of weakness. Finding none, he exhaled sharply.

"Ten minutes," the Marquess conceded, stepping aside with a reluctant gesture toward the interior. "You will find her in the drawing room."

"Thank you, my lord," Darcy replied, offering a curt bow before proceeding down the familiar corridor.

She was, indeed, in the drawing room, seated near the tall window, utterly still but for the charcoal moving deftly in her hand. She had not heard the door open. Afternoon light poured over her shoulder, softening the lines of her posture and catching in the snarled waves of her hair, but she remained intent, her head bent, her fingers smudged with gray. A thin square of paper was pinned at one corner, her wrist moving in quick, decisive strokes.

He paused just inside the doorway, watching her work. Her gaze flicked between the paper and something just beyond the frame of memory—no, not something.

Some*one*.

Him.

The likeness was unmistakable: his brow furrowed, his collar slightly askew, his eyes darker than he remembered them. She was still shaping the curve of his mouth, tracing and retracing the lines with such concentration that he could not help but smile.

She had drawn his mouth nearly half a dozen times. That fact alone pleased him in ways he could not quite name.

He took a slow step forward. She did not notice.

"Elizabeth," he said, gently.

Her head jerked up, the charcoal slipping slightly. She blinked at him, and color bloomed in her cheeks. "Oh! You startled me."

"Forgive me. I was... admiring your work."

She looked down at the sketch and then back at him, one brow arched. "You approve? I thought him a rather handsome chap, do you not agree?"

He grunted. "I believe I caught you studying my lips with alarming precision."

Her mouth twitched. "You are very difficult to capture."

"And here I thought it was *you* who was so difficult to capture."

She laughed and extended her hands to him. "You managed well enough."

"I got lucky." He crossed the room, taking her offered hands into his own.

"You call that luck?" She tossed her head, pretending to consider. "Oh, perhaps it was, at first, but I could have sworn you were almost the unluckiest man I knew."

He pulled her in closer—close enough to brush a tender kiss to her forehead. He had dreamed of doing that for so long... "Do you know," he whispered, "I think my luck has turned around."

"Oh?" She lifted her face to his, just enough to draw her cheek along his. "I would not call *that* luck. That was all my silly stubbornness."

"No, there... well, yes," he stammered. "And I shall bless your 'stubbornness' all the days of my life, but Elizabeth, I have news. I've just come from Carlton House."

Her brows lifted in intrigue. "Oh? And what has His Highness done now?"

He took a steadying breath. "The Prince Regent has decided to restore my family's estate and title. Pemberley is to be ours once more."

For a moment, Elizabeth simply stared, processing the magnitude of his words. Then, a radiant smile broke across her face and she leaped into his arms. "Fitzwilliam, that is wonderful!"

He huffed as she clung to him, so tightly that it nearly cracked his ribs. "It appears His Highness found our recent... notoriety rather entertaining."

"Oh, dear! So, our scandal is what finally moved the Prince into benevolence?"

Darcy shook his head as she pulled back to gaze up into his face. "Provoking, is it not? To think he held this power all along—and knew the truth, as well, do not forget that—and chose *now* to exercise it, seemingly for his own amusement."

She stepped closer, cupping his face with tender hands. "Let him have his amusement," she murmured before pressing a soft, lingering kiss to his lips.

In that moment, all thoughts of the Prince and his capriciousness melted away. Darcy wrapped his arms around Elizabeth, deepening the embrace, savoring the sweetness of her affection.

After a time, he reluctantly pulled back, resting his forehead against hers. "There is something you should know," he began hesitantly. "Pemberley... it is not what it once was. The estate will be in disrepair, the finances likely in ruin. Wickham may have sold off tenant farms, damaged furnishings... I have no way of knowing the extent of it yet, but I will almost certainly have to sell the townhouse to cover debts... if it is not already sold."

Elizabeth leaned back, a playful glint in her eye. "Fitzwilliam, have you forgot? I possess a dowry of fifty thousand pounds. That should keep us comfortable for quite some time."

Darcy blinked, confusion knitting between his brows. "But your father—he did not approve our engagement. He may have structured your dowry... Elizabeth, you may not have access to it until you are five and twenty."

She did not answer him immediately. Instead, she leaned in and cupped his face again, her thumb brushing once beneath his eye as though she could ease every worry from him by touch alone.

"We spoke last night," she whispered.

His eyes searched hers.

"It was not a short conversation," she added. "He sent for me after supper. The Duke and Duchess of Wrexham had been here—I think trying to help him perform damage control—or just contain his temper, perhaps—but they had left by then. It was just the two of us in that cold, terrible study of his."

Darcy swallowed. "And?"

"He poured brandy for himself. Poured sherry for me. I did not want it, but I drank it anyway, and I told him everything."

He blinked. *"Everything?"*

"Not tidily, not with grace, and not to make him see reason. Just truth. I told him—again—what I had seen in the House of Commons that day in May, and why I had to leave so suddenly. The fire that was supposed to kill me. What it was to run for my life. To fear every hoofbeat on the road behind me. To be pulled from a house in the middle of the night and thrown into a world where my name—my title—meant nothing. To be placed in your care—you, whom I never saw before that night. And how it was not only my life you saved, but my spirit."

She smiled faintly, almost bitterly. "And then I told him what it meant to be with the Bennets. To see a father who dotes on his daughters. Who laughs at them. Who listens to them. And who stays. And I told him that if you had been a lesser man—if you had given in to what everyone would have expected of you—I would be ruined now, and likely still have given you my hand willingly. But you did not. And so, I claimed yours, instead."

Darcy's throat worked hard. "And how did all that fall on his ears?"

"He said very little at first. Just sat there with his glass and stared at the fire. Then he asked what happened—how it ended." Her voice caught, just slightly. "I showed him the scars on my arms and legs, and told him the ones you bore were far worse. I told him what you risked for me. How you never asked for anything in return. And then, he... he wept."

Darcy stared at her. "He what?"

"Tears," she said simply. "Quiet, ungraceful, furious tears. He called himself a fool. And he said that perhaps love *can* be the fulfillment of one's duty."

"I... I do not understand."

Elizabeth blinked back a few tears of her own and laid her head on his chest. "He said that if he and my mother had tried harder to repair what had been broken, they might have managed another child—a true heir, as he was always meant to have, but they quit trying when I was five. Mother was still young, but..." She drew in a shaky breath and sighed against his shirt. "He said he had spent so long treating me like a political piece on a chessboard that he forgot I was someone with a heart."

Darcy exhaled, his own heart clenching.

She lifted her head and smiled up at him. "He will never be Mr. Bennet. But he said he hoped I would have the kind of marriage I wanted. Built on love. Not distance."

"And... forgive me for asking, but you said this long explanation was to do with your dowry?"

She grinned. "He is amending the terms. Already in process."

Darcy let out a shaken breath. Then his arms wrapped around her, crushing her close. He kissed her forehead once, and then pulled back just far enough to find her lips again.

"Elizabeth," he murmured against her mouth.

She kissed him back, laughing softly. "Well? Do I keep you in some comforts?"

"Fifty thousand pounds," he said, drawing her tighter. "I believe we can find one or two ways to make use of it."

She leaned back just enough to raise one brow. "Is that all I am to you now? A woman with a handsome dowry?"

He feigned solemnity. "And the very best criminal sketch artist in London. Let us not forget that."

"I suppose I ought to charge you for the portrait," she said, tilting her head toward the drawing still propped on her easel.

"You may frame it instead," he replied. "And hang it somewhere I can be reminded—daily—that your affections have always been somewhat fixated on my mouth."

Her cheeks flushed. "You noticed that?"

"I notice everything."

She shook her head, laughing as she nudged him lightly in the ribs. "You are the most pompous, ridiculous, prideful man in all England."

"And yet, here you are," he said, grinning. "Engaged to a man who once offered you a mattress stuffed with hay."

She tipped her chin up, pride and affection mingling in her gaze. "Yes. But only because he also gave me his coat. And his name. And his heart."

That quieted him.

For a long moment, he only looked at her—his Elizabeth. Alive with wit and fire and courage. A woman who had saved his soul just as surely as he had once saved her life.

He touched her cheek. "I have loved you in every corner of England. In forests and fields. In a stranger's attic and the back of a stolen carriage. But this—" he drew her close again, resting his forehead lightly against hers, "—this is the dream I dared not keep."

Her smile was luminous. "Then let us build it together."

EPILOGUE

July, 1816

THE SUN HUNG LOW over the Hertfordshire countryside, casting a warm, golden glow across the fields as the carriage rolled steadily along the familiar road to Longbourn. Inside, Elizabeth—rather, Lady Pemberley, his bride of four years, sat beside him, her gloved hand resting lightly atop his. Across from them, their daughter, a lively girl of three with his blue eyes and her mother's unruly curls, pressed her small hands against the window, delighting in the passing scenery.

"Is this the place where you lived, Mama?" Jane asked, her dark curls bouncing as she craned her neck to see out the window.

Elizabeth brushed a fond hand over their daughter's shoulder. "Only for a short time, love. Just long enough to learn something important."

Jane's eyes sparkled with curiosity as she turned. "What, Mama?"

Elizabeth's gaze drifted beyond the carriage window, past the hedgerows and blooming orchard, to the house that was fast approaching—a tidy country home tucked beneath the swelling green of Hertfordshire trees.

"That family is more than blood," she said. "It is safety. It is laughter. It is the place you run to when the world turns upside down."

The little girl made a thoughtful hum, leaning close to the windowpane with that expression on her face that Elizabeth always claimed matched his exactly. "Did you run away here?"

"Yes," Elizabeth said softly. "And someone came to find me."

Darcy had not spoken. He was watching... listening... soaking it all in. His cravat was slightly skewed—thanks to the tiny hands that had insisted on helping him dress—and his expression purposely hooded.

But Elizabeth could read him far too well, and she was already prepared to laugh at whatever he might say.

"You found Mama?" the girl asked, lifting her chin to him.

His brow rose, but his lips quirked. "I did," he said, voice dry and warm at once. "Though she made it very difficult. She is rather slippery."

"I am not!" Elizabeth laughed.

"You are," he said, settling one gloved hand over hers. "I am surprised I did not lose you entirely."

"You almost did," she replied.

He sobered. "Yes. Almost."

The carriage came to a gentle halt before the house, and the door swung open to reveal Mr. Bennet already standing on the front steps, his expression a mix of amusement and anticipation as he rocked eagerly up on his toes and back to his heels.

"Welcome home, Lizzy," he greeted, his eyes twinkling as they landed on Darcy's wife. "Darcy—or rather, Lord Pemberley, always a pleasure, but first, let me greet this young lady." He tugged at the fronts of his trousers and squatted slightly. "Do you remember me, Lady Jane?"

The child curtsied with practiced grace. "Grandpapa. Mama says you may call me Just Plain Small Jane."

Mr. Bennet chuckled, bending down to scoop her into his arms. "Well, now, Small Jane! An honorary grandpapa, am I? I shall make no complaints. You have grown since I last saw you. Have you been keeping your parents on their toes?"

Elizabeth laughed, linking her arm into Darcy's. "She has, indeed."

Darcy extended his free hand, which Mr. Bennet shook warmly. "Welcome, welcome, sir. The chess board is waiting, so which of you shall I have the pleasure of matching wits with first?"

"I shall claim the honor," Darcy replied with a respectful nod. "I fear once you play *her* again, I shall never see the two of you again for the rest of our visit."

Darcy followed Mr. Bennet into the familiar drawing room, the memories of past visits flooding his senses. The room was bathed in the soft glow of the afternoon sun, highlighting the subtle changes that time had wrought upon the Bennet household.

"Oh, my dear, dear Lizzy!" Mrs. Bennet exclaimed, enveloping Elizabeth in a tight embrace. "And Mr. Darcy! Such an honor to have you here. You are very welcome, very welcome indeed!"

Elizabeth exchanged a knowing glance with Darcy, who offered a polite smile. Over the years, Mrs. Bennet's effusions had become a source of gentle humor between them. Tea was called, and Darcy's fingers trailed just at the small of Elizabeth's back as he escorted her into the drawing room.

Jane Bingley sat on the settee, posture straight, hands folded neatly in her lap. Her expression was sweetly mellow as always, but her eyes followed every move her son made. Charles Bingley crouched beside her, balancing William on one knee while the boy galloped a wooden horse up his father's sleeve. The child's laugh broke across the room, high and clear, and Bingley's grin matched it without effort. They looked absurdly alike—same hair, same eyes, same wild energy barely contained in either frame.

Mary, now Mrs. Thornton, had returned to Longbourn for the evening. Marriage to the local rector had drawn gentler lines around her once-sober expression, and she sat with Elizabeth near the hearth, laughing quietly over some remembered absurdity. Their heads tipped close together, shoulders brushing now and again, the ease between them something that had not always been there—but had clearly been earned.

Lydia and Kitty had both married and settled in distant counties, their visits to Longbourn becoming increasingly infrequent. Their absence was felt, but the letters they sent spoke of contented lives and growing families.

Mrs. Bennet sat forward in her chair, hands clasped in rapture as she watched the two children in the corner—her grandson toddling after Small Jane with as much dignity as his little boots could muster. "Look at them," she said breathlessly, as if witnessing the first rays of dawn. "So dear. So companionable. Do you see how he lets her lead? And she does it with such authority—like a true lady. It would not surprise me in the least if they took a particular liking to each other. Mark my words, there is promise in that pairing."

Jane nearly dropped her teacup. "Mama, they are three."

Mrs. Bennet waved a hand as if Jane had missed the point entirely. "And yet so advanced for their age. I only observe. It is a very fine beginning."

Darcy, who had been studying his daughter's regal little posture as she directed her companion to 'guard the tea cakes,' let out a quiet laugh. "A very fine beginning, indeed."

Elizabeth turned to him slowly, one brow raised with suspicion. "Are you encouraging her?"

He lifted his teacup to hide a smile. "I am saying only that she has a discerning eye."

"For mischief," Elizabeth murmured.

Darcy tilted his head thoughtfully, watching Jane gesture to William as if conducting a miniature parliament. "Yes, and for strategy."

Mr. Bennet, having observed the exchange with amusement, rose and moved to the sideboard. "Well, let us toast to the future, whatever it may hold." He poured generous measures of port, distributing the glasses among the adults.

Bingley lifted his glass, his expression turning earnest. "To family and enduring friendships."

"Hear, hear," Darcy concurred, the warmth of the moment settling comfortably around him.

"How are the renovations at Pemberley coming along?" Bingley asked. "It has been nearly four years since you reclaimed the estate, and I imagine much has been accomplished."

Darcy's demeanor brightened at the mention of his home. "Indeed, much has been done, though there remains work ahead. The east wing has been fully restored, and the gardens are finally beginning to resemble their former glory. Mitchels says the orchard is recovering at last from ten years of neglect, so we expect a bounty this autumn, and we were able to purchase back two tenant farms that had been sold off. I regret to say the cottages both required extensive repairs, but all will be well in hand before winter. As for the drawing rooms and the study—you recall the state they were in before? You would hardly know them now. We have focused on preserving the character of the estate while incorporating some modern comforts."

Elizabeth smoothed her hand over his. "And the library has become a particular point of pride. My husband has taken great care in curating a collection that would rival any in England."

Darcy glanced at his wife, his heart fit to burst at his wife's tender boasts, and trying for all his might not to let it be obvious. He probably failed. "It is a joint endeavor. Elizabeth's discerning taste has been invaluable in selecting volumes that enrich our collection."

Mrs. Bennet clasped her hands together, sighing contentedly. "Oh, how wonderful it is to hear of Pemberley restored and thriving once more. You have both done a remarkable job, I am sure."

Darcy inclined his head. "Thank you, Mrs. Bennet. It has been a labor of love, and sharing it with family makes it all the more rewarding. I do hope you will all join us for Christmas this year. We feel it is finally fit to serve guests once more."

The lady of the house looked fit to swoon. "Oh, how splendid! We shall all come—shall we not, Mr. Bennet? Even Kitty might be coaxed to make the journey, if she believes there shall be music and mince pies."

Mr. Bennet gave a long-suffering sigh, but his eyes gleamed. "I shall come, so long as you promise not to force me to discuss lace and bows and the like while we are there."

"My dear, you do try my patience!" the lady sighed. And then she giggled.

Elizabeth laughed, tucking her arm through Darcy's. "I believe you are safe on that score."

Jane turned to whisper something to her husband, then stood, already gathering her son's little hand in hers. "Come, William. It is time we were back at Netherfield before the lamps are lit."

William groaned softly but obeyed, sleepily peeking up at Small Jane on the way out and whispering something about her toy pony.

"Goodnight," Jane said warmly, embracing Elizabeth. "We shall see you tomorrow."

Mary stood as well, and Elizabeth rose to embrace her. "Come back tomorrow," she said. "You shall help me officiate the rematch."

Darcy frowned. "Rematch? What is this?"

"I refer to your imminent defeat, and the vain hope you will cherish of vindicating yourself tomorrow," Elizabeth said, brushing his lapel. "We all know Mr. Bennet is going to trounce you at the chess board this evening. It is tradition now to keep score, as if it were sport."

"You mean to say you have been documenting my misfortunes?"

"Meticulously," Jane added sweetly.

Darcy turned toward Mr. Bennet with mock severity. "And you permit this?"

Mr. Bennet only sipped his drink. "Permit it? I encourage it. It is the closest I come to having my wits recognized."

"Come along then," Elizabeth said, gesturing toward the chessboard. "Your fate awaits."

Darcy offered a hand to Mr. Bennet. "Shall we?"

"You are awfully eager to lose," Mr. Bennet said.

"I am terribly fond of routine."

E LIZABETH CARRIED HER DAUGHTER up the narrow staircase with careful steps, Jane's small arms looped around her neck, her breath warm against her collarbone. The little girl had fallen asleep curled beside the hearth, her head tipping to Elizabeth's shoulder the moment she was lifted, one soft sigh escaping her lips before sleep reclaimed her.

The old guest room was waiting—cool, quiet, and filled with that peculiar mixture of lavender and beeswax that always marked Longbourn. Mrs. Hill had seen to everything. Fresh blankets were folded at the foot of the bed, a ceramic basin gleamed on the wash-stand, and a small oil lamp flickered in the corner, casting long golden shadows across the walls.

Elizabeth settled Jane down gently, brushing a kiss to her forehead before straightening. Four years ago, she had stumbled into this room half-intoxicated, disoriented, and run-ning for her life. This very bed had held her while she had hidden from the world—now it held her daughter, blissfully unaware of the storms her mother had weathered to arrive here.

She lingered a moment longer, watching the steady rise and fall of Jane's chest, her small hand fisted in the blanket. Then, with one last whispered goodnight, she turned down the lamp.

The hallway creaked beneath her feet as she padded toward the room Mrs. Hill had prepared for them. There had been no suggestion of separating her from her husband, nor would Elizabeth have accepted one. The room was simple, familiar. And it was the one she and Jane had shared that long-ago spring when the arrival of company necessitated it.

She undid her cuffs and stays by touch, the rhythm of it instinctive. A soft laugh es-caped her lips as she considered returning downstairs. She could picture them now—Mr. Bennet leaning over the chessboard with one brow raised, her husband frowning at his own side as if he could still commandeer a victory. Unless Darcy had finally learned to cheat, which was unlikely, his defeat was as inevitable as the tide.

So she turned instead to the small dressing table and removed the pins from her hair, one by one, setting them in a little porcelain dish. Her curls fell into loose snarls about her shoulders, and she crossed to the window to draw back the curtain.

Netherfield shimmered faintly in the distance, its windows lit like stars against the dark. The years had changed so much. And yet—here she was. Here *they* were. Safe. Together.

She exhaled and leaned her forehead lightly against the cool glass, the night quiet but for the rustling hedgerow beyond the orchard. Some while passed like that, as she pondered the whims of fortune and the things that mattered.

At length, the soft creak of the door behind her drew her attention. She did not move, only smiled faintly as she watched her husband's reflection in the darkened window.

Darcy entered quietly, his stride careful and almost impossibly light on the uneven floorboards. He removed his coat and laid it across the bench, then loosened the buttons of his waistcoat. His expression was thoughtful, content. He looked like a man who had, at last, come home.

He tugged at his cravat, pausing just long enough to glance toward the bed. He froze when he saw it empty, his brow tightening faintly. Then he looked toward the window and saw her there, haloed in moonlight.

"Still awake?" he asked softly.

Elizabeth turned, her smile deepening. "I was waiting for you."

He crossed the room in a few long strides, but she met him halfway. Her fingers found his suspenders, sliding them from his shoulders with the ease of long practice. Her palms splayed across his chest, warm through the linen of his shirt, and she stroked over the planes of his muscles. Heavens, he felt *good*... solid and strong and so very *hers*. And since he *was* hers, she might as well pull him in for a kiss, just to make sure he remembered.

He chuckled low in his throat. "Careful," he murmured against her lips. "The floor-boards groan. The bed creaks. And if you are not cautious, you shall have a red face come morning... and perhaps another child come spring."

She kissed him again, smiling against his mouth. Then she stood on her toes, her lips brushing his ear. "Too late for that," she whispered.

He pulled back slightly, brow furrowing—until she caught his hand in hers and pressed it gently to her stomach.

His breath stilled. His gaze searched hers.

Then—slowly, wondrously—he smiled. "Truly?"

She laughed, blinking back tears. "I have suspected for about a month. I hope it is a boy."

He touched her cheek, reverent. "I do not care what it is. The title can go hang. I am not anxious for an heir."

She kissed his nose. "Neither am I. But our daughter is wild and headstrong and far too clever. She may need a brother to keep track of her."

He grinned. "Ah. Am I no longer sufficient for that task?"

Elizabeth wrapped her arms around him, pulling him flush against her. "Your talents," she murmured, "are unrivaled. But you are mine alone, my love, and I do not intend to share."

He kissed her—softly, then more deeply, until she sighed into his mouth and felt him melt beneath her hands.

When at last he pulled away, he pressed a kiss to her palm and wrapped her tightly in his embrace. Together, they looked out the window.

"I kept watch here once," he said quietly. "From that very garden, just beyond the hedge. I stood there and wished with all my heart that I could be in this very room with you."

Elizabeth reached for his chin and turned his face back to hers. "And if you had been?" she whispered. "What would you have done?"

His eyes gleamed, and with a growl of pure affection, he swept her into his arms.

"I would have done this," he said—and carried her to the bed to prove it.

Hungry for more Darcy and Elizabeth sweetness? Lose yourself in *Make Your Play* and find out what happens when two old rivals make a marriage pact!

FROM ALIX

T HANK YOU FOR INDULGING with me and spending a little time with Darcy and Elizabeth.

I hope you've had a delightful escape to their world. I'd love it if you would share this family with your friends so they can experience a love to last for the ages. As with all my books, I have enabled lending to make it easier to share. If you leave a review for *Better Luck Next Time* on Amazon, Goodreads, Book Bub or your own blog, I would love to read it! Email me the link at **Author@AlixJames.com.**

Would you like to read more of Darcy and Elizabeth's romance? I have a sweet Rivals to Lovers tale for you to try next! Dive into **Make Your Play** and laugh along with our favorite couple as they find the love they were destined for!

And if you're hungry for more, including a free ebook of satisfying short tales, stay up to date on upcoming releases and sales by joining my newsletter: https://dashboard.m ailerlite.com/forms/249660/73866370936211000/share

MAKE YOUR PLAY

Coming June 30, 2025

They made a deal in jest, but love never plays by the rules.

Y EARS AGO, ELIZABETH BENNET and Fitzwilliam Darcy struck a reckless bargain on the <u>one</u> day they managed to get along: If neither of them were married within five years, they would marry each other. It was a silly, fleeting promise made in jest—and promptly forgotten.

Or so they thought.

As that fateful age looms, both are horrified to realize the other remembers their pact *perfectly*. Determined to avoid a lifetime with the one person who can unravel them with a single glance—or a sharp retort—they each set out to sabotage the agreement. Their solution? Help the other person find *anyone else* to marry, and fast. But in the process of orchestrating each other's romantic entanglements, they keep accidentally ruining every potential match.

Could their greatest obstacle be the very thing they're trying to avoid? Or is it possible that the heart has a playbook all its own?

"Make Your Play" is a witty, slow-burn Regency romance filled with sharp banter, unexpected alliances, and a love story that unfolds in all the delightful ways neither Darcy nor Elizabeth ever intended. Perfect for fans of spirited heroines, brooding heroes, and the timeless dance between love and pride.

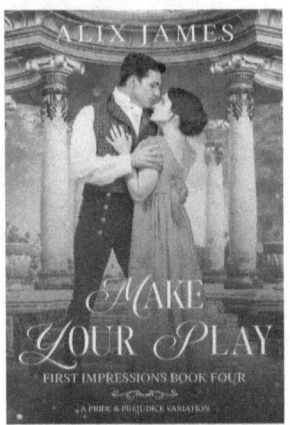

ALSO BY ALIX JAMES

The First Impressions Collection:

All Bets Are Off

Raising the Stakes

Better Luck Next Time

Make Your Play

_____

The Measure of a Man Collection:

The Measure of Love

The Measure of Trust

The Measure of Honor

The Measure of a Man Box Set

_____

The Mr. Darcy Collection:

Mr. Darcy Steals a Kiss

Mr. Darcy and the Governess
Mr. Darcy and the Girl Next Door

Mr. Darcy: Swoonworthy Collection

The Heart to Heart Collection

These Dreams
Nefarious
Tempted

Darcy and Elizabeth: Heart to Heart Box Set

The Sweet Escapes Collection

The Rogue's Widow
The Courtship of Edward Gardiner
London Holiday
Rumours and Recklessness

Darcy and Elizabeth: Sweet Escapes Box Set

The Sweet Sentiments Collection:

When the Sun Sleeps
Queen of Winter
A Fine Mind

Elizabeth Bennet: Sweet Sentiments Box Set

The Frolic and Romance Collection:

A Proper Introduction
A Good Memory is Unpardonable
Along for the Ride

Elizabeth Bennet: Frolic & Romance Box Set

The Short and Sassy Collection:

Unintended
Spirited Away
Indisposed
Love and Other Machines

Elizabeth Bennet: Short and Sassy Compilation

Christmas With Darcy and Elizabeth

How to Get Caught Under the Mistletoe: A Lady's Guide
The Scotsman's Ghost: Or How to Wreck a Yule Party
Mr, Darcy's Christmas Kiss

North and South Variations

Nowhere but North
Northern Rain
No Such Thing as Luck

John and Margaret: Coming Home Collection

Anthologies

Rational Creatures
Falling for Mr Thornton

Spanish Translations

Rumores e Imprudencias
Vacaciones en Londres
Nefasto
Un Compromiso Accidental

Reina del Invierno

Una Mente Noble

Cuando el Sol se Duerm

A lo largo del Camino

Reina del Invierno

Una Mente Noble

El señor Darcy se roba un beso

Cómo quedar atrapado debajo del muérdago

<u>Italian Translations</u>

Una Vacanza a Londra

ABOUT ALIX JAMES

Short and satisfying romance for busy readers.

Alix James is an alternate pen name for best-selling Regency author Nicole Clarkston.

Always on the go as a wife, mom, and small business owner, she rarely has time to read a whole novel. She loves coffee with the sunrise and being outdoors. When she does get free time, she likes to read, camp, dream up romantic adventures, and tries to avoid housework.

Each Alix James story is a clean Regency Variation of Darcy and Elizabeth's romance. Visit her website and sign up for her newsletter at AlixJames.com